STONE CRIBS

Kris Nelscott

St. Martin's Minotaur ⚹ New York

www.minotaurbooks.com

Library of Congress Cataloging-in-Publication Data

Nelscott, Kris.
    Stone cribs / Kris Nelscott.—1st St. Martin's Minotaur ed.
      p.   cm.
    ISBN 0-312-28784-4
    1. Dalton, Smokey (Fictitious character)—Fiction.   2. Private investi-
gators—Illinois—Chicago—Fiction. 3. African American men—Fiction.
4. Chicago (Ill.)—Fiction. 5. Rape victims—Fiction. 6. Abortion—
Fiction. I. Title.

PS3564.E39S76   2003
813'.6—dc21

2003050604

First Edition: February 2004

10 9 8 7 6 5 4 3 2 1

For Kelley Ragland,
editor extraordinaire

I appreciate all that you
have done for me, for
Smokey, and for my
work in general. Thanks
ever so much.

ACKNOWLEDGMENTS

Once again, I could not have written this book alone. My main support on these books, Dean Wesley Smith, also helped me with some of the more difficult details. I greatly appreciate the willingness of Paul Higginbotham to tackle reading this book during one of the more important and exciting events of his life. Many thanks to Steve Braunginn, who spent a lot of time on the manuscript despite serious health problems. (I appreciate it mucho, buddy!) Also, thanks goes to Merrilee Heifetz for being such a constant support and believer in my work. My research involved too many books and resources to mention, so I'll single out the most helpful, which was, once again, the staff at the Harold Washington Library in Chicago. I also need to thank the wonderful people at St. Martin's Press.

Surely the children of our society
deserve more than we are giving them.

—DORIS E. SAUNDERS, columnist,
Chicago Daily Defender,
March 11, 1969

ONE

Wind blew off Lake Michigan through the empty canyons of Chicago's Loop. The warmth of the afternoon was long gone, and the cold nights of early spring had returned.

As Laura Hathaway and I stepped out of the Sherman House Hotel, people surrounded us, talking and laughing. They were reviewing Ella Fitzgerald's concert, but not talking about the charity that had brought us all together.

The concert had benefited the Illinois Children's Home and Aid Society's new committee, the Committee for the Adoption of Black Babies. Events like this one overwhelmed me. Hearing about so many people in crisis—so many children in crisis—made me want to help all of them. Only to me, helping involved more than throwing money at a problem. Yet I couldn't see a real solution for orphaned and unwanted children, at least not a solution that I liked.

Apparently the benefit made the other four hundred and ninety-nine attendees uncomfortable as well. Even though the concert and dinner had raised more than fifteen thousand dollars, both in ticket sales and on-site donations, no one was mentioning the money or the children.

And neither were we. Laura and I were silent as we walked down the steps onto the pavement. I looked over my shoulder, an old habit, but I didn't feel as uneasy as I usually did in the Loop. All of the people around me, except Laura, were black. For the first time in this part of the city, I felt as if I belonged.

I slipped my arm around Laura, shielding her against the cold, and she stiffened, not leaning into me as she usually did when we were alone.

I wasn't sure if she was reacting that way because we were in a public place or because of the benefit. We tried not to touch when we were out in public—it simply invited too much trouble—but I didn't feel as if we were in public here.

Maybe Laura did. Or maybe she was still feeling stung from the reactions she had received inside the hotel. During the dinner, she had embarrassed me simply by being herself, and she had seen my reaction. However, I wasn't sure if she knew what she had done wrong.

She felt fragile against me, even though she wasn't. She wore her blond hair up, giving her an illusion of height. Her high heels and her elaborate hairdo made her seem almost as tall as I was, although flat-footed she was much shorter than my six feet.

The streetlights reflected off her pale skin. Her pretty features, accented by paler makeup, were set in a frown.

A dozen cabs, aware that there would be fares this late on Easter Sunday, lined up in front of the Sherman House's Clark Street entrance. Drunken patrons laughed as the valet whistled each cab forward.

The rest of us walked to our cars. Laura's was parked near the Chicago Loop Synagogue. From a distance, I could see the Hands of Peace sculpture hanging from the building's façade. They seemed appropriate somehow—helping hands—and I almost pointed that out to Laura. But one more glance at her expression reminded me to remain silent.

Her Mercedes 280SL was the only car on that block. It looked like the Hands of Peace were pointing at the vehicle.

This part of the street was empty. The other patrons had veered off, and Laura and I were alone.

My feeling of comfort left. The emptiness made me nervous, particularly since we were so well dressed. I was wearing a new suit, tailored to fit, and a topcoat of a type I'd only seen in movies. Laura wore a shimmering blue pantsuit that looked like a formal evening gown until she walked. Her shoes were open-toed. Her feet had to be cold now that we were outside.

In the distance, car doors slammed, a few taxis honked their horns, and people called good-byes and Happy Easters to each other. A man drunkenly sang the title line from "Between the Devil and the Deep Blue Sea," and a woman sang the next line, her voice not as drunk or as out of tune. Neither singer sounded like Ella Fitzgerald.

2

She had made the entire evening worthwhile. The dance floor in the old College Inn restaurant was lit with soft lights, the orchestra behind it. She used the space as if it were her own private stage until she got irritated that no one was dancing. Then she invited people forward.

And of course they came.

Laura's heels clicked on the concrete and my tight new dress shoes answered with solid taps. I wondered what Laura was thinking. Maybe Ella Fitzgerald's rich voice was reverberating in Laura's head the way it was reverberating in mine.

It wasn't the closing number that kept threading its way through my thoughts. Much as I liked "A-Tisket, A-Tasket," it wasn't my favorite Ella Fitzgerald tune. Instead, "Slumming on Park Avenue," with its sly lyrics about spying on the rich the way they slummed to spy on the poor, had captured my mood.

Ella Fitzgerald had segued into that song after an ill-advised set of rock 'n' roll tunes. When she introduced "Slumming," she had done so with a wide smile, knowing she was in a crowd of like-minded people.

"It's Irving Berlin's way of letting all those rich white folks know how despicable their behavior can be," she said, her eyes twinkling, the orchestra playing a musical backdrop behind her.

At that moment, several people glanced at Laura. She was well known among people who followed the society pages, and apparently a lot of the upper-class blacks who shelled out fifteen dollars per person to come to this event read not only the *Defender*'s society pages, but the *Tribune*'s as well.

As Laura and I reached the Mercedes, I scanned the area, looking for people in the shadows. Not a lot of pickpockets turned up for a black benefit, but I knew better than to ignore the silent streets.

I saw no one. The synagogue's stained-glass walls and street-level glass reflected the lights, the car, and nothing else.

Laura slipped out of my grasp. She pulled her keys out of her purse, brushed an escaping strand of blond hair away from her face, and walked toward the driver's side.

She unlocked her door, and peered at me over the car's dark blue roof. Her makeup hollowed out her cheeks, giving her a patrician air.

"You're angry at me, aren't you?" she asked.

"No," I lied and jiggled the car handle. I wanted to go home.

She pulled her door open and got inside. She braced an arm on the gearshift between the seats and leaned over, reaching for the lock. In the passenger-side window glass, my own image was superimposed over hers, and I looked as out of place as I felt—a burly, six-foot-tall man stuffed into a suit. The new scar I had along the left side of my face made me seem tougher than I felt. If it weren't for the topcoat, people would think I was a bouncer at a trendy nightclub.

Laura's fingers pulled lightly on the lock, clicking it open. I grabbed the door handle and pulled as she sat up, sticking the keys in the ignition. I slid inside.

The car's interior was warmer than the street had been, even though the leather seats still creaked with the cold. The solid metal frame blocked the wind. We weren't even rocking from its force.

I settled back, my knees bent under the dash. It felt awkward to sit on the passenger side, even though the car was hers. I was used to driving.

But Laura had insisted, just like she had insisted on everything else about this night. She had bought the tickets, helped me find the suit, and even managed to check the official guest list to make sure that there would be no one in attendance that I would have to avoid.

She had known that Easter was going to be a difficult holiday for all of us, and she had planned this to cheer me up.

Last Easter, I had been driving back roads with Jimmy Bailey, trying to keep him away from the FBI and the Memphis police. Jimmy had witnessed the assassination of Martin Luther King, Jr., and the shooter Jimmy had seen was not James Earl Ray. Jimmy, who had been only ten at the time, had reported the shooting to the large contingent of police officers nearby and they had tried to kidnap him on the spot.

If I hadn't arrived at just that moment, I had no doubt that Jimmy would be dead now.

We were hiding here in Chicago. No one except Laura, and Franklin and Althea Grimshaw, knew Jimmy's name was James Bailey or mine was Smokey Dalton. No one knew that Jimmy and I weren't blood kin. Everyone here thought we were related to Franklin, and I had identification in my wallet, claiming my name was William S. Grimshaw—a man with an eleven-year-old son named Jimmy.

I had focused most of my energies these past few weeks on Jimmy. The articles in the papers about King's assassination, the constant reminders on the television set, had made Jimmy's nightmares return. I had hoped the actual anniversary of King's death—which had been, ironically, Good Friday—would make the nightmares go away.

But they hadn't.

So I had agreed to let him spend Easter weekend with the Grimshaws, hoping that the celebratory church services, the Black Easter parade, and

Althea's delightful Easter dinner would help Jimmy focus on the present, rather than the darkness in his past.

It also gave me time with Laura, time we badly needed. In January of this year, we had resumed the relationship we began in Memphis, and it was proving as difficult as I had thought it would be. I was working with Laura now on a per-job basis, inspecting the buildings owned by the company she now ran. Laura had an amazing streak of somewhat naïve color-blindness, but no one else in Sturdy Investments did. The fact that she and I had an equal partnership disturbed almost everyone we came into contact with.

Then there was our personal relationship, which we were having trouble finding time for. I had Jimmy to care for, and Laura worked long hours. Sometimes we went a week without seeing each other, especially since I rarely went into Sturdy's offices.

Tomorrow morning I was supposed to pick up Jimmy, along with all of the Grimshaw children, and take them to school, so Laura and I were staying at my place to make the drive easier. I had wanted to spend the entire evening at home, but by the time I realized Laura was making plans, it had been too late.

Laura knew I longed for the music that had been part of the air in Memphis. My offices there had been on Beale Street, home of the blues, and every bar, every restaurant, had some form of music in the evenings. Even though Chicago was also a big blues town, it had its own style—a darker, moodier, more urban style that wasn't as accessible to me. The westside clubs were far away from my home and office, and I wasn't as free to go out at night as I had been in Memphis.

But I didn't want to go to a benefit. I had never liked the pretentiousness of the events, always wondering why people needed a special reward to give to charity.

I hadn't told Laura that, but she had sensed my mood on the way over. We pretended we were enjoying the evening, until we got up to dance. Then I felt the tension in Laura's body. She hadn't put her head on my shoulder like she had in the past. Instead, she had watched everyone around us, probably feeling the hostility they were directing at her.

She hadn't realized when she bought the tickets that she would be crashing an affair designed for blacks only. And I hadn't prepared her for the cattiness she would be suffering because she was a white woman who was clearly involved with a black man.

"It seems like you're mad at me," Laura said, obviously not willing to let the topic go. She checked the car's mirrors and turned on her lights before pulling onto Clark.

I was annoyed at the entire evening; I didn't like small talk and I had been subjected to hours of it. I had also been on alert for the first hour, making certain that no one who might have known me from Memphis, someone who hadn't been on the initial guest list, was in the room.

"I would have thought after my donation that people would have understood how serious I am." She kept her gaze on the road ahead, her hands in a perfect driver's V on the wheel.

In the middle of the evening, the organizers called for donations. People verbally pledged an amount, and most wrote checks to cover it right away. Laura had done so, and the hostility had grown worse.

I had no idea if she had noticed, however. I wasn't going to tell her. But I didn't know how to respond to her statement without patronizing her or starting a real fight.

Laura and I came from completely different worlds. She had been raised the wealthy daughter of a small-time crook who became a self-made businessman. She had been pampered and protected her entire life, stepping out of that world only after her mother had died, when a strange clause in her mother's will had led her to me.

My parents had been lynched when I was ten, and after that, I was sent away from everything I knew. My adoptive parents were good people, and they raised me well, but they could never erase the memories I held of my first ten years or of that time I spent hiding in an upstairs closet while my real parents were being dragged out of the house to their deaths.

"I understand that some people there found my question offensive," Laura said. "But I didn't mean it that way. I mean, if we're going to be a truly integrated society—"

"It was offensive, Laura," I said.

She looked at me. The dim light of the dash revealed the shock on her face. She hadn't expected me to side against her.

But she hadn't understood the situation. Even after listening to the speeches, the points apparently hadn't struck home. I had no idea how she had missed the evening's subtext, since the first speaker had outlined it with one sentence:

If we are really serious about black pride, if we really believe that black is beautiful, if we really believe that we are somebody, we black adults will do something about the adoption of black babies in Chicago.

Apparently Laura hadn't heard the phrase "black adults," or if she had, she had misunderstood it. I had a good view of her as I watched the speakers, and her eyes teared up more than once at the thought of over a thousand children who were unclaimed because of the color of their skin.

She had stood, hand up, during the question-and-answer section of the presentation, and waited a long time to be called on. I tried to get her to sit, but she shook me off. When the speaker finally turned his attention to her, Laura asked why no one had thought of finding white families to adopt black children.

The silence in the large restaurant had been deafening. For a moment, I had thought the speaker wasn't going to answer her. Then he had said, "It simply isn't feasible," and had moved on to the next question, leaving Laura red-faced.

She had sat back down and, to her credit, hadn't brought up the issue again the entire night. Until now.

"What did I say that was so wrong?" she asked.

I didn't want to have this discussion. I had imagined leaving Sherman House, driving to my apartment, and taking her in my arms. The last thing I wanted was tension between us.

I sighed. Laura wasn't going to let me brush her off the way the speaker had.

I said, "Let's leave out the fact that a hundred years ago, white people controlled the destinies of blacks and their children, often separating them and selling the children like cattle. Let's also forget that the social services available to whites, like maternity homes and other such places, are not usually available to blacks. And let's not even discuss the way the legal system treats black families who somehow find themselves in court. Let's just talk about what you suggested."

"Okay." Her tone was cautious, like Jimmy's often was when he knew he was about to get a lecture for something he didn't completely understand.

She turned the car onto Lake Shore Drive. Lake Michigan looked black against the night sky. Only the headlights, rippling in the water, gave any indication that the lake was there.

"If we allow white families to take black children, then we must assume that black families will take white children," I said.

"They won't?" she asked.

"They won't be allowed to," I said. "But that's not even the point. The point is that our children will leave our culture and our nest, and once again, white people will be determining our future."

"But the black children aren't being adopted," Laura said. "No one's taking them. I listened, just like you did."

"And there were some things we all knew but which weren't spelled out for people outside of the community," I said.

"Like what?" She kept her gaze trained on the road, but her jaw was set. She was angry, too.

Cars passed us. The street was busier than I would have expected at 10:30 on Easter Sunday.

"Black families do adopt black children, but have a tougher road of it," I said. "The model for a stable family is white. The woman is a homemaker and the man is the breadwinner, which is not the norm in black families. In black families, both parents work, and right there that makes the court assume that the household is unfit. If by chance the woman does stay home, then the white inspectors come and judge everything by their standards. They assume the neighborhood is bad because of the preponderance of blacks—"

"That's ridiculous," Laura said.

"I don't care if it's ridiculous, Laura," I said. "It happens. When I lived in Memphis, I used to do investigative work for attorneys who sometimes handled adoption petitions. More than once I had to prove that a black neighborhood, which looked dangerous to a white inspector, was actually safer than its economic counterpart in the white community."

Laura sighed. "So my donation made it seem like I was patronizing everyone there, then."

She finally understood. But I didn't want to upset her further, so all I said was, "I'm sure they knew you were sincerely trying to help."

"One thousand children without a place to go." Her voice was quiet. "That's a crime all by itself."

"I know."

We were heading into Hyde Park now, getting close to my street.

"I'm sorry," she said. "I wanted this to be a pleasant evening, Smokey."

I placed my hand on top of the one she had resting on the gearshift. Her skin was warm and soft.

"It was pleasant," I said, and it wasn't a complete lie. "It was fun to hear Ella again, and dancing with you—"

"Again?" Laura looked at me. She had chewed the lipstick off her lower lip, and more strands of hair had fallen around her face.

"I saw Ella a few times in Memphis."

Laura's carefully plucked eyebrows rose. I recognized the look. It was a combination of fear and panic.

"Does she know you?" Laura asked. "Could she have recognized you?"

I smiled. "Only as a familiar face in the crowd. We never spoke. I was just another nameless fan bebopping to the music."

"Bebopping." Laura smiled, too, and returned her gaze to the road. "I can't quite imagine you doing that."

Maybe not anymore. I hadn't had the lightness and relaxation I had enjoyed on those nights in Memphis for more than a year.

Laura had never seen me comfortable or lighthearted. From the moment I met her, I had been on guard, and then events conspired to make me serious, protective, and justifiably paranoid.

She turned the car onto my street, saving me from having to comment on my past. She expertly eased the Mercedes into an empty parking space a few yards from my apartment's main sidewalk.

Half of the streetlights were broken, sending uneven pools of light throughout the neighborhood. Most of the buildings were former houses turned into apartments or pre–World War II six-flats that had been allowed to run down.

I lived in an older building on the second floor, in the apartment first rented by the Grimshaws. Laura had found them a home more suited to their needs, and now Jimmy and I lived in three-bedroom comfort, at least compared with last summer's crowded conditions.

Still, the apartment was small and meager, especially when I thought of Laura's penthouse suite on Lake Shore Drive. Even though Laura claimed the difference didn't bother her, it bothered me. Every time I brought her here, I kept seeing how mean my circumstances were—and it made me wonder if each of us wasn't slumming in our own separate ways.

As she parked, worry must have shown on my face. Laura shoved the gearshift into Park, shut off the ignition, and then smiled at me.

"It's all right, Smokey." There was amusement in her voice. "I'm insured."

I never doubted that she was, but insurance wasn't really the point to me. I was used to taking precautions, and leaving a valuable car on a street filled with poor people didn't count as one to me. Sure, my rusted Impala wasn't pretty, but it belonged here.

I opened the door and got out. She did the same, and I waited for her to come around to my side. As she approached, I held out my hand, and wondered if she would take it.

She did. Her fingers were surprisingly warm. We walked up the sidewalk, hand in hand.

The six-flat regained some of its elegance in the darkness. The unkempt lawn was harder to see and the chipped paint covering the brick looked almost clean.

Still, this building was clearly a multifamily dwelling, with different curtains in each window, and the air of public property outside.

The door to the building was propped open, something I wished the other tenants wouldn't do. But as the weather got nicer, people liked to have a breeze fill the hallways, which got stuffy in the afternoons. Once the door was open, no one bothered to close it.

Laura and I stepped onto the porch. Last summer, I had discovered a body here, and each time I walked up the porch steps I thought of it.

That night was no different. Little ghosts haunted me everywhere.

We stepped inside. The hallway was wide at the entrance, with a staircase to our right—a wooden staircase with an elegant banister that once had been polished and lovely. Now it was dingy with years of dirt.

The main floor had two apartments, the first near the metal mailboxes that had been built into the wall. Both apartment doors were closed, and each had extra deadbolts, just like mine did, even though the neighborhood was considered safe by Chicago standards.

The hall smelled faintly of baked ham and melted chocolate. The remains of a chocolate bunny was mashed against the doorknob of the nearest apartment. Foil Easter egg wrappers glittered on the floor, proving that someone had had a sweet holiday.

Laura smiled when she saw the mess. Her hair was losing its height, and the change made her seem more like my Laura, instead of the glittery society woman I had taken to the benefit.

She headed toward the staircase, careful to avoid the foil wrappers.

"Don't touch the railing," I said. "Who knows if sticky little hands were there first."

"The chocolate should be hardening by now," she said, and reached for the banister.

Above us, something thudded. Something heavy had fallen. I didn't like the sound. Laura looked at me, a slight frown making a line between her eyebrows.

I shrugged. This apartment building had its share of odd noises. I had owned my own house in Memphis, and even though I'd been here nearly a year, I still wasn't used to all the sounds that neighbors could make.

I turned, closed the front door, and latched it, like all of the tenants had agreed to do after dark. Then I joined Laura on the stairs.

She slipped her arm through mine. The earlier tension had fled, and we were heading into that perfect moment I had initially imagined when we had left for the benefit. We took our time climbing up, as if we were heading toward a glorious suite in a fancy hotel instead of my dingy apartment.

Halfway up, she let go of my arm, and reached into the pocket of my topcoat for my keys.

Even though she and I had grown closer these last four months, I had not given her keys to my place, nor had I asked for keys to hers. Since I did most of my work out of my apartment, I wanted to be cautious about who came into my apartment and why. Keys to her place wouldn't have mattered, since I would never have used them. Even though the current building security was used to me, I was worried that some new overzealous employee would see a black man trying to open Miss Hathaway's door and act before thinking.

She managed to grab the keys, laughed, and with surprising agility for a woman in high heels, ran up the remaining steps. She thumbed the keys, looking for the square one that unlocked the top deadbolt.

The thud came again, closer, this time followed by a cry of pain. A door banged softly, as if it had been partially opened and had suddenly slammed closed.

Laura turned. She had obviously heard the sound, too. "Isn't that where your neighbor lives?"

The question wasn't as inane as it sounded. The only neighbor of mine that Laura had met was Marvella Walker, a stunning woman who had set her sights on me the moment I had moved into the building. Last winter, Marvella did her best to make Laura's visits hellacious, until I let Marvella know I wouldn't tolerate her behavior.

Laura was looking at the thick wooden door across the hall from mine. I took the last few steps two at a time and reached the top. There I could hear a woman's voice, making short sharp cries.

"I think she's calling for help," Laura said.

I didn't wait. I hurried to the door. The sounds were louder here. In between the cries were moans.

"Marvella?" I asked, reaching for the knob. "Marvella, it's me, Bill. Is everything okay?"

"Help . . . me . . . please . . ." This cry was louder than the rest, but I still wouldn't have been able to hear it if I hadn't been nearby.

I turned the knob and to my surprise, it opened. Marvella was usually as meticulous about using her deadbolts as I was. But the door jammed, as if something were pushed against it.

Through the crack in the door, I could see a woman's bare foot on the hardwood floor, a bit of satin robe, and a blood stain that appeared to be growing.

"Marvella?" I tried not to let the panic I suddenly felt into my voice. "Can you move away from the door? I can't get in."

She grunted. The foot moved, braced itself, revealing some leg. Blood coated the inner thigh, and had run down to the ankle. As she moved, the blood smeared against the hardwood floor, and I realized the stain was really a puddle.

"What's going on, Smokey?" Laura had come up behind me.

I held up a hand to silence her, and pushed on the door. It finally opened far enough for me to slip inside.

When she saw me, the woman on the floor moaned in relief. But she wasn't Marvella. She was small, her features delicate and elfin. Her skin had gone gray, and the area around her eyes was almost bluish, indicating a great deal of blood loss.

"Thank God," she whispered when she saw me. "I need some help."

"Where's Marvella?" I asked, uncertain what had happened. Most of Marvella's tidy living room was intact. The wooden sculptures, all of faces in an African style, remained on the surfaces, and the plants still covered the window seat in front of the large bay window. But the add-on kitchen was a mess of glasses and dirty dishes, and Marvella's normally pristine brown couch was covered with blankets, towels, and even more blood.

The woman shook her head, then closed her eyes and lay back down, as if all that movement had been too much for her. Next to her, a half-melted bag of ice added water to the blood puddle.

Laura pushed her way in behind me.

"Oh, my God." She crouched beside the woman, and put a hand on her forehead. "She's burning up. Smokey, we have to get her help. Now."

The blood was coming from between the woman's legs. She wore Marvella's white satin robe, and it was partially open, revealing a slightly distended stomach.

"Get towels from the kitchen," I said. "See if you can stop the bleeding. I have to make sure Marvella's all right."

I had visions of her dead or dying in the bedroom. I hurried toward the narrow hallway, wishing I had my gun. My topcoat flowed behind me, catching on the small table Marvella used to accent the space between the bathroom and bedroom, and knocking it over. The sculptures on top of it scattered.

Laura moved behind me, making soothing noises to the poor woman as she gathered towels.

The bathroom light was on. Drops of blood covered the white tile around the toilet, and more blood stained the orange rug in front of the bathtub. The brown and orange shower curtain was open, revealing a mound of wet towels in the tub. No towels hung on the racks, and a bloody handprint stained the white porcelain of the sink.

But Marvella was not inside.

I moved quickly to the bedroom and flicked on the light. I had never seen this room, but it continued the browns and oranges Marvella used to decorate the rest of the place. Instead of sculptures, though, big oil paintings of tribal figures covered the walls.

One painting was so large and narrow that the figure on it was life-sized. I caught it out of the corner of my eye, and had to do a double-take to make sure it wasn't a real person.

My heart was pounding. I made myself take a breath and slow down so that I could scan the room.

The batik bedspread had been pulled back and someone had removed one of the matching pillows. Women's clothing pooled near the closet, unusually sloppy in a very tidy room.

The bedroom smelled of Marvella's sandalwood perfume, and I realized that it was the only place in the entire apartment that didn't smell of fresh blood.

I checked the closet just in case, and saw nothing except rows of brightly colored clothing. Then I lifted the bedspread. Boxes of shoes, neatly labeled, were stored beneath the bed.

No one was in there either.

Marvella was missing and a woman was bleeding to death in her living room.

Something awful had happened here, and I had no real idea what that something was.

TWO

"Smokey, we have to get some help right now," Laura said.

She was kneeling between the woman's legs, on the ever-expanding puddle of blood, pressing a large wad of towels against the woman's genitals. Laura's hair had fallen out of its bun and trailed over her shoulders. Her hands were streaked with blood, and her shoes had slipped off the backs of her feet, refusing to bend with her toes.

She didn't seem to notice, and neither did the woman. The woman's eyes were closed, and she was still moaning. She was smaller than Laura, her hands folded beneath her breasts as if she were protecting her heart.

The robe had opened most of the way, and I saw no obvious wound, only a reddish area around the stomach. The woman's pubic hair had been shaved, but I couldn't see where the injury was because there was so much blood.

Her face seemed even grayer than it had before. She wasn't going to make it until help arrived.

"You've got to hold those towels against her," I said to Laura as I moved between the woman and the coffee table.

The blood puddle was seeping toward the kitchen—apparently the floor was downhill to the outside wall—and I had no choice but to step in the wetness. It soaked through my thin dress shoes, and surprised me with its chill.

Probably the melting ice. But even with it, the blood was still thick. The woman was bleeding heavily.

"What are you doing?" Laura asked. "We have to call for help."

"There's no time." I bent down, and slid my arms behind the woman's back, pulling the robe the rest of the way open. She moaned, but didn't open her eyes.

"Smokey!" Laura was protesting, but I didn't care.

I could feel the woman's skin through the back of the robe. She was too hot.

"Hold those towels in place," I said, and Laura didn't argue. "Move with me as I lift."

Laura nodded. She stood as I picked up the woman, making sure the towels didn't shift.

The woman was lighter than I expected. Her head draped back and one arm fell toward the floor. This time she didn't moan, and that had me worried.

Laura's pantsuit was covered in blood, and there was a smear of blood on her face where she must have wiped the hair out of her eyes. But she didn't seem to notice.

"We've got to get her downstairs," I said. "Your car is closest, but—"

"If you think I care about interiors at a moment like this, Smokey Dalton, you're crazy," Laura snapped.

"All right then." I adjusted the woman so that I could put one hand under her buttocks. That way, I could hold the towels in place and carry her at the same time.

There, the blood was slick, heavy, and warm. I hadn't felt anything like this since Korea. Then I had carried a friend off a battlefield as he bled to death from a gaping wound in his back.

Laura pulled the apartment door open, and I headed toward the stairs. My shoes squeaked. I knew I was leaving bloody footprints on the dirty wooden floor.

"You've got to go ahead of me," I said. "You have to open the front door which I so stupidly closed and then you have to unlock the car. Open the back passenger door so I can put her inside."

Laura nodded and ran down the stairs. Her shoes were slick with blood, and she was leaving a trail as well. She clung to the banister, using it to catch herself each time a foot slid out from underneath her. Her heel caught halfway down, and she lurched forward, grabbing the banister with both hands. For a moment, I thought I was going to lose her, too, but then she righted herself and continued the rest of the way down.

The towels grew wet under my hand. I pulled the woman closer to me, as if I could heal her just with touch. I kept one arm braced around her slender back, wishing she was conscious enough to hold on to me.

I thudded down the stairs, trying not to jostle her too much. I felt a desperate need to hurry—I didn't want her to die in my arms.

We were on the middle step when the woman shifted in my grasp. The towels slipped, and I almost dropped her.

Her eyes fluttered open. They were oval-shaped and dark brown, with an upward tilt on the outside edge. Beautiful, as much for the intelligence in them as for their shape.

"Marvella?" she asked me, her voice little more than a whisper.

"I don't know," I said, grunting the words as I thumped down the steps. "Do you know where she is?"

The woman shook her head slightly, her straight black hair catching on my topcoat. She slipped her arm around my neck, and I was grateful.

I didn't want to drop her.

"You'll be all right," I said, not knowing if the promise was true. "We're taking you to the hospital."

"No . . ." she whispered, but I ignored her. I didn't care if she couldn't pay for it. I was convinced that getting help was the only way to keep her alive.

I finally made it to the bottom of the stairs. My breath was coming in gasps, and my back ached. The woman's grip on my neck was loosening. She was losing consciousness again.

Laura had left a trail of heel prints that went from the stairs to the front door. She had propped the door open, and through it, her long, slender body bent at the waist as she tried to arrange the backseat for the woman in my arms.

I ran through the front door, across the porch, and down the sidewalk. I was wheezing. Even though I was in good physical condition, I wasn't used to carrying someone in such an awkward position.

Laura heard me coming and stepped aside. She bit her lower lip as she watched, her eyes wide.

I eased the woman into the car, propping her head against the backseat and tucking the rest of her inside.

"You'd better ride with her," I said, but Laura was already crawling in.

I pulled off my topcoat. Then I took the keys out of Laura's hand. She had turned away from me, trying to make the woman comfortable, and keeping one hand on the ruined towels.

"The towels are saturated," I said, handing Laura my coat. "You might have to use this."

She tossed the towels behind the driver's seat, and bundled up my coat with an efficiency that surprised me. I closed the door and loped toward the driver's side, finding the key as I moved, then got into the car, stuck the keys in the ignition, and flicked on the lights all in the same motion.

We sped toward the hospital. The nearest was only a few blocks away, but even that seemed too far. The woman moaned, and I was grateful to hear it. Somehow I felt that if we got her there while she was still somewhat conscious, she had a chance.

I swerved to avoid blue Volkswagen Beetle in an intersection. He honked, but by the time he'd taken his hand off the horn, we were another block away.

Laura murmured to the woman, using comfort words that meant nothing, and I tried to concentrate on the road. But all I heard were those thumps upstairs, the click-slam of a wooden door.

The woman had heard us come into the building, heard our laughter and our joking, and tried to call out to us. She had fallen—or perhaps she was already down and trying to get up—and she managed to get the door partially open before falling again.

We had been lucky to hear her. If we had been any louder, if we hadn't been paying attention, if I had truly shrugged off the sounds as part of apartment living, we would never have found her in time.

I yanked the wheel and spun around the corner, but the car's back wheels didn't even slide. The Mercedes moved like a dream. It was fast and responsive—the perfect car for this moment.

Then the hospital loomed before us, an entire city block of institutional brick surrounded by a parking lot. Lights were on in some of the windows, probably the corridors, and a yellow lighted sign with the hospital's name glowed above the main doors. A smaller sign, almost invisible in the darkness, pointed the way to the emergency entrance.

I had to make a 130-degree turn to follow the arrow on that sign, and took the narrow access road that led to a brick overhang someone had built above the emergency doors. Thin fluorescent lights illuminated the concrete beneath the brick overhang, and the two glass doors, with the words EMERGENCY ENTRANCE ONLY emblazoned in red.

I pulled the car haphazardly onto the ambulance parking ramp, thankful no ambulance was there ahead of me. Even before I stopped, Laura was out of the car. She ran across the concrete, her blond hair flowing behind her, her arms windmilling, and skidded to a stop in front of the doors. She grabbed them as if they weighed more than she did, yanked them open, and ran through them, shouting for help.

I left the keys in the ignition, and got out. By the time I got to the passenger side, two white male attendants, wearing green scrubs, hurried out of the hospital, pulling a mobile bed between them.

They stopped at the door Laura had left open.

The first man was already leaning inside the car, but the second peered at me. He was in his twenties, and he looked like he hadn't even started to shave yet.

"What've we got?" he asked me in a no-nonsense voice.

"I have no idea," I said. "She's bleeding badly, though. Be careful with her."

He nodded, and gently moved me aside as he went to help the other attendant. The other attendant had already pushed the seats forward so he could crawl into the backseat without hurting the woman.

I went around to the other side and pulled open the passenger door there as the attendant who had spoken to me grabbed the woman's legs.

"Has she hurt her head or her back?" the attendant closest to me asked.

"I don't know," I said. "I don't think so."

"Then grab her head. Don't let it drop."

"All right." I took her head between my hands. Her hair was silky soft, and her skull so small that I could've held it with my palm if I had wanted to.

Her eyes opened. They met mine, and I could see the fear in them.

"You'll be all right," I said, wondering how I could keep promising that when I had no idea whether she would be or not. But I had to say something.

The attendants eased her out of the backseat, and I climbed into the car as they did, crawling across the bloody seat on my knees. The second attendant kept pace with me, holding her back steady. Somehow he managed to get out of the car without bouncing her or hitting his head.

The first attendant had lowered the mobile bed so that we could ease her on it. I leaned forward, from inside the car, relinquishing my grip only when the attendant's hands met mine under her skull.

The woman's gaze stayed on my face, almost as if I were her lifeline. I gave her a weak smile, meant to be reassuring. Then they put one strap over her middle to hold her on the bed, and wheeled her away from me.

Laura hovered beside them, her hands twisting in front of her. She was running sideways, something I had thought impossible in high heels.

I was still kneeling inside the wreck of the Mercedes' backseat. Blood coated the leather. My topcoat was crumpled on the floor, and the front seats were pushed forward.

I doubted Laura's insurance covered something like this.

Then I got out, closed the back doors, and climbed into the driver's seat. I had to move the Mercedes away from the entrance—it was supposedly for ambulances only—but it felt awkward doing so. I should have been inside, helping Laura and the woman, making sure everything was all right.

I had left the car running, and hadn't even realized it. Fortunately, I also had had enough sense to put the car in Park and hit the emergency brake—even though I didn't remember doing that, either. All I remembered was my decision to leave the keys in the ignition while I went to the back to help the woman.

The hospital parking lot was dark. No one had thought to put lighting throughout the maze of parking spaces. Most of them were empty, although the ones closest to the emergency room were reserved for various doctors.

The streetlights guided me, and I finally parked the car at the street end of the parking lot, under a sign, hoping that the streetlights would deter anyone from trying to break in. This neighborhood was worse than mine, and there had been a lot of theft from this parking lot. It had become a joke—park here, gain your health, and lose your radio.

I got out of the car, made sure it was locked, and stuffed the keys in the pocket of my suit coat. Then I loped toward the emergency entrance.

As I reached the glass doors, I realized that Laura, the attendants, and the bed were still in the corridor. My stomach clenched. We had been too late. Even though the woman had been conscious, she hadn't made it any farther. I had misjudged just how serious her wounds were.

I hurried inside. Another person stood near the attendants—a short man in doctor's whites. He was younger than I was—early thirties, perhaps—and he had messy black hair over very pale skin. A white woman, wearing a nurse's uniform, clutched a clipboard to her chest. Her starched white cap was nestled in a bed of red hair, obviously being held up by an entire can of hair spray.

Laura's hair had tumbled around her face. Her pantsuit was black with blood, and yet somehow she managed to maintain an expensive elegance.

As I drew closer, I realized that the elegance came from her stance. Laura always stood tallest when she was angry.

"You will not take a confession from her." Laura's voice was low, but menacing. "You won't even know if she had an abortion or a miscarriage until you do a full examination."

I slowed down to a walk, and looked at Laura in stunned surprise. How did she know what was happening when I hadn't figured it out?

"Miss." The doctor stood across the mobile bed from Laura, and had to look up slightly to see her face. "We're only doing what the law requires."

Laura peered down her nose at him. I'd had her do that to me, and it was very intimidating.

"I don't give a good goddamn what the law requires," she snapped. "You have no right to withhold treatment from this woman."

The doctor, however, didn't seem intimidated at all. Instead he took a step away from the bed, as if he were going to leave the hallway altogether.

"I have every right to withhold treatment," he said, "and am required to do so until she tells us what happened."

I finally reached the bed. The woman was awake, her face shiny in the fluorescent light. I couldn't tell if the liquid on her cheeks was sweat or tears.

"If you don't treat her now," I said, "she probably won't survive."

The doctor whirled toward me. I had six inches on him and at least a hundred pounds, but he didn't seem intimidated by me. In fact, he looked relieved to be facing me instead of Laura.

He said to me, "We could lose our license if we don't do this."

Laura leaned across the bed, just as the woman raised her hand. Her thin fingers caught the lapel of the doctor's label coat. He looked down at her in surprise.

"Please," she whispered. "Please help me."

He pulled away from her, making her lose her grip. Her hand fell against the metal bedrail, the clang echoing in the corridor.

Laura winced.

I had had enough. "Are you the only doctor on duty?"

"Yes, and if you people would stop interfering, I could take care of this patient." The doctor pulled his coat closed. The woman's fingers had left a small bloodstain on his lapel.

Laura's spine straightened. She brushed the hair out of her face and raised her chin.

"Do you have any idea who I am?" she asked the doctor.

He didn't even look at her. Instead, he was reaching for the chart still clutched in the nurse's hands.

"No, miss," he said. "I don't know who you are. And frankly, I don't care. Your friend here is in trouble, and I can't help her unless she tells me what happened."

He took the chart and the pen someone had slipped under the metal clip, and started writing.

"Dammit," I said, but Laura held up a hand, stopping me.

The doctor looked up at the sound of my voice. "It's pretty clear," he said to me, "that a crime has been committed here. If you just tell me who this woman conspired with, then you'll minimize your own liability in this matter, and we can start treating her."

"Excuse me," Laura said. Her voice had an extra crispness to it. Her blue eyes flashed with anger. "You were initially talking to me, not him. And I was about to tell you why it would be a mistake to ignore me."

"I don't have time for this," the doctor said, bending over the chart again.

The woman's hand fluttered against the blanket, as if she were trying to reach for him, and couldn't.

Laura's gaze flickered down to the woman for only a moment before she raised her chin even higher.

"My name is Laura Hathaway," Laura said in her most aristocratic tone. "My father, Earl Hathaway, was a close friend of Mayor Daley's."

That was a lie, but not much of one. Earl Hathaway had ties to the Daley machine—ties that Laura hadn't pursued in the nine years since Earl Hathaway's death, ties which she was now actively repudiating. But the doctor didn't need to know any of that.

"If you refuse to treat this woman," Laura said, "I will personally sic the mayor's office on you. Everyone in this corridor will lose their jobs and you, sir, will never be able to practice medicine again. Am I being clear?"

The doctor sighed and shoved the chart at the nurse. She gave him a frightened glance. Another nurse appeared in a nearby doorway, watching the proceedings.

The attendants slipped down the hall, apparently not wanting any part of this.

The doctor faced Laura. Even though he was small, he had the same don't-fuck-with-me bearing that she did.

"Miss," he said, "abortion is a serious crime, and the law states that I need to get a confession first before—"

"I know the law, too," Laura said, "and what you want is called a deathbed confession by prosecutors. You're doing your goddamndest to make sure this is her deathbed."

The woman's hand clutched the blanket. I reached over the metal railing and smoothed her hair, hoping to give her some measure of comfort.

"I will have you up on charges of negligent homicide, Dr.—" Laura peered at his badge. "—Rothstein."

The doctor's face turned red, but his spine remained straight. He looked at me. "Are you the husband?"

"I never saw this woman before tonight," I said.

The doctor shook his head. "Then I can't—"

"Did you hear me, Dr. Rothstein?" Laura snapped. "Because if you don't take care of her right now, I will push this bed through the halls of the hospital, screaming for help until someone does something."

The doctor gaped at her. He seemed stunned that she had defied him. Laura grabbed the bed's back railing and the side railing, and bent over, trying to shove the bed forward.

Her hair swung over her eyes, and her cheeks turned red with effort. The woman put her hand on Laura's. I grabbed the railing, too, and started to push.

The doctor wrapped his hand around the railing, holding the bed in place. "You'll all be brought up on charges, you know that? Participating in an illegal operation is a felony."

"So is negligent homicide," Laura said, still trying to push.

I leaned into the bed, making it impossible for the doctor to hold it.

The doctor glared at me. His jaw clenched, then he looked at the woman. Her skin was even grayer, but her hand was firm over Laura's. The woman's eyes were open and sunken into her thin face.

The doctor's shoulders drooped. "Let's get her into one of the exam rooms."

"You'll do more than that." Laura maintained her grip on the railing. "You'll stop this bleeding. I'm going with you, and I'm going to make sure you follow your goddamn Hippocratic oath."

"You have a hell of a mouth on you, lady," the doctor said, but he started to push the bed down the corridor toward the exam rooms.

"My mouth'll be the least of your problems if this woman dies." Laura kept pace with him. So did I.

The red-haired nurse grabbed the railing beside the doctor, and the four of us pushed the bed forward.

The woman closed her eyes. She seemed to retreat inside herself.

The doctor looked over his shoulder at me.

"If you just met this woman tonight," he said, "you have no right to be here."

I had opened my mouth to argue when Laura said, "Go to the waiting area, Smokey. I'll join you when I can."

I let go of the railing and they pushed the bed away from me, Laura gripping its side as if she were the one in charge. The group went down the wide corridor with its bright lights, and turned right, into another corridor.

I stood alone, adrenaline humming through me. My breath was coming in short gasps, and I felt the beginnings of a headache. The world had changed in an instant. One moment, Laura and I were anticipating a quiet evening together, the next we were working in tandem to prevent a woman from dying.

"Excuse me?" a woman's voice said from behind me.

I turned. The young nurse who had been watching from the doorway had followed us down the hall. Her uniform was whiter than the other nurse's, suggesting newness, and the nursing cap tilted forward on top of her head. She wore large black fake eyelashes that made her green eyes seem too small. Her brown hair fell loosely about her face, as if the pins holding it in place had worked their way out during her shift.

In her left hand, she held a clipboard. It wasn't the same one that the other nurse had held.

"You can't stay here," she said. "Let me take you out front to fill out your wife's paperwork."

"She's not my wife," I said, disliking the misunderstanding more than usual. Perhaps it was because I had been anticipating a night with Laura, or perhaps it was because the assumption was based not on the way we were all dressed, but because our skin colors matched.

"Your girlfriend, then," the nurse said, coming toward me. She shoved the clipboard under one arm and reached out with the other as if she were going to take my elbow.

I moved away so that she couldn't touch me. "She's not my girlfriend, either. I don't know who she is. Laura and I found her."

The woman blinked, as if my words didn't quite register. "You have no idea who she is?"

I shook my head. "I've never seen her before."

But as I said that, a memory touched my mind, and then fled so fast I couldn't hold it. The woman *had* seemed familiar—something in those eyes. I felt like I had seen them somewhere before.

"Well, then," the nurse said, apparently not noticing my distraction. "You're free to go. If you leave your name at the front desk, we'll be able to contact you about her."

And for questions, should the police have them.

"I promised my girlfriend I'd wait in the waiting room," I said, deliberately describing Laura that way.

"But I thought you said—oh." The nurse blushed. "Of course. It's down the hall and to your left. I'll take you there."

So that I wouldn't go to the examination room and cause more trouble, the way that Laura had just done. I wondered if the doctor had sent this little nurse or if she had watched the whole thing, knowing what her duties were.

She started down the corridor, her rubber shoes squeaking on the tile floor. I followed. This part of the hospital was quiet. Apparently Easter wasn't a big day for emergencies.

I was glad that Jimmy was with the Grimshaws. I didn't have to call anyone or explain my absence or find someone to watch him while this new drama played itself out. The last time I'd brought a woman to an emergency room, I'd stayed all day.

We passed the corridor that veered toward the right. I thought I heard Laura's voice raised in protest. I turned in that direction, but the little nurse caught my arm.

"They don't need you," she said. "I'm sure they're taking good care of things."

I wasn't that certain. Considering how this visit had started, I wasn't sure they were doing well at all. But Laura seemed to be ahead of me on this particular crisis, and she had shown an earthy determination that I had never seen in her before.

In all the time I'd known her, I hadn't heard her swear like that or use her father's name to open a door. But she had done so here without any hesitation at all.

The nurse led me to a large room with plastic sofas, presswood coffee tables, and a few armchairs. Unlike the hospital I'd waited in last December, this hospital closed off the waiting room with a wall of glass.

I stepped inside and nearly choked at the stench of cigarettes. The waiting room had a bluish tint to it, the kind found in bars that hadn't had any fresh air for generations.

"Do you have a fan?" I asked the nurse, but she had already vanished down the corridor. So I propped the door open with a tall silver ashtray. The sand at the top was filled with half-smoked cigarette butts.

The last person who had been in this room obviously had been very nervous. He had also left that day's *Chicago Tribune*, and I picked up the pieces even though I had no real interest in it.

I finally had time to review what had happened. Marvella's absence bothered me. If this woman had truly had a miscarriage or an abortion, she shouldn't have been left alone.

It had looked like someone had been trying to care for her. Now that I knew what had happened, the clutter in the apartment had made sense. Marvella had made the woman a comfortable bed on the couch, had brought her food and liquid, and had tended her with towels.

I clutched the newspaper, still frowning. We hadn't left a note or anything. We'd left the apartment door open and a blood trail down the stairs. If Marvella had gone out for something—more ice, perhaps—and returned to that, she had to be in a panic.

I cast about for a telephone and saw none. So I walked to the front desk. It was long and it dominated a room filled with official wooden chairs and tables. A round clock hung on the wall behind a huge green plant.

No one seemed to be at the desk, but my sense of that changed as I drew closer. A typewriter rat-tatted importantly, then stopped. The desk was designed so that the employees were invisible when they sat down. The patient side of the desk was solid blond oak over five feet tall. Most people had to stand to see over it. I leaned on it.

The woman behind it looked up at me as if she hadn't expected me. She had gray curls and a round face. Her part of the desk was positioned so that she could work on it while sitting down. A phone with six lines sat beside her, and in front of her, a dozen patient records were open. She was writing in the top one, completing some kind of form.

"May I help you?" Her voice was cool.

"I was wondering if there's a phone here I could use."

"Pay phone down the hall, near the restrooms." She nodded toward a corridor on the other side of the desk.

I thanked her and walked in that direction.

This corridor was as wide as the others. The walls were painted an institutional green that no one had tried to decorate with paintings or pictures. The corridor dead-ended in a bank of elevators. Two bathrooms, obviously not for patients, were on one side of the hall. Two pay phones hung on the other side, their phone books neatly tucked in the metal slot beneath the phones themselves.

I went to the first phone, grabbed the book, and looked up Marvella's phone number. She was listed halfway down a page of Walkers, her full name as well as her address. Apparently she had decided it wasn't worth hiding her gender under an initial, not that such things fooled anyone.

I picked up the receiver and plugged the machine, listening as my dime ting-tinged its way through the coin slot. Then a dial tone started. I dialed Marvella's number, and waited for her to answer.

Instead, I found myself counting rings. Two, five, ten. My stomach clenched. Something had gone wrong. Maybe Laura and the doctor had been wrong in their interpretation of the mysterious woman's injuries. Maybe something else had happened, something that had affected Marvella as well.

I hung up the phone and leaned on the metal frame for a moment, trying to decide what to do. Even though I had known Marvella for most of the year, I didn't know her that well. Since she had started insulting Laura, I hadn't talked with her as much and I had stopped asking her to watch Jimmy for me during emergencies.

Outside of the people in the building, I had no idea who her friends were, how she spent her days, or where she might have gone. I wouldn't even know where to start looking for her.

If time was of the essence, I had already wasted a great deal of it.

I walked down the corridor until I could see the round clock near the front desk. It was a few minutes after midnight.

Not as late as I had expected. With all that had happened since the benefit, I would have expected half the night to have gone by. Instead, only an hour and a half passed since Laura and I had gotten into her car on Clark Street.

I walked back to the phones. My shoes had left little flakes on the tile floor. The blood I had stepped in had apparently dried, and was now coming off.

I returned to the same phone, and thumbed through the newsprint inside the phone book until I found the listings for Johnson. Marvella's cousin, Truman Johnson, was a policeman who had worked with me on a dangerous case last December. He was gruff and difficult, and he wouldn't like being awakened this late at night, but he was the only person I could think of to contact.

Johnson, at least, would know who Marvella's friends were. He would be able to make an effective search for her.

I found his number, and dialed it. Someone answered in the middle of the sixth ring, and then I heard an oath as the phone clattered to the floor. A man swore, then the line crackled as the phone was picked up.

"This had better be good." Johnson's voice, thick with sleep, sounded loud in my ear.

"Truman," I said, "Bill Grimshaw."

I had never told him my real name, and I wasn't about to. He had seen the FBI reports about me and Jimmy that listed me as Smokey Dalton, and Jimmy as James Bailey. The reports had crossed his desk last April, and, because Jimmy and I met the descriptions of the two people in those reports, Johnson had asked me about them in August.

I had lied to him, but I wasn't sure he was convinced, and even though we had worked well together, I didn't think I could trust him with something as important as Jimmy's life.

"Do you know what time it is, Grimshaw?" Johnson asked.

"I do, and I'm sorry, but I couldn't think of anyone else to call."

"We need to get you new friends," he mumbled.

"Look, Truman, it's about Marvella."

"What did she do now?"

"I don't know," I said. "She's missing."

I explained the circumstances—the woman in the apartment who was now here at the hospital, and the fact that Marvella hadn't been there then, and still wasn't answering her phone. I did not tell him what Laura and the doctor had been arguing about. All I mentioned was that the woman we found had been bleeding heavily, and we had taken her to the emergency room.

"I'm calling from the hospital," I said. "I was going to go look for Marvella, and then I realized I didn't know where to start. I don't even know who the woman we found is."

"She conscious?"

"She wasn't real coherent," I said. "Laura's with her, and the doctor's trying to stop the bleeding. I'm still not sure she's going to make it through the night."

"I told her she was going to get in trouble one of these days," Johnson said, and I knew he wasn't talking about the mystery woman. "Living alone, making people angry, not taking enough precautions. Hell, she doesn't have as many locks on her door as you do, Grimshaw."

I had noticed that, and last summer, I had thought I would do something about it. But our relationship had become so prickly, I had decided not to.

Now I wondered if that had been a mistake.

"I'll see what I can find," Johnson said. He sounded wide awake now. "Where'll you be?"

"Here until I can figure out what's going on. Then I'll be heading back to the apartment."

"Is the kid there?" He meant Jimmy.

"No, he's spending Easter with friends."

"Easter." Johnson said the word as if it were a curse. "You know what would be really nice, Grimshaw? If for one day, just one—Christmas, Easter, I don't care—all the world's problems would be put on hold, and I could get a decent night's sleep."

He hung up. I had known him long enough to understand that he was worried about Marvella, and the worry came out as complaint. But I wished he had told me what he had planned to do—if he was going to call his partner and make this a police investigation, or if he was going to look into it on his own.

I walked back down the corridor. Just as I reached the front desk, the woman looked up. She had fear-filled eyes, as if she didn't like sitting alone at night in the front of a hospital surrounded by strange men.

"Excuse me," she said, "did you bring in our Jane Doe?"

Caught. I had forgotten they would want information from Laura and I, in case the woman had had an abortion. If the hospital chose to prosecute, all of us could be named as accessories to an illegal operation, or worse.

I sighed. "Yeah."

The woman slipped me a clipboard. "Would you fill this out and bring it back? I know you don't know much about her, but anything you can tell us would be good for the record."

What a sneaky way of getting information for the police. Any Good Samaritan would have thought nothing of it, filling out the form, handing it back, and signing up for weeks of investigation or legal troubles.

"Do you have a pen?" I asked.

She handed me a blue ballpoint with the name of a construction company written on the side.

"Mind if I fill this out in the waiting room?"

"Be my guest," she said and returned to her work.

I carried the clipboard and pen back to the waiting room. It was still empty and the door was still propped open. Some of the blue haze had dissipated.

I set the clipboard on the table in the center of the room, then piled some magazines on top of it. I kept the pen, though, in case I got restless enough to scribble in the crossword magazines.

I picked up the *Tribune*, trying not to worry about what was keeping Laura. I thumbed through the pages, looking at the reports about the Martin Luther King marches and memorial services all over the country. I found myself shaking my head, stunned, even now, that my old friend Martin was gone.

So I paged on, past the articles about Saturday's anti-war demonstrations, past the picture of police in riot gear trying not to repeat last August's nightmare, and searched for something diverting.

I had finally found the comics when I heard footsteps outside the door.

"Bill Grimshaw?"

I looked up. Marvella stood there, a man I didn't recognize beside her. The man was almost hidden behind her, so I couldn't see him clearly.

Marvella was a statuesque woman. She had high cheekbones, a narrow chin, and the most magnificent eyes I had ever seen. In the past few months, she had let her hair go natural, which made her look like the drawings of African tribal goddesses.

Her clothes accentuated the look. She wore a short, dressy rain coat over black high-heeled boots. The boots made her as tall as I was.

I stood.

Her eyes narrowed. Even with the expression of displeasure on her face, she remained the most beautiful woman I had ever seen.

She crossed her arms. "Do you have any idea just exactly what kind of damage you've done?"

THREE

Marvella's words shook me. At first I thought she was referring to the mess in her apartment. But that shouldn't have made her so angry.

The man beside her stepped out of her shadow. His balding head shone in the dingy fluorescent light. He was shorter than Marvella, and rounder, as if he had been very well fed all of his life. He wore a black suit with a white shirt, and shiny black shoes. All of his clothes were clean and ironed so meticulously that they had no wrinkles.

I wondered if he had put them on recently or if he had worn them all day.

He didn't even seem to notice me. Instead, he looked up and down the corridor, as if he expected to be attacked at any moment.

"Where is she?" Marvella wore no makeup, but she didn't need any. Her anger had given her cheeks a dusky rose color that accented her almond-shaped eyes.

Her beauty was distracting, as always.

"Are you all right?" I still didn't know what had happened in that apartment. I also didn't know who the balding man was or why he was with Marvella. "I've been trying to call you."

My words couldn't convey the worry I had felt all evening.

"You brought Val here, right?" Marvella took a step into the waiting room. She held the door open with one hand, as if she were afraid the tall ashtray wouldn't hold the door's weight. "Where is she?"

"Val?" Finally the woman had a name, but it wasn't a familiar one. I had never heard Marvella mention anyone named Val.

"Valentina Wilson, the woman you carried out of my apartment, waking up everyone in the building."

The sound of my thudding feet, our yelling voices, the banging as we had left the building all returned to me. Of course we had woken people up. Of course they would have looked out to see what was happening.

And they would have seen me and Laura in our fancy clothes, carrying an unconscious woman into a Mercedes.

I wondered what they had thought.

Marvella was angry about this? She was angry that I had brought that poor woman to the emergency room?

"She was dying, Marvella," I said.

"So you're a doctor now?" Marvella let go of the door. She stalked into the room, clutching one hand into a fist. For a moment, I thought she was going to hit me. Instead, she yanked the newspaper out of my hand, and waved it in my face. "Tell me where she is or so help me God, Bill, I'll create a scene until I do find her."

The color in her cheeks had deepened. I had never seen her so angry.

"They took her to one of the exam rooms," I said. "I don't know after that. Laura's still with her."

But Marvella didn't seem to hear my last two sentences. She beckoned the man into the room. He looked up and down the corridor again before stepping inside.

Then he grabbed the ashtray and pulled it in with him, letting the door close behind him.

Even so, Marvella spoke softly when she turned to him. "You'd better see what's going on."

His eyes widened. The whites were bloodshot. He was sweating in that pristine suit. His body odor overwhelmed the residual odor of cigarette smoke.

"I can't, Marvella." His voice was deep and it shook. "It's someone else's case now."

Marvella shook her head once, almost as if she didn't want to hear any more.

She faced me again, blocking the balding man with her body, as if she were afraid I had already seen too much.

"The doctor treating Val," Marvella said. "Is he white?"

I knew where she was going with this. I had heard the argument before and I didn't agree with it. Some white doctors were bad, just like some black doctors were. But a person's color wasn't a good determination of his medical skill.

"He seemed competent enough," I said.

Her expression hardened. She looked at me with something akin to hatred.

Then she turned to the man behind her. He had moved sideways, so that he could watch the corridor through the glass wall.

Marvella grabbed his sleeve. He looked down at her hand.

"You know what they'll do," she said to him. "You have to go in there."

"There's no guarantee anything bad will happen," he said, without looking at her.

She pulled on his arm, and I finally caught a glimpse of her face as she looked at him. It was the face of a supplicant.

"Please," she said.

He sighed, just like the white doctor had when faced with Laura, and glanced at me. His eyes had a weariness that I hadn't expected. A weariness, and a sadness.

"Excuse me, Marvella," he said as he put a hand on her arm. He pushed his way around her, and stopped in front of me.

"How did you find her?" he asked. He was talking about Val.

I glanced at Marvella. She nodded, as if she wanted me to tell this man everything.

"She was asking for help," I said, even though I wasn't sure those small birdlike cries could be considered a request. They were more like the sounds of desperation, as if she had known she was dying, and was crying out to the cosmos for someone, anyone, to save her. "She was hemorrhaging."

"Bleeding?" He put an emphasis on the word. His manner reminded me of the emergency-room doctor's—a complete mistrust of all the information I was giving him, as if I wouldn't know the difference between a seeping wound and arterial spurts.

"Hemorrhaging," I said. "You know. You saw the apartment."

I was guessing on that last part, but I figured if Marvella had spoken to the neighbors, she had gone home before coming here.

He nodded. His expression was even more serious now. He had seen the apartment. He had seen the blood, and probably the empty ice bag. Perhaps he hadn't been able to determine how much of the mess on the floor was blood and how much of it was water.

I added, "Her skin color was poor and she was barely conscious. She couldn't stand, and she couldn't answer direct questions."

He let out a long breath. Then he shook his head. My answer seemed to defeat him.

"I would probably have had to bring her here myself," he said, but I couldn't tell if he was talking to me or to Marvella. "They'll do whatever is necessary to save her life."

She clutched his arm again. "I want you to watch them. I want you to make sure she's going to be all right."

He put a hand over hers. "Marvella, if I go in there, they're going to think she's my patient. They're going to think I did that to her."

"No, they won't. I'll tell them that you came at my request. I'll tell them—"

"I've got enough trouble already," he said, slipping his arm out of her grasp. "I can't invite more. Much as I want to help, I can't."

"But we have to make sure she's going to be all right." Marvella's voice shook and I realized, with some surprise, that she was close to tears.

"It's in God's hands now," he said, and squeezed her arm.

She pulled away and turned her back on him, her lower lip trembling. I had seen Marvella angry, but I had never seen her like this.

He looked at me, his eyes filled with compassion.

"You did the right thing," he said, and hurried out the door. He scurried down the hall, disappearing so quickly that it seemed like he had never been there.

Marvella bowed her head. I stood beside her for a moment, feeling helpless, then I put my hand on her shoulder. She was shaking.

"Tell me about it," I said. "Tell me what's going on."

She turned to me, tears in her eyes, and shook her head.

"Why don't we start with the easy questions," I said. "Who was that who just left?"

She swallowed. "Dr. Jetten. He's an old friend of the family."

"What was he doing here?" I kept my voice low, so that she would hear the comfort in it, and not shy away from my questions.

She shook her head.

"Marvella, I'm not going to do anything. I just want to know."

A tear ran down her cheek and hung on her chin, waiting to drip on her long, lovely neck. I resisted the urge to wipe the tear away.

Marvella didn't even seem to know it was there.

"When Val got worse," she said, "I went to find him. I didn't want to leave her alone, but I knew he wouldn't come with me unless I went to him personally. He has rules, you know?"

"Rules about what?" I asked.

"Bill—"

"Marvella." I kept my hand on her shoulder. She was still shaking. "You can tell me."

"No," she said quietly.

Rather than trying to drag the information out question by question, I decided to ask the most important one first. "Did Dr. Jetten give Val an abortion?"

"No!" Marvella sounded shocked.

"So she just miscarried?"

"Shh." Marvella whirled, looked at the glass wall, then scanned the room, as if she were making certain no one else was listening.

She wouldn't have been this worried if it were a simple miscarriage, would she?

"The only reason I'm asking," I said, "is that the emergency-room doctor thought Val had had an abortion. He was trying to find out who performed it."

"Son of a bitch." Marvella's legs wobbled, and she grabbed me to steady herself. "He made her tell him, didn't he? Just so that he would help her. He did that. Bastard."

"No," I said. "Laura stopped him."

Marvella looked at me in surprise. "Laura Hathaway, your pretty little china doll?"

"She knew what was going on, Marvella. I didn't. If your friend makes it out of this all right, it'll be because of Laura."

"She's family." Marvella's voice shook again. She wasn't talking about Laura. "Val's more than a friend. She's my sort-of cousin."

Now I remembered Valentina. The night I had met her had been so different from this night that I hadn't even put the two together. Marvella had introduced me to Val on the night of the Nefertiti ball in December, calling her a sort-of cousin even then.

It had been a giddy introduction. The women were wearing thin, white, Egyptian-style gowns, with gold bands under the breasts, around the waists, and over the hips. The gown had looked spectacular on Marvella, and just as stunning on her sister, but it had made delicate little Valentina look like a child playing dress-up.

I had flirted with her, telling her that she looked lovely.

She had gazed up at me with those unusual eyes. They were filled with suppressed laughter, most of it directed at herself.

I look silly, she had said, *but thank you.*

A woman with no illusions, a woman who knew herself. How had she traveled from that night to this one?

"I hadn't realized that's who she was," I said.

"She looks awful, I know. After all she's been through, you'd expect it." Marvella sank onto the nearest couch. The newspaper slipped out of her hand onto the floor. "She didn't tell any of us. That's the worst part. If she had just talked to me, I'd've sent her to Dr. Jetten. He hasn't lost a patient yet. But she went to some butcher. God knows what he did. She wouldn't tell me. But she was already so sick when she showed up this morning."

"It didn't happen today?"

Marvella shook her head. "Yesterday, I think, although it might have been Friday. She wasn't going to tell me anything."

"Why didn't you bring her here?"

Marvella's eyes widened. "Oh, for God's sake, Bill, how naïve are you? If she lives through this, they'll probably press charges, especially if she won't tell them who did this. Especially as close to death as she was."

I wasn't as naïve as she thought I was. I wouldn't have taken anyone to the hospital unless I thought the situation was an extreme emergency.

Marvella was the one who had risked her friend's life.

"What did you think was going to happen?" I snapped. "Did you think your friendly doctor was going to save her in your apartment without any equipment?"

Marvella stood again, the anger clearly giving her strength. She crossed the room and stood toe-to-toe with me. Not many women could look me in the eye, but Marvella could.

"He could have brought her in to any hospital as one of his patients," she said, her voice low and throbbing with anger. "He would have called it a miscarriage gone wrong, a pregnancy in trouble. No one would have thought anything of it. But you brought her in on her own, clearly in distress—"

"Dying," I said. "She was *dying.*"

"And now everyone'll know. Which is exactly what she didn't want." The tears were back in Marvella's eyes. She turned her head so that I wouldn't see them. "I'm going to find out what's going on."

She started for the door. I grabbed her arm.

"Wait a minute," I said. "Right now, they don't have her name. Laura and I didn't know who she was, and we gave out no information. If you go charging in there, telling them who she is, then the authorities will have everything they need. But if we wait, maybe we can finesse this."

Marvella stopped. She still faced the door, but she tilted her head, as if what I had said made sense to her. "Finesse?"

"When she was fighting with the doctor, Laura said that they wouldn't be able to tell if this was a miscarriage or an abortion without a thorough examination."

"I'm sure they did the examination, Bill."

"I'm sure they did," I said. "But a miscarriage is just a spontaneous abortion, and maybe, with a little inventive discussion, we can get the doctor to write it up that way."

Marvella looked at me over her shoulder. "Yeah," she said with deep sarcasm. "As if you and I could do that."

"We can't," I said, "but Laura might be able to. She got the doctor to stop interviewing your cousin and treat her. She might be able to do more."

Marvella turned toward me, slipping out of my grasp. She crossed her arms, clearly not believing me. "Why would she want to help someone like Val?"

"She already is," I said.

Marvella shook her head. "She's not helping. She's being a Good Samaritan. She hasn't taken any real risks so far. No one's going to think your rich white friend had anything to do with an abortion. But if she gets them to—what was your word? Finesse?—the medical reports, then she's as liable as the rest of us."

Marvella's mistrust of white people, and her dislike of Laura, was making it impossible for her to believe what I said.

"She'll help," I repeated. "And it won't cause any problems."

Marvella plucked at her coat. "You may put a lot of faith in that woman, but I don't. I'm certainly not going to trust Val's life to her."

"Marvella—"

She held up a hand to silence me again, and gave me a rueful look. "I have to take care of this, Bill. I'm responsible for Val. And I want to make sure she's all right."

Marvella pulled open the door.

"Marvella, wait."

But she didn't wait. She stepped into the hallway and strode away from me, arms swinging, heels clicking, looking like a warrior. I hurried out of the waiting room, but had trouble keeping up with her. Her long legs enabled her to move quickly down the hall.

She turned down the corridor toward the emergency area, and had already reached the corridor where Valentina and Laura had disappeared when I caught up.

Two nurses blocked Marvella's way. They must have heard her coming.

One of them was the brown-haired nurse who had confronted me. The other was a squarely built black woman who had both feet planted shoulder width apart.

Yet, she seemed small compared to Marvella. Marvella could have pushed her aside with a single movement, but she didn't. Instead she peered over both nurses, as if she could see what was going on down the hall.

"I'm sorry," the brown-haired nurse was saying as I approached. "No one is allowed down this hall, not even family."

"But that's my cousin down there," Marvella said, the strength gone from her voice. Her back was still rigid, though, and I could tell that this meek tone was a ploy.

"If you go to the waiting room, miss, I'll go check on her, and let you know how she is."

"Let me back there," Marvella said. "You already let someone else go with her."

I caught up to her then, and took her arm.

"She's distraught," I said to the nurses. "I'll take her to the waiting room."

The brown-haired nurse who had spoken looked up at me. Her eyes narrowed.

"Is this woman related to the woman you brought in?" she asked.

"Ye—" Marvella started, but I interrupted.

"We think so," I said. "We'll know more when she can see her."

"Not right now," the brown-haired nurse said. "They're prepping her for surgery."

"No!" Marvella launched herself forward. The black nurse grabbed her, keeping her from running down the hall.

I barely managed to keep my grip on Marvella's arm. I tried to pull her back, but she turned on me and pushed, shoving me backward. I grabbed her other arm.

"Calm down," I said, keeping my voice level. "This isn't helping anyone."

Marvella flailed against me. She wanted to be free, and she was very strong. It took a lot of effort to hold her.

"They can't take her into surgery, Bill," she said. "We've got to stop them."

"I don't think they had a choice." The black nurse was talking to me. "They couldn't stop the bleeding."

I nodded and pulled Marvella away from them, dragging her toward the waiting room. She resisted, trying to yank herself out of my arms.

"You don't understand," she hissed at me. "You can't understand. They'll destroy her."

It took all of my strength to get her down the corridor. Once we were out of the nurses' hearing range, I stopped.

"I do understand," I lied. I wasn't sure what Marvella was so afraid of, but at that moment, the worst thing she could do was throw herself into that operating room. "You're the one who is not seeing things clearly. If Laura and I hadn't found your cousin, she would have been dead within the hour. If the doctors have to operate on her to save her life, then that's what they're going to do. Anything is better than letting her die. Do you understand that?"

Marvella's entire body was rigid. Her lower lip trembled again, and she bit it. The trembling stopped.

"She made me promise," she said.

"Promise what?" I asked, steering her down the corridor toward the waiting room.

"That I wouldn't bring her here. That I wouldn't let anything bad happen."

I sighed. I'd made those kinds of promises too in my life, and I couldn't keep them. I hadn't even been able to keep them with Jimmy, whom I was trying to protect.

I slipped my arm around Marvella's back. It felt very different holding her than holding Laura. My arm naturally rested around Marvella's waist. With Laura, I was more comfortable with my arm around her shoulder.

The comparison caught me by surprise. I'd always found Marvella beautiful, but I was never attracted to her. I still wasn't. But I felt oddly guilty for holding her close while Laura was nearby.

"By the time we found her," I said, forcing myself to concentrate on the problem instead of Laura, "Val was begging us for help. I don't think she cared at that point what we did so long as we made the pain go away."

Marvella shuddered. "I hadn't even thought about the pain. It must have been awful."

It probably had been. Valentina Wilson's eyes had been glassy, and I knew from past experience that that kind of look didn't come just from blood loss, but also from extreme agony.

The waiting room was still empty, and some of the blue haze had cleared. The room was a mess, though, with the scattered magazines and the newspaper on the floor.

I pulled open the waiting-room door and Marvella walked in without my help. She sank on one of the couches, and put her face in her hands.

I sat beside her, rubbing my hand over her curved back.

"You tried," I said. "That's the best we can do."

"I know," she said, her voice muffled. "And obviously that wasn't good enough."

FOUR

We sat in the waiting room for another half an hour. Marvella rested her head on the back of the couch. She didn't even unbutton her coat. She wrapped her arms around her waist and stared at the ceiling. No matter what I said, she wouldn't respond. After a while, I grabbed one of the crossword magazines and searched for a page that looked challenging.

I was still looking when Laura came in. I had never seen her so disheveled. Her blond hair hung in strands over her face and was tangled in the back where it had fallen out of its bun. Her makeup was smeared and that streak of blood on her cheek had dried black. The front of her blue pantsuit—so elegant at the start of the evening—was completely ruined. Blood crusted the legs and coated the sleeves. More streaks covered her torso. Her blue open-toed shoes had turned black with blood.

I stood and extended a hand to her. Laura took it, and then used it to slip her arm around my back. She rested her head on my shoulder. She smelled of sweat and blood and Laura, and I found that very reassuring.

Marvella looked over at her, and her mouth opened slightly as if she were shocked at what she saw. She probably still hadn't believed me about Laura—at least, not until she saw her, covered in Valentina's blood.

I eased Laura onto the couch. She kept her head on my shoulder. Her body was heavy with exhaustion.

Marvella leaned forward, her arms no longer wrapped around her waist. "How's Val?"

Laura sighed, then ran a hand through her hair. Her hands were clean, as if she had scrubbed them in the exam room.

"Did they take her into surgery?" Marvella asked.

It was my turn to hold up a hand. "Give her a minute."

Laura shook her head, which still rested on my shoulder. Then she sighed again and sat up. "I don't need a minute. I'm just not sure how much I should explain."

Her tone wasn't condescending, but I stiffened anyway. Marvella usually took everything Laura said as maliciously intended.

"I'm probably better versed in female medical problems than you are," Marvella snapped.

A small, private smile crossed Laura's face. It was a sad look. "All right then," she said, and I was surprised at the mildness in her tone. After hearing Marvella's challenge, I would have attacked back. Apparently Laura saw no point in it.

Laura stood, her hands on her back as if it hurt her, and walked across the room to Marvella. Marvella watched her without changing position.

Even though I had seen the two of them together before, I had always been trying to stop a fight. I hadn't realized how much smaller Laura was. Her disheveled look made her seem younger, more vulnerable, than Marvella, although Marvella often hid behind her regal features.

Laura sat on the presswood coffee table, so that she could face Marvella. Laura's back was to me. I moved to the other end of the couch so that I could watch the interchange, and maybe learn something myself.

"Here's what happened." Laura folded her hands in her lap, looking prim and proper despite her ruined clothing. "The asshole who performed the abortion—"

"Shh," Marvella said.

Laura shook her head. "They know," she said. "And besides, we're alone here."

Marvella's gaze met mine, and I could see the frustration in it. She didn't trust anyone, not Laura, not the hospital. I averted my gaze, figuring I would get involved when Laura was done getting us up to date.

Laura looked from Marvella to me. When neither of us said anything, Laura continued. "That asshole tried a D&C. Either he didn't know what he was doing or she was too far along or both. Do you know how many weeks pregnant she was?"

Laura had Marvella's attention now.

"I didn't even know Val was pregnant." Marvella threaded her hands together in an unconscious imitation of Laura's position. "I hadn't seen her for a month. She would call, but we never managed to get together. The first time I saw her was this morning. What did he do?"

Laura ran a hand over her mouth, as if she didn't want to speak of the operation. Then she shook her head.

"To start," she said, her voice low, "he didn't get everything. He left a lot of tissue in the uterus."

Marvella's lips thinned. That hard expression had returned to her face. "So that's what caused the bleeding."

"Some of it," Laura said.

It was almost as if they were talking in code, as if I were only getting part of the conversation. I was astonished at Laura. She was speaking in a tired but clinical tone about things I had no idea she understood.

With her thumb, she scraped at the blood stain on her face. Some of it flaked off. I wasn't sure she was aware it was there.

"The doctor here," Laura said, "Rothstein, he's good. I fought with him a lot. He was trying the scare tactics, and when he realized she wasn't completely conscious, he tried them on me."

"Laura was tough out there," I said, so that Marvella would understand how hard Laura had fought.

Laura turned that tired smile in my direction. "This was after you left, Smoke."

That surprised me. I thought she had won the fight in the corridor. "He kept it up?"

That small, tired smile crossed Laura's face again. "Don't judge him too harshly. Val was in a bad way. He's required by law to find out what happened to her, and if the hospital or the police feel he wasn't diligent enough, they'll go after him."

Marvella wrapped her arms around her waist again, crinkling her black coat. "He was going to let her die?"

Laura took a deep breath. I recognized the tactic. She often used it to stall, so that she could think of the correct way to express her thoughts.

"At first," she said carefully, "I don't think he realized how ill she was. Not until we took her in the back, and removed the material I had used to stop the bleeding, did he understand how badly she was hemorrhaging."

The material was my topcoat, which I doubted I would ever see again, and which I knew I didn't want to.

"He was going to finish the D&C, but when he started . . ." Laura's voice trailed off. For the first time since she had moved to the coffee table, she looked at me. Her expression was pleading, but I didn't know what she wanted.

"What?" Marvella asked. "What's wrong?"

Laura bit her lower lip. She faced Marvella again. "He wasn't sure if all of the bleeding was coming from inside the uterus. He thought maybe there was a laceration on the cervix."

I winced. How could these women be so clinical about personal things? Men never talked like this—about anything.

"Did he dilate her?" Marvella asked.

"No," Laura said. "He set down the curette and, to his credit, turned to me and explained everything. Now granted, I'd been fighting him the entire time. The last thing I wanted him to do was punish her for this one mistake, so I wasn't going to let her go into surgery if I could help it. I think he knew that."

"Punish her?" I asked.

Both Laura and Marvella looked at me. They had identical expressions on their faces, and the expressions seemed tolerant and sad at the same time.

"They—"

"I'm—"

They spoke at the same time and stopped when they realized what they had done.

Marvella nodded to Laura. "You tell him."

Laura straightened her shoulders, leaning back slightly so that she could see me better. "I'm not sure if it's the doctor or hospital policy, but sometimes—"

"Always," Marvella said. "They always do it."

Laura shook her head. "Not always."

"On black women."

"And poor women," Laura said. "But some women manage to avoid it. Cook County's the worst, from what I hear. I thought maybe we were safe bringing her here, but when we got here I wasn't so sure."

There they went again, speaking in that code. "You were going to tell me how they would punish her," I said.

Marvella looked at me, her expression hard and her eyes flashing with something stronger than anger. It almost looked like hatred.

"They'll sterilize her," Marvella said.

I recoiled, from her tone as much as her words. I had never heard so much controlled anger in her voice.

"That's why I didn't want her in surgery, Bill. Because they're going to declare her an unfit mother or they'll say since she didn't want this one, she shouldn't have any, and they take away her chance to have children. Forever."

I let out a shocked laugh. "They can't do that."

"I don't know if they can," Laura said. "But they do. I know a woman that happened to."

"Me too." Marvella raised her narrow chin, a movement so like Laura's defensive gesture that it startled me.

"This is what you meant, Marvella?" I asked. "Is this why you thought I was so stupid to bring her here?"

Marvella's arms were wrapped so tightly around her waist that I thought she was going to rip her coat. "At least Dr. Jetten wouldn't have done it unless he had to."

"He couldn't operate on her in your apartment," I said.

"He could have done a new D&C there. I thought that was all she needed, when the bleeding didn't stop. I figured there was still tissue, and I figured he would give her something for the bleeding and penicillin for any infection. If it was really bad, he would take her in, like I told you, but as one of his patients, and no one would have ever known."

"That's why you were gone?" Laura asked. "To get a doctor?"

Marvella gave a small nod.

"You actually know someone who does this? Someone you trust?" Laura sounded surprised.

Marvella looked guarded, but she nodded again.

"So why did she go to someone so incompetent? Isn't she a friend of yours? Does she know that you know—?"

"Yes, she knows." Marvella hunched forward. "And she's my cousin. Sort of. And a friend. And I have no idea why she didn't come to me. She knows I wouldn't have told anyone. She knows I would have helped her. She knows. There was no reason to go anywhere else."

For a moment, none of us said a word. Then Laura put a hand on Marvella's knee. Her skin looked unusually pale against the black fabric of Marvella's coat.

"Sometimes people don't think too clearly when they're in this situation," Laura said.

I leaned back on the couch, obviously no longer part of this conversation—at least as far as they were concerned.

Marvella rocked, like a child trying to comfort herself. I wasn't even sure if she was aware of it.

"Val's one of the smartest people I know," she said. "If she had just come to me, everything would have been all right. Having kids was one of her main goals in life. If they take that away from her, I don't know what she'll do."

It was my turn to shiver. Just recently, I'd seen what that kind of despair did to people.

"There may be too much damage," Laura said. "If there truly are cervical lacerations or if that idiot abortionist punctured her uterus, then she might not have more children anyway."

"He couldn't have punctured the uterus," Marvella said. "She would have had a different reaction. Wouldn't she?"

Marvella raised her head. Her gaze met Laura's. Marvella wanted Laura to tell her everything would be all right, and I could tell from the set of Laura's jaw that she didn't believe it would be.

I caught my breath.

Laura shrugged. "The gaps in my knowledge are pretty huge."

Marvella still studied her. Then Marvella said, "Why are you helping us?"

"It was the right thing to do," Laura said.

"You didn't have to."

"Yes, I did." Laura ran a hand through her hair, messing it further. "And I want to apologize. I wanted to stay and argue, but I ran out of expertise. As far as I know, he was right this time, and she had to go into surgery. I told him that if he did anything unnecessary, he'd hear from my lawyers, but I don't know if that's enough. If it's hospital policy—"

"Then you'll have even deeper pockets to sue," I said.

"That won't make up for being sterilized, Bill." Marvella's voice was soft. "Nothing will make up for that."

There were tears in her eyes again. She blinked hard and looked toward the glass wall. Then she cursed.

I looked. Truman Johnson was walking down the corridor. His large, muscular body seemed even bigger against the institutional green walls. His chin jutted forward, as if he were clenching his teeth, and his fleshy face was lined with worry. His raincoat was rumpled and so were his dark pants, as if he had pulled them out of the dirty clothes pile when he put them on. He walked quickly, purposefully, as if he were using his strength to give everyone around him the message to leave him alone.

Marvella stood and crossed the room before Laura and I could move. She yanked the waiting room door open, and stepped into the hall, effectively blocking Johnson's progress. For a moment, I thought he would revert to his old linebacker status, and simply plow her aside, but he stopped.

He raised his head to look her in the eye. With her heels, she was almost as tall as he was.

"So, you *are* alive," he said, his deep voice rumbling.

Marvella's cheeks flushed. I stood too, and walked to the door. I had called Johnson, and I had forgotten to tell her about it. It was time for me to intervene.

"Of course I'm alive," she snapped.

I slipped into the hallway, and wedged myself between them. Johnson's raincoat was cold. He didn't budge as I brushed against him. Marvella was the one who stepped back.

"I'm sorry," I said to her. "I called him about midnight. I thought you were missing and since I had to stay here, he was the only person I knew who might know where you were."

As I spoke, her mouth opened and she looked around, as if searching for a way out. "You called him?"

"Yeah." I had no idea why this upset her. "I was worried. Your friend was injured, I thought. Laura hadn't said what was wrong, and your apartment was empty, so I thought the worst. I figured he would know how to find you."

Marvella stepped around me. She put a hand on Johnson's chest and shoved. "Go home."

I grabbed her arm and stepped between them again.

"You don't belong here," she said over my shoulder. "Go home now."

Johnson still hadn't budged. Marvella's shove had no effect at all.

"What friend?" he asked. I could tell from his tone that he already knew.

Marvella glanced at me. She had that trapped expression again. Even though she had stopped fighting me, I hadn't relaxed my grip on her arm.

"It's just someone I know," she said to Johnson. She was a terrible liar. Her cheeks flushed a deep red. "I'm sorry for the false alarm. Really, go home, Truman."

I wasn't sure what the problem was, but Marvella obviously didn't want Johnson to know who the woman was. Because of the illegal operation? Because she was afraid that Johnson would arrest Val?

"We were just getting ready to leave," I said.

"You're leaving?" He turned toward me. There was a challenge in his rumpled features. A challenge and something else, something I'd never seen before. I would have guessed he was drunk, but I knew better. I had awakened him just an hour ago. He seemed lucid, and he had been out searching.

"Yeah," I said. "There's not much else we can do—"

"You're leaving, too?" His voice rumbled with barely contained anger. He directed that last question at Marvella.

"No," she said. "I just got here."

"Laura and I," I said. "We're leaving."

"Laura?" Johnson repeated. Then I realized he had never met her. She stood and walked toward us.

He took in the ruined pantsuit, the blood, and her tousled blond hair. Then he looked at me and Marvella, as if he didn't understand how Laura was connected to this.

I could understand his confusion. Not only was she the only one covered in blood, but she was white as well. Maybe he thought she was here for another emergency.

"Go home, Truman," Marvella said, catching his attention again.

Laura came up behind me and slipped an arm around my waist. Her body trembled with exhaustion.

"You tell me what's going on first," Johnson said.

"A friend of mine got in trouble," Marvella said, and this time the words came out easier since she wasn't exactly lying. "She came to me too late. I was trying to get help when Bill found her and brought her here."

"She'll be all right." Laura was using that soothing tone again, and she was using it on Johnson.

He frowned at her, then turned away. He didn't care about her. He didn't seem to care about anyone except Marvella.

"A friend," he said again.

"Yes."

"I know all of your friends."

"No, you don't," she said.

"Stop lying to me, Marvella. It's Val, isn't it? Val's in there."

Marvella's mouth opened, then closed. "I—Truman, you have no right to be here. Just go home."

"No right to be here?" His voice rose with each word. "No right to be here? I have every goddamn right to be here. You should have called me, Marvella."

"You're forgetting yourself, Truman," she said.

"I'm not forgetting anything." He put his hands on her shoulders and moved her aside as if she were a rag doll. "And now I'm going to go see my wife."

FIVE

I had no idea Johnson was married, although it didn't surprise me. Cops rarely mentioned their home life or their families, and wives rarely answered the phone, because any time it rang, it was probably an emergency, something to do with the job.

What did surprise me was that Johnson's wife had a different last name than he had. I had never encountered that before.

Having moved Marvella aside, Johnson whirled and walked back down the hall. He had obviously been in this hospital many times before and knew where the exam and surgical rooms were.

He shoved his hands in the pockets of his rumpled coat, and strode with his head down, almost as if he were plowing through an imaginary defensive line.

Marvella put her hand on my shoulder, pushing me forward ever so slightly.

"Stop him, Bill," she said, "please stop him. He can't go down there."

"If it's his wife, then he has every right—"

"It's not," Marvella said. She gave me one more pleading look, and then hurried after him, her normally confident walk shaky on her high-heeled boots.

Laura and I stood side by side. She was still leaning against me, her arm around my back. She must have moved forward as I did when Marvella pushed.

"Do you know what's going on?" Laura asked.

"I don't have a clue," I said. "But if she got an abortion without his permission . . ."

I didn't finish the sentence. I couldn't. I'd seen Johnson in action. He had a temper and sometimes it ruled him. I could understand why a wife, set on getting rid of a child, wouldn't tell him anything.

Halfway down the corridor, Marvella caught up to Johnson. She leaned forward, grabbed his arm, and he shook her off. She stumbled, but kept after him. She grabbed him again, and he pushed her away.

Marvella slammed into the wall and stood there, hands pressed against the green paint as if it were holding her up.

"My God," Laura said.

I sighed. I didn't want to get involved in this domestic drama, but I had a hunch it would be me or hospital security. And in this case, with all of its legal ramifications, it would be better for me to be involved.

I eased out of Laura's grasp and hurried down the hall. Marvella hadn't moved. Johnson was looking around as if he were searching for the exam rooms.

"Truman," I called.

Johnson ignored me. He reached the second corridor.

"Truman, wait." I had nearly caught up to him.

He glanced over his shoulder, and saw how close I was. He frowned. "You don't know what this is about, Grimshaw. Butt out."

"I don't know and, honestly, I don't care," I said as I reached Marvella. Her breath was coming in short gasps. He had shoved her so hard he had knocked the wind out of her. "But there's more going on here than you may realize."

Johnson stopped walking. He crossed his arms, rumpling his coat further.

Marvella shot me a cautionary look. I glanced toward Laura. She was coming down the hall, too, her right hand clasped in a small fist. I wasn't even sure she was aware she was walking like that.

"Val's been wounded," Johnson said. "That's all I need to know."

He turned toward Marvella. She still hadn't moved. I wondered if he had hurt her.

Apparently he did, too.

"Look," he said, walking back to Marvella. She watched him, her back straightening as if she were bracing herself. "I went to your place. I saw it, all that blood, and then your neighbors said that Grimshaw had carried a woman out, and it sounded like Val. You were missing—or that's what I thought, until they said you showed up just before I did, and went off to the hospital. Do you even know what happened? Who did this to her? The neighbors didn't know. They didn't hear the break-in, just Grimshaw yelling as he got her out of the building."

Laura reached us, but hung back. Marvella gave me a sideways glance. Her face was full of anguish.

No one had told Johnson about the abortion. He probably hadn't even known about the pregnancy.

"Truman," Marvella said with great patience, "it's up to Val to talk to you."

"You people won't let me see her," he said.

"She's in surgery." Marvella took a deep breath.

"What happened?" he asked. "Marvella, I'll go crazy if you don't tell me. Please."

Marvella looked past me, at Laura. It was almost as if Marvella was consulting with Laura. I never thought I would see anything like it. Their relationship had changed in the space of a few minutes.

I looked at Laura, too, and so did Johnson. She was just a yard or so behind us. Somehow, even in her ruined clothing, she managed to look aristocratic.

She pushed her hair out of her face and shrugged. She obviously had no answers for Marvella.

Marvella sighed, then turned to me. "Bill, he's not her husband. They got a divorce two years ago. He just won't let go."

That was why the last names were different. Wilson and Johnson. Had Val gone back to her maiden name the way Laura had?

"I am her husband," Johnson said.

"Truman," Marvella said with the weariness that came only from long argument, "a court says otherwise."

"Val promised me," Johnson said. "She promised me before God. I don't care what the court says. In the eyes of God, she's still mine."

Laura grimaced. I bowed my head.

"It's not any of your business, Truman, and if I tell you what happened, she'll be really angry at me." Marvella took a step toward him. She didn't move like she was in pain. Maybe she had simply been protecting herself.

Johnson watched her as if he had never seen her before. Even though he was as large as I was, he looked small. His big shoulders hunched forward, his wrinkled clothing and his scuffed brown cop shoes diminished him. He wasn't a powerful policeman anymore. He was a man in love with a woman who didn't love him back.

"And if she doesn't survive," he said, his voice so soft that I almost couldn't hear the question.

Marvella started to reach for him, then stopped. "We'll deal with it then."

He shook his head. "You're stubborn, Marvella."

"If you love her, you'll leave her alone," Marvella said.

I was frowning, not liking how this sounded. I wanted to be anywhere else. I didn't like seeing inside of other people's lives, even though I sometimes got paid to do so. I especially didn't like it when I had gotten to know—and respect—the people in other contexts.

Johnson straightened. Marvella's words had revived his anger.

"I don't know why you're being so secretive," he said. "All I have to do is go to the front desk, tell them I'm her husband, and then I'll get all the reports. The doctors will deal with me. I'm trying to follow the rules here, Marvella, but if you won't tell me anything, I'll find someone who will."

He would, too. He was relentless. Marvella had to know that. He was her cousin.

Which was why she identified Val as her sort-of cousin. Because once Valentina Wilson had been her cousin-in-law. They had obviously remained friends after the divorce, and never lost the family feeling.

Marvella shook her head.

"Why don't we go back to the waiting room?" Laura's voice startled me. She spoke with the tone she used at Sturdy, the ones that got employees to jump.

Johnson looked at her as if he had forgotten she was there.

"It's probably better to have conversations in private." Laura's gaze met Marvella's. "Don't you agree?"

Marvella grimaced, then walked toward Laura. As Marvella passed me, she said, "I wish you had left him out of this."

I did too, now, but I had no idea that there were such tortured family relations between Johnson, Marvella, and Valentina Wilson. All I'd been trying to do was make sure Marvella was all right.

She continued walking, past Johnson, past Laura, heading back to the waiting room. After a moment, Johnson followed. Laura waited for me. As we walked, she slipped her hand in mine and squeezed.

"We should probably just go home," I said softly.

"We stay," Laura said.

"It's not our business."

"It's mine," she said. "I want to know if Val's going to make it."

I slipped my arm around her and pulled her close. She rested her head on my shoulder. "You don't think she will?"

"I don't know. But I don't think her chances are very good."

I wanted to argue with her. I didn't want to be in the middle of the fight that was about to start in the waiting room. But I wasn't sure what to say without sounding hard-hearted.

"Besides," Laura said, "I guaranteed her medical bills. I can't disappear now."

I stopped walking and held her back, too. I didn't want Johnson or Marvella to hear this.

"Laura," I said quietly, "you realize that could make you liable for more than just the money."

She raised her head and smiled at me. The smile was tired. "Let them try to take on Drew. Let them just try."

Drew McMillan was her attorney. He was as good as they got. "He's corporate, Laura. This would be criminal."

"And Drew's firm could take care of that. The publicity would be ugly, especially with that abortion bill being considered in the state legislature."

I had no idea any abortion bill was being considered in the legislature, but I didn't want to ask her about it. I didn't want a political discussion now.

"You've thought this through?" I asked. "I don't want anyone to arrest you."

"Oh, I'd love the publicity," Laura said. "Give me a microphone and let me talk."

I looked at her in surprise. I hadn't seen this side of her before.

She smiled up at me. "Come on," she said. "Let's get back there before World War Three starts."

We started down the hall, taking only a few moments to reach the waiting room. Marvella and Johnson were already inside, but they weren't speaking.

They were standing in the center of the room, a coffee table between them, and they were glaring at each other.

I could finally see the family resemblance. It wasn't in their features— Marvella's were classic African, and Johnson's were softer, without the high cheekbones or magnificent eyes. No, the resemblance was in their posture, and the defiant look on both of their faces.

Laura gave my waist an extra squeeze as we walked inside.

"Close the door," Marvella said.

I moved the silver ashtray and let the door swing closed. Laura continued inside. She stopped close to Marvella and Johnson, obviously ready to act as referee.

For the first time that night, Marvella ignored Laura.

"I'm letting Bill stay," Marvella said to Johnson, "because I need someone to control you, Truman."

My shoulders stiffened. I was a big man, but so was Johnson. And even though his ex–football player's frame was going to fat, I wasn't sure who would win in a one-on-one contest—him or me. I was stronger, but anger, weight, and sheer brute force might give him an advantage.

Marvella hadn't noticed my reaction. She was still looking at Johnson. "You have to promise me you won't take any of this personally."

He tilted his head back and crossed his arms. "Any of what?"

His stance didn't intimidate Marvella. She didn't move. "Promise me."

Johnson looked at me, as if I were going to support him. Instead, Laura said, "You're a police officer, right?"

He frowned at her. "How did you get involved in this?"

"She's with me," I said.

"I can see that, but I don't understand it."

"Yes, Truman's a police officer," Marvella said. "He's a detective."

"Then, Detective Johnson, we'll need your cool head, and your credentials, if you're willing to give them." Laura was the shortest person in the room, but she knew how to use her voice to take power for her. Her words were a command.

Johnson apparently heard that command and responded to it without realizing it. His chin came down, and he shoved his hands in his pockets.

"For what?" he asked. "What do you need my credentials for? What's happened?"

"You probably should sit down," I said, not because I was worried that he wouldn't be able to stand once he heard the news, but because I had seen his sudden reaction in the hallway. It would be easier to control him if he were off his feet.

Johnson looked from my face to Laura's to Marvella's. Whatever he saw made him comply. He sat down on the nearest couch, his hands cupping his knees.

"All right," he said. "I'm sitting."

Marvella walked to the other side of the room. She leaned against the far wall as if she were tired, but it was pretty clear that she wanted as much distance between her and Johnson as possible. She obviously didn't want to be near him when he heard what happened to Valentina.

I stayed by the door. I could reach him in two steps if I had to. Laura sat on the couch across from Johnson, her hands folded on her lap. She looked exhausted.

Marvella waited until all of us were in place before she spoke.

"I don't know everything," she said. "I only learned most of this today. Do you understand that?"

"I'm not an imbecile, Marvella," he snapped.

"I'm just being clear because you'll have a lot of questions, and I don't have most of the answers."

"I'm assuming then that this wasn't a break-in?" he asked.

"No," I said. "It wasn't a break-in."

Marvella looked at me. "Let me tell it."

I nodded, happy to comply. I crossed my arms and made sure I blocked the glass door. Johnson would have to work to go through me, and anyone trying to get in wouldn't be able to open the door.

Marvella pushed herself even harder against the wall. "Val showed up at my apartment about ten this morning. She was sick."

"Sick?" Johnson obviously hadn't expected that.

"She had a low-grade fever, and she was bleeding," Marvella said.

"Who hurt her?" He was halfway off the couch before he finished the question.

Marvella held up a hand for silence. "Don't go all he-man on me, okay? Let me tell this my way."

Johnson nodded. He sank back down to the couch. He was obviously confused and worried.

"Val took the bus," Marvella said, "because she was too woozy to drive. I have no idea how she managed to walk from the bus stop to my place. When I opened the door, she almost fainted. I got her to the couch, and realized then that she had a fever. I didn't find out about the bleeding for little while longer."

Johnson opened his mouth as if he were going to ask a question, but Marvella stopped speaking. She raised her eyebrows as if she were daring him to interrupt her.

He gripped his knees so tightly his fingers made indentations in his pants.

Marvella gave me a quick glance, and I saw a warning in it. She was going to tell him about the abortion now, and obviously she was afraid the entire idea would set him off.

"When I asked what was going on, Val started to cry. She was really sorry for not telling me sooner. I think she thought I was going to get mad at her."

"Like you think I will," Johnson said. His entire manner was that of rigid control.

Marvella studied him for a moment. "Yeah."

"I'll be good."

She shrugged slightly. She didn't believe him. Laura was watching him cautiously. I wasn't sure how I would feel if I had learned this about the woman I loved—even if the relationship was over.

"It took a while to get Val to talk to me," Marvella said, "and I won't lie to you, Truman. One of the conditions was that I wouldn't tell you anything. I'm breaking her confidence here, but I think it's better that you learn the whole story. The hospital won't tell you everything."

That caught my attention. What did Marvella know that the rest of us didn't?

"About nine weeks ago—what is that? January? February?" Marvella asked this last of Laura.

"The end of January, I think," Laura said.

"Around then," Marvella said, "Val got raped."

Johnson's grip on his knees grew so tight that his pant legs bunched. But he didn't move or say a word.

I was the one who did. "Son of a bitch. Who would do that to her?"

"I don't know, exactly," Marvella said.

"She go to the police?" This from Johnson. I recognized the tone he was using. He had slipped into cop mode, which was probably the only way he could cope.

"I don't think so," Marvella said.

"Stupid," Johnson said.

"Truman, this is why—"

"We'll never catch the bastard now. He's probably done a hundred other girls, and if Val had just followed the rules, then we could've caught him."

"Truman," Marvella said in a firm tone. "I'm not done."

He clamped his mouth closed.

Laura pressed her hands against her stomach and leaned back on the couch. She looked relaxed, but her entire body was rigid. I wanted to sit beside her and put my arm around her, but I didn't dare move away from the door.

"Val got pregnant," Marvella said.

Johnson closed his eyes.

"And she didn't feel like she could tell anybody about it." Marvella swallowed hard. This part seemed harder for her than the first part. She blinked a few times, and when she spoke again, I could hear the suppressed tears in her voice. "I think she pretended for a while that nothing happened."

Johnson nodded, but didn't speak. Apparently pretending nothing happened was not unusual for his ex-wife.

"Then she realized what was going on, and I don't know why she made the decision, Truman, but she just couldn't—"

"Have the baby," he whispered. He clearly knew. He knew now why Valentina was here.

He looked devastated, not violent. Still, I stayed by the door, uncertain now what to do.

"That's right," Marvella said.

She didn't say any more. We waited, in silence, but, for what, I didn't know. It just felt wrong to speak.

After a while, Johnson said, "Who did it?"

It took me a moment to realize he was referring to the abortion. Marvella, however, seemed to have no trouble understanding him.

She shrugged. "I don't know, but whoever he was, he did it wrong. Laura knows more."

Johnson whirled on Laura so fast that it startled me. I didn't know he had that kind of quickness in him.

"Where did you take her?"

"I didn't—"

"You shouldn't have taken her anywhere. There's ways of dealing with this. Good ways."

"I didn't—"

"You let her go to a goddamn butcher, and—"

"Truman," I said as forcefully as I could. "Shut up."

To my surprise, he did. He wilted into the couch as if his spine had melted. Then he put one hand over his face.

"Val did this on her own," Marvella said quietly. "She never spoke to anyone. I would've taken her to Dr. Jetten, if she had just come to me—"

"He's good," Johnson said through his hand.

"—and I might have even talked to you if that hadn't worked to find out which doctors have been paying protection lately. I wouldn't have told you, though, that it was for Val. I wouldn't have done that."

Johnson nodded. His hand still covered his face.

Laura glanced at me, as if she expected me to do something. There was nothing to do.

"Val was really sick when she came to me, Truman, and I tried to get Dr. Jetten by phone, but it's Easter." Marvella took a step toward him. The fear had clearly left her. "I couldn't reach him, and then I realized that even if I could, it wouldn't matter. He would have thought it was some kind of sting."

Johnson ran his hand slowly down his face, his thumb and forefinger making a trail from his eyes to his chin. Then he wiped his hand on his thigh.

His skin was blotchy, his eyes red.

"I could've got him for you," he said.

"She made me promise, Truman." Marvella stopped in the center of the waiting room.

He nodded.

"I thought maybe we could wait until morning, take her to his clinic, and let him deal with the authorities, but she got worse. Her fever spiked, and even though I put ice on her stomach like you're supposed to, the bleeding got worse."

Marvella reached the presswood coffee table. She sat on the end, and took Johnson's hands in hers. He didn't fight the movement; in fact, he seemed grateful for it. He looked at their hands, threaded together, and shook them a little.

"No one was around," Marvella said. "I tried to find someone to stay with her, but the only person I trusted is Bill, and he was gone."

She looked at me. So did Laura. But Johnson continued staring at the threaded fingers as if they were holding him together.

"So I tried calling Dr. Jetten again, and got his service. They wouldn't call his home, and he's not listed. But I knew where he lived, so I felt my only choice was to go there. I waited too long, I know, and I took too long getting him, but I never expected her to get so bad. Bill said she was really sick when he found her."

"She was hemorrhaging," I said quietly.

Johnson turned toward me, his eyes empty. Then he blinked and the cop returned to them. "Did they treat her?"

"They tried all the tricks," Laura said. "They were going to refuse until she told them who did the abortion. I'm not sure she was coherent enough to understand."

"Laura fought them," I said. "She threatened them with all kinds of things and they listened."

Johnson looked at her, then nodded. "Good work."

"They're probably going to charge her with participating in an illegal operation," Laura said. "You're going to have to do something to make the charges go away."

"I can do that," Johnson said. He didn't seem shocked by any of this.

Apparently I was the only one who didn't know how hospitals responded to women having trouble with an abortion. I also hadn't realized until this night how dangerous taking a woman who was miscarrying to a hospital could be.

"That's not the worst of it," Laura said, and paused. Johnson leaned away from Laura, but Marvella held his hands even tighter. He clearly wasn't ready for worse news.

Then the door hit me in the back. I turned, saw the doctor that Laura had been fighting with.

He didn't look so strong now. His lab coat was covered with blood, and there were strain lines around his mouth.

I stepped aside so that he could enter. No one protested, so I figured it was all right.

He turned to Laura. "May I talk to you, Miss Hathaway?"

"It's all right," she said. "This is the girl's family. You can talk in front of them."

He shoved the door closed and stepped around me like I was a dangerous animal. "How are you all related?"

"I'm her husband," Johnson said before anyone could stop him.

"And I'm her cousin," Marvella said.

I said nothing. I assumed the doctor remembered me from earlier. If he didn't, he could ask.

Instead he ran his hand through his hair. It was even more tousled than before. The gesture made him seem young and tired.

"I'm going to be honest with you," he said. "It was touch-and-go for most of the surgery. I really thought I was going to lose her on the table."

Johnson pulled Marvella closer. She moved to the couch and put an arm around his back. It seemed, at that moment, like she needed the hug as much as he did.

"She lost a lot of blood and"—the doctor turned toward Laura—"I want the name of the butcher who mutilated her. He didn't know a curette from a steak knife. He—"

Laura put a hand up, pointing toward the others. Johnson had gone so gray I thought he was going to faint. Marvella's mouth was open in horror.

The doctor remembered who he was talking to then. Apparently he had gained a lot of respect for Laura, because until that moment, he had been treating her like an equal.

"She was pretty cut up," the doctor said, turning back toward Johnson and Marvella. "I had to do a full hysterectomy and believe me, I wouldn't have in her condition if I didn't think it was warranted."

"A full . . . ?" Johnson's voice trailed off.

"But she's made it through the surgery, which is a victory all by itself. She still has a fever and she's very weak. She's not waking up, which is not a surprise given the amount of trauma she's suffered. Sometimes the body uses a light coma as a way to promote healing. We'll be monitoring her, so that we'll be alert to any change."

"She's alive?" Marvella asked, as if all of the information had confused her on that point.

"Yes," the doctor said. "But the next few days are critical. We're going to do what we can, but I'm not making any promises."

"What are her chances?" Laura asked.

The doctor shrugged. "A hundred percent better than they were two hours ago," he said. "But other than that, I can't tell you. Most women wouldn't have made it here, let alone survived the surgery. What we have to watch out for now is infection. We're giving her penicillin, since I'm pretty sure an infection started in all that tissue the butcher left, but whether she gets better is up to her."

"Can I see her?" Johnson asked.

"Not yet," the doctor said. "She's in post-op, and she will be all night. The best thing you can do is go home, get some rest, and come back in the morning."

Johnson stood, gave Laura a sideways look, then walked toward the doctor. The doctor looked up at Johnson as if he were a curiosity.

"There's a few things I need to talk to you about," Johnson said. "I'm a cop, and I just found out—"

"Miss Hathaway already discussed it with me," the doctor said. "The medical chart is simply going to list this as a traumatic pregnancy. She won't face any criminal proceedings."

"Damn right," Johnson said.

The doctor straightened. He wiped his hands on his lab coat and faced Johnson.

"I don't know you," the doctor said. "And I'm not inclined to help people commit crimes. You say you're a police officer, and so what I just told you could get me in trouble—"

"It won't," Johnson said. "All I was going to do was ask if you'd make sure no one hears about this. I don't want Val up on charges."

"I've already discussed this with Miss Hathaway," the doctor said. "I'm doing this as a favor to Miss Hathaway. You're lucky that she found your wife. Miss Hathaway's a courageous lady who knows more than she should about these things."

Laura's cheeks were red. Johnson didn't even look at her, but I did, and so did the doctor. He gave her a small nod and smile. She truly had gained his respect.

Then he turned his attention back to Johnson. "I am going to tell you something though, because I can't live with myself if I don't."

I positioned myself closer to Johnson. I didn't like the doctor's tone. This wasn't going to be about medicine now.

"Your wife is going to suffer a lot for this," the doctor said, "but she brought it upon herself. If she had made a sensible decision, none of this would have happened."

Johnson made a low sound in the back of his throat, almost a growl. I moved a little closer, ready to step in if Johnson grabbed the doctor.

But the doctor didn't move. He stayed toe-to-toe with Johnson, which I might not have done, given the look on Johnson's face.

"If you truly are a cop," the doctor said, "then I'm risking everything doing this for you and for Miss Hathaway. So I want some consideration in return."

Johnson studied him, but said nothing.

"First," the doctor said, "I want you to find the butcher who did this. I want you to put him out of business, and I want you to let me know that you did it. He shouldn't be loose on the streets. None of these people should, and you know it."

"If you take these people away," Laura said quietly, "then women will just do it themselves."

The doctor glared at her. "Better that you women take responsibility for your own actions and—"

Johnson's growl turned into a roar. He grabbed the doctor by the shoulders and shoved him against the glass. I threaded my arms through Johnson's and tried to pull him back.

But he was too strong for me. I couldn't move him. The anger that had been building in him all night was coming out at this doctor. I was afraid Johnson might beat him up, and then we'd all go to jail.

"He saved her life, Truman," I said. "Let him go."

The doctor put his hands on Johnson's, tugging futilely.

"You stupid ass, Truman," Marvella said. "Let go."

Johnson's eyes narrowed. I felt his muscles move beneath mine as his hand tightened. Then he let go.

The doctor reached for the door, but Johnson blocked it. He peered down at the doctor, and I prepared myself for more.

Instead, Johnson spoke in his low cop voice.

"Maybe you don't understand," Johnson said. "Val's the most responsible person I know."

"I wasn't implying—"

"Yes, you were," Johnson said. "You were very clear. You think Val's as low as some asshole out there who kills for money. You think she did this as a form of birth control. My Val's not like that. Do you understand?"

The doctor nodded, but the expression in his eyes didn't change. He was just placating Johnson.

Johnson saw it, too. "You treat her like a human being, or I swear to God, you'll regret that you ever met me."

"Truman, you're not helping." I pulled him backward, hitting the couch with my knees. I would have lost my balance if Johnson hadn't been so determined to threaten the doctor.

The doctor reached for the door again, only this time Laura's hand covered his.

He glared at her.

"I've just about had enough, Miss Hathaway," he said, his voice shaking. So Johnson had scared him after all.

"A piece of information," she said as if the doctor hadn't spoken, "so that you'll understand why the detective here got so upset at you."

The doctor's jaw worked, but he didn't say anything. He started to pull the door open, but Laura shoved it shut.

"You see, your saying that about responsibility, it was enough to make anyone angry." Laura's voice was cold. "It wasn't Valentina's behavior that caused her pregnancy. She was raped, Doctor, and she was only doing what she thought was best."

He looked at Laura. She removed her hand from his. Then his mouth thinned.

I braced myself.

"I don't care how she got pregnant," the doctor said. "That wasn't what I was talking about. She could have given the child up instead of mutilate herself."

Laura's eyes widened in surprise. She glanced at me, and I knew what she was thinking. She was going to tell him about the benefit, about the thousand children who couldn't find homes.

But the doctor wasn't going to stay in the room any longer. He pushed the door open and as he stepped through, he glared at Johnson, Marvella, and me.

"The thing about you people," he said, clearly not meaning us individually, instead meaning black people—God, how I hated that phrase—"is that you will never, ever understand there are better ways to take care of unwanted children."

I was glad I still had a grip on Johnson because he lunged for the door again. Laura blocked him as the doctor shoved the door closed. Johnson slammed into Laura—not full force, because I was holding him back—but enough to hurt her.

She slid down and Johnson, realizing what he had done, reached for her. Laura shook her head, keeping one hand up, holding him away from her.

I yanked him aside and was about to shove him into the couch when I saw his face. It was devastated. His eyes filled with tears.

I brought my arm down, then patted him on the shoulder.

He blinked, bowed his head, and moved away from me. Marvella still sat on the couch, and he sank down beside her. She put her arms around him and rocked him as if he were a baby.

I reached for Laura, helping her up. Color was coming back into her face. "You all right?" I asked.

"Fine," she said, and wheezed. "Stupid of me to get in the way."

"Stupid of that doctor to bait Truman," I said.

"Dr. Rothstein was just mad because he hasn't been in control since we arrived." Laura sat on the side of the couch. She wrapped her arm around her stomach and took a deep breath.

"Does that mean we have to keep an eye on him?" I asked.

"I'll check in," she said. "He's not going to be primary anyway after this. Her regular doctor should take over if she has one."

I looked at Marvella. She was patting Johnson on the back and still rocking him, but her gaze met mine. She had heard every word.

"Will your friend Jetten take this case?" I asked her.

She nodded.

"Do you want us to stay?"

She mouthed "no," and then added a silent "thank you."

"You know where we'll be," I said, then took Laura's free arm and helped her up. She wobbled a little as she stood, then she took another deep breath.

We started out the door.

"Laura?" Marvella spoke.

We both turned.

"I owe you an apology."

Laura shook head. "Past is past," she said. "Just let us know what happens here."

They studied each other for a moment. Then Marvella smiled at her—a real smile, for the very first time since they had met.

"Thanks," Marvella said.

"Don't mention it," Laura said, and led me out of the room.

SIX

The car stank of blood.

We got in and Laura scooted down on the seat, leaned her head on the leather, and closed her eyes. I drove the four blocks home, not knowing what to say.

It was almost 2 A.M. and the romantic evening we had planned on was no longer possible. The benefit felt like it had happened days ago. I was tired and so, obviously, was she.

I pulled up in front of the apartment building. I dug in my pocket for my keys and couldn't find them. Laura watched me for a moment, then gave me a sleepy smile.

"I still have your keys," she said.

I had forgotten I had given them to her. Everything had happened so quickly. All that had been on my mind once I had established that Marvella wasn't in her apartment and wounded was to get Valentina some help.

"Why don't you go on up," I said. "I'll be there in a while."

Laura frowned. "What are you going to do?"

"Wipe down the car. We can't let it stay like this. It's already bad enough."

She shook her head. "I'll pay someone to clean it, Smokey."

"It'll only take a minute."

"No." She took the keys out of my hand. "Let's just go inside."

I sat there for a moment, knowing that I should ignore her and just take care of it. I would save her a lot of money, and probably keep the seats from permanent ruin.

But it had been a long day after a long and stressful week, and I didn't want to spend the next hour cleaning up someone else's blood. Besides, I had to get up in less than five hours so that I could take Jimmy and the Grimshaw children to school.

After the week Jimmy had had, I wasn't going to miss that.

I sighed, opened my door, and got out. The wind had died down, and the night, though cool, was no longer cold. Laura got out as well, closed her car door, and walked toward me. Somewhere along the way, she had lost her coat.

She slipped her arm in mine, and together we walked up my sidewalk, bruised and bloodied, not the well-dressed couple who had made me so nervous earlier.

The front door was still propped open, and this time, I didn't pull it closed. We walked up the steps together. Someone had cleaned off our bloody footprints. The hall had the sharp scent of pine cleaner.

Someone had also closed Marvella's door and latched it. The people in this building did not socialize, but we did watch out for one another.

I liked the community, and felt it was important, not just for me, but for Jimmy.

When we reached my apartment, Laura leaned against the wall as I unlocked the three deadbolts. I opened the door, and as we stepped inside, I flicked on the overhead light. The apartment was neater than usual—I had cleaned up the night before—but looked as dumpy as ever. Paint peeled on the walls, and the carpet was threadbare.

The back of the couch served as a dividing line between the half kitchen and the living room. The kitchen table that stood off to our right also created a block between the kitchen and living room.

I had bought an Easter lily the day before, and placed it in the center of the table. The lily didn't brighten the room like I had hoped. Instead, it made the place smell like a funeral parlor. Still, the odor of fresh flowers was better than the apartment's usual smell—dirty dishes, stale milk, and unwashed clothes. Living with an eleven-year-old, even one as well behaved as Jimmy, left a lot to be desired.

Laura closed the door behind us and, to my surprise, walked into the half-kitchen. She opened the cupboard to the right of the sink, and removed two tumblers.

I hung my stained suit coat on the coat rack. I had moved the coat rack to the left side of the door after Christmas, since that corner looked bare without the tree. It was awkward, though. My instinct was still to take off a coat and hang it beside the table.

Laura stretched and opened the cupboard above the stove. That was where I kept my hard liquor, such as it was. I had some expensive bourbon, which Laura's attorney, Drew McMillan, had given me at Christmas, and a bit of whiskey for Franklin Grimshaw. I also kept some scotch that I had won at a raffle in February.

Laura grabbed the bourbon, then looked at me, as if waiting for me to tell her to put it back. I didn't. If ever we needed a nightcap, tonight was the night.

She poured three fingers' worth into each tumbler, then handed me one. The glass was warm. She led me to the couch, and we sat, blood-covered shoes on the scarred coffee table, staring at the silent television set.

"I thought you were going to fall asleep before we even got home," I said to her.

She took a tentative sip from her glass, then licked her lips. "I'm too wound up."

I slipped my arm around her shoulders and pulled her close. She leaned on me. Her muscles were tense. Her back felt like it was made of steel.

"You impressed me back there," I said. "I had no idea what was going on and you just took charge."

"It's becoming a habit." Her comment was dismissive. She didn't want to talk about the evening.

I did. "How did you know what to do?"

"Smokey." She shook her head.

The tight feeling in my stomach grew. "It's all right. Whatever happened to you—"

"Not to me," she said softly.

"Then who?"

"Friends," she said. "In college."

I frowned. "They told you?"

She sipped her scotch and continued to stare at the TV. Her voice was a monotone. "They had to. I was the only person they knew who could afford to help them."

Afford, as in money. She paid for abortions. It was my turn to take a drink. "That still doesn't explain how you know so much. You didn't have to go with them, did you?"

"It wasn't all of them at once," she said, and there was something in her tone, a deep thread of anger, maybe. Something I couldn't identify. "Just over time. You know. *Sex and the Single Girl.* Everyone was being so modern. Only there was no pill then and no one was thinking about the consequences."

"Still, you knew how to fight with the doctor—"

"Because a friend of mine died," Laura snapped. "Died, in the emergency room, because she was alone and too sick to make her stupid confession. The nurse told me later, when they called me because my number was in Susan's purse."

"I'm sorry," I said, but Laura didn't hear me.

"So from then on, I went with my friends if they needed my help, and most of the time I gave them enough money to go to England, where abortion was legal. But I started acquiring knowledge, because I ask questions, and doctors talk to me, like Rothstein did."

I finished my drink in a single gulp and resisted the urge to wipe off my mouth. "Marvella seems to know, too. I find that strange."

"I don't," Laura said. "It's self-defense. Doctors don't listen to women, so the only control we have is to know what they can do to us and try to prevent it. That's why I couldn't leave Valentina. It had nothing to do with guaranteeing her bill."

Her hand was wrapped so tightly around her glass that her fingernails had turned blood-red.

"I'm sorry," I said. "I didn't know. I—"

"Of course you didn't," she said. "Why should you?"

"Because I know what it's like to be ignored," I said quietly.

She closed her eyes, her lashes brushing her still-stained cheek. Then she turned inside my arm, and kissed me. There was need in that kiss, and exhaustion, and a desire for comfort.

I put both arms around her, pulling her close, not breaking off the kiss. Somehow she managed to set her glass down, and get mine as well.

This conclusion wasn't quite the way I had it planned when we left for Sherman House. Then I had hoped for fun and joy, and instead, we were impatient with need and fear and a sense of our own mortality. Eventually we moved from my springless couch to my springless bed, and long after we'd spent our passion, we held each other through the short, and for me, almost sleepless, night.

The next morning, I let Laura sleep an extra half an hour while I cooked breakfast and got ready for the day. I had to leave early to pick up the kids for school. Franklin Grimshaw and I shared that task, and even though Jimmy had been staying with them for Easter, I didn't want to give up my day.

Besides, I missed him.

I woke Laura with a makeshift tray of scrambled eggs, coffee, and toast. She gave me a bleary grin. I kissed her, then apologized for having to leave. She waved me away, saying that she understood.

The Grimshaw house was only a few blocks from the apartment, but it seemed like a world away. Instead of a neighborhood of apartment buildings like I lived in, the house stood in the center of a block of single-family dwellings.

The Grimshaws rented it from Laura's firm, Sturdy Investments, for an amazingly low price. When Laura had found them the place last fall, she had had to fight to allow them to live there. The management team at Sturdy had a vested interest in keeping rents high.

That was one of the many reasons that Laura staged a legal fight to reclaim her inheritance from her father. Now, as Sturdy Investments' largest shareholder and its new Chief Executive Officer, Laura was doing her best to reform the company.

Her problem was that she had to make changes slowly, so that she wouldn't destroy Sturdy's profitability, and invite a stockholder lawsuit. Unfortunately, as I feared and as she was discovering, much of Sturdy's profitability depended on its slumlord policies and its shady business practices.

Laura would be at this for years.

Still, she was able to do a handful of small things, like finding the Grimshaws a new home at a reasonable price. Together, she and I were investigating each property Sturdy owned. Her theory was that if she rebuilt the properties, made them comfortable homes with modest rents, the company would have a solid foundation instead of a shady one.

I hoped she would have the time to fulfill that dream.

I parked in front of the Grimshaw house. It was old and large, and with the converted attic space, had enough bedrooms for all five Grimshaw children, their parents, and Malcolm Reyner, the eighteen-year-old that the Grimshaws took in last fall.

A "Happy Easter" sign with some radio call letters, done by childish hands, decorated the picture window. Some green plastic Easter grass littered the wraparound porch. Three pairs of mud-covered shoes—none of them Jimmy's—sat on the mat beside the front door.

I felt a twinge of regret. Perhaps I should have been part of Jimmy's first real Easter, even though religion and religious holidays made me uncomfortable. It was part of being a family, and I had left that part of my duties to someone else.

I knocked on the door, then pushed it open. The odors of fresh coffee and toast greeted me.

"Hello!" I called.

Silverware clattered against plates in the kitchen, and Norene, the youngest, cried, "Uncle Bill!"

I walked through the dining room, which still contained remnants of the holiday—an Easter lily surrounded by seven partially empty Easter baskets, Easter cards, and more green plastic grass than I had ever seen in my life.

I had barely made it past the table when Norene caromed out of the kitchen and wrapped herself around my legs. She was six, and had more energy than I had ever had in my life.

"Uncle Bill!" she cried again. "The Easter Bunny was here."

"I see that." I detached her from me as gently as I could, then crouched. Her face was smeared with jam and her two braids were already twisting loose. She wore a plaid school dress with bright red tights, and in her left hand, she clutched the strangest stuffed bunny I had ever seen.

She shoved the bunny at me. "See what I got?"

I took him from her. He was eighteen inches tall and sturdy, with white fur that had miraculously avoided the jam—at least so far. He wore striped blue pants and a paisley shirt, and had a self-satisfied expression on his little rabbit face.

"Wow," I said, not knowing quite how to respond. "I didn't know the Easter Bunny brought stuffed animals. I thought he just brought eggs and candy."

"The Easter Bunny was quite profligate this year." Franklin Grimshaw stood at the door to the kitchen. He was still in the middle of breakfast because one napkin was tucked into the collar of his white dress shirt, and the remains of another napkin still decorated the belt that held up his dark pants. The napkin accented his slight pot belly, and made him look his age.

We had met when we were young men. It still startled me to see Franklin's thinning hair and his growing paunch. I recognized the aging in him better than I did in myself.

"Apparently," Franklin said, his tone dry, "Mr. Bunny believed that because we live in such a fancy house, we're rich enough to spoil the entire crew."

"Franklin!" his wife, Althea, said from the kitchen. I could feel her disapproval half a room away.

Norene was reaching for the bunny. I crouched, handed it to her, and hugged her. "Better go finish breakfast, honey," I said.

She didn't have to be told twice. She ran back into the kitchen, braids flying.

"I think the Easter Bunny's extravagance was more my fault than anything," I said to Franklin.

I was flush for the first time in nearly a year, and I had given Althea fifty dollars to cover Jimmy's Easter expenses, including new clothes for church and his share of the meals and candy.

"I don't care whose fault it is. I just don't like setting up the expectations for next year." Franklin swept a hand toward the kitchen. "Had breakfast?"

I nodded. "I just came for the kids. Am I early or are you guys late?"

"I think you're early," Franklin said. "It has to be some kind of record."

I glared at him as I headed toward the kitchen. He grinned and followed.

The coffee pot sat on top of the stove. Boxes of cereal littered the table, along with a large plate of toast, two containers of jam, and some peanut butter. A half-empty pitcher of orange juice sat beside a full pitcher of milk.

Norene sat on her special chair at the far side of the table. Her sister Michelle, whom we all called Mikie, sat next to her. The Grimshaw children were stairstepped, with about two years between all of them. Keith was Jimmy's age. Lacey, who would be thirteen soon, was the oldest girl, and Jonathon, at fourteen, was the oldest boy.

Lacey and Jonathon's places were empty. Malcolm sat at the foot of the table, shoveling giant spoonfuls of Cheerios in his mouth. He waved at me, like an oversized two-year-old.

"Where's Jimmy?" I asked.

"Upstairs getting his stuff." Althea was standing at the counter, mixing some cinnamon and sugar together. She was wearing a full-size apron over a dark blue dress, fancy clothing for her so early in the day. The dress slimmed her, but she would never be that slender girl I had met when she was first dating Franklin.

Apparently, she had somewhere to go this morning, just like the rest of us. She smiled at me, then frowned ostentatiously at Franklin, probably for his remarks about the Easter Bunny.

Althea set the cinnamon sugar mixture on the table. I took a piece of buttered toast, spooned some of the mixture on it. The Grimshaws had introduced me to this treat last summer, and I had become addicted to it.

"How was the parade?" I asked as I took a bite of toast. The butter mixed with the cinnamon and sugar added the right amount of flavor. I wasn't hungry, but I ate quickly nonetheless.

"Crowded," Althea said.

"Hot," Franklin said at the same time.

"Cool," Keith said.

"Too long," Lacey said from behind me. She was wearing a sweater that showed every curve of her developing body, a skirt that barely covered her knees, and boots.

"Nope," Althea said when she saw her.

"Mom, it's—"

"No boots, no short skirt."

"But, Mom—"

"Disagree one more time, and I'll dress you myself."

Lacey sighed heavily and stomped back up the stairs. I heard a thud and an "ouch" from above, and then Jimmy stepped into the kitchen, dragging the small suitcase we had packed for him on Saturday.

He glared at me. "You're early."

"I missed you, too," I said, and went over to hug him.

He moved away from me as if I were going to burn him. His eyes had deep shadows under them, and there were lines around his mouth.

Even here, then, where he was surrounded by people he loved, he hadn't slept well.

"How was Easter?" I asked, and then realized I shouldn't have. Jimmy had been raised mostly on his own. His mother, a sometimes-prostitute, would take off for months at a time. She had never identified his real father, and his older brother, who had cared for Jimmy initially, found drugs and gangs a lot more interesting. Because of that experience, Jimmy often had strange and sometimes offensive opinions about everything from Christmas to basketball.

He glanced at Althea, who was watching him closely. Then he said, "Look what the Easter Bunny left me," and shoved his left arm at me.

On the wrist, he wore a silver watch with a large face.

"Wow," I said, feeling as at a loss for words as I had been when I saw the rabbit. No wonder Franklin was a bit out of sorts. I'd never seen this kind of stuff at Easter. It seemed like a mini-Christmas.

"Nifty, huh?" Jimmy asked. "It winds itself."

I took a closer look. The watch was nice. "Too bad it's impossible to thank the bunny."

"I did my best." He glanced at Althea again. He knew who was responsible, just like he had at Christmastime. Only then, he had been willing to play along. Apparently Santa Claus was still cool to a fifth grader, but the Easter Bunny was not.

"Mikie got a bunny just like mine, only a girl," Norene said, her mouth full of toast. "And Keith got a watch, too, and Lacey—"

"Your Uncle Bill doesn't need the full rundown," Althea said, and put her hand gently on her daughter's head.

"All I want to know," I said as I stood, "is if there's any candy left."

"Yes," Mikie said, twirling her own pristine braid. "But we can't have any until after school."

"We're already rationing it," Malcolm said with a smile. "It's in little pouches in the cupboard, all labeled."

"Except Jimmy's," Norene said.

"Where's yours?" I asked him.

"Suitcase," he said, and patted it. Then he grinned, as if pleased that he didn't have to suffer the same rules as everyone else. I had a hunch he had lorded that point over everyone.

"Let's put your suitcase in the car, and then we have to get moving." I directed that last to the kids still sitting at the breakfast table. I caught Althea's gaze. "You'll have to tell Lacey that I don't have time for the full makeover. She's going to have to leave when we do."

Althea grinned at me, revealing that the pretty, fun-loving girl I had met all those years ago was still close to the surface.

I reached for the suitcase.

Jimmy shook his head. "I got it."

"Smokey?" Franklin had taken the napkin off his shirt. Althea made a slight hand motion around her waist and he pulled the last of the other napkin out of his belt. "Can the suitcase wait until the others are ready? I'd like a word."

Jimmy's face closed up. I put my hand on his shoulder.

"Your decision," I said.

Jimmy shrugged.

I asked, "Did you remember your books for after school?"

He blinked and then looked frustrated. Clearly he hadn't remembered to pack everything.

Malcolm stood, his cereal bowl empty. "I'll help you, Jim."

Jimmy gave him a grateful glance, but said, "It's okay. Me and Keith can get it."

"I'd like to see what Mrs. Kirkland has you reading anyway," Malcolm said, and came around the table.

"Okay." Jimmy set the suitcase down and went up the stairs two at a time. Malcolm followed him.

Franklin led me down through the second of the three doors that were off the kitchen. This one led down a small hallway. Off the hall was the house's only bathroom, and a cozy office.

We went inside the office, and Franklin closed the door.

"Jim had a rough weekend," Franklin said without preamble.

"He didn't start a fight or anything, did he?" I asked. Just before Christmas, Jimmy and Keith came to blows over the meaning of the holiday.

"Nothing like that." Franklin leaned on his desk. I leaned on the door. "Saturday night, he snuck out of Keith's room, and was sitting alone in the living room, crying. I found him, and offered to call you, but he wouldn't let me."

I nodded. "He hasn't slept well since we left Memphis. And all spring, the nightmares have gotten worse. Usually he wakes me up and we watch a late movie together or read a book until he falls back to sleep."

"I think he was afraid to turn on the television or a light here, afraid he would wake someone up."

"Did he wake you?"

Franklin grinned. "My bladder woke me. One of the perks of being middle-aged."

I smiled in return. Sometimes I thought there were no perks to turning forty, which was what I had done this year.

"Anyway, I think it was good the lights were out. I sat with him on the couch, and he talked to me."

I frowned, just a little. Jimmy wouldn't tell me about the nightmares. He never had.

"He's afraid they're going to get him," Franklin said.

"Who?" I asked.

"They," Franklin said. "The police, the FBI, whoever. The fact that he nearly got found last summer, and all this publicity about the anniversary have really upset him."

"I know," I said.

"I'm not sure you do." Franklin crossed his arms. "He's got it in his head that there are assassins out there, murdering everyone associated with King's death."

Franklin was the only person in Chicago, beside Laura, who knew why Jimmy and I were here.

"I've never lied to him," I said. "He knew his life was in danger when we left Memphis. And I've impressed on him the need for secrecy."

"I know," Franklin said. "But he thinks that these people are all powerful. He's afraid they're going to get you."

"Why would he worry about that now?" I asked. "We haven't had any problems like that since September. I don't think anyone knows where we are, and the more time we put between us and the assassination, the better chance we have of never being found or identified."

"I know that, and you know that, but he's still just a little boy," Franklin said. "It took me a while to get it out of him, but the problem is the news."

"What?" I asked.

"Grace Kirkland has had them read a newspaper every day as part of their homework. Jimmy's been reading the *Defender*—"

"Because that's what we get," I said, aware that he had this homework. I thought it was a good assignment. I approved of everything Grace Kirkland had done so far.

The parents in the area had hired her to take care of the children after school and to give them some one-on-one attention. The school they attended was underfunded, badly managed, and had a student-teacher ratio that made it impossible for the teacher to do much more than baby-sit.

Grace, a former teacher herself, took a group of children for three hours after school, and focused primarily on the basics: reading and mathematics. She insisted that the parents get involved.

Now, instead of watching a lot of television at night, Jimmy and I read a book together. And I was teaching him household math—how to budget money, how to price-shop for everything from clothes to groceries, and even complicated things, like how to double-check the accuracy of a phone bill.

He seemed to love all of this. Jimmy was one of the smartest kids I knew, which was how he attracted my attention back in Memphis. I didn't want that brain to go to waste.

"What's wrong with the *Defender*?" I asked.

"Nothing," Franklin said. "Except that it's been running more articles than the other papers combined about the anniversary of the assassination. A lot of them have been from people like Mrs. King and Ralph Abernathy, saying that they believe there was a conspiracy, and James Earl Ray was only a part of it."

I heard laughter down the hallway. If we weren't careful, we'd start running late.

"When the judge in the Ray case died last week," Franklin said, "Jimmy became convinced it was part of the conspiracy."

"What do you mean?" I asked. "The judge had a heart attack."

Franklin shrugged. "Jimmy's eleven. A death of someone powerful who was dealing with Ray, whom a lot of people are saying is only part of the problem. Jimmy believes—and it's an unshakeable belief—that eventually all the good guys on this case—his words—will get murdered. That includes you."

I sighed, and leaned my back of my head against the door. "He and I have had this discussion before. He knows I'm safe."

"You say you're safe, but your actions prove otherwise, Smokey." Franklin spoke softly, as if he were afraid of offending me. "You have a scar on your face because you nearly died in December."

"Which has nothing to do with the King assassination."

"But it does in Jimmy's mind. It's all connected, and he's terrified."

I let out a sigh of frustration. "We've been through this, Franklin. Nine times out of ten, the cases are routine, and I'm in no danger at all. Every once in a while things happen. But things happen no matter what to black men in this country. I'm in just as much danger going to the wrong part of Chicago."

"I know," Franklin said.

"I'm safer now than I've been for a long time. The work I do for Laura is easy, and the claims investigation I've been doing for Southside involve little more than photographs and paperwork. The personal cases—"

"Smokey, I understand," Franklin said. "It's Jimmy who doesn't, and logic isn't going to work with him."

I closed my eyes. I knew that. I was defensive because I knew that Jimmy wasn't coping well, that part of the problem was my work. But I was at a loss at how to make things better. It wasn't as if Jimmy's problems were the kind people dealt with every day.

"I was wondering if I could tell Althea what's going on," Franklin said.

I opened my eyes. He hadn't moved. He had the same concerned expression on his face.

"She's better with the kids than I am. She deals with them all the time. And she might have some good ideas."

I shook my head.

"He needs something, Smokey."

"I know," I said. "I love Althea. She's been marvelous with him. But the more people who know, the easier it is for word to get out."

"She wouldn't say anything."

"Maybe not intentionally," I said, "but I don't think we should risk it."

"Not even for Jimmy?"

"This is for Jimmy," I said.

Franklin studied me. "He's terrified, Smokey. I've never seen anything like it."

I had, but I didn't say anything. I had been Jimmy's age when my parents were lynched. I went to live with the people who became my adoptive parents, people whom I barely knew at the time. I had been that terrified for years, and I knew that the only way to get through it—the only way to get past it—was to let time go by.

"Maybe," Franklin said softly, "maybe you might consider having him stay with us. There are a lot of people here, and there's a lot of distraction. Althea's home all day."

I understood the argument. A stable family, a normal life. Jimmy could use that. But he also got a lot more attention from me than he would get here.

"You wouldn't have to worry about him all the time," Franklin said.

"I'd still worry," I said.

"Will you consider it?" Franklin asked.

"No," I said. "I promised him we'd stay together. I'm not going to break that promise."

"Not even if it's better for him?"

"I'm not sure it would be better for him," I said. "I don't mean to offend you, Franklin, but I don't know if anyone else could understand him as well as I do."

Franklin crossed his arms and sighed. "Well, you're going to have to do more than you have been. He's getting worse, Smokey."

"I know," I said, feeling the old worry come back. "Believe me, I know."

SEVEN

I thought about Franklin's offer as I drove the kids to school. I listened to them chatter about the holiday—the sunrise service that even Jimmy admitted that he liked, the Easter Egg hunt, the ham dinner with all the trimmings. Norene was still excited about her bunny even though Althea made her leave it at home, and Keith liked the delicate work of blowing eggs for an Easter Egg tree that they had put together out back.

Jimmy sat up front with me and remained quiet. Occasionally, he would touch his watch as if he couldn't believe he had it. Jimmy didn't look at the beautiful spring sunshine out the window, and he didn't say good-bye to Jonathon when we dropped him off at the nearby junior high school.

I wondered if Jimmy had overheard the conversation I had with Franklin. We'd been quiet, but the bathroom was nearby and even though the walls muffled sound, they didn't always block it.

But Jimmy didn't seem any different with me than he had been when I got to the house. I was just feeling guilty for even listening to Franklin's offer.

Although I had turned it down, I would have been foolish not to pay attention to Franklin's concerns. He got paid to see patterns and give people advice. Mostly he worked for the black politicians on the South Side. His positions always had different names—advisor, assistant, manager—but they resulted in the same thing, people paying him for what he saw. He was trying to use that skill for himself. By going to law school at night, he hoped eventually to become one of the people who got advice.

Jimmy's crying jag had shocked Franklin, and the boy's silence was bothering me. But I knew that changing his living conditions yet again was not the solution.

I pulled into the school parking lot and shut off the car. The lot was full of other parents, dropping off their kids. The school itself, a dingy brick building covered in graffiti, didn't inspire confidence. Neither did the gang members crowding the playground.

We had developed a routine during the winter, and the kids were used to it now. We walked to the door together. The schoolyard had become a hangout for the younger members of the Blackstone Rangers, and they tried to recruit from there, often using lies and intimidation.

Last winter, the gang had tried to recruit Jimmy and Keith, and ultimately failed. But I was sure the group would try again. And I meant to make sure that neither of them—or any other child under my protection—got involved with that group.

There were Stones on the playground as we got out of the car. They were easy to identify; they all wore their red tams, which they called "suns," and hung out in a cluster. Most of the Stones were older than the children who were filtering into the dirty brick building.

My charges gathered around me—even Lacey, who tried to pretend she wasn't related to the other children. Norene took my right hand, as she did every time I drove the kids to school, and Mikie took my left.

Lacey led the way down the sidewalk, with Jimmy and Keith behind her. The girls and I followed, as if we were in a small parade.

A teacher held the metal door open, shepherding students inside. She smiled when she saw me. She wasn't Jimmy's teacher, but I recognized her because she usually had door duty. I smiled back, waited until Jimmy and the Grimshaw children disappeared inside, and then walked back to the car.

I didn't want to give this up. Not the walks to the school, not the fierce protectiveness I felt whenever I saw Jimmy, not even the sullen silence with which he was treating me that morning. He and I had a tough lot, but he had become my family, and I was his.

If I took him to the Grimshaws', had him live there permanently, I would be abandoning him, just like his own father had before long before he was born, like his mother had a year ago Christmas, and like his brother had last spring.

I couldn't do that to Jimmy, any more than I could do it to myself.

I got into the car, and checked my mirrors before backing out of the parking lot. Every once in a while, the Gang Intelligence Unit parked a white van outside the school—ostensibly to keep an eye on the Stones. I could never figure out why the Unit was there, though, and I had a feeling it had more to do with something else, something I didn't completely understand.

They weren't there that morning, and I felt an odd relief. I didn't like that group any more than I liked the gang they were monitoring.

When I pulled up in front of the apartment building, Laura's Mercedes was gone. That must have been an unpleasant drive home for her in the filthy car. I had given her one of my shirts and a pair of pants that were too small for me, and I hoped she had worn them. At least then she wouldn't have had to put on the same blood-covered clothes from the night before.

I wished now that I had taken care of the blood in the backseat last night. It would have made at least part of this morning more pleasant for her.

I parked in the spot she had left open, got out, and went inside. Marvella's door was closed and her morning newspaper still rested against it. I wondered if she had ever gotten home last night. If so, I wasn't going to disturb her. I would find out later how Valentina was doing.

I went inside my apartment to find that Laura had straightened it. She had done the dishes, and she had also taken my suit coat with her, probably to have it cleaned. I would have to protest. She didn't need to spend money on things like that.

She had put my newspaper on the table inside the apartment. A large photograph of an elderly woman holding a black pom-pom in one hand and a poster of Martin Luther King in the other covered the bottom half of the front page. Apparently the elderly woman had been at the parade. If the parade had focused on Martin instead of Easter itself, then no wonder Jimmy was disturbed this morning. He couldn't avoid the memories of last year no matter what he did.

I left the paper on the table, poured myself a cup of lukewarm coffee, and took it into my office in the back of the apartment. My office was in the darkest room in the apartment. The window overlooked the building next door, and let in very little light.

I made up for it by having lamps all over the room—on the wooden filing cabinets and desk I had bought at a yard sale, and a standing lamp on the floor itself.

I sat down in the green office chair behind the desk. I had some paperwork to do before I headed back out again. In addition to the work I did for Laura, I also got steady jobs from Chicagoland Southside Insurance, a company that sold policies to blacks.

The two reports I had to file with the company were both auto claims.

Southside was worried that the claims had been falsified. With a little investigation, I determined that neither had. That surprised me as well. I had run across a startling number of false claims since I started this work.

I had done the same kind of work in Memphis for a number of insurance companies, and never encountered as much fraud as I had here. But Southside had recently been bought by black owners. Before it had been owned by whites. And Stewart Blakely, the new owner and the man who had hired me, believed—and I agreed—that incidents of fraud would decrease as the clients realized they were now dealing with people from their community, people who would treat them fairly instead of trying to bilk them for every last dollar.

I had just finished the first report when someone knocked at my front door. I tucked the report into a drawer, closed the other file, and went up front to answer it, glad that Laura had cleaned up for me.

Because I conducted business out of the apartment, I tried to keep the place neat. Jimmy's bedroom door remained closed—we had decided early on that his bedroom was his private place, and his private place was usually messy. But the rest of the apartment could have guests at any moment, and we tried to accommodate that.

We didn't always do very well.

But the apartment looked good this morning. It smelled of fresh coffee, and the only thing on any surface was the *Defender* I had left on the table.

I went to the door, looked through the spyhole, and started unlocking deadbolts the moment I recognized Marvella.

She didn't look well. Her eyes were so sunken from lack of sleep that not even the makeup she had slathered all over could cover the circles. Her face seemed haggard and thinner than it had just a few hours ago.

She wore a dark blue dress that accented the sallowness of her skin. The dress was the most conservative thing I'd ever seen her in—it almost looked like something Laura would wear to the office—and Marvella had made it more conservative by putting a string of pearls around her neck. They didn't look fake to me.

Somehow she had straightened her hair, and pulled it down around her ears. She hadn't worn her hair straight since the fall, when she used to iron it. Now she had used some kind of straightening oil, and the choice made her look older and less exotic.

I wondered if she had done that on purpose. I had a hunch she was going to talk to the hospital administration today or do other business in the white world, and she didn't want to look threatening.

I held the door open and she came in.

"How is Valentina?" I asked as I closed the door.

"She made it through the night, but they're making no promises." Marvella sat at the table and put the *Defender* on the chair next to her. "I called just a few minutes ago. She's not conscious yet. They don't even want visitors."

That wasn't a good sign. I went into the half-kitchen, emptied the coffee pot, and put new water in the base.

"Have you had breakfast?" I asked as I put some coffee grounds in the filter. I put the lid back on, set the pot on the stove, and turned on the burner.

"I don't need anything," she said.

I grabbed some bread and put it in the toaster.

"Do you have a minute, Smokey?" she asked.

That caught my attention. It sounded businesslike. "Yeah," I said. "I have a little time."

I was supposed to be checking a building for Laura that day, but I set my own schedule.

"First," Marvella said, looking down at her well-manicured hands, "I want to apologize for yelling at you last night. I wasn't thinking, I guess."

"It's all right," I said.

"No, it's not." She gave me a weak smile. "I didn't want to admit to myself that I might have killed Val by leaving her alone."

"You didn't make the choice to get rid of that baby."

"Now you sound like that damn doctor," Marvella snapped. "As if he understands what the hell she was going through—"

"I didn't mean it that way," I said. "All I meant was that she was ill when she came to you."

Marvella took a deep breath and nodded. "Sorry. I'm still shaky."

The toast popped up. I put it on a plate, grabbed the butter dish off the counter, and brought them to the table. Then I opened the silverware drawer, grabbed a knife and spoon, and set them in front of her.

"Eat something," I said. Apparently it was my day to feed the women in my life.

She looked at me.

"You're going to go do battle with the hospital, aren't you? I think you should eat before you go."

"It's that obvious?" she asked, her fingers going to the pearls.

"I've never seen you looking like a demure housewife before," I said.

She laughed. "Sometimes you have to put on a disguise to get what you want."

"And what do you want?" I asked.

"I want to make sure they don't press charges against Val. I also want them to let me take care of her bills."

"I thought Laura was going to do that," I said.

Marvella picked up the knife, and ran it through the soft butter. "She was great, your friend. I never expected that."

It was a sideways apology for all the ways she had verbally abused Laura.

"She's got a good heart," I said.

"I should've expected nothing less." Marvella shook her head. "It's been a rough twenty-four hours for me. Everything I thought I understood is wrong."

I opened the refrigerator and took out strawberry jam. The jar was sticky and left gunk on the metal rack. I wiped the jar with a cloth, then set it on the table.

"What do you mean?"

Marvella shook her head. "Val, your friend, even me. I thought I was good in an emergency."

"You are," I said. "You've helped me with Jimmy a lot. You've been real steady."

Until she got angry at my involvement with Laura. Then Marvella hadn't been steady at all.

"I can take care of things," Marvella said. "But this was an actual emergency, and I handled it wrong. Val would be better now if I had taken her to the hospital right away."

"You don't know that," I said. "They might have arrested both of you right then and there."

She spread the butter on her toast. The bread was already growing cold. The butter wasn't melting. "I would have mentioned Truman's name. They wouldn't have bothered us then."

"I thought you weren't supposed to tell him anything about this." I sat down across from her. "Do you really think you would have used his name with some white emergency-room doctor?"

Her shoulders slumped. "I don't know. I just keep going over it and over it in my head. I keep thinking I could have done something for her."

"You did. You took her in, and you tried to get her help. There's not much else we can do for other people."

Marvella sighed, and shook her head as if she didn't believe me.

"Does Valentina have health insurance?" I asked.

"I don't know," Marvella said.

"I think we might want to find out before we start haggling over her bills."

Marvella dabbed a spoonful of jam onto the toast, and spread that around as if she were making designs instead of breakfast. It almost seemed like she hadn't heard me.

"I feel awkward asking you this after the way I behaved lately," she said, "but I'd like to hire you, if you let me."

I leaned back in my chair. I hadn't expected her to say that. "Hire me? For what?"

"I want to find the guy who did this to her." She pushed the plate away.

"The rapist?"

Her breath caught, then she shook her head. "The so-called doctor. The one who cut her up."

I wrapped my hands around my coffee cup. "Let the police handle it, Marvella."

She shook her head. "That's just it, Bill. They won't. If this guy's smart, and most of them are, he's paying protection. No one'll get him."

"What about Truman?"

She looked down at her nails again. "Truman needs to stay out of this."

"Why?" I asked.

"Truman's not exactly rational when it comes to Val," Marvella said.

I didn't like how that sounded. "Not exactly rational. What does that mean?"

"It means he probably won't arrest the guy." Marvella grabbed her plate and pulled it close again. But she still didn't eat the toast. Instead, she took a piece, and started tearing off the crust. "I think there's been enough tragedy this week, don't you?"

Johnson would kill the man? Somehow that didn't surprise me. I'd seen Johnson's willingness to take the law into his own hands before.

"I don't know what I can do," I said. "I can't arrest the guy if I find him."

"No," Marvella said, "but you can give me his name."

"Why would I do that?" I asked.

"So that I can tell people to avoid him." She leaned over the chair and grabbed her purse. After she flicked the clasp open, she reached inside and removed two pieces of paper.

She slid them across the table to me.

I took them. On both pages, Marvella had written a series of names and addresses.

She bit her lower lip, then seemed to realize what she was doing and stopped. "I run kind of an informal clearinghouse," she said. "I tell women who to go to and who to stay away from."

"Women who want abortions?"

Marvella nodded.

"How come I didn't know about this?" I asked.

"You never needed me, Bill," she said, with a bit of a smile. "Seriously, though, it's not something I broadcast."

"Then how do women know who to call?"

She shredded more toast, only this time, she ate one of the pieces. "Some don't," she said. "But a lot of people know about me, women who've come to me before, relatives, a lot of nurses, and doctors who won't do the surgery themselves, but need someone to recommend. I've been doing this for a long time."

"Why you?" I asked.

She shrugged, not meeting my gaze. "It just kinda happened that way."

"You get paid for this?" I asked.

"God, no," she said. "Somebody just needs to keep track."

I frowned, still staring at the papers. I hadn't seen a long stream of women coming to Marvella's door. I hadn't noticed anything out of the ordinary.

But would I have, really? I wasn't even sure what I would have been looking for.

She got up, as if she couldn't sit any longer, and walked to the stove. "Mind if I have some coffee?"

"Help yourself," I said. "There's sugar on the counter and cream in the fridge."

"Thanks," she said, and grabbed a cup from the cupboard. She used to know her way around my kitchen pretty well, back when I had her sit for Jimmy. I had forgotten that, too.

"You know," I said, "you don't have to hire me for this. Just wait until Valentina wakes up."

"If." Marvella's voice was small.

"You don't think she'll make it?"

Marvella shook her head. "They're not telling me everything," she said. "They're talking to Truman, even though I keep telling them not to. But an infection's set in, and she's got an awful fever. I've seen this before, Bill. Most women don't make it. Especially after the surgery."

She brought the coffee back to the table and sat down. Her magnificent eyes were wet with tears. The water had gathered in her mascara, but hadn't fallen to her cheeks yet, making her eyes glisten darkly.

"I've known Val since we were little kids," she said. "We've been best friends our whole lives. Truman met her at my house when we were all little, and he followed her around like a puppy dog, even then, and I never understood it. I mean, she could think circles around him."

"Truman never struck me as dumb," I said.

"He's not," Marvella said. "He's just not book-smart, if you know what I mean. She always had a book in her hand. Still does, and she reads them faster than anyone I know. She also reads French and Spanish, and a couple other languages that I can't remember. She's brilliant."

"What was it then?" I asked. "He became captain of the football team and she was homecoming queen?"

"*I* was homecoming queen," Marvella said, "and proud of it, I might add. Val thought it was the stupidest thing in the world. 'Why would you want people to reward you for being pretty?' she asked me once. 'As if it's something you can control. And it'll just go away when you get older. But you can control how much you learn and how you put that learning to good use.'"

This didn't sound like a woman who had gone to a back-alley abortionist and worked as a legal secretary. I was intrigued, in spite of myself.

"I wish you'd met her then, Bill. I mean you would've—ah, hell." Marvella shook her head. "She would have liked you. You and all these books."

She swept her hand toward the small bookshelf we had bought when Jimmy started going to Grace Kirkland's class after school. I had picked out most of the books, and had been happy about it. I had missed my own collection, which I had left in Memphis.

Then she sighed. I wondered if she knew that she was talking about Valentina half in the present tense and half in the past.

I hoped that wasn't prophetic.

"I don't get it," I said. "If she's got so much promise—"

"Why did she marry Truman?"

"Actually, I was going to ask how she ended up as a legal secretary."

Marvella sighed. "I don't know exactly. She had this dream, you know? She was going to be a doctor. She was doing so well, too. She graduated college with some high honor—I can't keep that stuff straight, but it was cool, you know?"

I nodded, just to let her know I was paying attention.

"And then she applies to all the medical schools in Illinois. Get this, Bill. She graduates at the top of her class. She takes the track you're supposed to take for medicine."

"Pre-med," I said.

"Yeah, that," Marvella said. "She does all the applying stuff, and they get to the interview. Some places turn her down flat, but some guy at one of the schools—it might even have been the University of Chicago—says, 'What's the point? You're just going to get rejected somewhere else down the line. You've got two strikes going in. You're a woman *and* you're a Negro. Even if you graduate, what makes you think anyone will hire you?'"

I winced. I knew what that felt like. I had heard the male version of that speech a few times in my life. Mostly, I let the speech run off me, but every once in a while, it made me so angry that I wanted to hurt someone.

"There are black doctors," I said.

"Yeah," Marvella said. "But there was no convincing Val that she could be one of them. That's the problem with our Val. She's not a fighter. I think she just gave up and got married. That's what you're supposed to do."

"But she also got divorced. You're not supposed to do that," I said.

Marvella nodded. "It was a bad marriage. I don't think she ever really loved him. And I think he always knew, because he got more possessive and controlling as the marriage went on. She couldn't even come see me by herself without him getting all upset."

"So she left," I said.

"I wish it had been that simple." Marvella got up and poured herself some more coffee. "You know, not to make excuses for my cousin or anything, but being a black cop in this city is probably one of the worst jobs anyone can have. You get shit from the white members of the force who still call you a nigger and treat you like one, and then the folks you're trying to protect—all of us— assume you're a traitor for working with the cops, who we all know are the enemy. You can't win."

I nodded. I had seen that time and time again. And I even saw the effect it had on Johnson. It made him want to go around the system too many times to make me comfortable.

"So he's in this awful marriage, and he has this terrible job, and you know, he had all this promise. He was a football star once, and everybody thought he'd do great things."

"Like they thought Valentina would," I said.

She shook her head. "Most people didn't notice Val. I did. My sister Paulette did, and a few professors. But nobody else. I think that was Val's biggest problem, her ability to disappear. I think if she had been as tough as I am, she might never have gotten some of those talks."

"Or she might have ignored them."

Marvella nodded as she sat back down. "Anyway, Truman gets this case—this is around the time of the Watts riots in L.A., and things are really ugly here, and he's doing stuff he still won't tell me what it is, and one day, Val files for divorce. She couldn't stand his anger—not that he hurt her, he was just furious all the time at other stuff—and before Truman even knows what's really going on, he's single again, and she won't let him anywhere near her."

"But she stayed friends with you," I said.

"The worst of it is that I don't think Truman knows what went wrong." Marvella set her coffee cup down. "He's still possessive and jealous and insane about her. I don't know if you'd call it love. But you heard him last night. He refuses to acknowledge the divorce."

"Why hasn't she left town?" I asked.

"Friends, job, family," Marvella said. "I don't think she's been anywhere other than Wisconsin or Indiana on vacation. She's a timid thing most of the time. She doesn't strike off on her own. That's why she could be discouraged. If I could give her some spine, I would've long ago. I got plenty to spare."

I smiled. "You do."

She didn't smile back. "It's not fair what happened to her. I mean, if it should've happened to anyone, it should've been me. I'm the one who goes to all the places they warn you about. I've slept with the wrong men. I've lived the kind of life that my mother would've called trashy. Val's been a good girl, and the one time she tried to do something different than what she was taught, she got slapped down."

Marvella's voice wobbled. She wiped at her eyes with the tip of her little finger.

"I'm not sure she's got enough spine to make it through this," Marvella said. "Surviving something like this, it takes strength. Val's got too much brains and not enough guts. She might just think too hard and give up."

I thought about Valentina Wilson, the two times I had seen her. That first time, with her impish grin and her dry comment on her clothing, she had seemed petite and pretty and ever so bright. The second time, bleeding, dying, doing the best to save herself, she had seemed strong.

"She did everything she could to survive," I said. "That seems like guts to me."

Marvella shrugged and tried to clean her eyes again with that blackened finger. A tear hung off her eyelashes, and finally fell on her cheek, leaving a black-flecked trail through her foundation.

I extended my hand. She took it.

"I don't want this to happen to anybody else," Marvella said. "I've worked for years to make sure it doesn't, and then Val . . ."

She shook her head.

"How come she didn't come to you?" I asked.

Marvella blinked. Another tear fell. "I don't know, exactly. She didn't tell anyone about any of it. The rape, the pregnancy. I think she was afraid I'd tell Truman."

"But she had to know the risk," I said. Then I remembered what Marvella had told me. Valentina Wilson had been pre-med.

"I hate to ask this," I said, "but you don't think she did this on her own?"

"With a fucking coat-hanger?" Marvella snapped. "She's not stupid, Bill. I told you that."

"But she had some training," I said.

"Enough to know better." Then Marvella took a deep breath, as if she were rethinking her response. "If she had done it, her symptoms would have been different."

I nodded. My coffee had grown cold, but I took a drink anyway. Then I looked at the papers she had given me. "What are these?"

"The first list," Marvella said, "the ones with the stars, they're the people I work with. I send women to them. They're good folk, and I'm trusting you with their names. I know that Val didn't go to any of them, because if she had, she wouldn't have gotten in trouble."

"Abortions go wrong," I said. "All surgery can go wrong."

Marvella nodded. "But these people, they take care of their own."

Like Dr. Jetten last night.

"And the second list?"

Marvella set her coffee cup down. "They're the people I'd never send anyone to. The town butchers."

"I assume they pay protection," I said.

"Every last one of them." She spoke with such anger that I knew she'd tried to shut them down.

"Did Valentina know who they were?"

Marvella shrugged. "She knew what I did, but she never asked me about the people I sent women to. I have no idea who she knew and who she didn't."

"So this second list is my starting point," I said.

Marvella raised her gaze to mine. "You're going to take the job, then?"

"I don't know," I said. "Honestly, I can't figure out how to start. I mean, who's going to confess to butchering a woman?"

"Oh, shit, I almost forgot." Marvella wiped at her face, then reached into her purse again. "You'll need these."

She handed me some photographs. Three of them were Polaroids. Two were graduation photos, and one was a snapshot. The snapshot was a good picture of Valentina. She was laughing.

The others were photographs of women I had never seen before.

"I've been thinking about this all night," Marvella said. "One way this'll work is if you tell these people you know me."

I frowned. I hadn't expected that.

"Like I said, a lot of people know what I do, and they know that I keep track of who does a good job and who doesn't," she said. "Most of the people on the second list, they're in this for the money. They know a good recommendation from me gives them more clients."

I set the photos on the lists.

"What you do," Marvella said, "is that you tell them that you work for me, and that you know that these women recently had good experiences with doctors I'm not familiar with. Then you show the pictures and ask which one that particular doctor worked on."

"These other women have had bad experiences?" I asked.

Marvella nodded. "And I don't know with who."

"Why would anyone who worked on Valentina tell me? Wouldn't this doctor know he hurt her?"

Marvella shook her head. "Most of her symptoms would show up later. Unless she called him for help, he probably has no idea where she is."

"And why wouldn't any of these women know who operated on them?"

"A lot of these doctors use fake names. They also move around. Many come to the woman's apartment."

"But they're paying protection," I said. "They're known to the police."

Marvella nodded.

"How do women find them?" I asked.

"It's all word of mouth," she said. "Sometimes a friend calls, sometimes you get a contact name who then calls the doctor for you, and sets up the meeting. It's pretty elaborate."

I couldn't imagine it, being operated on by someone whose name I didn't know, in my own unsanitary apartment—a person I might not be able to find again.

"If you already have a list of names," I said, "why should I even try? I thought you just wanted to know who this was."

"Because," she said. "I have a hunch the person who did this to Val is someone I don't know."

"You want me to eliminate these suspects first?"

"I want you to find the guy," she said. "The other thing you can do is pretend to be the boyfriend of a woman in trouble, see who you can find. You'll probably come up with names I haven't heard of yet."

"This seems like a lot of work for no real payoff," I said.

Marvella glared at me. "Right now, that butcher is probably operating on some other poor unsuspecting woman. God knows how many he's already killed."

"And knowing who he is won't stop that," I said, "not if he's paying protection."

"I'm going to give his name to Rothstein," Marvella said. "Maybe that high-and-mighty doctor can shut him down."

"Maybe," I said, but I didn't believe it. "You're not going to go after this guy yourself, are you?"

"If I wanted him dead," Marvella said, "I'd tell Truman."

She got up, put her cup and plate in the sink, and then turned to face me. Her perfectly made-up face was ruined, and there was a mascara stain on her blue dress.

"You'll take the job?" she asked.

"I can't promise anything," I said.

"But you'll try," she said.

I nodded. "I'll try."

EIGHT

Marvella's request did seem like a lot of work for very little payoff, but part of me was happy to do it. I didn't like the helpless feeling I'd had since we found Valentina lying on Marvella's floor.

However, I wanted time to think about how I wanted to approach the people on Marvella's lists. I wasn't sure if Marvella's plan was the best method. I also wanted to see what I could find out on my own. Marvella might trust the people on her "good" list, but I didn't.

I knew also that I would have to fit this search in around my other work. I couldn't stomach charging Marvella much for this, if anything. She was right, after all. Getting this butcher off the street would be a community service.

Much as I wanted to, I couldn't devote all of my time to finding the person who hurt Valentina. I had work to do for Laura as well, work that would benefit a lot of other people over time. The more buildings we cleaned up for Sturdy Investments, the more available and affordable housing there would be.

So I would have to balance my desire to search for Valentina's butcher with all of my other work.

That morning, I was supposed to check an apartment building on the West Side. It took me half an hour through minor traffic to make it from my apartment to West Monroe Street.

By midday, Easter Monday had blossomed into one of those glorious spring days found only up north. Just ten days before we had had a surprise spring snowstorm, and remnants of it still huddled against buildings and in dark corners of alleyways—bits of dirty snow that had iced over and looked like filthy smoked glass.

What hadn't melted yesterday was melting today. The jacket I had worn out of the house was useless. I flung it in the backseat and drove with the windows open.

The radio told me we were one degree off seventy, and I wasn't the only one enjoying the weather. People ate lunch outside, sharing benches or even curbs, their own coats thrown down to protect their workday clothing from winter's dirt that still covered the sidewalks.

Sturdy Investments had a lot of holdings all over the city, but the ones it held in the ghettos on the South and West Sides were in terrible shape. The rents that Sturdy charged, however, were three times what they were in better areas. Because most of the tenants were poor and black, they were usually denied housing in other neighborhoods. These tenants became captives of their own poverty, and companies like Sturdy took advantage of that. Often they didn't fix complaints until the buildings literally collapsed around the tenants' ears.

In the past five years, tenants had been burned out of their buildings because of faulty wiring, had fallen through floors because the boards had rotted, and had lived without heat through most of a Chicago winter. These were facts documented not by Sturdy but by reporters for the black papers or by the tenants themselves using Polaroids.

Laura and I had uncovered some of this before she angled to take over Sturdy. The rest we had discovered in the past three months. And, we knew, we were just beginning this quest. Sturdy Investments, as run by her father and then by his cronies, was one of the biggest slumlords in a city filled with slumlords.

Perhaps the biggest frustration for Laura was that the people who were supposed to act as watchdogs in these cases did not. City building inspectors were easily bought. She had reported two in January who had been receiving the bulk of the payoffs from Sturdy. To her disgust, neither man had been fired. They had just been moved to other parts of Chicago.

By February, she realized that exposing these people wouldn't stop the corruption. Instead, she quietly took the remaining building inspectors off the payroll by handling all inspections herself. No more bribes, no more payoffs.

Now the money went to me for my reports. I was supposed to be as accurate as possible. Laura's goal was to fix each dilapidated building, charge reasonable rents, and slowly make an honest profit. I wasn't sure her plan would work, but I was willing to try.

I turned on to West Monroe and entered a different world. The Loop had been filled with workers trying to enjoy the day off. Monroe, which ran through the Loop, changed from a business street to residential, eventually becoming the part of Chicago everyone pointed to when they talked about slums, urban decay, and inner cities out of control.

The city fathers considered the South Side, where I lived, the oldest ghetto in Chicago. The description wasn't really accurate; there were people of various income levels living there. While certain neighborhoods were in decay, others were being rebuilt—or had never decayed in the first place.

But the West Side was different. Franklin called it the place where dislocated families went, people without connections, and people without a lot of hope. The anger here was palpable, as well as the frustration. It seemed like every time this part of the city made some progress, something happened to make that progress go away.

Since I had moved to Chicago, there had been a number of incidents here—incidents the city didn't want to call riots. A real riot started last Thursday night, but the city had been prepared for it. Hundreds of police in riot gear had flooded the area but, remembering the bad press from the Democratic National Convention, had not beaten people senseless—at least not in front of the cameras.

Thursday's riot, a reaction to the anniversary of Martin Luther King's assassination, was nothing like the riot a year ago that erupted the night Martin died. More than two square miles of the West Side burned. Fire didn't cause all the damage: there had been looting and fighting as well.

Hundreds of buildings were destroyed. Even more had been looted and nine people had died. Those statistics had been raised again in the past few weeks in the white press as the anniversary of Martin's death loomed, and I practically had them memorized.

In the white press, it seemed, that was all Martin's death signified: destruction blacks wreaked on themselves. As if a black man had murdered Martin. As if blacks were responsible for all the bad things that happened to them.

Sturdy Investments had lost fifteen buildings to the fires. Many of the remaining buildings in the riot area that the company still owned had been damaged, and Laura couldn't find any evidence that the buildings had been repaired.

I was supposed to inspect those, but I hadn't gotten to most of them.

Going through a building properly took time, and since these buildings were so run-down, some of them took days instead of hours.

The 2300 block of West Monroe looked, at a distance, like the solid old middle-class neighborhood it had once been. The apartment buildings, some of which had started as single-family dwellings, extended as far as the eye could see. Large trees that had clearly stood in the same place for generations still looked imposing, despite their winter barrenness.

The cars parked along the street, however, were the first clue that the neighborhood had fallen on hard times. Here, my rusted Impala was one of the more expensive vehicles. It ran and it was semi-clean. The other cars were older and rustier, looking like they might fall apart in a good wind. One or two brand-new sports cars sat among the others, untouched, clear signs that they had been stolen, and that their new owners were people that no one wanted to mess with.

Another block north, on West Madison, the Black Panthers had their headquarters in an old storefront. It was easily recognizable. On the main level, someone had painted two black panthers, facing each other as if they were about to begin a fight.

I had, so far, been able to avoid that building. I figured a group like the Panthers had to have at least one FBI informant hidden in their midst. The last thing I wanted to do was call attention to myself, and bring the FBI down on Jimmy and me again.

The apartment building I was supposed to inspect had lost its last tenant at the end of March. I would have gotten to the building anyway, just not as quickly. Laura put a priority on the empty buildings, hoping that we could take care of them first, without disturbing any tenants.

The buildings on this block were close together, and it took me a moment to find the one I was supposed to inspect. It was only two stories high and quite narrow, nearly disappearing between its larger neighbors.

Its size made me relax a little. Perhaps I would get through the inspection in half the normal time. That would allow me to move to the building I had been planning to inspect on Division for the past month now. Maybe I might even be able to get more than two buildings completed this week.

The street was remarkably empty, considering what a warm, sunny day it was. No one sat on the stoops, and no one was on the sidewalks. No young children played in the front yards, even though there had to be children who were too young to go to school on this block.

However, I knew I was being watched, and probably from several of the buildings. There had to be some Black Panther Party members living here, since it was so close to the headquarters, but there also had to be a goodly number of families.

As I got out of the car, I thought I saw movement in one of the apartment buildings across the street. A large bay window on the top story had curtains that were still twitching.

Whoever had been watching probably didn't consider me a threat, probably didn't even know if I was a resident of the neighborhood or not. When that person realized I was black, he probably relaxed.

I had a hunch others still watched me, however, trying to figure out what my business was. I debated getting my gun out of the glove compartment, and then changed my mind. I wasn't being threatened by anyone, and the neighborhood, while obviously full of caution, wasn't as bad as some that I had been in.

I generally used a clipboard for notes, but in some neighborhoods did not carry it. The worst thing I could do here was look official. I slipped a small notepad in my shirt pocket along with the pen, so that I could make notes while inside. Then I'd transfer everything to the form when I got back home. I also picked up my industrial-size flashlight, and clipped it onto my belt.

I got out of the car, closed the door, and locked it. Anyone with determination and a coat hanger could get into this car, but it would take some doing. And often, simple barriers like a lock and a rolled-up window was enough to keep a casual thief out.

People had stapled flyers to the large streetlamp near my car. A few of the flyers advertised the Black Panther Party. One of them showed a giant white rat wearing a hat decorated with the stars and stripes running out of an alley, a giant black panther in pursuit. Below the image were the words, "Defend the Ghetto."

As I walked up the cracked sidewalk, I pulled the keys Laura had given me out of my pocket. I doubted I would need them. The front door hung crookedly in its frame. Even if it wasn't unlocked, one good kick would open it.

Before I went inside, I inspected the foundation. The building had initially been built as a three-flat with one of the apartments in the basement. The basement windows were grimy and cracked, certainly not enough to keep the cold out in the winter. If any kind of storm brought wind from the north, I was pretty certain that snow or rain fell through those cracks into the apartment below.

No one had stuffed the windows with rags or tried to board them up, so I assumed that apartment had been empty at least through the winter.

The windows were surrounded by large bucket gutters, also made of stone, which had to make the water problem worse any time those gutters got clogged. One of them was filled with dirt, and someone had actually tried to plant flowers in it. All that remained of the flowers were hard brown stalks and some trailing leaves.

I walked around the building. The foundation itself appeared pretty solid. It had very few cracks, and most of those had been caused by time, not by any structural flaws. The place was made of stone and had been painted brown some time in the last ten years. The paint was flaking away near the ground, revealing other generations of paint, one of them a very bright blue.

The alley in the back was littered with garbage. The buildings facing Adams Street appeared to be the same kind as the ones on Monroe, and from the same generation. Only two of them were badly scorched, and one was only a foundation filled with charred beams of wood.

I couldn't tell if the fire had been an isolated one, or had happened during last year's riots. The ruins had no smoke smell, though, so the fire hadn't happened too recently.

I scooted across the alley and gazed up at Sturdy's building. The back stairs on the upper floor had rotted away, and the window that opened onto them was gone. Only shards of glass remained. The stairs leading to the main floor apartment—which was nearly six feet off the ground back here— were pulling away from the building.

There were no drain pipes, and the overhanging roof had holes in it that were visible from below. The foundation might have been solid, but the rest of the building was a mess.

I slipped through the other side, stepping through last summer's dried weeds, piles of unmelted snow, and a lot of broken glass. When I reached the front of the building, I mounted the stone steps and tried the door.

As I suspected, it opened easily. I stepped inside and caught the faint odor of rot and decay. The floorboards were soft, and covered with more garbage.

There was no light in the hallway, but that could have been because the bulb was broken. I unhooked my flashlight and turned it on, shining the beam along the ruined floor.

Wooden stairs, which had once been grand, swept up toward the second floor. The stairs shared a wide design and ornate banisters with the stairs in my apartment building, but here, no one had kept the wood polished. It was gray with age, and most of the spindles attaching the banister to the stairs were broken or gone.

I trained the beam upward. The landing had a large hole in the center, as if someone had fallen through, and the wallboard had a corresponding hole about arm-height.

I shook my head, thinking about the poor souls who had lived here until a week ago, wondering how they had put up with all of this filth. They had given notice on the first of March, like responsible tenants, but the notice hadn't included a forwarding address. Had they had enough of Chicago? Or had the rent, even for a dump like this one, proven too much for them?

Moving the beam away from the stairs, I trained it down the hall, revealing two doors. The building had a three-flat design, but someone had converted the original apartments into two apartments, making this into the six-flat my documentation said it was. The apartments had to be very small and cramped.

I tried the first door, startled to find it locked. According to my records, the last tenants had been in the apartment at the end of the hall, not in this one. Apparently people were a lot more responsible than I expected them to be. Whoever had been here last made sure that the apartment was locked.

It took me a few minutes to find the right key. When I finally found it, it turned the deadbolt easily, and the door swung open.

Sunlight filled the main room. The light's brightness startled me. Even though the bay window was filthy, it still let in enough light to make this room attractive.

A thin carpet covered the floor, and the walls were painted white. Bookcases, made of oak, lined the sides of a bricked up fireplace. An ancient radiator stood in front of the fireplace as if, decades ago, someone had failed to get the message about not making fires.

The windowseat built into the bay window still had pillows on it. The pillows were clean enough that I could discern their color—a bright orange that had probably been offensive before dust and sunlight had faded it back to cheerful.

The odor wasn't bad in here. The apartment smelled of garlic, mildew, and cigarette smoke. I closed the door behind me and stepped farther inside, releasing a horde of dust motes that caught and reflected the sunlight.

This had been a very pleasant place in its day, and probably could be pleasant again, given enough time and work. No one had destroyed the main room. The wallboard was solid, and so were the floors. The ceiling had a water stain above the window, but other than that, I saw no damage.

I would come back to this room and do a more thorough search. But first, I wanted to get a sense of the rest of the apartment.

The original railroad design would have put everything else behind me, but I wasn't sure how they had cut up the space. I turned around.

What would have been the dining room had been divided into two parts—the kitchen, which opened onto the living room, and a closed door that had to lead into the apartment's only bedroom. A small bathroom was probably off the kitchen, sharing its pipes.

I went into the kitchen first, found the light switch and tried it. To my surprise, the lights came on. So the electricity to the building hadn't been shut off, or someone had jury-rigged it to pull power off of someone else's meter. Yet one more thing for me to check.

The kitchen was unexpectedly clean. The stove had grime on its surface, but no real dust, and the sink was marred only by a giant rust stain near the drain. The refrigerator—a Frigidaire older than I was—kicked on behind me, startling me.

Something scuttled in the cabinets near the sink, probably mice, even though I couldn't smell them. That wasn't a surprise. They were probably nesting upstairs, where no one had lived since last summer, and were used to coming downstairs for their food.

I left the kitchen and headed toward the bedroom to finish my cursory search of the first apartment. The bedroom's door was a thin plywood, the kind that was made in the fifties. The remodel of this building had happened when Laura's father was alive. Perhaps he had even ordered it.

I grabbed the doorknob, and turned. It was stuck. But these doors were easy to open, no matter what. I shoved, hoping to force the latch, and the door moved inward slightly.

It should have moved all the way, given the force I had put on it. Something was blocking the door. Apparently all the damage was in the bedroom. I had encountered that before.

I shoved again, and this time, the door flew open. I staggered forward as someone screamed.

A small form wrapped itself around my waist, pushing its head into my stomach and pushing me back.

I was already off-balance because of the door. The momentum of the small body, shoving me, propelled me backward. I tried to clutch the doorframe but wasn't able to get my hands around it in time. My legs came out from underneath me, and I hung suspended in midair for what seemed like an eternity.

As I did, I saw a skinny girl, her hand over her mouth, clutching a young child, holding her away from the door.

Then I fell, landing with a whomp that reverberated through the entire building. The whomp reverberated through me, too. The air left my body in a painful rush.

I lay on my back, gasping as that same small form started pounding me in the stomach.

I managed to grab one thin wrist, and then the other, holding them above me until I was able to catch my breath again. A young boy no older than Jimmy tried to squirm out of my grip.

"Lemme go!" the boy yelled. "You lemme go!"

I shook my head, still too breathless to talk.

He managed to get his knees underneath him. It would only be a matter of seconds before he got to his feet. Then he would probably use those feet as weapons. I would have, in his place.

I twisted him sideways and sat up, even though it hurt my back and my oxygen-starved lungs. I wrapped his arms around him and pulled him close, holding him in place against my chest.

"Someone want to tell me what's going on?" I asked.

"This's our house. You get out. Get out." The boy started slamming his head against my already aching chest.

"Doug, that's enough," said the girl, and as she spoke, I realized she was older than I had initially thought. She was small and too thin. I could see the bones in her arms.

She bent over, picked up my flashlight, and held it out to me. Her cotton shirt and denim pants were so thin I could see her skin through the material.

"If you let my son go, mister, we'll get out of here."

The boy slammed me in the chest again. I slid one hand over both of his arms and held them tightly. Then I put the other hand over his forehead and pushed it against my ribcage.

"Please, mister," the girl said. I couldn't quite think of her as a woman, even though she had two children. She didn't look much older than Lacey, although that was probably due to the fact that she was small-boned and starving. "We won't bother you if you just let him go."

If I let him go, they would run from here and I wouldn't see them again.

"Who are you?" I asked.

She shook her head. "Please. We didn't mean nothing. We just needed a place to stay and somebody said this place was open. We ain't took nothing, and we didn't do no damage."

In fact, she had probably cleaned the apartment up as best she could. That was why the pillows on the windowseat looked so bright. Either they had been in the apartment and she cleaned them up, or she had scavenged them from somewhere to provide one of her children a place to sleep.

"You gonna stop pounding on me, Doug?" I asked.

He tried to nod under my hand. I let go of his head, but kept him wrapped up and against me.

"Please let him go," his mother said. "Please. We'll just disappear and you won't have to worry about us again."

I studied her arms for needle tracks. I didn't see any. In fact, I saw no evidence of drug use.

"How long have you been squatting here?" I asked.

"Just a few hours." Her dark cheeks, already flushed with fear, grew even darker. She was as bad a liar as Marvella was. "It was a mistake. We're really sorry."

"It's all right," I said. "I work for the building's owner, and we have a policy about squatters—"

Doug slammed that sharp little head of his against my ribs, making me gasp. I grabbed his forehead and held him in place again.

"As I was saying," I said, sounding a lot more breathless than I had before, "we have a policy about squatters—"

"I know," the woman said, "and I'll do anything, just don't take me to the police. Please. They'll call welfare and that'll be the end. They'll take my babies. Please. Don't call anyone."

I sighed. I had run into this before. Apparently Sturdy—the old Sturdy—had been vicious when it found squatters. The company wanted people to stay out of their buildings if they couldn't afford the rent.

The reputation had gotten around. But that didn't stop desperate people, like this woman, from squatting anyway.

"That's the old management," I said. "Now what we do is take people to a place on the South Side that'll give you some food, a shower, and a bed while we find you a place to live."

She put a thin hand over her mouth, then shook her head. "I can't afford nothing."

"I know," I said. "We're not asking you to pay right away. We try to help people get back on their feet."

This was not another branch of Sturdy, but a private shelter Laura, Franklin, and I had set up through one of the community organizations.

After I had found nearly a dozen squatters in one ruined building with no heat in January, I had called every social service in town. The Salvation Army hadn't had an open bed since the cold weather set in during November, and the missions had filled up at the same time. A lot of the other War on Poverty organizations—little branches of philanthropy run with government grant money—had had to close when Nixon cut off their funding as one of his first acts in office.

I went to the churches next, only to discover they were as stumped as I was. Most of them had desperate people sleeping in their basements or on the floors of the church-run soup kitchens. The churches apologized and told me to contact the organizations I had already contacted, leaving me with a dozen homeless people and no place to put them.

So I had called Franklin, hoping he could use his connections, and he had suggested having Laura rent a space for these people until he could find a way to help them. Franklin knew everyone of import in Bronzeville and he was able to set up a small organization, which we called Helping Hands Incorporated. We staffed it mostly with female volunteers, who took in the squatters I found every month, found them homes or jobs or medical help, whatever they needed to get back on their feet.

Drew McMillan, Laura's attorney, had set up a nonprofit corporation to handle everything, and did the fund-raising himself, so that Laura's involvement would remain quiet.

It was a way, she later told me, of taking care of her conscience while moving so slowly on reforming Sturdy.

But I couldn't tell this poor family that history, and I wasn't sure they would believe me if I even tried.

The woman was looking at me as if I were crazy, and the boy was struggling in my arms. The little girl, who wasn't much more than a toddler, clutched her mother's leg, looking terrified.

"If you can promise me that your son won't hurt me anymore, I'll hand him over to you," I said.

"I can promise that," the woman said.

"And," I said, "if you can promise that you'll stay, I'll prove that I can help you."

Her gaze flicked to the door. She was measuring the distance, whether or not she would be able to get past me.

"I can promise that, too," she lied.

I didn't let him go. Instead, I said, "I'm quick. You won't make it to the door before me, not with a toddler in tow."

"She's three," the woman said softly.

I looked at the little girl again. She was so small, it was almost impossible to believe she was older than eighteen months. She wore what had once been a pink dress. The dress had been taken in, but was still too big for her. She had large blue eyes and skin as dark as her mother's. She would be beautiful one day—if she lived long enough.

"How long have you been on your own?" I asked the woman.

She shrugged. "I dunno. Always, I guess."

She sounded so sad. The boy kept squirming in my arms. I released him and he almost fell off my lap. He caught himself with one hand, started to run toward his mother, and apparently decided against it.

He turned toward me. "You don't hurt her."

"I wasn't planning to," I said.

I stayed on the ground so that I wouldn't intimidate them, but I drew up my legs so that I could get to my feet quickly if I had to.

"Let me tell you what we do now when we find people staying in our vacant apartments." I avoided the word "squatter" with its negative connotations. I didn't want the woman to feel any more uncomfortable than she already did.

I explained to her the system we had devised, how I would take her and the children to the South Side office, and how the women there would find them a place to stay, and help her find work.

"I can't work," the woman said. "I don't got no diploma, and I can't leave my babies."

"Your son should be in school," I said, "and they'll figure out a way for you to work and take care of your daughter."

"I'm not going to school," Doug said. He was rubbing his forearm where I had held him. I could see the imprint of my fingers in his skin.

"What do you say?" I asked the woman.

She studied me for a moment. "What if I say no?"

"Then I'm authorized to give you twenty dollars and the address of the Salvation Army. They might be able to help you. They might not."

"Twenty bucks?" she asked, and the way she said it, she made it sound like a fortune.

I leaned forward and pulled my wallet out of my back pocket. I reached inside, found the petty cash I carried for various needs around the building—including this kind of thing—and handed her a twenty.

She stared at it as if it were ten times that much.

"You can have it anyway," I said. "But if you come with me, it'll last longer."

"How do I know you ain't gonna hurt us?" she asked.

I didn't blame her for asking. She didn't know me at all. I could have been anyone, and I could have been making up this story to get her into my car, and into some kind of trouble.

"I'll give you a dime," I said. "There's a pay phone on Madison. You can call the police station and ask for a Detective Sinkovich. You don't have to tell him your name. Just tell him mine, which happens to be Bill Grimshaw, and ask him if he'll vouch for me."

Usually I had Truman Johnson do that, but I doubted Johnson was in. Jack Sinkovich had been on desk duty off and on for the past three months, so I was pretty sure he would be in to answer the phone. He was going through a nasty divorce, and his volatile temper made him almost impossible to work with. But he had also made some spectacular arrests during this time, and the department couldn't just shove him aside.

The woman was still staring at the twenty.

"Honestly," I said, "with two kids to protect, I don't know if I would trust me, either. Take them with you, make the call, and come on back if you want my help. Otherwise, you have your twenty, and you can find another place to stay."

She shoved the twenty in the pocket of her jeans. "What are you going to do?"

"Rest for a minute." I looked at Doug. "That's one powerful tackle you have."

He nodded, but he didn't trust me enough to smile at me.

"Then I'm going to finish inspecting the building. That's what I was hired for. I'm supposed to figure out whether this place is livable or not."

"People been living here," the woman said. "The last official ones moved out last week."

"Are there other unofficial people?" I asked.

"No," she said, and it didn't seem this time like she was lying.

"Because," I said, just to make the point, "I really am not sure I can take another tackle like that."

"We got the good place," Doug said, apparently taking my tackling remark seriously. "Nobody knows the other apartment's empty, and everybody hates upstairs. Downstairs is cold and wet most of the time, so it's not much better than being outside."

His mother gave me a defeated look. His answer proved that they had been here quite a while.

I flicked her a dime. "Go check. You'll feel better."

She caught it with her free hand. Then she nodded at me. "How long're you gonna be here?"

"For a couple of hours at least. So you have plenty of time."

She nodded, and hugged her little girl closer. Then she put her fist, still clutching that dime, against Doug's back. She led her little troop out of the apartment without another word.

I stayed on the floor until I heard the front door close. Then I eased myself up. I was sore from the fall, and I would be bruised. I wasn't lying to that boy. He had a stupendous tackle—and he had been lucky. Most adults couldn't get me off my feet, but I had been so unprepared that his momentum and his height had worked in his favor.

I turned in time to see them through the bay window as they crossed Monroe, heading toward Madison. I hadn't even gotten her name.

She disappeared between the buildings across the street. I sighed and returned to my work, hoping she would come back, knowing that she probably wouldn't.

NINE

Even though I wasn't finished, I moved from the family's apartment to the newly vacated apartment in the back for reasons I didn't entirely understand. I almost felt as if I didn't belong in their living quarters, although they hadn't paid rent, and technically the quarters belonged to Laura.

I left the apartment door open, so that the family could find me if they returned, and so that I could hear if anyone else entered the building.

The second apartment on the first floor was dark and dingy, and I couldn't imagine anyone living in it for a week, let alone years like the previous tenant. That faint odor of decay was present here, along with the smells of garlic and mildew. There was only one window in the living room, and it had a view of the building next door. There was almost no natural light in here, even on a sunny day like this one.

I found empty apartments in buildings like this depressing. They spoke of failed dreams and loss, of lives lived with no hope at all, of desperation made all that much worse by the loneliness that surrounded it.

I was in the apartment's only bedroom, looking at the white mildew on the carpet beneath the window, when I heard voices. I made my way back to the door.

". . . see? Told you he was gone." That was Doug, with all the confidence of a ten-year-old.

"You talking about me?" I asked as I stepped into the hallway. The little family was inside their living room, the woman holding her daughter on her hip.

The little girl smiled at me, a tentative, worried smile, as if she was afraid she was doing something wrong.

"Did you get ahold of Detective Sinkovich?" I asked.

The woman looked at me, and shook her head. I felt my shoulders tighten.

"I thought it was kinda weird, you know, having me call a cop. But it's pretty effective. I mean, you can't set up all those official voices and all those people talking in the background." She spoke rapidly. Apparently she had been shaking her head at my methodology, rather than answering my question.

"That's why we did it that way," I said. "I knew a few people wouldn't want to call the police, but I figured it was a lot safer than having them not believe me, especially if I gave them some random number."

She nodded. "He says you're a stand-up guy, even if you are a royal pain in the butt."

I smiled. That sounded like Sinkovich.

"And he wanted to know who I was, and why I was asking about you."

"What did you tell him?" I asked.

"I hung up." She gave me the same fear-filled, wide-eyed expression that her daughter had had a moment ago.

"Good for you," I said. "Are you going to come with me, then?"

"We gotta get our stuff first." She looked at Doug. He huddled next to her, and I realized he was small, too. He frowned at me, as if to warn me away from them, then went into the bedroom I hadn't gotten to yet.

I wouldn't get to it that afternoon, either. Taking care of this small group would use up the rest of my work time. But I didn't mind. I was pleased that I had somewhere to take them. I wouldn't have kept doing this work if I had to constantly turn out squatters who then had nowhere else to go.

The woman walked to the bedroom door, keeping the little girl on her hip.

"Need help?" I asked.

"Yeah," she said. "Can you get the pillows?"

I knew which ones she meant, the ones on the window seat. I picked them up. They smelled of child-sweat, sunlight, and dust. I turned around to find Doug behind me, spreading out an army blanket.

"Put them on there," he said.

I did. He then grabbed a pile of neatly folded clothing and put that on top of the pillows.

"You just gonna stand there?" he asked.

"What else do you need?"

"Tie it up," he said.

"Say please," his mother yelled from the bedroom.

"Please," he growled, and then ran back to the bedroom door.

I tied the blanket into a makeshift duffel. I had done this a few times in my own life, mostly as a young man, and the movement was a familiar one. I even left a bit of material so that there was something to hold on to.

The filled blanket was light. I carried it into the bedroom, saw the woman on her hands and knees packing a few more belongings into another, smaller blanket. The little girl clutched a Raggedy Ann doll that looked filthy.

Doug set a tattered Bible in the middle of it all, and then started to tie up the second blanket.

I wondered if they would have left all of their belongings because I had found them, or if they would have snuck back during the night. It looked like they had been here for a long time, long enough to spread out and make this home.

"Got everything?" I asked as I helped the woman up.

She nodded, then bent down and picked up her daughter. Doug hefted the second tied blanket over his shoulder.

"Let's go then," I said.

I led them into the hallway and locked up both apartments. Then I marched them down to my car. While I had been inside, someone had left a flyer on my windshield, attached by the wipers.

All of the cars on the block had flyers on them. That caught my attention. I had never seen anything like it. The flyers weren't mimeographed or hand-done. They had been produced at a print shop at considerable cost.

Attention Drug Addicts, the flyer said. *Are you tired? Would you like to stop using DOPE?*

There was more, but I didn't feel like looking at it. I crumpled it up and tossed it onto the floor behind the driver's seat.

"Problem?" the woman asked.

I shook my head. "Someone just mistook me for a drug addict, that's all."

She let out a small laugh, and Doug looked at her in surprise. It was as if he'd never seen her do that before.

"They didn't get a good look at you, then, did they?" she asked.

"I don't think they got a look at me at all." I swept my hand toward the backseat. "You all can ride in back if you want, or one of you can ride in front. I don't care which."

"Watch your sister," the woman said to Doug. "I'm sitting up front."

She helped the children into the back, then tucked the makeshift duffels around them. She also locked the doors. Then she went around to the front and got in.

I got into the driver's side, and turned the radio off before starting the car.

"You know my name," I said as I stuck the keys in the ignition. "Mind if I ask yours?"

"Helen," she said softly. "And that's Doug and Carrie in the back."

I turned to them, nodded as formally as I could over the seats, and said, "Pleased to meet you."

Carrie put her small hands over her face, giggling behind them, but Doug just glared at me.

I swiveled back in the seat and started the car. "They're going to ask you a lot of questions down at the Helping Hands. You don't have to answer them if you don't want to. It's just for their information. One of the men who set this up sometimes works with local politicians. He figures the more he knows about the ways that people get in trouble, the more he can do to prevent it."

I checked my mirrors, then pulled out. No one had driven down the street, and no one was walking by. Even though someone had put flyers on the cars, no one else seemed to be anywhere around.

"What kind of questions?" Helen asked.

"Things like how did you get here, not to this apartment but to this living situation, stuff like that."

Her face closed down. "They're not gonna use this to take my kids, are they?"

I had dealt with this question before. It was an important one to all of the parents I had encountered because the State of Illinois required mothers to maintain a "suitable" home to get welfare benefits. In Cook County, that could mean anything from a two-parent household with the wife as homemaker to limiting the number of children inside the household. I had only been doing this a short time, and only with people I happened to find in Sturdy's buildings, and I had already heard countless horror stories.

"This place I'm taking you has nothing to do with the government," I said. "It's privately run. They're not interested in taking your kids. They're interested in helping you get back on your feet."

Her expression hadn't changed. "What does that mean?"

"They'll help you figure out what you're good at, probably help you find a job, definitely help you get benefits, and make certain you have enough money to make it through each month."

"I can't get no job." Her fingers clutched the edge of the car seat.

Through the corner of my eye, I could see Doug. He had one hand on his sister's back, and he was frowning at me, as if I were the reason for his problems.

Carrie's small face had become serious again. She looked from Doug to me and then back to Doug. Clearly his attitude worried her.

"Why can't you get a job?" I asked Helen.

She stared straight ahead, but her hands gripped the seat even tighter. "I gotta take care of my kids. Carrie's too little to leave alone."

"You don't gotta leave her alone," Doug said.

Helen's mouth tightened, but she continued as if he hadn't spoken. "I didn't graduate high school, and I don't got no experience."

"You've never had a job?" I asked.

We were in the Loop now. The streets were filled with shoppers and businessmen who walked with their coats off. A lot of people headed toward Grant Park, probably to enjoy the warm weather as they got off work.

"I waitressed for a while, but that was in Milwaukee," Helen was saying.

"Is that where you're from?"

"Yes, but it don't matter. My folks told me when I left for Chicago that they wasn't going to have nothing to do with me. They didn't like Carrie's dad."

"Where's he?" I asked.

She stared out the window, and didn't answer me. I wasn't going to push. Even though she had believed me enough to get into the car, she wasn't going to tell me everything. I doubted she would tell the volunteers at Helping Hands everything, either. It would be a long time before she trusted us.

Besides, a lot of the questions I was asking were similar to the ones a social worker would ask.

I turned south and traffic got worse. It was bumper-to-bumper on both sides. Honking horns echoed in the building canyons, and the sun seemed thinner here. Exhaust made the air thicker, and hotter, not that I minded. After the deep cold of mid-winter, this breath of spring felt good.

No one spoke while we were in the Loop. Helen's silence made it pretty clear that she wasn't going to answer any more questions. She was tense now, as if she regretted coming with me.

What she didn't realize—what I probably hadn't made clear—was that she had a real chance now to turn her life around. But it would depend upon her. Helping Hands Incorporated would get her started, and then she would be on her own.

"What's going to happen over the next few days is this," I said. "The volunteers will find you a place to stay tonight. By the end of the week, you'll have your own apartment. The first month will be paid for by Helping Hands Incorporated. After that, they'll pay for whatever your job and assistance can't cover."

"Said I can't get no job," she muttered.

I ignored that. "Eventually, the idea is that you'll be able to afford the apartment or a place like it on your own. They help you, but they won't pay your way indefinitely."

"If I gotta get a job to make this work," she said, "you gotta let us out here. I ain't gonna leave my babies alone."

"The job is just one option. There may be benefits you qualify for or other things that will help you make your bills, things you may not be aware of."

Things I wasn't aware of, either. I didn't have the patience for this sort of thing, which was why I was glad that Laura and Franklin found a way to take it out of my hands. I was already getting exasperated with Helen, and I knew that she needed help desperately.

"We was doing okay on our own," she said.

"I know that." It was easier for me to agree with her than disagree. "And you can say no to the help at any point."

That seemed to reassure her. We drove into Bronzeville in silence. As we reached Hyde Park, she spoke up again.

"We was doing okay." She wasn't looking at me. She was looking out the window. "It was the fire."

I glanced in the rearview. Doug had his head back, his eyes closed, but I couldn't tell if he was asleep or not. Carrie clearly was. She was lying sideways on the plastic seat, her thumb in her mouth.

"What fire?" I asked, hoping Helen didn't mean the riot-started fire after Martin died. That would have meant this family had been on the streets for a year.

"Our building. It burnt down. Nothing left." Helen shook her head. "I got the kids out, though. That's the main thing. But the manager, he didn't refund our rent, even though it was the first of the month, and the welfare people said they'd hold my check till I got another address, and I couldn't get another address till I had some money. I didn't have nothing to sell—except, you know, what a woman's got to sell, and I ain't never been that low—and everybody I know, they was all burned out or broke or wanting something I wasn't willing to give. So I went to the mission on Pacific Grove, and they helped for a few nights, and one of the ladies there, she even tried talking to the welfare people, but it didn't do no good."

Helen wrapped her arms around herself.

"And they got some rule there about not staying real long. So before they kicked us out, I started looking for places. Found a few. But never got a real address, so we never did get our ADC again."

"How have you been eating?" I asked.

She shrugged. "What we can find. That new program the Panthers got, the kids been doing real good on that."

"The Breakfast For Children program?" I asked. I had seen it in the papers, but I hadn't realized that it was actually working.

"They gotta listen to some weird speeches, but I think it's worth it for them to get a full stomach. They started it last week, and Doug's been taking Carrie every day. It was just a few blocks away. So if we can't do nothing at your Helping Hands place, I wanna go back to that neighborhood, see what I can find. Free food for the kids ain't something you find a lot of."

I nodded. "I'll make sure you can get back if that's what you want."

"Yeah."

No wonder she was so thin. She probably hadn't had a good meal since she got burned out of her apartment. Her food obviously went to the children, unless there was enough to spare.

I didn't want to ask any more questions, and she didn't volunteer any more information. We drove the rest of the way in silence.

Helping Hands Incorporated had its offices in Woodlawn. The office was small, nestled between a drug store and a five-and-dime. The "L" divided the street, providing shade where none was needed.

People crowded the sidewalks, looking harried and busy, as if they didn't have time to enjoy the sunny day. In between the heavyset matrons with their shopping bags and the tall men in tattered coats were teenage boys, smoking and standing in clumps. The boys wore the red tams of the Blackstone Rangers. The rest of the crowd either ignored them or gave them a wide berth.

I didn't want to set up Helping Hands in Stones country, but the rent was reasonable and Franklin argued that the people we wanted to help were more likely to show up in Woodlawn than they were in Kenwood—a place where, the joke went, blacks and whites united against the poor.

I parked in front of the office, and helped Helen get out. She picked up the sleeping Carrie as if the little girl weighed nothing. Doug grabbed both makeshift duffels, shrugging me off when I tried to help.

It seemed warmer down here and the air smelled of sweat mixed with overheated metal from the "L" tracks. I led the three of them through the crowd, and pulled open the office door.

The office was little more than a boxy room with a desk, a few comfortable chairs, and some plants. Another door led to the back room, which had a hot plate, a refrigerator, and a water cooler, as well as a bed for anyone who needed it.

The office was cooler than outside, and smelled faintly of rosewater. Only two people worked during the afternoon—a volunteer and one of three paid staff members.

I didn't recognize the volunteer, a slender middle-aged woman who wore her hair in a beehive. Cat-eye glasses hung around her neck instead of jewelry, and her simple white dress looked perfect for the weather.

She had just gotten herself a glass of water. She crossed the room, and sat behind the desk, looking official. Then she smiled, and I saw why she had been hired.

Her smile was the brightest thing I'd seen all day.

"I'm Bill Grimshaw," I said, extending my hand. "I found these nice folks living in an apartment on West Madison."

I gave the volunteer the address, and I made introductions. Then I excused myself, planning to leave.

Helen caught my arm. "Ain't you staying?"

I shook my head. "This nice lady will help you now."

"But what if I wanna go back? Who'll drive me?"

I had told her that she could go if she had to.

"Give it a night," I said, "and if you're not happy here, have someone call me. I'll drive you back to the west side."

"Before breakfast?" she asked. "They serve at six."

I suddenly understood her concern. This was an office building. She was used to shelters that had kitchens and beds. Office buildings meant welfare workers and prying questions, no food, and loss of dignity.

"You'll get breakfast tomorrow," I said. "All three of you. If you want to go back, we'll do it after lunch. That way I know you got two of your three squares."

"Are you hungry now?" the volunteer asked. "I have some food in the back. I can get you something to eat."

Helen licked her lower lip. I wasn't sure if she was aware she had done so. But she didn't turn around.

Doug, to my surprise, said nothing. But he looked at his mom with longing.

"They're hungry," I said, "but go easy. They haven't had a lot to eat lately."

The volunteer nodded.

I carefully pried Helen's hand off my arm. "You'll be all right," I said.

"These people will take good care of you. And you know how to get hold of me if you absolutely have to."

"I do?" she asked.

I nodded. "You just make the same call you made earlier. Detective Sinkovich'll track me down."

I had learned in February not to give my home number out. A woman I had found in an apartment on South Cottage Grove had called fifteen times one night. She had seemed stable when I first found her, but it turned out that she was withdrawing from some drug, and thinking that everyone was against her. Everyone but me.

Helen stepped back slightly and put her free hand on Doug's shoulder. "Okay," she said. "We'll give it one night."

"And food?" Doug whispered, apparently thinking he was quiet enough that only she could hear.

"Yes," she said to him.

I said my good-byes and slipped back out into the sunshine. As the door closed behind me, I did not turn around or wave. I already had the image of the three of them—Carrie asleep against her mother's thin shoulder, Doug a small but serious guardian beside them—firmly in my mind.

I wished I hadn't.

It seemed, no matter how much I did, it wasn't even a fraction of a drop in the proverbial bucket. And, as a result, I had to get folks out of my mind, as best I could.

Still, I could feel the three of them watching me through the office's grimy window as I got into my car. I drove off, wishing I had spent the day sitting on a beach, enjoying the weather with Jimmy instead of delivering a family to Helping Hands Incorporated, a family who might be right back where I found them less than twenty-four hours from now.

TEN

had about two hours before I had to pick up Jimmy. That wasn't enough time to drive back to West Monroe and finish the house. So I pulled Marvella's lists out of my pocket, and checked to see if there was an address nearby.

There were several, and not all of them on her "bad" list. I drove to the closest, which was in a bad neighborhood of Woodlawn.

I was venturing into gang territory. I didn't like it, but I knew I would be better off alone. My rusted Impala fit right in, and if I looked like a worried boyfriend, people might think I was looking for the abortionist.

The street number belonged to a five-story brick apartment building. Most of the windows had been knocked out, a few of them replaced with cardboard. The door was open and unlocked, and several teenagers loitered on the front steps.

As I got out of the car, I caught the sickly sweet smell of marijuana.

The teenagers made no moves when they saw me. They didn't scatter, nor did they try to hide their joints. I walked past them without acknowledgment. In this neighborhood, where the Blackstone Rangers ruled, I could get in trouble just for saying the wrong thing.

The smell of pot was stronger inside, mixed with the stench of urine. My skin crawled. I couldn't imagine coming here, feeling helpless and worried, to end a pregnancy. If I had brought a girlfriend here, I would have turned around before reaching the stairs.

The apartment number was on the fourth floor. I climbed the steps quickly. A bundle of rags on the landing between the second and third floor turned out to be a woman as skinny as Helen, lost in her clothing. She stank of cheap whiskey, and mumbled something as I stepped past her.

By the time, I reached the fourth floor, I had a feeling I was on a wild goosechase. I walked across the trash-filled hallway to the door of number 407.

The door was partially open. I pushed it open the rest of the way. The apartment was empty. The stench of urine seemed stronger here, along with an older smell of dried blood. The beige carpet was covered with brown stains, and I hoped that wasn't where the blood smell came from.

The windows had been broken long ago. The sills were covered with dust. I wandered from room to room, but found nothing except rat droppings and sneaker prints, probably from the teenagers below.

I took Marvella's sheet and looked at the address again. I hadn't misread it. Marvella had said that abortionists moved around a lot. I wondered if this place was used occasionally as a surgery, maybe by some kind of appointment.

I glanced out the window. More teenagers stood across the street, a number of them wearing red tams. They didn't seem to be doing anything other than enjoying the sunny day.

I turned around and walked to the door. No one had followed me inside. No one had noticed or cared that I had come here. In that way, this was the perfect place for an illegal operation.

The drunk woman hadn't moved from her position on the second floor landing. This time when I stepped over her, she didn't even groan, but she did move enough so that I knew she was still alive.

When I reached the front door, I made sure Marvella's list was in my pocket. I stopped near the teenagers.

"You guys know Ike Jackson from 407?" I asked.

"Who wants to know?" One of the boys, not much older than Jimmy, leaned against the brick wall, and eyed me carefully.

"I was told he could help my sister," I said. I didn't know where the sister thing came from. It just felt better than mentioning a girlfriend.

"He ain't been here for months," the boy said. "You gots to go to Stony Island. I heard he moved down there."

"Where exactly?" I asked, as if I really were a concerned brother.

"Hell if I know," the boy said.

"Then how do you know he's there?" I asked.

"That's what he said." The boy shrugged. "Figured anybody who gots to ask is probably a cop. Right?"

I got that question often enough that it worried me. Especially on a case like this. I might need some help with it, someone who didn't have whatever it was that made me seem official.

"You know anybody else who can help me?" I asked.

"You mean your sister?" one of the other boys asked. He was acne-scarred and malnourished. His eyes were bloodshot.

"You know what I mean," I said.

"You go see Sister Mary Catherine at the Salvation Army," he said.

"She's a nun?" I couldn't keep the surprise from my voice.

All of the boys laughed.

"Hell, no," the second boy said as the laughter died down. "She's a sis-tah, you know. One of us. She works on Wednesdays and Thursdays in the Woodlawn store. You got that?"

"I do," I said, beginning to understand that this underground network was no different from any other I'd come across. "Thank you."

"You got it, bro," the second boy said, and they all laughed again. I made my way down the steps before the smell of marijuana made me high.

Mary Catherine at the Salvation Army. I would write that contact down. I suspected I would run into a lot of people who knew someone who knew someone else who maybe knew the person who could help a woman in trouble.

I had been right; this search I was conducting for Marvella would be a long one.

ELEVEN

I drove past the Salvation Army store in Woodlawn, but it was closed. I still had time before I had to pick up Jimmy, but not enough to effectively pursue another lead. I could have gone home and finished the second report for Southside Insurance, but my mind really wasn't on it.

Instead, I decided to go to the hospital to see how Valentina Wilson was doing.

Part of my decision to go was self-defense. I had a feeling she wasn't going to survive. I wanted to be armed with the news when I saw Marvella again.

The hospital parking lot was full when I arrived. I parked curbside across the street, and went in the hospital's front door. The air was stuffy and smelled of disinfectant. Last night, I hadn't noticed how hot it got inside. I suspect the warmth of the past two days had caught the maintenance people by surprise; they probably still had the heat running.

I followed the signs past the gift shop until I got to the main desk. Several women staffed it this afternoon, most of them taking information from distraught-looking people who kept glancing down the hallway.

A white woman stood behind the counter, thumbing through some charts. I walked up to her.

"Excuse me," I said, "I'm looking for a patient brought in last night. She would either be listed as Valentina Wilson or Valentina Johnson."

The woman raised her carefully plucked eyebrows at me. "Why the problem with the name?"

"The people who brought her in didn't know her by her married name." I figured that answer, while only partly true, was simplest.

The woman nodded, as if that made sense to her. "You need her room number?"

"If I could."

She went to the back and dialed the switchboard. I couldn't hear what she had to say. As she looked up Valentina's room for me, I leaned across the counter, to see if I saw her name on any files.

I didn't.

The woman who was helping me had picked up a headset. She was talking to someone, a frown on her face.

My stomach tightened.

The woman hung up the headset, bowed her head for a moment, then came out from behind and stopped in front of me.

"We have a Valentina Johnson who arrived last night." The woman spoke softly.

Her expression and her tone of voice made me brace myself for bad news.

"I'm afraid she's not in a room, though," the woman said. "She's still in recovery. They took her back into surgery this morning, and she hasn't woken up yet. Are you family?"

I shook my head. No sense lying about that, especially if there was family here.

"Then I can't tell you much more," she said.

"She's a close friend," I lied, making it sound like Valentina Wilson and I were involved with each other. "Can you tell me anything about her prognosis?"

The woman looked down at the desk, as if she were consulting a file. She wasn't. She obviously didn't want to meet my gaze. "Her doctor will have to tell you that. Or you'll have to talk with the family."

"Is there any family here?" I asked.

"I don't know," she said, "but if there is, they'd probably be in the waiting room down the hall."

Where I had been the night before. I thanked her and walked toward the waiting room, thinking I might find Marvella. I would tell her how my first encounter went and see if she had any other ideas.

The corridor seemed different in the daytime, smaller, narrower, filled with people. Nurses, attendants, security guards, and people like me who seemed to have no purpose there at all.

The waiting room was full, the air so clouded with cigarette smoke that I could barely make out the people inside. A few were reading. A man sat near the door, chain-smoking, and another paced, with cigars in his pockets, obviously waiting for fatherhood.

I didn't see Marvella and I was about to go back to the car when a solitary figure caught my eye.

In the very back of the room, a large man sat, his hands folded between his knees. It was Truman Johnson.

That tight feeling returned to my stomach. I wanted to walk past as quickly as I could, but I knew that I wouldn't be able to forgive myself if I did.

Johnson had always seemed like a strong man to me, but the man in there didn't look strong at all. He looked like he had lost everything.

I pulled the door open, and clouds of cigarette smoke billowed over me. My eyes watered, and I resisted the urge to cough as I walked into the blue haze.

Once I passed the chain-smoker, the air cleared a little. There was room on the couch beside Johnson and I took it, putting a hand on his shoulder as I did so.

He jumped, startled, and the look on his face before he masked it was sheer panic.

"Grimshaw," he said, and there was gratitude in his voice. He was wearing the same clothes he had worn the night before and, if anything, they looked even more wrinkled than they had then.

"How is she?" I asked.

He shook his head. "They found more bleeding this morning. Something that didn't get sewn up or that got nicked in the—you know—in the thing that brought her here, and it didn't get caught. She almost didn't make it. I mean, if I hadn't asked how come she was looking so gray, then maybe they wouldn't've noticed. I want to move her, but Marvella says there's no place better."

I had no idea if that part was true. But I did know that a lot got missed in hospitals and, at times, that there was nothing a doctor could do.

"Have you had your doctor come in?" I asked.

"The guy Marvella went for last night?" Johnson asked. "He's not our doctor. He's just someone I know who specializes in, you know."

I nodded.

Johnson's eyes were red-rimmed and he looked exhausted. He kept looking down at his scuffed shoes as if they held a secret all their own.

"What's the prognosis?" I asked.

"The prognosis is that it's a goddamn miracle she's still breathing, so I should stop asking what the prognosis is. They act like I'm in the way." He folded his hands again, as if he didn't know what to do with them.

He probably was in the way. If he used any of his detecting skills, he was probably irritating the doctors and the nurses.

"Where's Marvella?" I asked.

"Talking to those pricks Val works for, trying to find out if she has any insurance." Johnson glanced at the door.

I had no idea how he could see through the glass. I could barely see to the glass, what with the chain-smoker starting his second pack since I entered the room.

"She's still covered on my policy, but Marvella says that's not right. I figure let her keep busy, and I'll take care of things my way." Johnson rubbed his eyes with his right hand.

"Have you been home yet?" I asked, even though it was clear from his clothing he hadn't left the hospital at all.

He shook his head. "Called in this morning, let them know that I have a family emergency. If they don't like it, that's their problem."

He was talking about the precinct now. He wasn't tracking. I had a hunch he hadn't slept or eaten anything since I had left him the night before.

"Let's go down to the cafeteria," I said. "You can fill me in."

"The doc expects me to be here."

"And if he needs to find you, he'll look in the cafeteria for you around mealtime. That's how these places work," I said.

Johnson sighed. "All right," he said after a minute, "but only because I want to talk to you, too. I got a proposition for you."

I didn't like the sound of that. I glanced at the watch the pacing man was wearing. I still had a few minutes before I had to pick up Jimmy. I would make sure Johnson had something to eat, then I would leave, using Jim as my excuse.

Johnson and I threaded our way out of the waiting room, past the pacing man, a woman in tears, and the chain-smoker. The chain-smoker didn't even seem to see anyone else. He kept lighting cigarettes with the butt of the previous cigarette and staring at the smoke he was creating.

As Johnson and I stepped into the corridor, I asked, "How long has he been doing that?"

"All day," Johnson said. "His daughter was in a car crash this morning. They're rebuilding her legs. The only time he's been out of the room was to go to the gift shop for more cigarettes."

I took a deep breath, trying to clear my lungs. I had only been in the room for a short while, but I carried the odor of cigarette smoke with me. Johnson probably smelled like a smoker himself.

"I can give you the lowdown on everyone in that room if you want," he said. "The expectant father—he's afraid of twins. It happened the last time and this time was an accident. The crying woman, her mother's got a brain tumor. Not expected to survive the surgery. Then the quiet teenager in the corner—"

That startled me. I hadn't even noticed him.

"—his girlfriend is the chain-smoker's daughter. They're not talking. I think the kid was driving the car. He's got a bruise on the side of one arm that looks like it needs medical attention."

Johnson coughed, as if he were clearing an irritated throat.

"I can't read, can't sleep, can't do anything but wait, but I can still assess people. That's what I been doing all day, watching people come in and out of that room, figuring out what the crisis is in their lives. You ever been married, Grimshaw?"

I would have thought that last question a non sequitor except for the way he glanced at me when he asked it. He meant that last sentence as a challenge.

"No," I said.

"Never even come close?"

"A few times," I said.

"What went wrong?"

I led him around a corner, following the signs to the cafeteria. I really didn't need to. The smells of boiled beef, reconstituted gravy, and industrial-strength coffee pointed the way.

"I don't know what went wrong," I said. "It was different each time."

All three times, all of them years ago. I hadn't even given them much thought lately. I wasn't even certain if I had told Laura about them.

"Because you're too private, I'll bet. Keep things in, don't want to worry anyone." The present tense clued me that Johnson wasn't talking about my past, but his. "She can read anywhere, you know that? Anywhere, any time. Doesn't know why I watch people all the time. Says I don't trust anybody."

"It's kind of hard to trust in your job," I said.

"Yeah."

We stepped into the cafeteria. It was large, filled with gray tables and wooden chairs that had seen better days. Along two walls were steam tables, manned by androgynous people wearing white, their hair hidden under nets.

Interns sat in one corner, a pair of nurses in another. Some patients were scattered throughout the room, identifiable by their robes and slippers. It felt strange to see people wearing such private clothing in such a public place.

Several other people, obviously visitors, filled the rest of the tables. About ten were in line, getting food or beverages.

I led Johnson to the stack of trays at the beginning of the food line. At first he shook his head, but I grabbed one of the gray metal trays and forced it into his hands.

He opened his mouth to argue with me, then seemed to think the better of it. Instead, he set the tray on the metal bars in front of the steam trays and stared at the food as if it all looked inedible.

Actually, it didn't look half bad. The macaroni and cheese had a lot of sauce, the mashed potatoes seemed to be real instead of a mix. The corn was pale from overcooking and the cooked carrots looked more like orange goo. But as I followed Johnson through the line, my stomach actually growled.

I gave in when we reached the desserts and took a slice of chocolate cake that seemed to be fresh.

Johnson reached for his wallet, but I had mine out. I paid for his meal over his protests. Then I got us both some coffee, before finding a table in one of the emptier sections of the room.

"I can afford my own dinner," Johnson said as he sat down.

"It was my idea to come here," I said.

He didn't argue anymore. Instead, he tucked into the beef roast, mixing the corn and mashed potatoes together with his gravy to make mush. Looked like he had been in the army, too, but I didn't ask him about it—not because I wanted to spare him, but because I didn't like talking about it myself.

I ate the cake, which was surprisingly good, and drank the coffee, which wasn't. Johnson shoveled food into his mouth like he hadn't eaten in years.

After a few minutes, his plate was empty. He washed everything down with coffee.

"Okay," he said. "I know. I should've done that hours ago."

I didn't say anything.

"But this morning, I wasn't thinking too clear." He shook his head. "I kept thinking if she lived through this, I'd change. I'd win her back. I'd do everything she wanted."

He wiped his mouth and then tossed his napkin on his plate.

"But I'm not sure she's going to make it through, and if she does, I don't know how she'll be—you've seen stuff like this, right? You know." His gaze met mine.

I had seen cases like this. Women never came out of it the same.

"Yeah," I said quietly, giving no details.

He burped, and did not excuse himself. Then he leaned forward, and I cursed silently. He had remembered his proposition after all. I had hoped, with the meal and the conversation, that he would forget.

"There isn't much I can do to make this better," he said. "If she wanted me in her life, she would have asked for help. She would've let me go after that creep or find her a real doctor. She would've told me what was going on."

Then again, she might not have. A lot of women never told their husbands about the private things in their lives or things they were ashamed of, particularly strong, can-do husbands like Johnson.

But I didn't argue with him. After the conversation I had had with Marvella, I had a hunch Johnson was closer to the truth of his relationship with Valentina than he had been for some time.

"She's going to need a lot of love and support," I said.

"She's got that. She knows she's got that," Johnson said. "I just can't sit much more, you know. And I'm scared to leave, scared she'll die on me and I won't be here."

"You can't be beside her right now," I said.

"Yeah, but I'm here. I'm in the same building. Marvella wants me to go home, and maybe I will, but it's like, I don't know. I've got to do something. You know?"

I did. I hated that helpless feeling as much as Johnson did. It was one of the reasons I had decided to help Marvella.

I had known from the moment I met Johnson that we were similar in some ways. We both liked solving things, making problems go away, and we both knew that life wasn't that simple.

"There's not much to do here," I said.

"Here, yeah, there isn't a lot to do." Johnson looked at his hands. They were big and scarred, the hands of a man who had always worked for his living. "But I'm not too good at sitting around."

I nodded. I didn't know anyone who was—at least in these circumstances.

"All day I've been thinking I should go to my strengths." He rubbed his hands together, then looked at me. "No matter what, no matter how much I want it, I'm not getting Val back. I know that. And this might change it, I know that, too. She'll need someone to take care of her for a while. I can do that."

I didn't argue with him. I didn't really know Valentina Wilson and, as he said, people changed after traumatic events. Maybe she would want him at her side again. He would certainly be a good protector.

"But if she doesn't make it, and I have a hunch she's not going to, I still got to help. I've got to find a way to be useful here."

This time, when he used "here," he didn't mean in the hospital. It was a Chicago colloquialism, one that was creeping into my speech as well.

"So," Johnson said, "this is my proposal. I want you to hear me out before you say anything."

"All right." I folded my hands on the tabletop, wishing I could bolt.

"This is what I figure," he said. "Val's here because of two problems. First, there's the person with the knife pretending to be a real doctor. What galls me most is that Val paid money to this person and ended up here."

"You know that for a fact?" I asked.

"You were going to wait until I was done," he snapped.

I nodded. He wasn't in a mood to be trifled with.

"Second," he said, frowning at me as if he expected me to talk over him, "there's the asshole that caused this problem in the first place. Marvella says she don't know anything about it, but I think she's lying. Doesn't matter. I'll find this guy—"

"And then what?" I asked.

Johnson glared at me.

I held up my hands. "I know, I know. I wasn't going to ask questions, but Truman, even if you do find him, it's Val's word against his. There's no police report from the incident, which had to be two months ago or more. And there's probably no witnesses. Hearsay won't stand. So there's no real way to charge him."

"You gonna listen or not?" He spoke very softly. "Because if you're not, I'm going to get up, I'm going to thank you for this lovely meal and for coming here to check on my wife, and I'm going to walk away."

It was my opportunity. I could say that I didn't want to hear any more— and I didn't—or I could tell him that I needed to pick up Jimmy, which I would have to do soon anyway.

But I didn't take advantage of the moment. As difficult as my relationship with Johnson had been, he had come through for me. I could at least listen to him, and maybe try to talk him out of something he would later regret.

"Sorry," I said.

"Okay." He leaned back in his chair, and did a sideways glance around the room. He didn't even move his head as he looked. It was a cop maneuver, and he was good at it.

When he seemed satisfied that no one was listening, he continued.

"I know the problems," he said. "I'm saving the other guy until she wakes up. Then Val can direct me. If he's a drifter, someone who's clearly not in town anymore, then I'll let it go. But if he can hurt her again, I'm going to make sure he doesn't. Whatever it takes. You got that?"

128

I nodded once, biting back the question I wanted to ask. I wasn't sure what "whatever it takes" meant. I wasn't sure how far Johnson would go to protect someone. Marvella had seemed convinced that he would kill someone who had hurt a person he loved.

And she knew Johnson better than I did.

"So," Johnson said, "I figure I'm going to start with this so-called doctor. I know who Val knows. I'll see if I can track this person down, and put him out of business. That's where you come in."

"Me?" The question slipped out before I could stop it.

He didn't seem to notice. "See, here's my problem. A lot of these guys—most of them—pay protection, so I can't just go in and arrest them without stepping on someone else's turf."

I gripped my hands tightly together. Johnson spoke so calmly about "protection," as if it didn't bother him. It bothered me. I hated the way that cops took money to look the other way.

"Besides, if I get in too deep and I piss someone off, they'll come looking for why, which'll lead them to Val. I have the doctor here working with me—"

"I remember," I said.

"—so right now, Val is covered. But if I start looking under these particular rocks, then someone will find her. I don't want her charged. Hell, I don't want her embarrassed, and she will be if this ever gets out."

He paused and took a pretend sip from his empty coffee cup. When he got the dregs out, he stood.

"Be right back," he said, and went to pour himself another cup.

I could have used one, too, but I didn't follow him. I didn't like the direction in which this was heading. I didn't want to tell Johnson that I was already looking for the abortionist. Then Johnson would want to help me.

As volatile as he was right now, he would only get in my way. Or he would ask me to do something I didn't want to do.

Johnson had asked me to play vigilante for him in the past, and I had always refused. I knew that I confused him. I didn't follow a lot of the legalities and formalities of the world, but I liked to think of myself as a man who believed in justice. And, much as I hated the system, I always felt it was best to try going through that system first. If the system failed, then sometimes a man had to take things into his own hands. But even then, the rule wasn't absolute. As far as I was concerned, only in times of dire emergency could a man become a law unto himself.

Johnson returned carrying a full coffee cup and a chocolate-chip cookie. He took a bite, wiped the crumbs off his face, and said, "A guy like the one that mutilated Val this weekend leaves a trail. Lots of injured women, maybe even a death or two. Here's where you come in. You're good at this kind of digging. If we can find those, we might have a case against him. Then we start looking for Asshole Number Two."

I didn't know how to say no without mentioning Marvella, so I argued with his methodology instead. "So," I said, "it's all right to drag these other women through the hell of public exposure, but it's not okay to mention Val, a case against this person, whoever he is, that we actually have dead to rights?"

"I'm not going to do that to her," Johnson said.

"Why not? She made the same choice as the other women."

Johnson glared at me. "Val stays protected."

"And these other women aren't worth protecting? They probably have families, too, people who care about them, people who probably don't even know what they've done or why. Why should we drag those people in? Is it fair to step into their lives when you're not willing to do the same thing in your own?"

Johnson flattened his hands on the table. The movement jostled the coffee cups, slashing coffee all over the surface.

I grabbed a napkin and started to clean up. Johnson grabbed my wrist hard enough to cut off the circulation to my hand, making me stop.

"I'm a cop," he said softly. "She's a cop's wife. How is that going to look, especially if she has to sit in front of some judge and explain what happened to her?"

His fingers dug into my skin, but I didn't look at them. Instead, I met his gaze.

"Are you worried about her or about yourself?" I asked.

"About her," he said.

"Then stay here. Wait for the doctors to tell you she's going to be all right. When she wakes up, see what she wants."

"Meantime, this butcher mutilates how many other women?" Johnson asked.

That was Marvella's argument, and the reason I was helping her. But this wasn't going to be as fast or as easy an investigation as either Marvella or Johnson thought it would be.

"What this guy does and who he hurts is a different issue," I said, "and one you guys should think about every time you take protection money."

I regretted the sentence the moment I uttered it.

Johnson let go of my wrist. "You guys?"

"Figure of speech," I said, resisting the urge to rub my skin where his fingers had dug into it. But my opinion had slipped out. I didn't approve of the fact that it was the police who allowed this corruption to continue.

Without police protection, abortionists like the one who had hurt Valentina Wilson would be out of business.

"You think I'm on the take?" Johnson asked.

"I didn't say that."

"You said I take protection money." His voice was so soft I barely heard it.

"You're the one who brought it up," I said.

"I didn't say I took it. I said that I worried about getting into other people's turf."

"I know what you said." I leaned closer to him. Even though we were speaking softly, we were attracting attention. Probably because we were two black men, obviously angry, in the middle of a room full of people. "If you're worried about their turf, then you're helping them protect it."

"No," he snapped, "I'm protecting mine. They'll go after Val."

"It looks like someone already did."

That silenced him. The spilled coffee started dripping onto the floor, making an annoying splat-splat sound.

I used my sopping napkin to soak up what I could, then I went to the counter beside the trays and got a few more napkins. By the time I came back, Johnson was gone.

I let out a small sigh. I had handled that badly. All I had tried to do was keep Johnson from investigating—and prevent him from finding out that I was investigating.

Instead, I had made him angry.

I wiped up the mess, including the floor, then piled the sodden napkins onto a tray, and carried both trays to the window that opened into the kitchen. Then I walked out of the cafeteria into the corridor. Even more people filled the hall, apparently visitors who had just gotten off work, and were coming to see friends and family.

For a moment, I debated returning to the waiting room, and seeing if Johnson was all right. I stopped, looked in that direction, and realized that Johnson wasn't the only one who was angry.

If I went to the waiting room, I'd just continue the fight. And even though I knew a lot of Johnson's fury and frustration came from the situation, I wasn't sure I was level enough to remember that when he started demanding things of me.

He needed to focus on Valentina anyway. He wouldn't be doing anything else that night. Then Marvella would force him to get a good night's sleep, and by tomorrow, he might have forgotten this crazy plan.

At least that was what I hoped as I walked toward the front door, not realizing how wrong I was.

TWELVE

That night, I fielded several phone calls. One was from Southside, which had three more jobs for me even though I hadn't finished the most recent two; another was from a man who wanted me to help him find some missing land deeds; and one was from a man who wanted someone to tail his wife because he thought she was having an affair.

I put the insurance jobs off until later in the week, which was fine with Southside. The company was in no hurry. I told the man who needed the land deeds that I could help him, but he would be better off with an attorney. He said he would consider that, and get back to me. And I told the final man that I didn't do divorces—which wasn't exactly a lie, since I hadn't done one yet in Chicago, although I had done quite a few in Memphis—and gave him the name of the best black detective agency in town.

Jimmy didn't say anything, even when I wasn't on the phone. He ate his dinner in silence, no matter how I tried to draw him out. He said he wasn't angry at me—even seemed shocked at the idea of it—but he wouldn't look at me, either.

And this avoidance was different from what he had done earlier in the winter, when he had been embarrassed about being recruited by the Blackstone Rangers. Then he had spoken to me, just avoided certain topics.

Now he wasn't talking at all.

So I watched him eat, as if by studying him I could see what was wrong.

He was bigger than he had been a year ago, and he was starting to get that lankiness that came with adolescence. He still had a little boy's face, though, with its soft skin and round cheeks.

I wanted to rub my knuckles against those cheeks, a gentle gesture, just so that he would know he was loved, but I knew better. He had pulled away from me all day. I didn't want him to do so again.

I wasn't sure my heart could take it.

He ignored my stare and finished his dinner. Then he did his homework, and wanted to settle in for our nightly reading session. We had started reading *The Wind in the Willows* the week before, even though Jimmy had complained that it looked like a baby book.

I had thought it looked too young for him, but Grace Kirkland had pulled me aside in early March and recommended that I read fantasy novels to him.

He gets enough reality in his own life, she said. *He needs some kind of escape.*

She had given me a reading list that I was dutifully working my way through, despite Jimmy's protests. Still, he was the one who dragged out the thick green-covered book every night and waited for me. He hadn't done that with anything else we had read. He also put the book away in his room when we were finished, so no one would see it.

I didn't allow phone calls to interrupt dinner or the reading, which we shared—him doing what he could (without me correcting him) and me taking over when he got tired. But the phone rang four times during supper and five more times during our reading session, and that wasn't unusual.

What was unusual was that I wanted to answer, worrying about Marvella and Johnson, and their reactions should Valentina Wilson die.

Finally, Jimmy went to bed. As I turned out his light, the phone rang. It was Laura.

"You need an answering service," she said with a laugh. We both knew how likely that was. "I've been calling all day."

"Problem?" I asked, mostly because the day had been about problems. Hell, the last twenty-four hours had been about problems.

"Not really," she said. "I just wanted to find out how our friend is."

She meant Valentina Wilson. So I updated her, although I didn't tell her about my discussion with Johnson. However, I did tell her that Marvella had hired me.

"Is that wise, Smokey?" Laura said. "I mean, what are you going to do when you find this guy?"

"Marvella says she'll make sure no one goes to him. She's also going to tell Rothstein, to see if he'll press charges." Although I was beginning to realize, after talking with Johnson, that that particular ploy wouldn't work. Johnson didn't want Valentina's experience to become public knowledge.

"I wish her luck," Laura said.

"She gave me a list," I said. "Two, actually. One of people she recommended and one of people she didn't. Can you do the same for me?"

There was a long silence, then Laura said, "I haven't done this for a while."

"It doesn't matter," I said. "I'll cross-check, maybe get some leads from a few other people. I feel like I'm looking for a needle in a haystack as it is. Maybe if I have a few more names, I might be able to make some headway."

"I'll see what I can do," Laura said. "There are some women I know who are trying to do what Marvella's doing, only in a more organized fashion. I'll get some names from them."

"Thanks," I said.

"It's the least I can do," she said. "I hate problems like this. There seems to be no real solution."

"I know," I said. It seemed, lately, like my life was full of those kind of problems. I found myself wishing for a simple problem with a simple solution.

But those didn't come along much anymore. I wasn't even sure I'd recognize them if they did.

The next day dawned cloudy and muggy, with the threat of rain in the air. I was still on driving duty, and somehow, even though Jimmy and I were both running late, we managed to get to the Grimshaws' on time.

Lacey wasn't feeling well, and was staying home from school. Unfortunately, her father had called her illness the "girl flu" to explain it to me. Norene and Mikie had overheard him, and spent the drive to school asking if they would contract it.

I kept reassuring them that they wouldn't—at least, not for another few years, but I didn't tell them that last part. I was a friend of the family, not the person who was supposed to explain the facts of life. I would have to do that for Jimmy soon enough, although I suspected he knew more about the facts of life than I did, thanks to that mother of his.

Jimmy and Keith spent the entire drive in discussion about the new baseball season. It was good to hear Jimmy talk to someone, and so while I fended off the little girls, I enjoyed listening to his conversation.

As we pulled up to the school, the playground was full of boys wearing red tams. I hated the Stones' presence here, but didn't know how to make it go away. At least, since I had traded information with them last year, they were living up to our agreement and leaving all of the Grimshaw children alone.

I had no idea how long that particular truce would last.

Once I got the kids safely into the building, I headed back to the West Side. If I finished with the house, then I could work on Marvella's case for the rest of the week. I knew finding the man who had injured Val might take days—or maybe even weeks.

I hoped by then she would be awake. I didn't want to think about what would happen if she died.

It took me nearly an hour to get from one side of town to the other. Morning traffic was tied up in the Loop, reminding me why I usually spent the first few hours of my day in the apartment finishing paperwork.

When I finally got to Monroe Street, it was empty. I was beginning to wonder how many of the buildings were inhabited. The cars also had an abandoned look. Most of them still had the flyers on the windshields. Several of the flyers had found their way to the gutters, where they waited, along with last fall's leaves, for someone to clean them up.

I parked in the same spot I had the day before, and returned to the house. This time I brought the Polaroid that Laura had given me, so that I could document some of the things I found, particularly the foundation. The fact that this place was so solidly built intrigued me; I wanted to have the pictures to convince Laura that she needed to find someone else to confirm my findings.

I hung the camera around my neck, attached the flashlight to my belt, and grabbed my clipboard. I had been here two days in a row without seeing any locals. I figured if they were bothered by an official presence, I would have learned that already.

Then I locked up the car and went inside the house. I spent nearly three hours in there, marking each crack in the wall, each rotted floorboard, on my chart.

I found a dead rat on the floor of one of the apartments upstairs. The rat was so old that it was mostly bones and fur. The smell of decay had seeped into the carpet and the room, and stayed there, like a bad memory.

But I didn't find anything worse than things I had found in other empty Sturdy buildings. Each one seemed to have a long and impressive list of damaged ceilings, clogged toilets, and scorched stoves.

Still, I believed that this building's frame was solid enough. Its interior needed gutting and rebuilding, but once that was done, the exterior would probably survive an inspection from a trained building inspector—one who hadn't been bought off.

When I went back outside, the air was still muggy, but cooler than it had been inside. A light breeze had kicked up, not enough to blow away the humidity, but enough to swirl it around.

A large dog that looked like it was part Lab and part Greyhound dug in the makeshift flower bed in front of the basement window. The dog was big and skinny, but his coat had a shine to it, and he wore a collar.

He wasn't a stray, then, but he was big enough that I didn't want to interrupt him.

I walked down the steps, keeping my distance from the dog, and stopped in front of the other basement window.

Some teenage boys, who looked young enough to still be in school, sat on a stoop across the street, smoking cigarettes and watching me. Two young men wearing black leather jackets despite the heat and the berets of the Black Panthers walked down the sidewalk.

A middle-aged woman stepped out of a car down the street. She wore a maid's uniform, and carried her little white cap in one hand. As she walked toward the front door of a small red building, she whistled.

The dog's head went up. His muzzle was brown with dirt. He whined, as if in protest.

She whistled again, then called, "Here, Star. C'mon, boy."

The dog whined again, louder this time, and looked at the mess he had made in the dirt.

"Star! Here, Star!"

The dog shook himself, then ran at full lope toward the woman. Apparently the call of the person who fed him was a lot more important than whatever he had been seeking in the dirt.

I made my way around the building, using up one expensive roll of Polaroid film as I did. I asked Laura for a real camera with real film, but she said she preferred Polariods. They were more immediate, they couldn't be "gussied up"—her words—in the development process, and they had a shabby veracity to them—not exactly her words, but her sentiment at any rate.

The dog barked and I looked up, startled. The dog was jumping around the woman, tail wagging. She had a hand on its head, trying to keep it down.

"All right, Star." Then she shook her head. "God, you stink. That's why I never let you run like this. If I figure out who let you off your leash . . ."

I smiled. Sometimes Jimmy begged me for a dog, but we couldn't have one in the building. Even if we could, it wouldn't have worked with my job and his schooling. I barely had time to take care of him.

The last Polaroid turned colors in my hand as it developed. I had five more packages of film in the car, and I would get them before the afternoon was done. I carried one extra in my pocket. I stopped in between the buildings, clipped the photographs I had already taken to the clipboard, and loaded the new roll of film.

I circled around to the front, the camera to my eye, looking through the lens at the stone foundation. As I did, something crunched beneath my foot.

I let the camera drop to my chest and looked down. The dog had scattered the small bones of a dead animal all over the brown lawn. I lifted my foot, saw that I had stepped on one of the bones, snapping it in half.

Something about the bone made me stop. Flesh still clung to it—flesh that didn't appear to have any fur on it.

My mouth went dry. I stepped around the trail of bones the dog had made and walked to the area where it had been digging.

The dog had been digging in the dirt someone had used to fill the stone gutter, the dirt where I thought, with one quick glance the day before, that someone had planted a makeshift flower bed. But the dog had shoved the dead plant on top aside, and I saw no roots. Instead, someone had placed that plant there, the way a person would lay flowers on a special spot.

On a grave.

My breath caught. I hoped I was wrong. Still, I crouched and, careful not to touch anything, peered into the hole the dog had left.

The first thing I saw were small curved bones that were so recognizably a rib cage that my stomach turned. Dirt had fallen between them, but there was still some meat there, and some bug activity. But the bones went all the way around, like a tiny circle, and ended in a spine.

The dog had shoved the dirt aside, apparently trying to get to whatever was in the middle of those ribs. Instead, he had gotten to an arm, pulling it apart.

Mercifully, I couldn't see the skull or the rest of the body, but what I could see was bad enough: the tattered remains of a jumper, once white, that closed with snaps and was decorated with tiny blue bunnies.

A baby.

Someone had buried a baby out here in a grave shallow enough to let a dog dig up the remains. That someone had also cared enough to place flowers on the surface.

I put my face in my hands, and didn't move for a very long time. Then I got up, and went to look for a phone so that I could call the police.

THIRTEEN

I hated to have contact with the police. I felt like every time I did, I exposed myself and Jimmy. There were a few officers I could trust to a small degree—Truman Johnson and Jack Sinkovich—but I didn't want them to ever suspect I was anyone other than Franklin Grimshaw's cousin, Bill.

I wasn't sure if I should call one of them. Johnson had his own concerns at the moment, and Sinkovich, while he was a good detective, was unpredictable.

Besides, I wasn't sure I wanted a good detective on this case—at least, not until I had spoken to Helen and her little boy, Doug.

Those were the thoughts that haunted me as I looked up and down the street for a phone. I suppose I could have knocked on doors, asking to use a phone, but I didn't think I would be welcome company with my camera and clipboard. I also could have driven away, made the call from somewhere else, but an irrational part of me didn't want to leave that baby alone a moment longer.

I didn't see a pay phone. This block was residential, and so were the next few. I had no choice but to go to West Madison, which was a commercial block.

As I crossed Monroe, the teenagers sitting on the steps stood. They signaled to the Panthers who had been pretending to stroll by.

I ignored them. They were just protecting their neighborhood. I had more important things to deal with.

The alley between the two streets would have dead-ended into storefronts with apartments on top, but most of them had been burned out over a year ago. The blackened ruins of these buildings remained, not even roped off to warn children away.

The city was going to let this section of town fall apart until they could bulldoze it and start all over again. Sometimes the Panthers' rhetoric about keeping white folks out of the ghetto made a lot of sense.

If I called the general police number, uniforms would show up, probably black officers, since white ones hated working this part of town. No matter who I called, though, they would probably log in the complaint, get the coroner to come take the body, write it up for the white papers as something expected in this part of town and forget about it.

If I called Sinkovich, he would do his best. He would also draw attention to Helen. She would be back in the system, this time as a murder suspect, and someone would take her children away.

But someone did want to keep that baby's death secret. With just bones and bits of clothing, I wouldn't be able to tell if the child was murdered or not. But I had seen enough babies to know that a ribcage of that size occurred in a newborn. This baby wasn't a fetus. This child had been alive and breathing at one point.

I reached Madison, and stopped. Directly across from me stood the party headquarters with the two black panthers flanking a sign that read ILLINOIS BLACK PANTHER PARTY. Posters littered the windows, and the main door was open.

The pay phone stood in front of the Scientific School of Beauty Culture, which didn't look like a school at all to me. A single door led up a flight of stairs, and another sign with the same logo—a black woman's sculpted head next to the word "beauty"—graced the upper windows.

The last thing I wanted to do was call the police from a phone in front of the Panther offices. I didn't want any Panthers overhearing me talking to the people they called Pigs.

Instead, I turned left and jogged to the end of the block, following a neon sign that pointed to a liquor store. Just as I suspected, there was a pay phone outside.

I grabbed the plastic phone. It was grimy. I fished in my pocket for some change, then set the money on the metal surface beneath the phone.

As I did, the Panthers who had been patrolling Monroe came out of the alley. They looked both ways, as if searching for me. I leaned against the liquor store window.

They didn't seem to see me.

I stuck a dime into the machine and listened to it *cling-cling* its way down. After a moment's hesitation, I dialed Sinkovich. I didn't want this case hushed or dismissed as another way that blacks treated their families. I wanted that child taken care of.

Someone had cared enough to bury this child. The least I could do was make sure that, once the investigation was over, the child got a proper burial.

The dispatch picked up right away, and I asked for Detective Sinkovich. His line rang for a long time. I was almost ready to hang up and call for a squad when he picked up.

"What?"

"Jack, it's Bill Grimshaw." I spoke softer than usual. The Panthers had seen me and were walking down the sidewalk. "I've got a problem."

"Yeah," he said. "What is it with women calling me, asking if you're a decent man? Can't you get dates on your own?"

"Not that kind of problem," I said. "Hang on a minute."

The Panthers walked past, and one of them raised his eyebrows, as if he were amused by me. I didn't recognize him. The other Panther slid his hand back, revealing a gun beneath his leather jacket.

A car sped past, honking its horn.

"What the hell's going on?" Sinkovich's voice sounded tinny through the receiver.

I said, "One more second."

And then the Panthers were out of listening range. They crossed the street and lounged against a discount loan office. The taller man pulled out his gun, holding it with the muzzle toward the sidewalk as he watched me.

They thought I was a cop, and here I was, acting like one. All the rhetoric I had heard from them came back—slogans like "Off the Pigs," and how the Panthers had the right to shoot any representative of the law who ventured into Panther country, out of self-defense.

I wished I hadn't left my own gun in the glovebox of my car.

"You okay?" The lighter tone had left Sinkovich's voice.

"For the moment," I said. "I'm on West Madison, across from the Black Panther offices."

"Jesus H. Roosevelt Christ," Sinkovich said. "How the hell do you get yourself into these places?"

"I needed a phone." I slid so that my back was now pressed against the brick between the two buildings. I didn't trust the glass. Whoever was inside that liquor store could see the two Panthers through the window. If one of them gave a signal, I could have been shot without even realizing I was in danger.

"Okay, spill," Sinkovich said, "and then get the hell out of there."

Good advice, which I had already been planning to take. I glanced down Madison at Panther headquarters. So far, no one had come out. The two across from me appeared to be alone.

"You know that I'm doing some inspection work for Sturdy Investments," I said.

"No, I didn't know, but that's okay," Sinkovich said.

"I go through recently vacated buildings to see if they need renovation."

A heavyset man wearing plumber's green came out of the liquor store carrying a case of beer. He glanced at me, took in the Panthers across the street, and turned away from us, hurrying down the side street to Monroe.

"You're full of surprises," Sinkovich said into my silence.

"Sorry about that," I said. "Don't want to be overheard."

"No shit. Don't want them to know you're talking to the Pigs."

Somehow hearing my thoughts reflected in Sinkovich's words did not make me feel better.

I lowered my voice even farther. "I'm inspecting a house on West Monroe, and—get out a pen. I'll give you the address."

"I'm ready. Shoot."

I rattled off the address.

The Panthers passed the gun back and forth, carefully keeping the muzzle pointed down. Whoever didn't have the gun looked at me, the long, uncomfortable stare of someone issuing a challenge.

"You need to come out here," I said, "and you need to bring some investigators with you along with the coroner."

"What happened, Grimshaw?" Sinkovich was all business now.

"I was taking pictures of the outside of the building when I noticed a dog digging in some dirt. I went to see what he was pawing at and I found a grave."

"As in a people grave?" Sinkovich asked.

"As in a baby's grave," I said.

"Son of a bitch. Murdered?"

"Can't tell. What I saw was mostly bones. I'm going back there now to wait for you."

"You know," he said before I could move the receiver away from my ear, "you calling white cops ain't gonna be that popular in that part of town.

How come you're bringing me into this mess? This one's gotta go to John-son."

"Johnson's ex-wife is in the hospital. They say that each minute she's still alive is a miracle."

"Crap," Sinkovich said, and I couldn't tell if he was referring to Valentina Wilson's situation or his own, being stuck with this. "You sure this corpse is human?"

"Ribcage looks human," I said, "and so does the little jumper with its tiny blue bunnies."

"Holy fuck, this is just what I need. I'll be there in thirty." And then he hung up.

Thirty minutes. That was a long time for me to stand alone in front of the Monroe Street house. But I would. I didn't want that dog to get back into the gravesite, and I couldn't just leave the child alone.

I wasn't sure where that irrational impulse was coming from. I knew it made no difference now, that the appropriate time to defend that baby had been when it was alive, not after its death.

But I had been around long enough to know that logic didn't always apply.

I had also been around long enough to know that keeping information from Laura about her properties would also be a bad idea.

The Panthers watched me hang up, then plug the machine again. The tall one stuck the gun back under his jacket. Either I wasn't that interesting anymore, or they had just changed the rules of the game.

I dialed Sturdy, identified myself, and asked for Laura. The operator put me right through.

"Laura Hathaway." Laura's voice had a this-better-be-important tone she used whenever she picked up the phone at Sturdy. It sounded nothing like her regular speaking voice, but I suspected it was effective—especially with people who didn't expect the CEO of a major corporation to be a woman.

"Laura, it's Smokey."

"Hey, Smoke—"

"I don't have time for pleasantries."

One of the Panthers walked down the street toward headquarters. The one with the gun stayed. He leaned against the streetlamp and watched me.

"I have a problem down at the building you sent me to on Monroe," I said.

"How bad?"

"Bad enough that I just called the police. It's going to be in the news, most likely."

"Smokey, are you all right?"

"I'm fine," I said.

"Then what is it?"

I told her. In quick, blunt terms, I told her about the baby and that I had called Jack Sinkovich, the other man who had helped me with the case last December. Laura hadn't been involved—she had been out of town for most of it—but I had told her about it when she asked about my scar.

I also told her about finding Helen and her children, something I hadn't remembered to do the night before.

"The thing is," I said, "I don't know if that family I found here yesterday is involved or not."

"You think that woman with the two children buried another one out front?" Laura sounded shocked. I suppose I would have, too, if I had had someone to talk to when I had found the body. But I had had some time to accustom myself to the idea now, and I realized there were a lot of possibilities.

Four Panthers came out of their headquarters and stared at me. I pretended not to notice.

"I don't know what happened," I said, "and I'm not going to make any assumptions. I just want me to be the one to tell Sinkovich about Helping Hands Incorporated and about that family, all right?"

"You think I'll be talking to him?"

"I know you will," I said. "Let me take care of that part of it. Jack Sinkovich is a good cop, but he isn't always the most sympathetic person. I don't want him to take action because he got information at the wrong time in his investigation."

"I'm not sure what you're worried about," Laura said, "but I promise, I won't say anything unless you tell me otherwise."

"Thanks," I said, and hung up.

The six Panthers crossed the street in one big lump. They were all younger than me by at least twenty years, but none of them were as big. As if that mattered. They had me outnumbered, and definitely outgunned. I wanted to walk away from them and get back to the house, but I knew that was the worst thing I could do.

I remained in my position against the wall, watching them approach.

The short one in the front wore thick black glasses. He wore his hair in the fashion most barbers were calling natural, cut short with no grease or pomade to pull it straight. He was the only one not wearing a beret.

"Hey, Daddy-O," he said, stopping in front of me. "You got business with Madison Liquors?"

"Just using the phone," I said.

The Panther pushed his glasses up his nose with his forefinger. "We don't like Uncle Toms."

"That's good," I said. "I'm not real fond of them, either."

"You sayin' you ain't one, with that camera and clipboard?"

I hadn't realized I had carried the clipboard with me. I had it tucked under my left arm. The camera was still around my neck.

"I work as a building inspector for Sturdy Investments."

"You mean you work for the Man," the Panther said.

"No, I work for Sturdy."

"That who you be callin'?" one of the other Panthers asked.

"Yes," I said.

"And who you call before that?" Glasses asked.

"A guy I work with sometimes," I said.

They looked at each other, and I wondered what they heard.

"Why you call him from here?" the other Panther asked.

I had had enough. I stood up straight, so that I could move quickly if I had to. "I don't think that's any of your business."

"Anything happens here is our business," Glasses said.

"Do you harass everyone who comes to this neighborhood or just black men with cameras?" I asked.

"We bother you, Tom?" Glasses asked.

"Yeah," I said. "At the moment, you're acting like a bunch of thugs instead of the revolutionary leaders Fred Hampton makes you out to be."

"You know Chairman Hampton?" That surprised the tall Panther, the one with the gun.

"I've met him," I said. "I heard him speak at the Circle Campus last December and I was impressed."

That wasn't a lie. I had been impressed. Hampton had a gift for leadership. I didn't agree with most of what he said, but he had a charisma that I hadn't seen since I first saw Martin speak at Boston College.

"You don't look like a revolutionary, Brother," said Glasses, but he sounded doubtful.

"I have a kid," I said. "I need a job. So I do what I can, and I keep my politics to myself most of the time."

I wasn't agreeing with them. I couldn't, in good conscience, do so. But I wanted them to think I did.

"You get fired for listening to Chairman Hampton?" Glasses asked.

"I wouldn't get fired for listening," I said. "But if I wore the uniform, sure, I'd get fired."

"We don't like Toms coming down here with cameras and lies," Glasses said.

"I need the camera for my job. The clipboard, too. You want to see what I'm doing?"

I handed him the clipboard, and was happy to see that the photographs were still attached.

"Pictures of the foundation to the house. Sturdy thinks it's time to fix up this place, now that it's empty."

"Sure, and pigs fly, man."

They were flying. Sinkovich had said that he would arrive within thirty minutes. My internal clock was ticking, telling me that time was running out.

I had to get past these guys, and make sure they didn't follow me. I didn't want them to think I had called the police. The only way I could avoid that was to make sure these six stayed here.

"I just do what they tell me," I said.

Glasses was reading the clipboard. It was my checklist, and I had it turned to the second page.

"What is this crap?" He shoved the clipboard at me, pointing to the list.

The second page started with the words:

Roaches or mice?

"You guys plant this crap?"

I smiled. "As if we have to in a building like that. You know better than to ask stupid questions."

He thumbed through the rest of the pages, reading some of the reminders out loud.

"Does the toilet flush and empty completely? Is the toilet bowl chipped or cracked? Does the shower drain?" He handed the clipboard back to me. "Man, you got a shit job."

The others laughed, apparently at his terrible pun.

"It feeds my kid," I said.

"You should be bringing him to our program," the second Panther said. The antagonism was gone now. "He could be learning about Black Power with his Wheaties."

"You bring your kid," Glasses said, giving my arm a friendly slap. "We'll make sure he gets treated right."

I didn't know how I had gone from a suspicious Uncle Tom to a guy whose kid needed indoctrination along with his cereal, but I wasn't going to argue. I had a hunch once the police showed up, I'd be back to my Tom status.

The others punched me lightly or winked as they walked past. They crossed Madison in the center, stopping traffic, and headed back to their headquarters.

I adjusted the pictures on my clipboard, and made myself look as nerdy and nervous as possible. I stalled for a moment longer, giving them a chance to go inside, before I turned the corner and walked back to Monroe.

Someone had called the Panthers—or had gone to get them when I drove up. They were protecting the neighborhood, and they had seen me as a threat.

I hoped they decided to stay on Madison. The last thing I needed to do was initiate a clash between the Panthers and the police.

FOURTEEN

Sinkovich was already there when I reached the house. He had shown up in an unmarked car, and he wasn't wearing a uniform. Despite the muggy day, he wore a raincoat with the collar turned up, and a wide-brimmed hat. His hands were in his pockets, and from the back, I couldn't see a shred of white skin.

Sometimes he was a lot smarter than I gave him credit for.

"Jack," I said, as I walked up the cracked sidewalk.

"Grimshaw." He turned toward me. He was even thinner than he'd been when I met him eight months ago. He had shaved off his mustache and, even though it hadn't flattered him, its loss made him look naked. "I was just getting ready to give you what for. I woulda thought this was some kinda set up if it weren't for that mess down there."

He nodded toward the body.

It was just as I had left it. Some of the smaller bones were scattered, and the rest lay in the dirt, looking frail and vulnerable.

"I got sidetracked by some Panthers," I said. "I hope I convinced them not to come over this way. Didn't you tell anyone else to come?"

"You think I can snap my fingers and make the coroner appear at my beck and call? I had to come out here, see if you knew what you was talking about, and call it in from here. You know the drill, Grimshaw, I know you do."

I did. I was just hoping he could circumvent it. But now that he was here,

I didn't have to worry so much about the Panthers. They wouldn't think that I had called the police. They would assume that Sinkovich was from Sturdy Investments and, when they realized he was white, they would think he had called the police.

I wasn't sure if Sinkovich had done this to save my butt, but I was glad he had.

He crouched near the hole, hands on his thighs. He leaned forward and peered around the corpse, but didn't touch anything.

"I'm thinking this kid's been in the ground a while," he said, "but I ain't no expert."

He wasn't. When I met Sinkovich last summer, he had been working in Vice. After a spectacular, newsworthy arrest this winter, he was promoted to Homicide, but mostly for show. His supervisors kept him on the desk most of the time.

"And," he said, still peering, "we had one hell of a flaky winter. No snow till January, then that awful cold, and the March from hell. Don't know how that would affect decomposition."

"Well," I said, crouching beside him, "the ground froze in late November. Burying the child, even this shallowly, would have been hard after that."

" 'Cept they didn't have to bury him." Sinkovich pointed at the stone window well. "They coulda just poured dirt in here, then put the kid in the dirt, and put more dirt on top."

"You're right." I hadn't thought that through. I had been so disturbed by finding the body that I hadn't looked closely at all the details. "We're going to have to check out the basement apartment, see how much dirt is on the floor and if it can tell us anything."

"You called me, Grimshaw, which makes this a police matter now. This ain't one of your special cases. I already put the coroner's office on notice that I might need them. There's gonna be an official inquiry."

"I know," I said. "I wanted it that way."

Sinkovich gave me a sideways glance. "Since when do you want white cops involved in your life?"

"First," I said, "this isn't my life. Secondly, I called you, not some generic white cop. Third—"

"Shit," Sinkovich said. "I wasn't looking for some weird speech. I just meant you're not normally an official guy. I was just wondering why this time you decided to be. And in such a nice neighborhood, too."

I found it hard to swallow. There was something in my throat. "The body." My voice sounded odd, even to me. "I couldn't leave it. This isn't right."

Sinkovich nodded. "Never did understand folks who can do crap like this—not, mind you, that it's unusual. They found some kid in an abandoned garage on Forty-second this morning. Took it over to Michael Reese Hospital. Little girl, not even a day old."

"Christ," I said.

"And we get, you know, one of those a month, sometimes more. Dead, mostly. This little one, she was lucky. Had good lungs from what I heard. I was listening to the radio in my car when it come through dispatch. Guys sounded shook."

I recognized that feeling. It hadn't left me. I tried not to look at the tiny white jumper, because that disturbed me most of all.

"And it ain't just you people," Sinkovich said. "White folks do the same damn thing. I don't get it."

I bit back an angry response. In the past few months, Sinkovich had come a long way toward changing his attitudes toward "my" people. But the words like that still came out of his mouth, always making me worry about how much I could trust him.

I stood and surveyed the area. The teenagers still sat on the stoop, watching us, but I saw no sign of the Panthers.

"What we need to do," I said, "is make sure no one tampers with this area—at least until the coroner arrives."

"I'm thinkin' it's way too late for that," Sinkovich said. "I mean, you said there was a dog in here, mucking things up—"

"And we don't want it to come back."

"I'm just sayin the chance of finding evidence here is between slim and none." He stood, his knees cracking. He wiped off the bottom of his pants legs.

"The reason I asked you here, Sinkovich, rather than just calling an emergency number and leaving, is because I thought you would have a decent chance of figuring out what happened here. This child deserved better—"

"Hey!" Sinkovich said. "I didn't do nothing. I'm just sayin' that the scene's already compromised. If it wasn't, I woulda made you stay back. That's all."

He studied me for a moment. He wasn't quite as tall as I was, but he didn't have to look up at me, like most people did. His pale gray eyes were serious and, it seemed, filled with a compassion I'd never seen before.

"I'm not gonna let this little guy stay here too long, and I'm gonna make sure there's justice if we can have it," he said. "I'm just sayin' that we're already at a disadvantage. Abandoned building, buried baby—God knows how long it's been here—and this fuckin' neighborhood. You shoulda waited for Johnson, you know. Ain't nobody gonna tell me nothing."

"I doubt they'd tell him anything, either," I said. "Or me, for that matter."

"But you got ways of findin' things out," Sinkovich said. "And you got that kid who sometimes helps you—what's his name? The one that was in the gang?"

"Malcolm," I said. "And he never really was that involved in the Black Machine."

Sinkovich rolled his eyes and shook his head. "I was watching them, Grimshaw. He was involved, least for a while. Good thing you pulled him out, too. They hooked up with the Stones a month or so back. If I was you, I'd be getting the hell out of the South Side. I been hearing rumors of some kinda gang war heating up."

I looked at him in surprise. Sinkovich wasn't that tied into the black community. The only community he knew well was the Polish Catholic neighborhood where he grew up—and they certainly weren't tied to the black community, either.

"Where did you hear that?" I asked, trying not to let him see how disturbed I was.

He shrugged. "It's been the word for a while. That's why they're trying to get Conlisk to lift his ban on automatic weapons."

Conlisk was the Police Superintendent. Last fall, he had banned not just automatic weapons, but blackjacks—the long black nightsticks that the police had used so viciously against demonstrators at the Democratic National Convention.

"Who's asking?" I tried to keep my voice level.

"Haven't been paying that much attention," Sinkovich said, "but you know how you hear stuff. Me, I don't want that crap no more. I'm still having nightmares—"

He stopped himself, but I knew the end of the sentence. He had been a part of that police riot at the Democratic National Convention, and he had beaten students with bird pellet inside his gloves.

Ever since, he had had nightmares, about the sound, he said, of those gloves hitting a teenager's head.

I had been the first person to challenge him on his behavior that night, and ever since, he had come to me as if I were a father-confessor, embarrassed by what he had done and, at the same time, extremely defensive about it.

But it had changed him. The reason his wife left him was because he had returned to his original sense of right and wrong. He had made a choice that hurt his status in the neighborhood, but had saved the life of a young black family.

"Who's asking?" I repeated.

"Jesus, Grimshaw, I don't know."

We stood there for a minute, letting the silence surround us. This neighborhood was too quiet for my tastes.

I looked down at the window well. From this angle, I couldn't see anything except a hint of bone and a bit of jumper.

Sinkovich put a hand on my arm, startling me. "When I was working Vice, we found stuff like this all the time. Babies born addicted, babies born dead. Babies neglected in ways you don't wanna think about. The things people do when they're on something—sometimes they don't even think of the babies as living at all."

"I know," I said, resisting the urge to stare at his hand on my sleeve.

"Then you gotta know that this baby might not be from here. Some hopped-up freak might've thought she was putting her kid to bed, not covering it in dirt, you know? And she might've just been passing through."

I shivered, and wished I hadn't. Sinkovich felt it through my sleeve. He squeezed my arm, then let his hand drop.

"If that happened, someone would have seen it," I said. "You can't bury someone in the front yard of a building and not get noticed."

"Yeah, but here?" Sinkovich looked around.

I did, too. The neighborhood wasn't bad. There were worse not far from me on the South Side. "People live here. Good people. They'd notice."

"I suppose." Sinkovich didn't sound convinced.

"I can get you a list of the former tenants in the building," I said. "I'm not sure how accurate it'll be, but it'll be a place to start."

"I'm gonna be starting by hearing what the coroner says. There's a lotta criteria before we even start an investigation."

"Criteria?"

"Cause of death. That's a biggie. If this kid ever took a real breath."

"It's wearing a jumper," I said.

"Yeah, and I've seen heroin addicts dress up ice-cold corpses like dolls."

I winced.

"Sorry, Grimshaw, but this happens enough we got procedure on it, and believe it or not, the procedure ain't half bad."

He glanced at his watch. I looked at the teenagers, still smoking on that stoop. They didn't seem that interested in the two of us at the moment.

"I gotta call this in, get the coroner here," Sinkovich muttered, almost to himself. "Tell you what, Grimshaw. I'm thinkin' it'd be better if you vacate now. I mean, you can stay and represent the property owner, but if you do, I got a feelin' you ain't gonna be able to ask nobody about nothing. They're gonna know you called us."

Again, he was being a lot more astute than I had given him credit for. Still, I wanted to stay, to see how the police handled the crime scene.

Sinkovich must have seen the hesitation on my face. "I looked up the rotation. The coroner we're gettin's a deputy. He's good, but he ain't gonna listen to you. He's probably gonna treat you like you done something wrong, 'specially if you get in his face. Now, I know this's important, and I'll do what I can to make sure you get all the information. You okay with that?"

I had called them. I had been the one to put this in the police's hands.

"Promise me you'll make sure this child doesn't get cremated and tossed out," I said, even before I realized I was going to speak. "Promise me that we'll be able to take the body and have some kind of service."

"Gettin' soft on me, Grimshaw?" Sinkovich had no malice in his tone. He was a realist, and he was right. Children got discarded every day. Jimmy had, but he had been old enough to fend for himself.

"Maybe," I said.

Sinkovich studied me for a moment. "If we release this kid to you, you got enough ready cash to make sure it gets taken care of proper?"

I looked at him in surprise. "Yeah."

"Okay, then I'll make sure nothing else goes wrong for the poor thing. Deal?" He extended his hand.

I took it. His skin was cold. "Deal," I said.

FIFTEEN

I gave Sinkovich my keys to the abandoned building, with the promise that he'd make copies and return them later that evening, along with a report about the day's events. I felt odd leaving him at the house alone. A white man was conspicuous in that neighborhood, but he told me he could take care of himself.

He was going to stand guard over the little grave until the coroner showed up. Then he was going to inspect the basement, and see if he found any clues as to what had happened.

By the time I drove away, the teenagers had disappeared, leaving a pile of cigarette butts behind.

It wasn't yet noon, and my plan for the day was shot. I had expected to remain at the building, maybe even finish it up, not deal with something like this.

I had to go see Laura and tell her what had happened, but before I went anywhere near Sturdy Investments, I needed a shower. I had a hunch I smelled a lot more like dead rat than I knew.

I hadn't told Sinkovich about that, nor had I mentioned the holes in the stairwell. My mistake. But I supposed he would find all of that soon enough.

My apartment building was empty when I arrived. The main door was shut and locked, and the interior of the building was stifling. Marvella, usually the only other person home during the day, probably wasn't in. Her

Defender was gone, but when I knocked, hoping to get an update on Valentina, no one answered.

My own apartment was unbearable. The heat had kicked on. The radiator clanged merrily, as if it were forty below instead of seventy and humid outside. I opened every window, found the fans that Franklin had left me, and scattered them around the apartment.

Then I climbed into the shower, throwing my filthy clothes into the laundry bag. I would have to find time to go to the launderette sometime this afternoon as well.

The shower cooled me down, but didn't help my attitude. Finding that corpse had brought up anger I hadn't even realized I had buried. At first, the anger felt general and formless—anger at that faceless person or persons who had allowed a baby to die, and who didn't even have enough respect for the poor thing to give it a decent burial.

Then I thought about all the children I had known who had been left behind by someone, all the children no one wanted, like the thousand unwanted black children Laura and I had learned about on Sunday night. Not to mention what had happened to Jimmy—and, at the bottom of it all, what had happened to me.

I came to that last thought with one hand braced on the green tile wall of the shower, the water turning cold. My final memory of my parents—the pounding at the door, my father whispering, *Hide, son* as he carried his shotgun down the stairs, the darkness of the crawlspace in the back of my closet where I heard all the angry voices, my mother's, shrill and frightened, shouting, *It ain't so! It ain't so!* and then the silence, the hideous awful silence that went on, it seemed, even until now.

I shut off the water, and rested my head on my arm, water dripping down my skin. It seemed like my entire life was about other people's children. My parents had died because someone thought they had kidnapped a white child. I escaped Memphis because the police and the FBI wanted to kill a black child. Cases over the years, from Roscoe Miller begging me to help his daughter to the death of Brian Richardson last summer, always forced me to put me and mine second, and someone else's child—someone else's crisis—first.

With my wet hand, I wiped the water off my face. Somehow these cases came to me, probably because I understood them, because, even though they didn't intend it, my parents abandoned me that night—protected me, yes; saved me as well; but they never came back because that choice was taken from them, just like it had been taken from me.

That was why I reacted so strongly to that small grave. Why I couldn't leave those bones, that bit of skin, and that pathetic little jumper to the animals and the elements. Why I had to have the small corpse released to me, so that that tiny child wouldn't be abandoned again.

I grabbed a towel, dried myself off, and then dressed. I had an afternoon of tracing names on the list Marvella gave me, looking for people who didn't want to be found, something I was not in the mood for, at least, at the moment.

I invaded Jimmy's room, grabbed his dirty clothes, and packed them with mine. Then I left the apartment for an exciting hour of lunch and laundry.

The skies were black with thunderclouds. The mugginess had grown even worse, and it had brought out little black bugs that liked to fly in circles. I had no idea where the bugs came from or how they survived in this city filled with concrete and steel, but they managed somehow.

The heat was worse in the launderette, so I sat outside while everything spun in various washers and dryers, watching lightning illuminate the clouds, and listening to more thunder rumble far away. The promised storm never hit this part of the city, although after a while, the air smelled like rain.

By the time I returned to the apartment, I was calmer. I hung up our clothes, stared at my desk, and then remembered that I had promised to talk to Laura.

I had planned on driving there, but I didn't want to go back to the Loop. Instead, I called.

Apparently, she had been waiting to hear from me because she sounded relieved when she heard my voice.

I updated her, then I asked her if she could get me a copy of the tenants list.

"I'll bring it over later along with a pizza," she said, "unless you have an objection."

I wasn't ready to see Laura. I was still feeling a bit raw. I started to tell her that I needed some time alone with Jimmy, then I realized that Jimmy and I had been alone the night before, and I hadn't gotten him to talk to me. Maybe he would talk to Laura. He sometimes told her his fears, things he wouldn't tell me.

Besides, he idolized her. Laura was the only person in his life who, even though she had had to leave him, promised she would come back—and had.

"Can you bring the other list, too?" I asked. "The one I asked you for last night?"

"Sure," she said. "I haven't been able to reach everyone, but I can always update it for you as I get more information."

"That would be great," I said.

"See you around six, Smokey," she said, and hung up.

I hung up, too, feeling inexplicably better. The decision to have her come over was the right one, even though I wouldn't have made it without Jimmy. In my life, I had gotten too used to spending time alone, particularly when something disturbed me.

This past year, I was learning brand-new methods of coping, and they still felt strange to me.

I spent the afternoon chasing names on Marvella's lists. Most of the addresses were old, just like the one I had found the day before. They took me to abandoned buildings, or burned-out buildings or, in a few cases, non-existent buildings.

I was beginning to get discouraged, and wondered how anyone found one of these so-called doctors.

Marvella's lists weren't working. I was going to have to find a new method, or maybe get an update from Marvella. Perhaps she didn't realize how dated her information was.

Around four, I found myself near Helping Hands, and decided to stop. When I pulled up outside, lightning still flashed across the sky. Here, the sidewalk was wet, as if I had just missed a downpour.

There weren't as many people on the streets as there had been the day before. Everyone wore raincoats, and a few carried newspapers above their heads like umbrellas. I saw no tams this afternoon. The Stones had to be waiting out the bad weather somewhere else.

As I opened the glass door, I looked inside the office. A different volunteer manned the desk that afternoon. She was older. Her gray hair had been ironed thin, and she wore too much makeup. Her black dress—which looked too warm for that humid afternoon—had lace flowers decorating the neckline, a touch of frivolity that almost seemed out of place.

"May I help you?" she asked as I stepped inside.

The door closed behind me, and I wished it hadn't. The office was hotter than my apartment had been. A rotating fan sat beside the typewriter on the credenza, but all it did was blow the hot air around.

"My name's Bill Grimshaw," I said, leaning over the desk and extending my hand.

She took it in her moist palm and put her other hand over mine. She didn't even try to shake.

"It's a pleasure, Mr. Grimshaw," she said. "I can't tell you what an honor it is to be a volunteer here. I feel like I'm doing the Lord's work."

I wondered if she was one of the people Althea had recruited from the church or if she had come to Helping Hands from another route. However, I wasn't curious enough to ask.

"I was wondering if you could check on something for me, Miss . . . ?" I let my voice trail off.

She smiled, patted my hand, and let it go. "I'm Anna Shay."

"Mrs. Shay," I said, "I brought a woman and two children in here yesterday. The woman said her name was Helen, and her children were Doug and Carrie. I never did get their last names. I was wondering if I might be able to visit them. I have a few questions for Helen."

Mrs. Shay's smile faded. "Now you know that's not procedure, Mr. Grimshaw."

I nodded. I had helped develop the procedure, although I didn't want to tell her that.

"I understand," I said. "It's just that something's come up, and I want to see if Helen knows anything about it."

"Procedure dictates, Mr. Grimshaw, that I tell her of your request to talk with her and let her decide what she wants to do."

I almost smiled. When we set up Helping Hands Incorporated, I sat across from Drew McMillan, who was helping us draw up guidelines, and said, *The last thing we want is for the police or anyone official to use this organization as a way to get information or to mistreat the people we're trying to help. We need to hire volunteers who'll enforce the rules we set up, no matter who asks them to change those rules.*

It seemed I had gotten my wish in the person of Anna Shay.

"Fair enough," I said. "Please ask Helen if she's willing to meet me here. Let me give you my phone number, just in case she is, so that we can set up a time."

Mrs. Shay shoved a piece of paper at me, and I wrote my phone number on it. Then I handed it back to her.

"Can you tell me one thing, Mrs. Shay?" I asked. "Obviously Helen and the children decided to stay yesterday. Are they doing all right?"

"I saw them this morning before I started my office shift. That little boy is fierce. No one gets near his momma or sister. I just want to hug him, and tell him that he's going to be all right now." She shook her head. "At that age, children should be joyful. I'm hoping we'll be able to help him recover that joy."

If he ever had it in the first place.

"Did the interview go well? Are we going to be able to help Helen become financially independent?" I was asking too many prying questions, but better to have one of the volunteers tell me than to ask Helen the following day.

"The interview did not go well," Mrs. Shay said. "She doesn't trust anyone, Mr. Grimshaw. But another volunteer discovered this morning that your friend has an amazing talent for sewing. It seems her mother was a seamstress, and young Helen learned at her knee. We're seeing if we can use that somehow. Although I don't know how, in this day of ready-made dresses, she would ever be able to earn a true living from sewing clothing."

The news buoyed me up, although I wasn't sure why. Perhaps I had assumed that Helen had no skills at all.

"Well," I said, "please ask her for me if she's willing to talk briefly tomorrow. If she's not, that's all right. But it would be helpful."

"I'll ask, Mr. Grimshaw," Mrs. Shay said. "But I make no promises."

"I can't ask for more." I smiled at her. "It was a pleasure to meet you, Mrs. Shay."

Then I let myself out the door.

It was fifteen degrees cooler outside, at least, and for the first time that day, I didn't mind the humidity. The air had droplets of water in it, but they hadn't yet become rain.

Still, as I walked to my car, I noticed that it was beaded with tiny drops of mist, just enough to make me turn on the wipers and smear the windshield.

It was nearly five, so I drove to the church where Grace Kirkland held her afterschool lessons.

The kids were just coming out of the church as I pulled up. Two dozen children of all ages, carrying books, laughing, and shouting at each other. No gangs waited on the lawn, no barbed-wire fences cordoned off the area, and no graffiti decorated the church's brick walls.

This was what school should be. The fact that Chicago didn't provide it for its black children angered and disturbed me, and I wasn't alone. Parents were up in arms all over the city, but unfortunately, each neighborhood seemed to have different issues.

I made sure my doors were unlocked, and leaned across the seat as the kids ran to my car. I grabbed the door handle and pushed the passenger door open.

Norene got in, filling the car with the scent of grape bubblegum. She had some in her hair, something Althea would hate. Mikie got in beside her.

Everyone else piled into the back. All of the kids said hello to me, even Jimmy, although he glowered as he did so. He hadn't laughed with the rest of them as they had piled out of the church, and he had kicked at the sidewalk as he walked.

All the way home, I listened to conversations about the importance of fractions ("because you need to know how much a half is, stupid!"), and whether or not Crispus Attucks was a hero.

I didn't join in. I figured they would learn fractions whether they wanted to or not, and Grace wouldn't be happy if I weighed in with my opinion of Crispus Attucks, the first man to die in the American Revolution. That he was a black man seemed to me the first defining moment in United States history: a black man stood up for freedom—and got shot for his efforts.

But that view was too cynical for this group, so I kept quiet.

It didn't take long to get to the Grimshaws', and by the time the kids piled out, the car grew deadly silent. For the second day in a row, Jimmy did not move to the front seat.

As we pulled away, I said, "What's going on, Jim?"

"Nothing," he said.

I glanced in the rearview mirror. He was looking out the window.

"Is someone bothering you at school?" I asked.

"Nope."

"You seem awfully quiet."

He shrugged, and I swerved, realizing that I had better keep my gaze on the road instead of in the backseat.

"Something's wrong," I said.

"Nah." But he drew his legs up to his chest.

I sighed and drove. I had no idea how to approach him.

"You'd tell me if it was the Stones, right?" I said.

"You already asked me that."

"And apparently the answer didn't stick."

"It's not them," he said, but I wasn't entirely convinced.

We pulled up in front of the apartment. Laura's car wasn't there yet. I waited for Jimmy to get out, and then we walked inside together. I didn't say anything as we went up the stairs and as I unlocked the door, but the moment I closed it, I said, "Jim, whatever it is, you can talk to me. I—"

"No, I can't," he said with more ferocity than I had ever heard from him. Then he stalked to his room and slammed the door.

I stood by the front door, my heart pounding. I wasn't certain what I had done to deserve that much anger. I wasn't certain if I should go after him or if I should let him sit alone for a while, to get some distance between us.

But distance was what we had. So I walked through the living room, picking up bits of the newspaper I had left lying around, and then I knocked on his door.

"Go away!" he said.

"Jim, I just want to find out what's going on."

"Nothing! Just go away."

I opened the door. He was sitting cross-legged on his bed, his books spread out before him. He glared at me.

"What happened to 'our rooms is our private space'?" he said, lapsing into the bad grammar that he had learned from his family in Memphis.

"It is. I just wanted to—"

"If it's private, then go away and close the door. You wasn't invited in. Go away." He spoke with such force that spittle flew from his mouth.

I nodded, feeling my cheeks heat. I had broken one of our cardinal rules, and my concern for him was no excuse. Or rather, I wouldn't have let it be an excuse if he had broken the rules with me.

I pulled the door closed, dropped the newspapers in my office, and sat down at the desk. Every moment with Jimmy was unknown territory for me, a man who had never had children. But this was even more unknown. Most of the shapes and influences he'd had in his life had nothing to do with me. I had only been a part of his life for the last few years, and directly involved only for the last year. I had no idea where those facts were going to take us as he made his way to adulthood.

As if that were the problem. The problem, right now, was that he was angry at me for reasons I didn't understand. And he refused to talk with me about them.

I couldn't let this slide, but I wasn't sure how to press it, either.

I felt like I was losing him, and I didn't know how to stop it.

SIXTEEN

Laura's arrival brought Jimmy out of his room. He heard her knock on the apartment door, and ran down the hallway. I heard him instead of the knocks. By the time I came out of my office, Jimmy was taking hot pizza boxes out of Laura's arms.

She had changed from her work clothes. She wore tight blue jeans with ripped hems and appliqué flowers, a woven peasant blouse that accented her braless state, and she had her hair down.

She looked so different from the woman who had entered this apartment in the wee hours of Monday morning. I liked her many incarnations, all of her different sides. She intrigued me like no one else ever had.

The apartment smelled of cheese and tomato sauce. She had brought four large pizzas, apparently remembering the last time, when Jimmy had eaten most of a pizza all by himself.

"Pop tonight?" Jimmy asked me, and his eyes were bright. The sullen boy I had brought home seemed to have vanished. But I had a hunch that if I said no to his request for soda, the sullen boy would be back.

I didn't have a chance to answer. Laura said, "I have root beer in the car. I just wasn't able to carry it up."

"I'll get it," Jimmy said.

"It's not the usual car," she said. "It's the big ugly black thing parked behind your dad's."

"What happened to your car?" he asked.

Laura glanced at me, and I realized with surprise that I hadn't said anything to Jimmy about our adventures at the hospital on Sunday night.

"Got some major stains in the back," she said, covering pretty well. "I had to take it in for cleaning."

"And they just gave you another car?" Jimmy asked.

"Yeah," Laura said. "They do that as a courtesy."

"Especially when you've just bought a new Mercedes from them," I said.

Laura frowned at me as if she didn't approve of the comment. But Jimmy had to know that perks weren't for everyone. If I took my rusted Impala back to the dealership where I had bought it and asked for a loaner car while someone cleaned mine, I would have been laughed out of the place. Of course, anyone with any sense would have laughed at me just for bringing the car in for cleaning.

"It's not locked, is it?" Jimmy asked. "I can get the root beer?"

"It's not locked," Laura said. "But lock it before you come up here."

"Okay," he said and ran out the door.

She waited until he jumped on the bottom step before saying, "I thought you said he's been down lately."

"He screamed at me to leave him alone not fifteen minutes ago."

"Wow." She peered out the door as if she could get the answer just from his behavior now. "You'd never know it to look at him."

I took the pizzas off the chair where Jimmy had set them, carried them into the half-kitchen, and set them on the counter.

"You planning to feed the entire building?" I asked.

"I couldn't remember what Jimmy liked, so I got half-and-half of everything in weird combinations." She shrugged. "I figure he'll probably eat the rest tonight and tomorrow anyway. Growing boy."

"Yeah," I said. That was as much a part of the problem as anything else.

I got out plates and handed them to Laura. She had a touch of color in her cheeks, and her blue eyes sparkled. She looked beautiful, and I couldn't resist. As I set the plates in her hands, I kissed her.

"Yuck," Jimmy said as he came in the door. "Mushy stuff."

We both grinned at him. Then Laura set the plates on the table. Jimmy brought me the root beer, and I got out three glasses.

Even more than pizza, Jimmy found soda for dinner—a staple before he moved in with me—to be a special treat.

"Before I forget," Laura said, "I have both lists for you."

She slung her purse off her shoulder and reached inside.

"What lists?" Jimmy asked as he got the ice cube trays out of the freezer.

"Laura brought me a list of former tenants at the building I'm inspecting," I said.

"Somebody steal something?" Jimmy took the metal prong from the middle of the tray, pulled it, and emptied the ice into a large plastic bowl we had inherited from the Grimshaws. The outside of the bowl was grimy with Jimmy-sized handprints. I hoped that Laura didn't notice.

"I guess you could say that," I said.

"What, then?" He grabbed the tongs and picked up ice, dropping cubes into each glass. Usually I had to remind him to do that.

"It's more like they left something behind," Laura said.

"That's not the same thing." Jimmy gave me the same glare from earlier, only he made certain that his back was to Laura, so that she couldn't see it.

I opened the ringtop on one of the Hires cans and poured the root beer into all three glasses, letting the foam rise. The sweet smell of root beer tickled my nose.

"You said two lists," Jimmy said.

"The other one is for a case I'm working on," I said.

The root beer foam receded, and I filled the glasses a little more.

"You know, I'm not a baby anymore," Jimmy said. "You don't always got to hide stuff from me."

"I've never treated you like a baby," I said.

Laura handed me the lists, and Jimmy snatched them from my hands.

"Jim," I said, warning in my tone.

"They're just lists." Laura kept her voice level. "Nothing suspicious."

"How come one's typed and one isn't?" Jimmy asked, looking at both pieces of paper.

"One was done at the office by my secretary," Laura said. "I did the other."

"How come your secretary didn't?" Jimmy asked.

"Because I didn't have time to give it to her to type." Laura reached for one of the glasses. She obviously did it so that Jimmy couldn't see her face. Her voice handled the lie well, but the frown between her eyes gave away her concern.

"It's all names." Jimmy shoved both pieces of paper at me.

"That's what a tenant list is," I said.

"What's the other one?" Jimmy asked again.

"It's a list of some doctors I know," Laura said, carrying her glass to the table. I grabbed the other two and set them near the plates.

"You sick?" Jimmy asked me, his tone changing from belligerent to worried.

I shook my head. "Like I said, it's a case."

"Who're you working for?"

"You're not supposed to ask me that," I said. "You know that."

"Laura knows," Jimmy said.

"Yes, she does," I said. "She was there when I got the case."

"It's not fair, you know," Jimmy said. "Everybody knows stuff but me."

"It's not about being fair," I said. "It's about me handling my cases with professionalism."

"And telling me isn't professional?"

"No," I said. "It's not."

Jimmy's mouth opened, and then he slammed a fist on the table.

The glasses shook. One almost toppled, but Laura caught it.

"Do that again," I said, "and you're heading to your room without supper."

Jimmy slid into his chair, his lips a thin line, his eyes narrowed. He made it clear that he had more to say, but he wouldn't—at least until he had finished eating.

I was so angry that I was shaking. I took the papers into my office, set them on the desk, and stood there for a moment, catching my breath. If only I knew where Jimmy's anger was coming from, I could address that, rather than fight about little things. It was too easy to respond to his challenges, and I knew if I didn't handle them right from the beginning, they'd only get worse as he got older.

It took me a moment to gather myself, but I finally felt calm enough to return to the living room. Jimmy was still in his chair, and Laura had set napkins next to the silverware. Two of the pizza boxes, their lids cut off, sat like serving trays in the middle of the table.

"Dig in," Laura said.

The pizza did smell good, and it had been a long time since that launderette lunch. I sat in my chair, and reached for a slice of pepperoni, as someone knocked on the door.

"Damn," I said.

"No cursing at the table," Laura said quickly—so quickly that I knew it was an automatic phrase, probably one she had heard as a child.

Jimmy was staring at her in startled surprise. Apparently he had never heard anyone talk to me like I talked to him.

I slid my chair back, went to the door, and looked through the spyhole. Marvella stood there, wringing her hands together. I wasn't even sure if she was aware she was doing so.

No one had locked the deadbolts, so I pulled the door open. She was wearing sandals, blue jeans, and a sweater. Her hair had reverted to its natural state.

If it weren't for her wringing hands and the shadows under her eyes, I would have thought she was looking better than she had the day before.

"Come on in, Marvella," I said.

"Bill, I was wondering how the—" She stopped herself when she saw the food on the table and Laura standing in my kitchen as if she belonged there.

Marvella had cooked for me a few times, shortly after the Grimshaws had moved out, and then once when I asked her to baby-sit Jim. Her meals were elaborate and delicious, and I had felt, when she served them, like I had stepped into a television program of the perfect family.

Laura serving us pizza was something those TV moms frowned upon. You never caught June Cleaver serving pizza instead of a well-rounded meal.

But then, neither Laura nor Marvella was June Cleaver. Nor were they like any other woman portrayed on TV.

Jimmy had gripped the edge of the table. When I saw that, I realized that my back muscles were tense. I, too, had braced myself for Marvella's snide onslaught against Laura.

Instead, Marvella gave me a weak smile. "I'm sorry. I didn't realize you were eating. I'll come back."

"There's no need," Laura said. "Sit down. Tell us how Valentina is."

"Valentina?" Jimmy asked me.

"A friend of Marvella's," I said softly. "She's in the hospital."

"No," Marvella said to Laura. "I don't want to impose. I'll come back."

"Please," Laura said. "I insist. There's plenty of food—too much, as Smokey told me when I showed up."

"You brought the pizza?" Marvella said, and Jimmy and I braced ourselves again, although Laura, who had taken the full brunt of Marvella's wrath in the past, didn't seem all that disturbed.

"The working girl's emergency meal," Laura said with a grin. "I couldn't even trouble myself to make a salad."

She took out another plate and set it on the table, along with an extra napkin.

"What will you have to drink? We have lots of root beer, some milk, and I could make coffee. But Smokey doesn't keep beer, and I don't know what else goes with pizza."

Marvella let Laura steer her to the chair. I had never seen anything quite like it. In the past, it had been Laura who was at a disadvantage with Marvella.

"I guess . . . root beer," Marvella said.

"I'll get it," Jimmy said, but I put a hand on his shoulder.

"Eat," I said.

"Well, you guys gotta, too."

"We will," Laura said. "I'll get the root beer. Sit down, Smokey. Keep Marvella company."

I sat down too, feeling out of control in my own kitchen. Two of the pepperoni pieces were already gone, and only one of them was on Jimmy's plate. The crust of the other one sat on his napkin.

"What do you want, Marvella?" I asked. "We have sausage, pepperoni, sausage and pepperoni, cheese—"

"It doesn't matter," she said as I took her plate. I gave her a slice of sausage. She took the plate with the piece on it, and stared at it for a moment. "You know, I didn't mean to impose."

"You're not imposing." Laura set the root beer glass in front of Marvella, then sat down. Laura served herself some pepperoni. "I, for one, have been wondering how your cousin is."

"I thought she was a friend," Jimmy whispered to me.

I took a piece before the pepperoni vanished forever. "It's complicated."

"I hate it when you say that." He glowered at me, but it didn't seem like the angry glare from before. He was too interested in the conversation to nurture his anger at me.

Marvella cut her slice with a fork. "She's still not awake."

"My God." Laura bit her piece of pizza, a big bite that squeezed tomato sauce onto her chin. "What's the prognosis?"

"Every day, every hour, that she keeps breathing is another step forward," Marvella said. "But nobody's promising anything."

Laura nodded, wiped the tomato sauce off her chin with a napkin, and then took another bite.

"Fever gone?" I said.

"No," Marvella said. "But the infection seems to be better. The penicillin seems to be working, but I'm not even sure about that. No one's talking, which has me worried."

"Not even to Truman?"

"He left this morning," Marvella said. "He sat around as much as he could, but I finally got him to go home, take a shower, and get some sleep. Maybe they'll talk to him when he comes back tonight."

"Is that the cop?" Jimmy asked.

"Yeah," I said.

"What, he arrest her or something?" Jimmy asked.

Laura looked at him, startled. She always seemed startled when his old life showed up in his questions. It was still more natural for him to think of a cop arresting a woman than being related to one.

"He's her ex-husband," I said.

"What happened to her?" Jimmy asked.

We all looked at him, uncertain what to tell him. Then the women looked at me. Jimmy missed their reactions. He was focusing on devouring his third piece of pizza.

"She was hurt in a crime," I said, realizing how lame that sounded. "And things got worse. She had to have surgery."

"Hurt?" Jimmy said. "Mugged?"

He wasn't going to let up.

"No," I said.

"Beat up?"

"Kind of," Laura said.

"Some guy, huh?" Jimmy said. "He done stuff to her?"

Marvella's eyes widened and she stared at me. I wasn't about to tell her that Jimmy's mother had been a prostitute. I had no idea why I had even tried to protect him. He probably knew more about this stuff than I did.

"Yeah," I said. "He hurt her pretty badly."

"They catch him?" This he directed to Marvella.

"Not yet." Marvella stopped, stabbed her fork into one of the cut pizza pieces, and ate it. "Which was what I initially came here for. Have you got anything yet, Bill?"

So much for keeping things from Jimmy.

"No," I said. "I'm finding that a lot of the people on your list aren't on the address that you gave me."

"She gave you a list?" Jimmy asked.

"Jim," I said, a bit more sharply than before. "It's business."

His cheeks flushed. He set down his piece of pizza. "You'll talk business with everyone but me?"

"It isn't like that," I started, but Marvella spoke over the top of me.

"He's finding some stuff out for me, Jimmy," she said.

Jimmy looked from her to me, and then back to her. "You're working for her?" he said, his voice low and angry. "You don't even like her."

It was my turn to flush. "That's enough!" I said.

"It's all right," Marvella said, setting down her fork. "I haven't been the nicest—"

"This isn't about you, Marvella," I said. "It's about Jimmy and me. He's doing everything he can to piss me off, and it's working. Apologize to her, Jim."

"For what? Telling the truth?" He looked at her. "You made him really mad—"

"Jimmy, that's it." I stood, took his plate away and carried it to the sink. It took all of my strength to stop myself from throwing it against the wall. "You're done with dinner. Go to your room."

"You can't order me," he said.

"I can, and I will," I said. "You're excused."

He stood up, grabbed one more slice of pizza and a napkin, and started for his room. I debated grabbing the slice from him, decided it was too petty, and let him go.

"Wow," Laura said. "I've never seen him like that."

"Neither have I." I sighed and sat back down. "I don't know what to do."

Then I looked at Marvella. Her cheeks were still flushed, and she was pushing the pizza around with her fork.

"I owe you an apology," I said.

"No," she said. "He's right. I've been awful."

"We discussed it," I said. "You apologized. I just didn't tell him. I—"

"It doesn't seem like you can tell him anything right now." She looked up and gave me a smile that her heart clearly wasn't in. "I should go."

"Not yet," I said. "I need to talk with you about the case."

She nodded.

"If that's all right," Laura said, looking at me, knowing that she was stepping into an area that was mine and mine alone. "Sometimes things can be overwhelming and—"

"It's okay." Marvella took a deep breath, squared her shoulders, and faced me. "What have you found?"

"Nothing yet," I said. "As I was saying before Jimmy got in the way, the addresses on your bad list are out of date. I can't even find anyone who knows these people."

"I was afraid of that." Marvella picked up her drink and took a sip. "A lot of those names were old. I never send anyone to them, so I don't really keep it updated."

"You have a list of providers?" Laura asked.

Marvella nodded.

"Good ones?" Laura asked.

Marvella nodded again.

"May I have a copy?"

"Sure," Marvella said.

"I'm thinking," I said, "that I might need a new strategy, at least to get names. Maybe posing as the boyfriend of someone who needs help."

"Let's find these known providers first," Marvella said. "Chances are it's one of these. You can dig for them, can't you? Like you do for other things?"

I took another piece of pizza for myself. My stomach, which had been churning, was finally settling down. "I can dig," I said. "The problem is that it'll take time. And I thought you wanted answers sooner rather than later."

"I do," Marvella said. "But nothing's working out the way I want it to. So keep going."

"She might be awake before I find out who her so-called doctor was," I said.

Marvella gave me another fake smile. "We can only hope."

"I don't think it matters if she's awake or not, Smokey," Laura said.

I looked at her. Marvella hadn't moved. "Why not?"

"Because she's not going to tell, is she, Marvella?" Laura shifted in her chair so that she could face Marvella directly. "You've already asked her, haven't you? And she was too embarrassed to tell you, afraid somehow that it's her mistake."

Marvella's eyes teared. "Yeah," she whispered.

"So just keep looking," Laura said. "Believe me, you'll do more women favors than you know."

I studied both of them. They had seemed so different just days ago. And now, they seemed to have the same opinions, the same goals. I would never have expected it.

"All right," I said. "I'll do what I can."

SEVENTEEN

We spent the next half an hour brainstorming ways to get additional information. Laura and Marvella compared notes about doctors they had heard of, and I mostly listened. It was still a new world for me, and I needed all the information I could get.

We had just put the last pizza on the table when someone knocked at the door. I couldn't remember a night this busy in a long time.

"Excuse me," I said and stood. I went to the door and looked through the spyhole for the second time in less than an hour.

Sinkovich stood outside. He wore the same raincoat he had had on at the crime scene. This time the shoulders were damp with rain.

I had forgotten that he had said he was going to come over to pick up the tenant list.

I pulled the door open. "Jack, I—"

"Don't worry," he said, holding up a six-pack of Old Milwaukee, "I got you covered. I brought beer since, as I recall, you're not enough of an American to keep some on tap for the good citizens."

He stopped when he saw Marvella and Laura. He hadn't met either of them before, and his mouth dropped open at the sight of them sitting side by side.

Because I was so afraid his next words were going to be offensive, I said the first thing that came to mind. "Care for some pizza?"

"You had pizza without beer?" he asked, recovering. He bowed slightly. "Ladies."

"Laura, Marvella, this is Jack," I said.

"Officer Sinkovich?" Marvella asked, putting two and two together. Johnson, Sinkovich, and I had worked a case together last December. Obviously, Johnson had told her about it.

"Detective now," he said. "You Johnson's sister?"

"Cousin," she said.

"And you're the Hathaway," he said to Laura.

That twinkle came back to her eyes. "Yes," she said, "although I've never been referred to quite like that."

"The kid, he told me you and Grimshaw was pals, but I never totally believed him. Kids tend to idolize their dads."

"Do not," Jimmy said from the hallway. He had apparently left his room to see who was at the door. I was going to tell him to return to his room, but Sinkovich spoke first.

"I seen how you look at him, sport. No sense lying to Uncle Jack." Sinkovich pulled off his coat and hung it on the rack. He wore a bowling shirt underneath that didn't go with his dark pants.

"You're not my uncle," Jimmy said.

"Jim," I said, not wanting him to tangle with Sinkovich when he was in this mood. Even at the best of times, they had a tendency to rub each other the wrong way.

"And," Jimmy said, "I'm not sport."

"Sorry, kiddo," Sinkovich said. "My dad called me sport. Old habits die hard, you know?"

"No, I don't know," Jimmy said. "What're you doing here, anyway?"

"Your dad and I got some business."

"More stuff I don't know about?" Jimmy turned toward me.

"Listen, kid, you ain't entitled to know everything your old man does," Sinkovich said, staying true to form. He apparently hadn't realized that Jimmy had directed this last to me.

"This ain't about you," Jimmy said.

Sinkovich's eyes widened. "What's got into you?"

"Like you care," Jimmy said.

I was about to step in, but Laura touched my arm. The movement was subtle. I doubted anyone else had seen it.

"Try me," Sinkovich said.

Jimmy swaggered toward him. That lankiness served Jimmy well. He came up to Sinkovich's chest now. Jimmy had a look of challenge on his face, an adult look, one that dared Sinkovich to mess with him.

"Okay," Jimmy said. "I been thinking about something all week, and I bet you can't say nothing about it."

Sinkovich frowned. He recognized the challenge.

Laura tightened her grip on my arm, holding me back, even though she didn't have to. Sinkovich, in his inept, belligerent way, might have just opened the door to Jimmy.

"About what, kiddo?" Sinkovich asked.

"About what's the point?" Jimmy had entered the living room now. He wasn't standing that far from Sinkovich.

"The point about what?" Sinkovich asked. He looked at me as if I understood what Jimmy was talking about. I hoped I didn't. I didn't like hearing that kind of despair coming from an eleven-year-old.

"About being a good man," Jimmy said.

Laura let out a small breath beside me.

"You see, I been thinking about it, and it seems to me that the better you are, the worse you get treated."

"I'm not following, sport," Sinkovich said.

"You know, like Mr. King," Jimmy said. "Smokey says he was one of the best, and they shot him."

My stomach clenched. I didn't want Jimmy to say any more about that. He wasn't even supposed to talk about the assassination.

"So Althea, she says I got to go to church, got to learn to be like Jesus, because he's the best man ever, and what did they do to him?" Jimmy stopped in front of Sinkovich.

Sinkovich looked like he wanted to be anywhere else, but, to his credit, he didn't back away from Jimmy.

"They killed him. Just like Mr. King."

"Jesus rose up," Sinkovich started.

"So what?" Jimmy said. "So what? Mr. King didn't. I wouldn't, if they killed me because I was so good."

Laura's hand slid down my arm, and into my hand. I clenched my fingers around hers.

"You don't know that, sport," Sinkovich said. "The Bible teaches that all good people will rise—"

"That's not what I'm talking about, and you know it." Jimmy's voice shook. "I'm talking about here. About now. What's the point of being good if they're just gonna shoot you for it?"

Sinkovich stared at him in dumbfounded shock. Marvella leaned back in her chair as if she didn't want to be in the room. Laura's hand quivered in mine.

My mouth was dry. Sinkovich had no idea what he was dealing with here. He had no idea that Jimmy had actually seen Martin get killed, had seen the greatest man this community had produced get his throat shot clean away—and worse, Jimmy had seen the man who had done it.

"Well, sport," Sinkovich said after a moment, "I mean, Jimmy. You don't know it, since you were doing it to be a big man, but you probably asked the only person in the room who's also been thinkin' about the same thing."

Jimmy blinked at him in surprise. I had no idea what Jimmy had expected—probably platitudes or clichés—but he obviously hadn't expected Sinkovich to take him seriously.

"I ain't been the best person I could be," Sinkovich said. "Not by a long shot. And one day, I woke up, thought, I don't like who I am no more, and so started living the way I think I should live. Thing is, people don't like that. My wife, she took our kid away because she don't like the new me. My boss, he says I'm going rogue. My friends, they say they don't know me no more."

"So why do it?" The challenge was gone from Jimmy's voice, replaced with curiosity.

Sinkovich shrugged. "It's a good question. I been asking it a lot myself. And what I come up with is this: I do what I can live with. And I couldn't live with the way I was before."

Jimmy frowned. The rest of us were so silent, I couldn't hear us breathe.

Sinkovich looked almost naked as he waited for Jimmy's response.

"I don't get it," Jimmy said. "If you do what you think is best, how come other people'll—like your wife. How come she don't love you no more?"

"I didn't say that, sport. I said she's mad at me. Different thing."

"So how come she's mad?" Jimmy asked.

"Because maybe when I looked in the mirror and really saw myself, and started to change," Sinkovich said, "maybe by accident, I was holding up a mirror and forcin' her to look at herself, and maybe she didn't like what she saw."

"Why would that make her mad at you?" Jimmy asked.

"Maybe she didn't want to change," Sinkovich said. "Obviously, she could live with the things the way they was. Maybe she even liked it that way. And then I started messin' with it."

"Like Mr. King," Jimmy said.

"Only he wasn't takin' on just one family, Jim, or one little corner of Chicago. He was takin' on everybody. The way we all grew up. He had the biggest damn mirror in the country, and when we looked in it, what we saw was some kinda ugly."

"But he couldn't live with himself if he didn't do something?" Jimmy asked.

"I think that's probably right," Sinkovich said. "I'd be the last guy to speak for him, but I would guess you probably got it in one."

Jimmy looked at me. His eyes were red rimmed, but I wasn't sure if that was because of what Sinkovich said or because he had been crying in his room. "You think that's true, Smokey? About Mr. King?"

"Dr. King," I said, because I couldn't help myself. "And yeah, I think Jack's exactly right."

Sinkovich shot me a grateful look.

Jimmy grunted, apparently satisfied with that. He walked toward the kitchen, grabbed my plate off the table, and then turned to Sinkovich again.

"You want some pizza?" he asked.

Sinkovich grinned. "Thought you was never gonna ask."

"That's some kind of kid you have," Sinkovich said to me an hour later.

We were in my office with the door closed, and the fan blowing muggy air around the tiny space. Marvella had gone home, and Laura was reading to Jimmy in the living room.

I had peeked out there before Sinkovich and I got started to make sure everything was all right. They were sitting on the couch, Laura holding the book, and Jim cuddled up against her, his legs tucked beneath him, looking younger than his eleven years.

"Yeah," I said to Sinkovich. "He constantly amazes me."

"Well, you gotta tell me what you been feedin' him, because the last thing I want is for my kid to ambush me like that someday. Jeez, talk about thinkin' on your feet."

"You did fine," I said, and hoped it didn't sound patronizing. Actually, Sinkovich had done a lot better with Jimmy's questions than I would have.

"Moments like that I'm scared I'm gonna miss with my kid, you know?" Sinkovich's cheeks turned pink. He looked at the open window, even though there wasn't much of a view.

Sinkovich's wife had taken his son to her parents' vacation home in Michigan, and started divorce proceedings. He wanted custody of his son, but knew he didn't have much of a chance—not with his job, his performance record, and the hours he had to keep. He couldn't really afford an attorney, either, but he hired one anyway, one that at least promised him joint custody and a minimum of alimony.

"Well." Sinkovich clapped his hands together with a false bravado. "Let's talk about this list you got."

I handed him the tenant list that Laura had brought. "I haven't had a chance to go over this," I said, "but it's the list of the most recent paying tenants."

"Interesting choice of words," Sinkovich said. "You got non-paying tenants?"

"We've had squatters in all of the buildings I've been inspecting. You know that, before Laura took over, Sturdy was considered one of the biggest slumlords in the city."

"I know it still is," Sinkovich said. "Rumor is it's letting buildings fall down so that it can bulldoze them, and build something more profitable at the site."

"I don't know how anything can be more profitable," I said. "They charge three times the rent charged anywhere else for places they don't fix up."

"I been hearing they want some of that model cities money that Mayor Daley's dishing out."

No wonder the management team put in by Laura's father had fought her so hard for control. I wondered how much of that money they had planned on pocketing.

"Doesn't matter," I said. "It's not going to happen now."

"I'd be shocked if one broad can change the corporate culture," Sinkovich said.

"You've met the broad in question," I said. "She's tough."

"She'd have to have brass ones to pull this off." He scanned the list. "Don't see no names that ring any bells."

He flipped to the second page. I started to look as well. The names were arranged by apartment number. Often each number had only one name behind it, which, I would assume, was the person who actually signed the lease.

"Wait," he said. "Here are a few. Coupla small-time hoods, some dealers I know. Mostly guys."

I looked up from my list. "You sound disappointed."

"Naw, not disappointed." Sinkovich flicked the list with his fingertips. "Just don't know how relevant this is, that's all."

"What do you mean?"

"I didn't tell you because of your kid and all—you know, this ain't dinner-party conversation—but the coroner, he didn't find nothing."

"Didn't find anything?" I asked. "The corpse wasn't human, then?"

"Oh, yeah," he said. "It was human. Probably male, judging by the pelvic area, though on something that young . . ."

"How young?"

"Few days at most. Maybe not even. Coroner couldn't exactly tell with what was there. He can't, of course, give me nothing official because that takes time. He don't think he's gonna get much more anyway—it's not like someone's gonna come forward and confess or nothing."

"What did he find?" I asked.

"Not a whole hell of a lot," Sinkovich said. "He dug up the rest of the body, and we got a skull, some skin, not a lot of much else. He took the dirt with him, which was pretty easy, considering it was in that bowl thing."

"The window well," I said. "I thought it was a flower bed yesterday. There were even some dead flowers on top."

Sinkovich frowned at me. "You didn't say nothing about that."

"We didn't have a lot of time to talk this afternoon."

"Here's the problem." He templed his fingers and looked at me, like a doctor about to make a diagnosis. "The baby's got no obvious trauma, and unless we find something in the house, we might not find what it died of. I mean, coulda been natural causes. Lots of these kids starve, and the parents ain't got enough money for a proper burial, or they're afraid we'll call welfare—which we will—and take the other kids from them. So they don't do nothing. They bury the kid in the backyard, or the front yard in this case, and just go on with their lives."

I tried not to think about that tiny form in the dirt, the jumper that meant someone cared just a little, the flowers on top of the makeshift grave, meaning that someone had tried to honor the child beneath.

"I mean," Sinkovich said into my silence, "it's not like the parents—usually the mom—don't try, it's just that she ain't got no hope in hell, especially if she ain't gettin' enough food. Formula's expensive, and if she's starvin', she can't breast-feed."

My mind flashed on Helen's excessively thin arms as she clutched her daughter to her side.

"And these little guys, we think they're tough, you know, can make it through anything." Sinkovich folded the list once, then twice, then a third time, his fingers creasing it. "But if the mom's had a few kids already, and ain't well-nourished herself, the kid's weak coming in. Then there's no food, and maybe even no heat, and the child ain't got no chance at all, no matter what the parent does."

I had known that, deep down. I had known it, but I hadn't completely understood it. "What's police procedure in cases like this?"

"No obvious sign of trauma on the corpse," he said. "No way to know how the kid died without talkin' to someone. I doubt, since there ain't much of this corpse left, the coroner's gonna find anything."

"Right," I said.

"We don't assume, just because we found the kid in a window well, that he's a murder victim. We get too many of these things."

I felt cold, despite the room's mugginess. "What's next, then?"

Sinkovich folded the list in half again, using his thumb and forefinger.

"Procedure is first we figure out if it's murder. In the cases of skeletal remains, we don't got a lot to go on. We look for bullet wounds or fractures or something like that. We don't got that here. Then we try to figure out if it's negligent homicide. The drug mothers, most of the time that's what it was. And then we decide if it's prosecutable."

That shiver ran through me again. "How do you figure that out?"

"Higher-ups usually make that decision. But mostly, we put these ladies away in some kind of mental-health place, detox 'em, at least the first time. Then if they have another kid, and the same thing happens, we put the bitch away for life."

"You'd let another child go through that?" I asked in spite of myself.

"First offense, tough to prove," Sinkovich said. "Even a public defender can handle one of those. Babies die for no reason all the damn time. I had a cousin, she had a perfectly healthy baby. Put it to bed one night, next morning she comes in and the baby's blue. They did a damn autopsy on that kid, at my cousin's insistence, and didn't find nothing. The kid just stopped breathing for no apparent reason. And this was in a nice, middle-class house where the kid was fed regular. It's a lot worse in places like this, where there's rats the size of dogs and bugs everywhere, and filth in the fuckin' air."

This time, I slid back in my chair. I'd understood LBJ's War on Poverty. I'd seen the kids outside of Memphis with the bloated stomachs and the big eyes. I used to give money to the church relief programs, and donate food every Thanksgiving. But I never really thought about day-to-day living, not until I started inspecting houses for Laura.

Even then, I wasn't sure the reality of these lives penetrated. I did what I could and then walked away.

"We get a second offense," Sinkovich said. "You know, the second kid dies the same way—starving or something—we can prosecute. Usually, it don't come to that. Usually with the detox, we introduce these women—girls, really—to someone they can go to if they get pregnant again. If they're on dope, then they might not even remember the act what got 'em pregnant, and they're more than happy to give up the baby."

"What if they're not on dope?" I asked.

"Jesus." He shook his head. "Then it's usually something sad. Can't afford medicine for a kid with a fever, baby didn't breathe right from the minute it was born, that kinda thing. Most these women can't afford a hospital at all. They don't get care in the beginning, and they have the baby at home, in all that dirt. So the kid contracts something, dies, and then what? You can't afford to go to the doctor to have a baby, you sure as hell can't afford to bury the thing."

The pizza wasn't sitting too well in my stomach. "And the procedure?"

"Those cases?" Sinkovich crumpled the list, then realized what he had done. He smoothed it out again. "Depends. We always try to find out the whys, if we can, but we don't put a lot of effort into it. And if there's no evidence of wrongdoing, what're we gonna do? Charge them with illegally burying a corpse? It's a friggin' misdemeanor. What does that get us?"

I nodded toward the list. "So you didn't need this after all."

"I'm not plannin' to do much," Sinkovich said. "First off, I can't. Not with my life the way it is, and my standing at the job. But even if I could, I wouldn't. Too much heartache for everyone. So I'll wait for the official coroner's report, if I ever get it, and maybe call one or two of these people on the list, then, you know, something else'll come up."

I nodded, feeling sadder than I had in days.

"You gotta let this one go, Bill."

I started. I wasn't sure he had ever used my first name before.

"I learnt that from early on," Sinkovich said. "That's why cops get so hard, especially those what work in the bad parts of town. You can't think about the kid."

"Someone has to," I said.

"Sure, and you are," Sinkovich said. "You're gonna take him when the coroner's done, and you're gonna make sure he gets a nice little funeral. And that's what you can do. Because there ain't no justice in this one. Not for him, not for you, certainly not for his family."

I stood up. I couldn't sit any longer. The room seemed tighter and closer than it had before.

"You gotta concentrate on the living." Sinkovich shoved the crumpled paper into his pants pocket. "My old partner told me that first time we came across one of these. Pissed me off royal back then, but he was right. You gotta concentrate on the ones that's left."

I shoved my hands in my pockets, not sure I truly agreed with him.

"Look, I'll make good case notes. I'll go over that list, give this a little time. Maybe we can put a name on that grave you'll be payin' for. But that's probably the most we can hope for, and we may not want even that."

He stood and clapped a hand on my back.

"Sorry, Grimshaw," he said, and let himself out of my office.

I continued to stand there for a moment. I heard him talking to Laura in the living room, their voices soft, but I couldn't hear Jimmy.

Looking out for the living. Wasn't that what I was doing with Jimmy, when he actually held the secret to Martin's death? Martin was a great man, but he was gone. And if I put Jimmy out there so that he could testify against unknown men, he might not survive the week.

Looking out for the living.

It sounded easier than it actually was. There was no justice in it, only survival.

But sometimes, survival was all we had.

EIGHTEEN

The next morning, Franklin had driving duties. He picked Jimmy up at seven-thirty, and I was left alone to face a new day.

I hadn't slept well. Sinkovich's words echoed in my mind, and I felt like I was missing something important. Laura had not stayed. We didn't sleep together around Jimmy, something we had never discussed. It had simply become a habit which neither of us questioned.

I found it fascinating; in some ways, we were more old-fashioned than we cared to admit.

I cleaned up the breakfast dishes, and made a grocery list, since we were out of nearly everything except beer. Sinkovich had left his Old Milwaukee behind—*Grimshaw,* he'd said with a grin, *some of your snobby friends might actually enjoy a brewski instead of that hoity-toity stuff you keep around here*—and try as I might, I couldn't get him to take his brewskis home.

When I finished the list, I wandered into my office and stared at the paper Laura had given me the night before. Her list was shorter than either of Marvella's, but none of the names overlapped. Since Laura had clarified Marvella's reasons for wanting this investigation—her fear that Valentina, even if she came out of the coma, would never tell her who this butcher was—everything seemed clearer to me.

I also realized that I might be investigating these names and others for a long time.

The night before, Marvella, Laura, and I had brainstormed ways for me to approach people to find out who some of the other abortionists were in Chicago and the surrounding areas. The women had devised an entire script for me, which, after my encounter with the teenagers near the Castle Church, made a lot of sense to me.

I planned to use the script that afternoon, as I started digging into the rest of the names and searching for the ones who had changed location. My first plan, however, was to do the most simple thing in the world. I was going to go through the phone book, looking for the names on the two lists.

Sometimes the most obvious method was the one that worked.

But first I had some household errands to complete, and I would use the morning to finish those before spending my afternoon on Marvella's case.

After I cleaned up the kitchen, I called Chicagoland Southside Insurance. They owed a check for the two reports I had finished for them, and they had more work for me as well. I put off the work for another week, but did tell them I would stop by for the check.

By early afternoon, I had Southside's check in my wallet and was unloading groceries out of my Impala. As I did, I toyed with the idea of going to the hospital to check on Valentina Wilson. She, more than Marvella and Laura, was my motivation for this case.

It was the second stormy day in a row. Even though the weather wasn't as muggy as it had been the day before, thunderstorms had rolled through with amazing regularity, shaking buildings, and dropping sheets of rain for fifteen minutes before stopping.

I had avoided getting drenched, mostly by waiting out the storms, but the ground was covered with large puddles. By the time I got to my apartment building, my cuffs and shoes were soaked.

As I crossed the porch, thunder boomed again and lightning zigzagged across the sky. A few drops of rain splattered on the sidewalk behind me, so loud that they sounded like slaps.

I knew what was coming next. I hurried inside as the heavens opened for the fifth time that day.

Even though I moved quickly, I still got wet. I shook off at the entry, checked the mailbox, and found only an advertising circular. Then I started up the staircase.

As my eyes adjusted to the dim indoor light, I realized someone was sitting at the top of the stairs. I frowned, wondering what was going on, and then I recognized Jack Sinkovich.

He looked as bedraggled as I felt. His clothing was soaked. He had been sitting in the same spot long enough to create a puddle of his own. His hair was plastered to his skull, and he looked grim.

"Bad news?" I asked.

"You haven't heard, then?" His voice was flat.

I shook my head, balancing the groceries in one arm and fishing for my keys. "Did the coroner find something on the baby? I thought he wasn't even getting to the case for weeks."

"No," Sinkovich said. "It's not the baby."

Something in his tone made me stop. I was still six steps from the top, so that we were able to look at each other face-to-face.

He looked like he had lost fifteen pounds overnight. His eyes were blood-shot, and his cheeks were hollow. He hadn't even looked this bad the night his wife threw him out of the house.

"It's not Jimmy, is it?" I asked.

Sinkovich shook his head.

"Laura?" I didn't like how my voice sounded. Strangled, frightened. Not my voice at all.

"I figured no one would tell you," Sinkovich said. "So I come over soon as I heard. Get your rain gear. I'll tell you on the way."

My mind was still running scenarios. What would get Jack Sinkovich to my front door because he was concerned about me?

I couldn't come up with anything.

"Tell me first," I said.

He studied me for a long moment, then said, "They found Johnson."

Whatever I had expected him to say, it wasn't that. "Truman Johnson?"

"Yeah."

"Found him?" I said. "I didn't know he was missing."

"They found him," Sinkovich said again, "outside Greenwood's Tavern on the Gaza Strip. He'd been shot."

I felt a surge of adrenaline "Where'd they take him?"

"Nowhere yet," Sinkovich said.

It took a moment for his words to sink in. "He's dead?"

Sinkovich nodded.

I had to struggle with the grocery bag to keep from dropping it. "Who did it?"

"They don't know." But his tone said that someone did.

"They have a guess, though, right?"

"Grimshaw, he was shot on the Gaza Strip. Outside of Greenwood's. Of course they got a hunch."

I felt slightly dizzy, as if I had forgotten to breathe. "They think it was a gang hit? On Truman?"

"All I know is what I got from dispatch, and it's got all the markings."

"Why would the gangs gun for him?" I asked.

"Dunno," Sinkovich said.

My mind flashed on Truman Johnson, sitting in that smoke-hazed waiting room, his hands clenched between his knees.

"This can't be right," I said. "He wasn't even working this week."

"It's him, Bill." Sinkovich stood. His clothing dripped onto the fine old wood. "Get your rain gear. I'm taking you down there."

NINETEEN

They called the neighborhood around Sixty-fifth Street and Woodlawn the Gaza Strip because it was the most hotly disputed gang territory in Chicago. The Blackstone Rangers ruled all of the South Side to the east, and the East Side Disciples ruled the west.

Their territories met at Sixty-fifth and Woodlawn, which was often no-man's land. Lately, I had heard, it had become Stones territory, but who knew how long that would last. When I had first heard of the Gaza Strip last summer, it had been in the hands of King David and his Disciples.

No one went down there without a good reason. No one in his right mind, not cop, not working adult, passed through, no one except teenagers bent on destruction. A lot of gang murder victims were found there—killed somewhere else and dragged into a gutter at the disputed turf near Sixty-fifth and Woodlawn.

But that wasn't what crossed my mind as Sinkovich drove us south from my apartment in his beat-up Ford. What went through my mind was Johnson, the man I had known. The man I had worked with on two separate occasions.

He may have been difficult, but he was a good cop. And good cop rule number one was to never venture into gang country all alone.

Twice Sinkovich had to pull over as water poured from the sky, turning the streets into rivers. Sinkovich sat patiently, his hands on the wheel, while the car shivered and shook with the force of the rain.

He kept the radio off—whether to protect me or because he had no interest, I didn't know and didn't much care. As we got into the car, he turned his police band down, so all I could hear was the occasional crackle of static.

He was off duty, which gave him a certain amount of freedom. I asked—in the apartment, in the car, I wasn't sure which—if they minded our coming to the crime scene, and he said that he doubted it. Whenever a cop died, the others came as if it were a holy site.

It didn't feel as if we were traveling to a holy site to me. I felt shaken and slightly hollow, unable to believe that Johnson was dead. I had just seen him two days before—and we had parted badly.

What had he done then? Gone back to his desk?

"You're sure it's Truman?" I asked on one of our pullovers.

"Dispatch's been pretty clear," Sinkovich said.

"Gang country." I shook my head. "That doesn't sound like him."

But I wasn't sure who he was. We weren't really friends. I hadn't even known he was married—or divorced—until Sunday, and I knew even less about the rest of his family. I only had one sense of the man, a professional sense. And in the middle of that was a certain recklessness that had startled me.

Was that what had brought him to the Gaza Strip?

Sinkovich didn't say anything. He had been amazingly quiet since he followed me into my apartment. He had been the one who had put away my groceries, and had found my raincoat, along with a battered hat, which had probably once been Franklin's since I didn't recognize it. Sinkovich even found some galoshes, which I refused to wear. My shoes were already wet. I didn't need to risk another pair on this weather, even with protective rubber around them.

While Sinkovich searched for my gear, I called Franklin and just managed to catch him before he left the office. I asked him to keep Jimmy for the evening, feeling guilty the entire time.

I knew how important it was to be with Jimmy these days. I also knew that Franklin disapproved of the way I was taking care of Jim. This was just one more nail in that coffin.

As we waited out the rain, I realized I could have called Laura. She would have been happy to take Jimmy for the night. But relying on her had never been my first reflex. When I had first come to Chicago, she and I were estranged. I had never gotten into the habit of asking her first to step in on an emergency basis.

It took Sinkovich and I nearly a half an hour to get down to the Gaza Strip. I could have walked quicker in that driving rain, but I needed Sinkovich to get me on that crime scene.

I had a feeling—maybe it was a hope—that the body wasn't Johnson's, that someone had made a mistake. I would go in and disprove the initial claim, and then the investigation would go on from there.

The Gaza Strip looked like a war zone. Burned and gutted buildings—not from riots, but from everyday living, everyday fighting—covered both sides of the street. A few taverns remained open, as well as a pawn shop, and an all-night grocery with barred windows and doors.

The rain-created river on Woodlawn carried all sorts of trash in its waves—needles, crumpled paper, beer cans. No one seemed to care that so much stuff was floating toward the rain gutters, and disappearing into Chicago's sewers, maybe forever.

Sinkovich pulled up on the sidewalk not far from Greenwood's. It looked like a place that had long ago lost its soul. On one side, a burned building tumbled into itself. On the other, a three-story apartment building rose like the desiccated survivor of an unspeakable tragedy.

The police had set up a makeshift tarp tent over the crime scene, and official-looking people in official clothing were taking pictures inside, creating miniature lightning flashes that echoed the large ones still splitting the sky.

I counted five official cop cars, parked in a U so that no one could get around them. Another half a dozen cars parked haphazardly on the street, lights on, flashers creating red reflections in the muddy water.

Some rusted cars were parked against the far side of the street, reminders of what the neighborhood really was. A woman with mottled skin, wearing nothing more than a robe, smoked a cigarette on the balcony of the building across the street, and watched the proceedings as if they were a TV movie. A few other people peeked through windows.

But the only people on the street were the police themselves, some in uniform, most not.

Before we got out, Sinkovich said, "Stay close. If you don't say anything, they'll think you're from my unit. Not everyone knows everyone down here."

I nodded, opened the door, and stepped across the stream that swirled toward the gutter. Cigarette butts, newspapers, and candy wrappers circled before they poured over the metal lip into the sewer below.

The rain had stopped, but the sound of it continued, since water dripped off everything, eaves, signs, doorways. The top of the makeshift tent sagged inward. A giant puddle had formed in the middle, threatening to collapse the entire thing.

Sinkovich led the way, and I kept pace beside him. As we splashed close to the tavern, my gaze caught something white in a nearby alley. I looked closely and saw the Gang Intelligence Unit's unmarked white van parked next to the tavern's back door.

"What're they doing here?" I asked Sinkovich, nodding toward the van.

"Gang killing," he said. "They're the specialists."

"I didn't know they specialized in homicide," I said.

"Everything to do with gangs," Sinkovich said. "And given the rise in killings lately, that's gotta include homicides."

His voice was soft. As we got closer to the site, walkie-talkies hissed and spit, interrupted conversations blaring through them like half-heard voices on distant radio stations.

No press had arrived yet. Even though Sinkovich had gotten the information from a dispatcher, the news hadn't gone out in a way that reporters would understand.

Either that, or they were afraid to come down to the Gaza Strip, even for a story.

I didn't recognize any of the officers guarding the site, nor did the detectives who were conferring near one of the squad cars look familiar.

Sinkovich's face formed into hard lines as he watched someone he knew, but he didn't say anything to me. I wondered if he would when we returned to the car.

The water wasn't as deep here. The sidewalk was wet and covered with puddles, but nothing ran. Still, any evidence that had been here was long gone. I hoped the crime-scene technicians had arrived soon enough to find something. Not even a tent would have protected the site from such an onslaught.

Sinkovich only had to show his badge once as we approached the tent, and that was to a new officer who got a reprimand from his partner for asking. A number of the cops greeted Sinkovich in lackluster tones—*Hey, Sink; Hell of a thing, Sink; What've you been downgraded to, shitholes these days, Sink?*

Sinkovich answered it all with grunts and nods. If I hadn't known how well he paid attention to things around him, I would have thought he didn't even know who was talking to him.

We stepped into the circle of cops lining the tent. The tavern door, down a flight of concrete steps, was open, and the smell of cigarettes and beer floated out as if it were trying to escape.

I peered over the iron railing into the tavern and saw mostly darkness. Neon lights flashed on a jukebox in the back, and candles burned in red bubbleglasses on a few tables. The bar was recessed, invisible from my vantage point, and the place looked empty. Not even cops had gone inside.

"Hey, Sink, ain't this dead guy the guy you partnered with on that bust down here?" someone asked.

Sinkovich didn't answer. He stepped past a uniformed officer who was watching the proceedings from the front of the makeshift tent.

"Sink?" said the same voice. I looked over, saw Chaz Yancy leaning against the tavern's brick wall. He wore black T-shirt with the sleeves torn off, revealing dark, muscular arms. The shirt blended into his black pants, which ended in black boots. "You knew this guy, right?"

Sinkovich looked up. "Have a little respect, Yancy."

Yancy's eyebrows went up when he saw me. "If it ain't the protective daddy from over to the elementary school."

He and I had had several run-ins when the Blackstone Rangers were trying to recruit Jimmy last winter. The Gang Intelligence Unit's white van had been parked outside the grade school during most of Jimmy's encounters, and the cops inside had watched as the teenage gang members tried to recruit from the ten- to twelve-year-olds.

Naïve me, I had thought the police would want to stop that sort of thing, but the Unit had some other, more important plan. Or so Yancy had told me.

"C'mon," Sinkovich said to me under his breath. He ducked out of Yancy's visual range, and so did I.

The uniform held the tent flap back for us, and we stepped inside.

The interior was crowded. Two photographers took pictures, their flashbulbs blinding in the close space. A detective crouched, writing on a notepad, and another man was taking measurements.

None of them seemed to be paying attention to the body on the sidewalk.

Truman Johnson looked smaller in death, so small in fact that for a moment I thought my fantasy was right, that it couldn't be Truman Johnson. Truman Johnson was an ex-linebacker going to fat, a man with so many muscles that they strained out of his clothing.

He wasn't that pile of flesh and bone and blood sprawled on the wet concrete, facedown, mouth open, eyes staring at nothing.

I recognized his shoes first, the same brown shoes he had worn in the hospital. Cop's shoes, comfortable and cheap, scuffed from too much use. One was bent in the middle, as if he had been taking a step when he fell forward. The other was twisted sideways in an unnatural position.

His pants were black, a pair I didn't recognize, and his shirt—what I could see of its natural color—was blue. His arms were flopped beside him, hands open. He hadn't even had time to reach for a gun.

A gun. I looked for it, didn't see it, but did see the shoulder holster that a man would normally wear beneath a coat.

"You see a gun?" I asked Sinkovich quietly.

He shook his head.

No gun, and for that matter, no coat. I crouched beside the body. The blue shirt was navy on the sleeves where the water had soaked it, sky blue on the collar untouched by anything, and purple on the back where there was shirt at all.

I made myself look away from the torso. I would give myself a moment before studying that. Instead, I looked at the face—really looked—and my fantasy of this being the wrong body, the wrong man, died.

The sightless eyes, chocolate brown, lacked the sharp intelligence they usually had. The mouth was open, pursed, as if he had fallen asleep in the middle of a conversation. But the features all belonged to Truman Johnson, a man who, no matter what he said, had helped me a lot more than I had helped him.

You gonna listen or not? he had said to me during that last conversation, so softly that I had to strain to hear him. There was anger in his voice where before there had been gratitude. He had been thinking about me all day, counting on me.

I have a proposition for you.

"You okay?" Sinkovich asked.

I blinked up at him, then nodded.

"They said there was a lot of blood. Mostly gone now."

I made myself look at the torso. There would have been a lot of blood.

The shirt was coated, gaping holes blown into—or perhaps out of—his skin. The blood had clotted black in some places, and in a few others, the shirt was blown outward, ragged and protective.

"What the hell happened?" I asked.

"Gang shooting," the detective across from me said. He was thin, white, with sandy hair and narrow, beady eyes.

"How does everyone know that?" I asked. Sinkovich put a hand on my shoulder. Apparently my frustration had found its way into my voice. "Location? Number of wounds? What?"

"Witnesses," the detective said and looked back at his pad, dismissing me. He probably thought of me as a friend, another member of the Afro-American Patrolmen's League, someone who lied to himself, saying he was coming here to help, when he was actually coming to confirm what he didn't want to know.

Actually, that wasn't too far from the truth.

"Where's the gun?" I asked again.

This time, no one answered. Sinkovich's hand tightened on my shoulder.

"Maybe we should let them do their jobs," he said quietly.

"Where's the gun?" I asked louder.

The detective looked up at me. "What gun?"

I pointed at the shoulder holster. "Truman's gun. He had to have one. He wouldn't be stupid enough to come down here without one."

"Haven't found it," the detective said.

"What about his coat?" I asked.

The detective frowned at Sinkovich. "Your friend gonna let me do my job or is he gonna kibitz?"

"C'mon, Bill," Sinkovich said, and I knew he used my first name, not out of sympathy like before, but because he didn't want to give everyone here too many clues as to my identity.

"You see, I figure that there's no reason to wear a harness like that if you're not going to wear a jacket over it," I said, resisting the urge to shake Sinkovich's hand off my shoulder. "So where's the gun and where's the jacket?"

"Dunno," the detective said as if I were asking directions to the nearest gas station. "Probably in his car."

"Probably in his car?" I said, my voice rising. "You're not going to check?"

Sinkovich tugged on my shoulder, pulling me to my feet. "We're leaving," he said.

"We got witnesses," the detective said. "We already know what happened."

"Care to enlighten me?" I asked.

"Not really," he said, and bent over his notebook a third time.

Sinkovich pulled me backward. I nearly tumbled into the uniformed officer still peering through the tent flap.

I shook Sinkovich off. "Just because they have witnesses, doesn't meant they shouldn't—"

"Not here," he said, pushing me out. "If I'd've known you were gonna go nutso on me, I wouldn't've brought you here."

"I haven't gone nutso," I said.

I looked at the uniformed officer, who couldn't have been more than twenty-five. He was a skinny redhead, his nose and cheeks dotted with freckles. His gaze met mine, and I recognized fear in his eyes.

"And," I said to that officer as if we had been conversing all along, "there's water on the roof of this crappy tent you guys put up. It's about to collapse, which won't do your crime scene any good."

"Like we have a crime scene." Chaz Yancy spoke from his position against the brick wall.

Another man stood beside him, wearing a conservative coat over the same black pants and black boots that Yancy wore. The man's skin was coffee-brown, set off by a wispy goatee that hung to his chest. He watched me with avid black eyes.

"I don't know what else you'd call it," I said to Yancy. "You have a body in there."

"And we've had more rain in the last hour than Noah saw during the flood," Yancy said. "If there was any evidence, it already got washed away."

"How come it wasn't collected?" I asked. "You've been here awhile."

"You sound mighty informed, Mr. Grimshaw." Yancy reached into the pocket of his T-shirt and removed a pack of cigarettes. "You know, you always show up at the most interesting places."

"So do you," I said. "And at all of them, you just watch. Do you ever work?"

"Bill." Sinkovich's whisper was urgent.

"What's your connection to Johnson, Grimshaw?" Yancy asked.

"I live across the hall from his cousin," I said.

"The luscious Marvella," said the man with the avid eyes. He had a nasal voice that grated on me. "You met her?"

"That woman's related to Johnson?" Yancy raised his eyebrows. "She's fine."

My fist clenched. Sinkovich grabbed my arm, as if he thought I was going to throw a punch.

But I wasn't going to. I wanted information more than I wanted to bash Yancy's head against the wall. "So who are these witnesses and what did they see?"

"Oddly enough, me and Jump." Yancy pulled a cigarette out of the open pack with his teeth. "We were near the van when the kids went by."

I wasn't sure I had heard him right. "Kids?"

"You know the drill, Grimshaw." Yancy slipped his lighter out of his pocket. "You're so smart about gangs."

"What're you talking about?"

"The hit." He flicked the lighter and a small flame burned blue. He

194

cupped his hand around the flame, leaned forward, and lit his cigarette without removing it from his mouth. Then he inhaled, let the lighter go out, and stuck it in his pocket. "Surely a man as smart as you knows about the hits."

"And this was a hit," said the man with the avid eyes, the man Yancy had called Jump.

I didn't even look at him. I had no idea who he was and I wasn't going to give him any attention, at least not yet.

Yancy exhaled lungfuls of smoke. "Two boys—maybe twelve, maybe younger—ride by on a bicycle. One is on the handlebars, the other is pedaling like his life depends on it. You see it every day, every neighborhood in the city."

The cigarette smoke floated toward me, ghostly white.

"No one thinks anything of it, two kids, going about their business. Not even down here. Me, I'm trained to look at them, and I see that Handlebars is holding something on his lap. I call out to Jump and we start up the alley."

"We shoulda got in the van," Jump said. "We weren't thinking."

"Now most folks wouldn't've even run. To them, it just looks like boys trying to make it home before the next storm hits." Yancy took another puff off his cigarette.

He was watching me closely, as if he were gauging my reaction. He seemed to enjoy telling this story.

"We make it to the mouth of the alley, just as your friend Johnson comes out of the bar. The bike blocks him, startles him, and the kid on the handlebars jumps off, and shoots him, point-blank, shotgun."

My breathing was shallow. I didn't move.

"We're running toward him, shouting," Jump said. "I've got my heat and we're gonna shoot—"

"But we never have a clear shot." Yancy took his cigarette out of his mouth, and tapped the ash on the ground. "The bike keeps going, like nothing's happened. The shooter runs for the curb. A car's waiting there. He gets inside, we're shooting like it's the O.K. Corral, and the car drives off, fishtailing in the wet."

"If we'd gotten the van, we might've been able to follow," Jump said.

"But there was no chance," Yancy said. "They turned off at the first corner, and disappeared."

"You could've gone after the bike." I was shaking. They were right here. Right here, and they didn't do anything.

"Jump here ran to the corner just in time to see the kid drive the bike into the back of a van. They were all gone in less than a minute."

"License plates?" I asked. "Descriptions?"

"Got them," Yancy said, taking another puff off the cigarette, "not that it'll do any good."

"Why not?" I asked.

"Chances are everything was stolen."

"But you haven't run it yet," I said. "You don't know."

"Shit, we haven't run anything yet. We've been here, first trying to save your friend there, not that he had a chance, and then trying to make sure the evidence didn't find itself in the Chicago River."

Yancy sounded annoyed for the first time since I started questioning him. He finished his cigarette and stubbed it out on the brick wall.

I was trying to process the information. "These kids, they're a hit squad?"

"It's a great method," Jump said with more admiration than I liked. "The Main 21 doesn't get blamed at all. It's just children running wild."

"They get paid, usually in candy bars or toys, something they really want," Yancy said. "A lower-down sets the kids up, sometimes even gives them the bike, shows them how to use the gun, and the kids go after their marks, at least until they get arrested and new kids get recruited."

Fury ran through me thick and fine. "They're twelve?"

"Or younger." Yancy's gaze was flat as it met mine.

"How long have you known about this?" I asked.

"This shooting or this trick?"

"This so-called hit squad?" I asked.

"Years. They've been doing it in one form or another for years." Yancy flipped the lighter over in his hand.

Some of the other cops had gathered around us, watching us instead of taking care of the crime scene.

"Years," I repeated. "So when the Stones were trying to recruit my son in December, and you advised me to leave them all alone, you knew about this?"

"Sure." Yancy smiled, his gold front tooth looking dull in the dim light.

"They could've taught my kid to be a killer and you didn't fucking care?" My voice was going up again.

"I care, Mr. Grimshaw," Yancy said. "I just figure there isn't much I can do one-on-one."

"That's for damn sure," I said. "That's a friend of mine on the ground over there, and you didn't do anything."

Yancy's smile left his face. "We tried to stop it. We came out of the alley—"

"The moment you saw the bike, right," I said, not believing him. "You didn't come out until you heard the shotgun blast. You didn't see any car get away, and you didn't run to the curb. You didn't even try to do anything to help Truman."

Yancy took a step toward me. Sinkovich tried to move between us, but I wouldn't let him.

"What the hell do you know?" Yancy asked.

"I know what I see," I said, "and I see a lot of discrepancies in your story."

"Oh, really?" Yancy asked.

"Don't do this, Bill," Sinkovich said so softly I wasn't sure if anyone else could hear him.

"Really," I said, ignoring Sinkovich. "First of all, for a boy to jump off a bike and keep his balance, the bike has to be going relatively slowly. If you were at the mouth of the alley . . ."

I swept my hand toward it.

". . . then you weren't that far away. Any man could have caught up with the bike rider before he reached the corner, grabbed the back of the bike, and stopped him."

"You weren't here, Grimshaw," Yancy said. "You don't know what the hell you're talking about."

Two of the uniforms, though, looked at the alley and then at the corner. Then they glanced at me. Both of them looked pale.

"Secondly," I said, "neither of you have a drop of blood on you. If you tried to help Truman like you say you did, then you'd be spattered."

"It fucking poured, man," Jump said.

"Yeah, it did," I said, "and you're not even wet. Explain that to me."

"Who the hell is this guy?" Jump asked Yancy. "Internal Affairs?"

"C'mon," Sinkovich said. "You're upset. Let's go."

"You're right, Jack, I am upset," I said. "There are a lot of questions that I can see that none of these so-called trained professionals seem to care about."

Yancy was ignoring Jump and Sinkovich. He was staring at me. "You think you're so goddamn smart. I've never liked that about you."

"You don't know me," I said, "but you'll get to know me if you don't work on solving this murder."

"We've done what we can. It's Homicide's now."

I nodded. "And you're going to tell them why you're not carrying the guns you allegedly used to shoot at the car and the van?"

"The first officers on the scene confiscated our weapons." Yancy's entire face was only a few inches from mine. "Just like they're supposed to."

I nodded toward his tight clothing. "Where did you carry the weapon? I don't see any holster. Did you have it stuck down your pants?"

One of the officers behind me snorted, then put a hand over his mouth as if he hadn't reacted at all. Yancy's gaze flicked toward him, and the officer let his hand drop.

"I was carrying it. In my hand."

"I see," I said. "You had time to get your weapon from wherever you keep it, but you didn't have time to get to the scene to save Johnson."

"I already had it," Yancy said.

"Oh?" I asked. "Why? Was something else happening?"

He poked a finger into my breastbone. His fingernail was long and sharp against my skin.

"You're just a civilian," he said. "Illegally on a crime scene. I can make your life hell."

"Are you threatening me because I questioned your behavior?" I asked. "Or because you're lying?"

He shoved me and I shoved back. Sinkovich got between us. Two uniforms grabbed my arms and held them tightly. Yancy came at me again, and I kicked him, missing his balls, which I was aiming for, and getting his thigh.

He staggered backward.

"Come at me again," I said, "and I know you're lying."

"Stop it." Sinkovich moved away from me and put a hand on Yancy's chest. "This doesn't solve anything. Grimshaw's upset about Johnson's death. He doesn't know what he's saying."

"Oh, yes, I do," I said.

"He's a goddamn asshole," Yancy said, pushing against Sinkovich's hand. "He thinks he knows everything."

"All I know," I said, "is that you're covering something up, probably your own incompetence. You can't be a hero all the time, Yancy."

"I'm not trying to be a fucking hero." Yancy was still pushing at Sinkovich, but not as hard as before. "I'm not the only witness, you know."

"Yeah, you and your friend here with the interesting name."

"That's Sergeant to you, asshole," Jump said, giving me at least his rank. Next, I would try to get his real name.

"Not just us," Yancy said. "There were people in the bar, and a few on the street. They're being interviewed. They saw the whole thing."

"And if they're from this neighborhood, they're not going to identify anyone because they don't dare. The last thing they want to do is get between the Red Squad and the Stones," I said, using the derogatory name the black community called the Gang Intelligence Unit.

"You can question every fucking thing I've done," Yancy said, pointing his finger at me over Sinkovich's shoulder. "But my word is gold around here. I'm clean. I'm not the one who makes deals with gangs."

Everyone looked at me, including Sinkovich, as if I had suddenly sprouted a red sun on my head.

I knew what Yancy was referring to, and I wasn't going to go into a long defense. There wasn't much I could say that would be useful or would put me in a good light.

"I told them to leave my son alone," I said. "They have."

"They don't listen to anyone. You gave them something," Yancy said. "You gave them us."

My eyes narrowed, but I didn't know how to respond. On the afternoon I met with some of the members of the Blackstone Rangers Main 21 leadership, I had seen the Gang Intelligence Unit van a few blocks away. I had used the van as proof that I knew what I was talking about. In exchange for leaving Jimmy alone, the Stones wanted me to provide them with information. I made something up, something plausible, giving them the impression that I would filter more information to them when I had it.

I found it curious that Yancy knew I had made that promise.

"If I had given them you," I said, "you wouldn't be standing here."

Yancy stared at me for a moment, then shoved Sinkovich's hand away and stalked off. Jump followed, with a nervous glance at me over his shoulder.

The uniforms continued to hold me. I didn't struggle.

"What the hell are you doing?" Sinkovich wasn't even trying to keep his voice down. "Do you even know what kind of people you're pissing off?"

"You gonna take a swing at me?" I asked him.

Sinkovich looked confused, as if he didn't know what I was talking about.

"Because if you're not," I said, "I'd like the use of my arms again."

"If you fuckin' stay here and don't go pissing off any more people. Jesus, Grimshaw." Sinkovich shook his head.

The uniforms seemed confused since Sinkovich did not give them a direct order. After a moment, the guy on the right released my arm. I moved it, flexing it, and the guy on the left let go, almost like he was afraid I would hit him.

"We've got to figure out who exactly is in charge of this investigation," I said to Sinkovich, "because it stinks."

"I don't know how you can say that," he said. "For crissakes, Bill, he's still lying there. No one's double-checked the statements, sure, but the wounds match up. And so does the story. Everyone knows about the assassin squads."

"I didn't," I said.

"But you knew they recruited kids, sometimes taught them to kill."

"I didn't know it was so organized," I said.

Sinkovich opened his hands as if he were appealing to a higher power. "I swear to Christ, you're ignorant sometimes."

"And you have the ability to close your eyes at the exact wrong time." I moved closer to him. The uniforms still crowded us, listening, maybe, or perhaps they were protecting Sinkovich from the large, pissed-off black male they suddenly found in their midst.

"There could be a thousand reasons for those things you say are important," Sinkovich said.

"All right," I said. "What if I give you that?"

"What do you mean?"

"Let's say I believe them."

"Okay," Sinkovich said. "Then there's nothing."

"There's everything," I said. "Think about it, Jack. If those boys were truly assassins, they were gunning for Truman. They knew he was going to be here."

Sinkovich's gaze met mine. He shook his head slightly.

No one else around us spoke.

"And somehow," I added, "they knew when he'd be standing right outside."

TWENTY

"You can't know that," Sinkovich said.

"I can't?" I asked. "It's logical, Jack. If these boys are coming by to do a hit on a bicycle, they're not going to come inside a bar, especially one in a basement. The hit doesn't work that way. Imagine a twelve-year-old walking in, carrying a shotgun. Everyone would see him, everyone knows they're in the Gaza Strip, and everyone would duck."

"Shit," someone whispered behind me.

"So unless you're going to try to convince me that this is a random event, that little boys on bicycles just shoot passersby for sport, and have getaway cars waiting for them on the same block where the so-called random shooting takes place, then I'm saying this was a setup."

Sinkovich looked over at Yancy and Jump, who were talking to a thin white man at the mouth of the alley. I didn't recognize him, couldn't even tell if he was a police officer since he was wearing brown pants and a white shirt with the sleeves rolled up.

They glanced at me once, then continued their discussion.

Sinkovich turned back to me. He scanned the cops standing around us. His lips were thin with fury and there were two bright spots of color on his cheeks.

"We're getting the hell out of here," he said to me.

"You can leave if you want to," I said, "but I'm staying."

"For what?" he asked.

"There's a few things I want to check out," I said.

"Why?"

"Because," I said, "I owe Truman."

"Well, I sure as hell don't," Sinkovich said, "and I'm the one with the car, so you're leaving with me."

"I'll catch you later, Jack," I said, and headed toward the tavern.

No one flanked me. No one seemed to care that I was still inside the police lines. The coroner's truck had arrived, and several uniforms were scrambling to their own cars, trying to move them so that the coroner could get close to the body.

I wanted to look at Johnson's body one last time, but knew, now that the coroner was here, that I wouldn't get the chance.

Instead, I walked down the steps into the tavern itself.

Greenwood's, like so many taverns in Chicago, was built below street level. The floors above had once been stores or a restaurant or storage. It was impossible to tell now, with the door that led to the upper level sealed off. But the tavern door was still open. The candles still burned in the red bubble glasses, and the jukebox's flashing lights invited me to pick my favorite song.

The place was silent, though—no radio playing, no voices. The silence was unnerving in a place that should have been filled with conversation.

I stepped inside. The smell of beer was stronger here, and the cigarette odor, while present, had faded—especially compared to Yancy's fresh smoke. A Budweiser sign was lit up in the back corner, and someone had pasted posters of alpine meadows on the brick wall beside the door where a window would have been if the bar was farther above ground.

I heard footsteps behind me and turned quickly. Sinkovich came down the stairs two at a time, his jaw set.

"I ain't never doin' you another goddamn favor," he said as he came up beside me.

A third man hovered near the top of the stairs. Aside from Yancy and Jump of the Gang Intelligence Unit, he was the only other black man on the site. He wore a uniform that was rumpled and rain-spotted. His hair had lost its straightening oil to the storm, and was beginning to sprout tight curls.

He peered down at us as if he couldn't see us clearly in the tavern's darkened interior.

I moved Sinkovich away from the door.

"What're you doin' in here?" he asked.

"Looking around," I said.

He glanced up the stairs. "Can't even see the street from in here."

"That's how it's designed," I said. "So that you can forget about the world."

"Who the hell would come here, right here on the Gaza Strip?"

I didn't answer him. I was certain there were regulars who felt comfortable here or perhaps the tavern itself was a gang hangout. I wasn't going to make any assumptions.

Still, the interior was nicer than I expected it to be. The tables were all polished wood, and they had expensive cutglass ashtrays next to those candles.

Around a glass brick divider just inside the door stood a coat tree, and on it were two denim jackets and a man's suit jacket, black and large. I left it alone for a moment, not wanting to draw attention to it, and walked deeper into the tavern.

The fresh scent of lemons cut the beer smell the closer I got to the bar itself. I blinked as my eyes adjusted to the dimness, and saw a black man behind the well. He was trim, broad-shouldered, and narrow-hipped, which made him look younger than he was. I suspected he was my age, even though he looked about thirty.

He wore a green bowling shirt with *Greenwood's* on the breast pocket. He had twisted himself so that he wasn't visible from the doorway, and his back was protected by a stack of glasses piled nearly three feet high.

He was cutting lemons with a very small, very sharp knife.

"Excuse me," I said. "You been here all afternoon?"

"Not like I'm able to leave," he said with just a touch of bitterness.

"Is this your bar?"

"Part of it," he said.

"Which part?" I asked.

He shrugged. "My brother and I inherited it from our dad."

"So you saw what happened this afternoon," I said.

He picked up the cutting board and slid the lemon slices into a bowl near the well. He didn't look at me as he answered. "I didn't see nothing."

"Heard it, then?" I asked.

"The jukebox was on. Modern shit. Always too loud for my tastes." He picked up a lime and started to slice it, the knife narrowly missing his fingertips.

"A shotgun blast and you couldn't hear it?"

This time he looked up. His eyes were bloodshot. "My dad left this place to me and my brother," he said. "That's all he left. And despite the neighborhood, business is good. Especially on the weekends."

I sat on one of the stools and wiped my hand across the bar's polished wood surface. "The man lying facedown out there is a friend of mine."

"I'm sorry, man," the bartender said, although it didn't sound as if he meant it.

"There's something strange about what went down," I said.

He shrugged.

Sinkovich prowled the tables, pacing, guarding my back and obviously waiting for me to finish, all at the same time.

"You know that the guy who died today was a cop," I said.

The bartender picked up the cutting board and shoved the lime slices into a different bowl. "Not the first time this year that's happened around here. They never get resolved, neither, even though we all know what's going on."

"What is going on?" I asked.

He looked at me as if I were crazy. Sinkovich stopped pacing.

I held out my hands. "I'm not a cop. You won't get in trouble for talking to me."

The bartender shook his head. "It's not trouble I'm worried about, man. Not on this one."

He looked past me at Sinkovich.

"It's a goddamn war, Bill," Sinkovich said. "Thought you knew that."

"Between the Disciples and the Stones, sure," I said.

Sinkovich glanced at the door before saying anything. "Between some of the cops and the gangs," he said, his voice very low.

"Some of the cops?" I asked.

"Christmas Day," the bartender said, "found one cop wounded at the Southmoor Hotel. He wouldn't say what happened."

The Southmoor Hotel was one of the Stones' headquarters.

"But the next week, eight Stones were picked up by cops at various times, driven across the Gaza Strip into Disciples' territory, and pushed out of the cars. The cops told them to walk home." The bartender set his knife down. "They never made it."

I looked at Sinkovich. He looked down.

"You think Truman was connected to all this?" I asked him.

Sinkovich shrugged. "I don't know what he worked on. We're from different precincts."

"Had you ever seen him before?" I asked the bartender.

"The guy that was shot?" he asked.

"Yeah," I said.

"No." The bartender set the knife in the sink, turned on the water, and scrubbed his hands. Then he wiped them on a bar towel.

"Do you still have his gun?" I asked.

Sinkovich's eyes widened. The bartender started, then tried to cover the movement by shifting some glasses around.

"What are you talking about?" The bartender's voice was slightly higher pitched than it had been before.

"Well," I said as I got off the bar stool. "He came in here, took off his coat and hung it on the coat tree, just like he had been told to do. He's still wearing his shoulder holster. It was there when he died."

Sinkovich stared at me. The bartender kept his head down. He used the bar rag to wipe off already clean glasses.

"The gun is visible, which isn't that much of a problem here because you're used to weaponry. You have to be, to keep this place open."

Sinkovich tilted his head, as if I were a fascinating bug. The bartender turned his back on me and put the glasses on top of the pile. But he was listening. He was listening closely. He just knew he couldn't hide his expression from me, so he wouldn't let me see his face.

"Still, you mention the gun, and he says it's okay because he's a cop."

The bartender stopped moving.

"Then the guy he's meeting comes in. They talk for a minute, while they're at the bar. You offer them drinks, and before they order, they both put their guns on the bar itself. One of them asks you to hold the guns until they're done—a gesture of good faith—which you agree to do because you've done it before."

The bartender turned around. He looked shocked.

"So why don't you give the gun to me?" I asked. "Because if you don't, someone's gonna take it, file off the serial numbers, and use it on some poor unsuspecting kid down here. You know it, and I know it."

I wasn't going to accuse him of wanting to pawn the gun. I was certain that hadn't crossed his mind—yet. Although it would when the cops didn't press him for the weapon.

"You said you're not a cop," the bartender said.

"I'm not," I said. "I'm a friend, so I actually have an interest in solving this."

The bartender glanced sideways at Sinkovich. "You a cop?"

"Maybe not after today," he said.

"Why don't you get me two evidence bags, Jack?" I said.

"What?"

"It'll only take you a minute," I said.

"I don't think I should leave you—"

"I've already caused my trouble for the afternoon," I said, deliberately misunderstanding him. "If you get me the bags, you can take the gun and Truman's coat to property, put it in a box, and retrieve it if we need it for evidence."

"Shit," Sinkovich said. "You'd never make it in the Chicago P.D., you know that? You're too by-the-book."

But he went, sprinting out of the tavern, and hurrying up the stairs.

"You're by-the-book?" the bartender asked.

"No," I said. "I just figured you might talk a little more if you aren't worried about a badge listening in."

"How do I know you're not one?" he asked.

"I'm a half-assed private detective, not even good enough to get licensed. You can check up on me if you want. My name's Bill Grimshaw."

He frowned. "Related to Franklin Grimshaw?"

Only by fictional bloodlines. But I never admitted that. "Cousins."

"Your cousin is one of the reasons my dad had this bar to leave us," the bartender said. "You got proof that you're related?"

"I've got a driver's license with my name on it," I said—and I had paid well for that. It was as real as a license could be, even though it didn't list Smokey Dalton as my name. It called me William S. Grimshaw. "Otherwise, you'll have to call Franklin."

The bartender bent his fingers twice in a show-it gesture. I leaned forward, pulled out my wallet, and flipped it open to the license. He studied it, and then he sighed.

"I don't know the name of the guy he met with," the bartender said. "But I will tell you this. They didn't like each other at all."

"I figured that from the guns," I said.

"It was a setup. These things always are. Those goddamn kids aren't human anymore. Or maybe they never were. They think the whole thing is a game."

"He met with a kid?" I asked.

"Oh, no. That guy was an adult. But the kids are the shooters. Two of them on a bike, one on the handlebars with a shotgun wrapped in a towel. And they're deadly shots, too, close range. I never know who's gonna get hit."

"But you know a hit's coming?"

The bartender shook his head. "I try not to pay attention. We actually remodeled the bar so that it's in this corner. See nothing, do nothing, have no fucking liability."

I studied him, feeling my stomach turn. But I was better at hiding my expression than he was.

"Usually," the bartender said, leaning across the bar, his voice low even though we were alone, "they get them out of here by promising dope. You know, saying let's meet the dealer outside—he hates coming inside where people can see him, that sort of thing."

The bartender wiped part of the surface, then frowned.

"It took me a while to catch on to that, but I did. And if someone says something like that now, I try to convince them not to go out. Some folks trust me. The rest think I'm a narc." He shrugged. "You do what you can."

If, I supposed, tolerating gangs and drugs and murders for hire in exchange for a small inheritance made you feel like you were doing something.

"Your guy, though, I don't know what the other guy promised him. They were over at that table." The bartender waved his hand toward one of the tables beneath the alpine meadows posters.

I looked, trying to imagine them there. It would have been a squeeze for Johnson if he sat between the table and the wall. If he took the other chair, though, he would have fit just fine. That implied—although I couldn't be certain—that the other guy was thinner, smaller.

"The next thing I know," the bartender said, "they were walking out the front door. Your friend calls to me, says they'll be right back."

"Who's first?" I asked.

"How's that?"

"Who was first out the door?"

"Couldn't see it. Would've thought the other guy, because your friend waved to me, but don't know that for sure."

I nodded.

"All I know," the bartender said, "is they left their guns and coats."

"You have both guns?" I asked.

"Not anymore. The other guy came back in, got his coat, got his gun, and was outta here like a shot."

"Which way did he leave?" I asked.

The bartender grabbed a glass, and scooped some ice into it. "Dunno."

"What do you mean you don't know? You were right here. You gave him his gun."

"And I make it a habit not to look too hard at anything," the bartender said. "I already gave you more than I'd give most."

He filled the glass with a soft drink and downed it. Then he filled the glass again.

"You want something?" he asked me.

"Just my friend's gun."

He made a face, then grabbed the bar rag and reached under the bar. He lifted the gun, wrapped in the rag, and set it on the bar just as Sinkovich came back down the stairs.

His skin had turned a sallow yellowish-green. I'd never seen a human being that color.

"They're taking Johnson out," Sinkovich said, handing me the evidence bags. "No one saw me get these."

He must have stopped and watched them remove the body.

"It's bad, huh," I said.

"It didn't look that bad when we got there, but Holy Christ, the front of him . . ." Sinkovich shuddered.

"The rain cleaned most of it up," I said. "We were lucky."

Although I didn't truly believe that. If the rain hadn't fallen so heavily and so hard, cleaning the sidewalks and everything around, then I might have gotten a few more answers from Yancy and Jump. Just from the way they looked, and from their shoes. I hadn't noticed anything on their shoes.

"That the gun?" Sinkovich asked.

I nodded.

"Let's bag this stuff and leave before we get into more trouble." He reached for the gun, but I pushed his hand away. He wasn't thinking clearly, and he wasn't going to be cautious.

I slid the rag toward me, then used it to pick up the gun. I put them both in the evidence bag. Then I pulled the rag out before we sealed the bag.

"Better label it," I said.

"Got a pen?" Sinkovich asked the bartender.

I took the other evidence bag to the coat tree and pulled down the jacket. It was clearly big enough to be Johnson's, although I hadn't seen him wear one like it.

While Sinkovich was preoccupied with labeling the evidence bag, I went through the coat's pockets. I found two gum wrappers, a movie ticket, matches from Mr. Kelly's, and thirty-five cents. In the other pocket, I found a bank withdrawal slip with numbers handwritten in ballpoint in the columns, and a torn piece of paper with part of an address on it.

I pocketed all of it before tucking the coat into the other evidence bag.

Sinkovich hadn't noticed. He was writing on the first bag, and cursing because the pen didn't work the way he wanted it to. I tossed the other bag at him.

"Better do that one, too."

"Who died and made you God?" he asked, but he did it.

The bartender watched us. When Sinkovich handed him the pen back, the bartender said, "You guys aren't gonna shut me down, are you?"

"Have we in the past?" Sinkovich asked.

The bartender shook his head.

"Then we ain't now." Sinkovich stuck the bags under his slicker and turned to me. "We're leaving, Grimshaw. I ain't taking no for an answer this time."

"Fine," I said.

I let him lead the way up the stairs. The tent was gone, and the medical examiner's truck had left as well. There was a trail of blood across the sidewalk, and a large stain in the center that was spreading.

Rain dripped from the sky. Dark clouds rolled in, promising yet another downpour.

A few cops remained, mostly picking up after themselves. I didn't see Yancy or his friend Jump.

The black uniformed officer hung near the stairs. As I reached the top, he caught my arm.

"Word?" he said.

"Jack," I said, mostly because I didn't want to say no to the uniform, but I didn't want to get too close without some backup. "Be right there."

"Jesus, Grimshaw, I said we was leaving." Sinkovich turned, saw the uniform's hand on my sleeve, and grimaced. "Fifteen seconds. I swear to God that's all you got."

He was standing awkwardly, almost as if the evidence bags were weighing him down. At that moment, I wished that I had taken them.

I slid my sleeve out of the young cop's grasp. "I guess we got fifteen seconds," I said.

He looked both ways before speaking. "What you said about the kids, the logic?"

"Yeah?"

"You believe that?"

"Do you?" I asked.

He glanced at the stain. "I was second squad to arrive. Just before the downpour. There was blood and guts and everything all over everywhere. Then the skies open, and it looked, for a minute, like something out of the Bible. A river of blood."

I couldn't help myself. I shivered.

"I start going for the trace, I mean, it's a crime scene, right? And no one else does. They already know what happened, they figure they're not gonna get the exact kids, and they don't really care." He looked back at me. He wasn't much older than Malcolm. "But it's a cop. They should care, right?"

"What's your name, son?" I asked.

"LeRoy DeVault," he said, tapping his badge. "Officer DeVault."

"Well, Officer DeVault," I said, giving him the respect of his title, "you're right. They should care about every corpse they find, not just a cop's. Doesn't mean they will."

He frowned and glanced at the spot on the sidewalk, the stain of blood, cloth, and tissue that was the only evidence of Truman Johnson's murder.

"So how come you care?" he asked. "Because he was your friend?"

I studied the young officer for a moment, wondering if I had ever had that same mixture of naïvete and cynicism, that same wary look that dared me to chip away at his innocence.

But he wasn't asking me about his innocence. He was asking me about my own reasons for barging into a crime scene even though I wasn't a cop, for taking evidence and trying to force others to be more professional.

My own motives were so complicated, I wasn't sure I could explain them to myself.

"I don't know if you could ever have called us friends," I said to DeVault. "I'm not sure either of us would have been happy with that label."

I gave him a rueful smile, and then I turned away, hurrying down the sidewalk after Sinkovich. When I reached the car, the heavens opened, and the deluge started again.

TWENTY-ONE

What the hell am I supposed to do with this stuff?" Sinkovich asked as we pulled out.

He was driving even though the rain was coming down so hard the windshield was a sheet of water. All I could see was the reflected lights from streetlights that had come on due to the afternoon's darkness.

"Shouldn't we pull over?" I asked.

"We're getting the hell out of this neighborhood." Sinkovich reached under his coat and pulled out the evidence bags. He steered with one hand, using the other to toss the bags into the backseat.

I longed to reach over and grab the steering wheel myself, but I didn't. That would be even more dangerous than Sinkovich's blind drive.

We swerved under the "L" tracks and for a blessed moment, we could see. We were the only people on the road. Water flowed around us. The gutters had backed up, unable to take the excessive rain, and garbage swirled in the headlights.

"The car's going to stall," I said.

"We're not gonna stall," he said, and turned right. The car's wheels slid— we were hydroplaning—but we didn't stall.

The sheets of water coated us again, and Sinkovich leaned forward, as if getting closer to the windshield would help.

"I don't know why I do these things," he said. "My wife, she says I got a death wish, and I'm beginnin to believe her. I think, Grimshaw's gonna be upset when he hears about Johnson. I'll take him to the site, maybe he'll see a few things, tell me later. Instead, you take on the Red Squad, for chrissake, and then one of the assistant chiefs who's been gunnin' for me ever since last winter shows up just as you drag us into that fuckin' tavern. We pull evidence from the scene—"

"No one else had taken it," I said.

Sinkovich turned his head toward me, nearly hitting his chin on the steering wheel because he had been sitting so low. The car swerved again, and he didn't seem to notice.

"Maybe they hadn't thought of it yet," he said. "Maybe they'll be back and maybe that creep of a bartender'll tell 'em we got the goddamn evidence for a case that ain't even ours."

"Maybe we should pull over."

He glared at me, still not looking at the road. "Maybe you should stop being such a pussy."

"Maybe you should take your own advice."

"Jesus." He swung the car toward the curb—or where I thought the curb was—and we fishtailed again. The wheels bumped something solid, and for a brief moment, the windshield cleared.

We were on the sidewalk which was, fortunately, empty.

"I don't wanna hear it," he said and drove back into the street.

Thunder boomed overhead and lightning flashed almost at the same moment. And then the rain became hail, pounding on the car like a hundred angry fists.

He yanked the steering wheel to the left and swung under the "L" tracks again. The hood of the car had hail melting in the middle of a dozen tiny dents.

"Just what I need." He made a fist and rested it against the steering wheel.

"At least it didn't dent the windshield," I said.

"You shut up," he said. "I don't need any more mouth from you."

The hail pelted the ground around us, missing us. Another car crawled by, its back window shattered. No one else was on the street.

Thunder boomed again, but it didn't sound as close. Gradually, the hail stopped.

Sinkovich ran a hand over his face. He didn't move the car.

"What'm I supposed to do with those fuckin' bags?" he asked. "They're like a confession that I've been tampering with a crime scene."

"You already labeled what they are, right?" I asked.

"The case don't have a number yet, at least that I know of. I just marked what they are and where I found them."

"Good," I said. "Put the wrong case number on them."

"Oh, yeah, so some prosecutor can find them when he goes to trial on that other case."

"He won't," I said. "You already told me he won't."

"What are you talking about?" Sinkovich frowned at me.

"Put the baby's case number on them, and put them in Property. Then you and I will know where they are if we need them."

"Why would 'we' need them?" Sinkovich asked. "You gonna track some gang kids down yourself?"

"If I have to," I said.

"And then what? I get in trouble again with the department for messing in a case that's not mine, you draw attention to yourself which, forgive me, I thought you didn't want after some of the stuff I heard you say over the last few months. And for what? What're we gonna gain? Truman Johnson was a victim in a goddamn war, and that's all. He's just one of the opening shots."

I shook my head. "I don't think this is a war."

"Then you're fuckin' blind," Sinkovich said. "What do you think that order was to allow cops to carry bigger guns? It was a volley. There've been over a hundred and fifty shootings down here since January, and a bunch of kids murdered. Truman ain't the first cop to die down here this year, and he ain't gonna be the last."

"So we should just let it go?" I asked.

"I don't wanna volunteer to become a target, do you?" Sinkovich said.

"That's not it, is it?" I asked. "What else is going on, Jack? What aren't you telling me?"

He closed his mouth and turned his head toward the window. The sun was shining through the "L" tracks now, illuminating the wet streets. Water was still backed up in the grates, but it only swirled along the curbs, not in the middle of the street.

"I been hearin' talk, okay?" he said.

"What kind of talk?"

"Rumors, you can ask all you want, but I dunno where they're comin' from. Could be anywhere."

"All right," I said.

He sighed, and looked at me. His face was lined with streaky light from the window. "Policies ain't been workin' and the gangs are gettin' big. There's four thousand people in the Stones, and that's conservative. Then the

Panthers come in, and they're talkin' about killin' cops, which we don't take too kindly to."

"I know," I said. "Although looking at how they behave, I'm not sure they mean it. I heard Fred Hampton speak—"

"I don't care what you heard. I'm tellin' you what I heard, okay?"

"Okay," I said.

"I'm hearin' talk about declarin' a real war. Now that Nixon's in office and the country's leanin' toward law and order, the city thinks maybe it's got a shot at takin' harsher measures. You can't deny there's a problem down here."

"True," I said, feeling cold.

"And it's gettin' worse. Now, I ain't sayin' this to anyone but you, but I think it's gettin worse on purpose. The gangs ain't doin' nothin' but respondin', protectin' their turf."

I turned toward him in surprise. Sinkovich had come a long way since August. He would never have noticed this sort of thing then.

"The Red Squad had twenty-one guys six months ago. It's been recruitin'. It's got nearly two hundred now, hired from all over the place, and I gotta tell you, most of these guys ain't thinkers. They're troublemakers, bein' moved to the part of town most likely to let them earn their trigger-happy reputations."

"Truman wasn't one of them," I said. "He was Homicide."

"He was a cop, and he was down here."

"I still don't get it," I said. "If this is the case, wouldn't it be better to find the shooters, make an example of them, and take advantage of all the press?"

"And take away their excuses?" Sinkovich asked. "Right now, a cop down here can shoot at any two kids on a bike with one on the handlebars, thinking they might be preventing a hit. They can shoot at any teenager wearin' red, claimin' he was a Stone. They can shoot the driver of any van, sayin' he was the getaway driver in a bunch of shootings—and who the hell is gonna contradict them? The gangs? Even if they do, who cares? No one'll pay attention."

I leaned back against the cracked car seat. What had I been thinking when I brought Jimmy to this town for his safety? He wasn't safe. Even doing a simple kid thing like riding a bicycle made him a target.

"They want to use Truman as an excuse?" I asked, still trying to comprehend this.

"They can't solve it. If they solve it, they're sayin' it's normal life down here, not a war zone. See what I mean?" Sinkovich said.

214

I did understand what he meant, and I didn't like it. "Do you even believe Yancy's story, then?"

"Oh, yeah," Sinkovich said. "I seen the corpse up close and personal. That was done with a shotgun. Johnson was in the wrong place at the wrong time."

"That's what you think, then? This was random?"

"That's what I think," Sinkovich said.

"Even with the third guy," I said.

"Maybe the kids were gunning for him," Sinkovich said, "the guy Johnson was meeting. Did you think about that?"

"No," I said.

"Don't get us involved in this, Grimshaw. You're steppin between the city and the gangs, and that ain't no place to be. We won't live through it."

"Who'd kill us?" I asked.

"Who wouldn't? We'd be convenient victims," Sinkovich said. "I don't know about you, but I wanna die in my chair in front of the TV, my hearing aide turned off and my teeth out, at the age of ninety."

I shook my head. "Truman asked me to help him with something."

"So?" Sinkovich said.

"He wouldn't've gone back to work."

"That don't mean work didn't come to him. You don't know what he was doing before. This coulda been related to an old case, or something he got called on just today."

"It could have," I said.

"Or it could've been wrong place, wrong time," Sinkovich said. "What I'm tryin' to tell you here is that we can't be involved. We don't dare."

"I heard you," I said.

"Your kid won't like it if you get killed outta misguided loyalty."

"Misguided?" I looked at Sinkovich. "What's misguided about this? A man was murdered today, and you're telling me to ignore it."

"I'm tellin' you to let the authorities handle it," he said.

"You're telling me they're going to use it as one more excuse to escalate the gang war."

"Let 'em," Sinkovich said. "A man's gotta look after his own."

"Whatever happened to 'a man has to do what he can live with'?" I asked.

Sinkovich winced. "Don't do this to me again, Grimshaw."

"You think something stinks here, too, don't you? That's why you brought me along. You wanted me to see this, you said so yourself."

"I was being a friend," Sinkovich said.

"To me or to Johnson?"

"Shit," Sinkovich said. "Shit."

He put the car into drive and pulled onto the street. Another car zoomed by, honking. He didn't seem to notice.

"I'm takin' you home," he said. "I'll put the goddamn bags in the wrong case file, and then I'm done. You're on your own, you got that?"

"So if I call and ask you to check Johnson's logs to see what he was working on, you won't do that?"

"I'm not involved," Sinkovich said. "Whatever you choose to do, you choose to do it without me. I got a kid, too, and a divorce that I'm losin' and a job that I'm barely hangin' on to. I'm not takin' on my department, and I'm not goin' back to the Gaza Strip. You got that? You're on your own."

"I got that," I said, leaning back in my seat. "I got that loud and clear."

TWENTY-TWO

Sinkovich let me off in front of my apartment building and drove off without another word.

Hail covered the ground like snow, making the sidewalk slippery. I made my way across it, the hail crunching beneath my feet.

I was drenched and miserable, soaked through even though I hadn't stood in the rain that long. I was also shaken. Johnson hadn't deserved to die, and he didn't deserve to become a faceless statistic in a made-up war.

The apartment building's front door was closed and locked. I fished in my pocket for my keys, found them, and let myself in.

The interior still had the afternoon's mugginess. Wet footprints went down the hall and up the stairs, left by various residents coming home from their day's work.

I climbed the stairs slowly, my shoes making an unpleasant squishing sound. I left footprints, too, bigger than the others, and as I looked at them, I thought again about Yancy and Jump's clean clothing.

A shotgun blast at close range would have sent pellets and blood and guts flying in every direction. If it had been a dry, sunny day, they might have picked gore off the sidewalk across the street.

Those men should have been covered with it, and despite the rain, some of it should have stuck to them, the way it stuck to the sidewalk.

No matter how much Sinkovich wanted me to, I couldn't let this go.

I reached my floor. The stairs turned and went up, and so did the footprints I was following. I had hoped they were Marvella's. I looked at her door. There was no indication that she was home.

Then again, there was no indication that she wasn't.

I crossed the hall and knocked. I didn't want to be the one to break the news to her, but I would if I had to. I wanted to find out what she knew about Johnson's plans these last few days.

The knock sounded hollow. It echoed through the empty hallway. I listened, but didn't hear anyone come to the door. I knocked again, for good measure, even though I knew now that Marvella wasn't home.

I crossed the hall, unlocked my three deadbolts, and went inside. The clean apartment startled me. I had forgotten that I had planned to spend the evening with Jimmy.

I couldn't do that now. The first few hours after a murder were the easiest time to solve it. The longer I waited, the less chance Johnson had for justice.

Then I snorted. Justice. Justice would've been Johnson alive, not face-down on the Gaza Strip, a victim of a shooting who was about to become a victim of the city's propaganda.

Was I doing this because he was a friend? Hell, no, Officer DeVault. I was doing it because I felt guilty. Because, in the words of Jack Sinkovich, I couldn't live with myself if I didn't.

But I was going to keep that clearly in mind, not fool myself that I was seeking justice.

I was trying to clear my conscience for failing to help a man who had helped me. Nothing more.

I pulled off my wet coat and hat and hung them on my coat rack, staring at it for a moment. I had mentally accused Sinkovich of being unfocused at the crime scene, but I had been, too. I hadn't asked about the denim jackets that hung on the rack, and I had forgotten to ask for a description of the third man.

I would probably have to go back there, alone, and that was the last thing I wanted.

But first, I had to figure out what got Johnson there in the first place, and all I had to start with was the bartender's story, a withdrawal slip, half an address, and Johnson's plan to find the abortionist who had nearly killed Valentina.

Had Johnson given up on that? Or had he followed up? I had been near that neighborhood just the day before, searching for someone on Marvella's list. Maybe Johnson had found him.

Or maybe he had realized how difficult the task would be, just like I had. Maybe he had gone back to work just to keep his mind off Valentina. And if that was what he had been doing, how was I going to find out?

My socks were so wet that I could see my feet through them. I walked across the ratty carpet to my bedroom.

I was chilled, even though the apartment was warm. I peeled off my clothes, dumping them on the floor like Jimmy would, and found new clothes. I had them half on when I realized that I was putting on all black, like a cat burglar.

Like Yancy.

I slid boots over my cold feet, scooped up my wet clothes, and hung them in the bathroom to dry. I transferred my wallet to the new pants, then went to my wet coat, getting the withdrawal slip and the torn piece of paper out. I stuck the withdrawal slip and the paper in my wallet and walked to the phone.

I had dialed the Grimshaws almost before I realized what I was doing. I had initially planned to go over there and talk to Jimmy myself, explain to him why—yet again—I was foisting him on someone else.

But I couldn't. Jimmy had met Truman Johnson, and while he may not have liked him, he knew that I had worked with him. He also knew that Johnson was a cop. It had been my way of showing Jimmy that not all people in authority were bad.

I wasn't sure how I would tell him about this, especially after his good-man speech last night.

And worse, I wasn't sure I could justify my plan to solve this case on my own to Jimmy. So I wasn't going to try.

The phone rang five times before someone answered. It was Franklin, who boomed away from the receiver,

". . . my phone, Lacey. I'll answer it if I want to." And then he said, "Hello?"

"Franklin," I said.

"No," he said. "Don't tell me. All night."

"It's just—"

"You can't keep doing this, Smokey. It's not right." Franklin's voice was low, probably because he didn't want anyone else to overhear. "He's already unhappy that you're missing dinner."

"I may miss more than dinner," I said.

"No, Smokey. It's—"

"Truman Johnson's dead."

"What?" Franklin forgot to keep his voice low. "The cop?"

"Yes, and don't let Jimmy overhear because he knew him."

"Overhear what?"

"Truman was gunned down in Woodlawn this afternoon."

"Jesus," Franklin whispered. "They know who did it?"

"They think they do."

"Smokey, if the police think they know—"

"They're not investigating it, Franklin. They're assuming it was a gang hit."

"Maybe it was a gang hit."

"There's too much wrong."

Franklin sighed. "This isn't any of your business. Jimmy is your business and he needs you."

"It is my business," I said. "Truman made it my business a few days ago. He asked for my help and I said no."

"And so what?" Franklin asked. "You're going into gang turf to see if you can find the lost soul who wielded the gun?"

"It was a hit, Franklin," I said. "Someone set him up."

"Tell the police." Franklin sounded muffled. I heard a door close. He must have moved into his office and closed the door on the phone cord. "Let them handle it."

"I tried," I said. "They're not going to. They didn't even interview the witnesses. It's complicated, Franklin."

"And dangerous. Have you forgotten why you're here in Chicago, Smokey? You can't go against the Chicago Police."

"Truman helped me out," I said. "I owe him."

"And he's dead," Franklin said. "Pay attention to the living, Smokey. They're the ones who need you. Jimmy needs you."

I closed my eyes and leaned against the couch. I knew that.

"Give me twenty-four hours," I said to Franklin. "If it looks like I can't resolve this or if it looks too risky, I'll quit."

"Twenty-four hours? Smokey—"

"Franklin," I said, opening my eyes. The apartment looked empty. I could hear Johnson's voice behind me when he first walked in here, months ago.

What will you do? I had asked him about that first case, the one we'd met on.

Whatever I can, he had said.

"You want me to call Laura?" I asked Franklin.

"No, no," he said. "Jimmy's always welcome here. You know that."

"Twenty-four hours, Franklin," I said. "That's all I'm asking."

"I hope you know what you're doing," he said.

"I hope so, too," I replied.

TWENTY-THREE

I started at the hospital. It was just past dinnertime, and the entire place reeked of boiled cabbage. It was enough to turn my stomach; I had no idea how anyone truly ill could have tolerated the smell.

Valentina was still in the ward for the critically ill, which was on the fifth floor. I took the elevator up, leaning against the pressboard walls. The doors closed, and I saw myself reflected in the shiny steel.

Dressed all in black, I looked large and dangerous, the scar along the left side of my face even more noticeable than usual. The expression in my eyes didn't help, either—they seemed flat and cold, almost empty.

If I had seen someone with that expression, I would have thought him lethal—which, I supposed, I was.

The elevator stopped on five, and the doors opened slowly, distorting my image before it vanished altogether. The cabbage smell was worse here, mixed with the odors of urine and sickness.

I stepped off and started down the hall. Valentina's room was down the corridor to my right, past the nurse's station. No one manned the station, although a phone line blinked repeatedly, and a call button ponged every few seconds.

All the room doors were open, and the sounds of television came from several of them. In one, a man moaned in pain, and another person coughed so hard I thought his lungs might come out.

Valentina's room was at the far end of the hall. I wouldn't have been able to tell that as I walked, except for the fact that Marvella stood outside it, her arms crossed.

She wore blue jeans and a different sweater than she had worn the night before. The sweater was too big, and the sleeves were rolled up to her elbows.

The curtains were drawn over the room's small window and the door was closed tight. Marvella effectively blocked it with her long, lean body.

Her face was drawn and haggard, her hair sticking out in clumps. Her eyes were swollen, and she clutched Kleenex in her right hand.

"You heard," I said. It wasn't a question.

She nodded. "One of the guys from the station came down shortly after it happened."

"I'm sorry," I said.

"He was a stupid son of a bitch. Gangs. What was he thinking?" She wiped at her eyes with the tissue, and looked up at me. "I'll tell you what he was thinking. He was thinking he couldn't do anything here, so he might as well go back to work. That was his solution to everything. Work."

Marvella's voice broke, and the next thing I knew, I was holding her. She sobbed silently, her entire body shaking.

I patted her back, feeling nothing.

After several minutes, she pulled away. "I'm sorry."

"It's all right," I said.

She blew her nose and tucked the tissue into her sleeve. "And I was going to call him. Val's getting better."

"Is she awake?"

"Not really. She's restless, talking, but not really tracking. Not yet. Still, the doctor doesn't want anyone upsetting her. So I've been out here. I'm afraid she'll overhear, and it'll set her back . . ."

"Well," I said. "Her getting better, that's some good news then, right?"

Marvella nodded. Then she blinked and looked up at the fluorescent lights, trying to control her tears. "I sent him home."

She had returned to Johnson's death. I was probably the first person she could talk with about it.

"I tried to get him to go home the night before," I said. "It was the right thing to do."

She shook her head. "If he stayed here, I could have kept an eye on him."

"Even you were smart enough to go home, Marvella. You can't be here all the time."

"I didn't tell him to go back to work," she said.

"No," I said. "He might have gotten that idea from me."

Suddenly I had her full attention.

"He wanted me to help him find the . . ." I stopped, remembering where I was. "The person who, you know."

Her lips thinned. "What did you tell him?"

"Nothing," I said. "I never told him that I was already looking. Maybe I should have."

"You think he went looking?"

I shrugged. "I don't know anything right now."

"Gangs don't do this," Marvella said. "It's not their thing."

I sighed. Part of me had hoped that the gangs had a sideline in illegal operations. That would have explained Johnson's death.

"He didn't work with gangs, did he?" I asked.

"I don't know what he did day to day," Marvella said. Then she frowned. "You don't think they killed him."

"I know they killed him," I said. "I was at the crime scene."

"Was it bad?" Her voice sounded small.

I nodded.

"Jesus, Truman," she said again, as if he could hear her. "And it was the gangs?"

"Yeah," I said.

"Then why are you asking me these strange questions?" Marvella asked.

"Because," I said, "it was a hit. A gang hit. They knew he was going to be there."

She shook her head as if she couldn't comprehend it. "Why would the gangs go after Truman?"

"I thought maybe you would know."

She glanced at the room behind her, almost as if she were worried that Valentina could overhear us. "I don't know much about his work. He never said much. Why are you asking?"

"I want answers," I said. "The police aren't really investigating."

She frowned. "They said they were."

"No," I said. "I told you I was there, and there were a lot of things wrong at that crime scene. No one really cared about it."

"They have to care about Truman. He was one of the best detectives on the force," she said.

I shrugged. "Something changed."

"Or maybe I don't know what was going on," she said. "He always filtered everything. He didn't want the women in his life to be tainted by his job."

I remembered how protective he had been of Marvella. He had checked me out when we first met, knowing that she was interested in me.

She gets in trouble with men, he said. *She mentioned someone new. I wanted to find out about him.*

I reached into my back pocket and pulled out my wallet. Marvella was frowning at me.

"I found these in Truman's coat," I said. "Do you recognize either of them?"

I handed her the withdrawal slip and the piece of paper with the address. I had already checked. The address didn't match any she had given me, but I still had hope that she might recognize it.

"Five hundred dollars," she muttered, citing the sum in the withdrawal line on the slip. "Wow."

She frowned, staring at it some more.

"It's our bank," she said after a minute. "Truman banks there. But that's a lot of money to withdraw. On Friday. What would he need—?"

She looked over her shoulder at the room again.

"I can't tell you anything about this," she said.

But I looked, too. For some reason, she thought the slip was related to Valentina.

"You think he took the money out for her abortion?" I asked.

"Shh," Marvella said. "And no, I don't. It's just weird that it's the same day that Val would have had to get her money."

Marvella handed the slip and the paper back to me.

"What about the paper?" I asked.

"It's an address," she said, "but I don't recognize it."

I sighed. Even though I had expected it, I still had hoped that she would know what these two pieces of paper meant.

"Look, Marvella," I said, "I know this is a bad time, but did he say anything, anything at all that might be able to help me?"

"About what? About gangs? He knew them. He knew some Rangers—Stones, whatever you want to call them. He put some away." She shrugged. "He helped a few go straight. He had mixed feelings, just like anyone who lives down here, but that's all I know."

"What about anyone else?"

"Why would anyone else matter?"

"Trust me," I said.

"God, I don't know," she said. "He was a cop. He must have had a hundred people who hated him. Not to mention some of the white guys on the force who hated a nigger getting promoted over them."

226

The word sounded odd on her lips, odd and bitter.

"He told you stories about that?" I asked.

"He didn't have to," she said, "any more than I have to tell you."

"Did he keep stuff at home? Work papers, things he was working on?"

I was reaching, but to my surprise, she nodded. "When he helped you out on that last case, he had stuff at home. And before that. He wouldn't let anyone in his study, except maybe Val."

I felt something for the first time since that afternoon. Curiosity, hope, something. "Can you take me there?"

"To Truman's? No." Marvella glanced at the door behind her again. "I'm staying here. I've got hospital permission. I'm not letting press come here or family or anyone who's going to mention Truman in her presence. I don't want to lose her, too."

Her voice broke. What a week she was having. First, her closest friend, and then her cousin.

But I needed her help. I needed to move quickly on this. I only had twenty-four hours before the time I'd bargained with Franklin would run out. I knew he wouldn't help with Jimmy after that.

"How about giving me Truman's address then?" I asked. Maybe I would turn into a cat burglar. Maybe I would break in just to find out what was in Johnson's private files.

"Truman was a cop, Bill." She almost smiled. "He didn't hide keys under his mat."

"I didn't expect him to."

"You're very serious about this."

I nodded. "I owe him. He asked me to help him find that butcher on Monday and I said no. I'm thinking now maybe if I had let him help me, he would still be alive."

"And maybe if I hadn't sent him home, he would be, too." Marvella's eyes glistened. "We can't do this to ourselves, Bill. He's dead. We're going to have to accept that."

"I've been doing an awful lot of accepting this past year," I said, and was surprised to hear the anger in my voice.

Marvella raised her eyebrows. "What're you going to do, raise him up? Easter was Sunday. I think we missed our chance."

A tear ran down her cheek, belying her sarcastic tone. I wiped the tear away, and she tucked her face into my hand. I pulled her close again, but she didn't cry. Instead, she leaned on me.

She hadn't had anyone to lean on, not for the past several days. She had done this alone, and with courage, and now she was second-guessing herself.

"It probably had nothing to do with us," I said.

She nodded against my neck.

"It might be in those case files," I said.

She pulled back, rubbed her hand on the wet spot she'd left on my skin. Then she looked at me.

"What are you going to do if you figure out who ordered the hit?"

"Report it, I hope."

"You hope?"

"I'm hoping someone'll listen," I said.

"If they don't?" she asked.

"I'm taking things moment by moment right now."

She nodded, apparently satisfied with that.

"I can't take you to Truman's," she said, "but I can help you."

"How?" I asked.

I expected her to pull a key out of her pocket. Instead, she said, "Paulette."

"Paulette?"

"My sister, Paulette Shipley."

"What about her?"

"She lives just two blocks away from him. She can let you in. It's probably better that way, anyhow. The neighbors won't think anything of it if she goes inside."

Good point. "Can you call her for me? Have her meet me there?"

"Yes," Marvella said.

I smiled at her, and rubbed my fingers down her face. "You're amazing."

"It's about time you realized that," she said, and gave me Johnson's address.

TWENTY-FOUR

Truman Johnson lived on a tree-lined street in one of Bronzeville's better neighborhoods. The houses had all been built around the turn of the century and were made of stone, in keeping with Chicago's strange city ordinance.

After the famous fire of 1871, Chicago forbade wooden structures inside the city limits. It created a great world of stone—making the entire place look harsh and elegant at the same time.

Johnson's neighborhood retained that elegance. The homes weren't grand, but they had been kept up. The surrounding trees were almost as old as the houses, creating a comfortable canopy over the wide street.

I didn't like the shadows the trees cast. The streetlamps were large here, illuminating a wide circle around their base, but the trees interfered with that circle, leaving too many patches of deep darkness. One of them was the walk that led up to Johnson's house.

I parked in the driveway as if I belonged, uncertain what to do next. I didn't see Marvella's sister anywhere, and I didn't want to stand in the middle of Johnson's yard.

I didn't want to call attention to myself.

The storms still passed overhead, but the thunder rumbled far away. Lightning illuminated the black clouds, but didn't fork downward any longer. The air smelled fresh and clean, like it should after a strong rain.

After a few minutes, I heard footsteps on the sidewalk. I looked out my side window and saw a couple walking down the street arm in arm. They carried a flashlight, its tiny beam illuminating the cracked concrete before them.

I got out of the car, figuring that they might think it suspicious to see a man just sitting there, ignition off, lights gone. The couple might notice, too, since they had a flashlight and could look inside.

I let the car door thunk closed. Then I started for the front door. It wouldn't hurt to knock, pretend that I didn't know anything about the day's events.

"Mr. Grimshaw?" A woman's voice floated across the air.

I turned. The couple stood at the foot of the driveway.

"Paulette Shipley?" I asked.

"Yes," the woman said and the couple came forward. The man held the flashlight. He ran its beam over my body, letting it linger on my face.

The light hurt my eyes. "You don't need to do that."

"Sorry," Paulette said. "This is my husband, Mike. He's a bit protective."

"Probably a good thing right now," I said. "I'm sorry about Truman."

Paulette nodded. I couldn't see her face in the dim light. "I guess it's not unexpected. I mean, he's a police officer and all."

"It was unexpected to me," I said.

"Tell me why you want to get in his house," Mike Shipley said. He had a deep voice that carried across the quiet street.

I opened the back car door and took out my gloves. "I don't know how much Truman talked to you. He and I worked on a few cases together."

"You're a cop?"

"Private," I said.

"You solved those murders last December," Paulette said. "The ones that were bothering Truman so much."

"Yes," I said. "I was at the crime scene this afternoon, and a few things don't add up."

"What do you mean, they don't add up?" Shipley wasn't going to give me any quarter. He was as tall as I was, but whip thin. I couldn't see his face clearly, either.

"I don't know what Marvella told you," I said.

"Nothing," Shipley said.

"Enough." Paulette spoke with an authority that silenced her husband. "She told me it was a hit, that someone ordered it, and you're going to find out who because the police aren't interested."

"I don't know how you know this stuff," Shipley said to me.

So I explained it to him as quickly as I could. I kept my voice down because I didn't want the entire neighborhood to learn what was going on, but I felt it didn't hurt to tell the family. They might be able to get the city to take action if I couldn't find anything.

"I still don't see what Truman's house'll tell you," Shipley said.

"Marvella said he kept records here. I just want to see them. You can supervise me the entire time."

"Mike," Paulette said, "Marvella trusts him."

"Yeah," Shipley said. "And she trusted that bastard ex-husband, too."

I wasn't going to let them continue bickering. I had things to do.

"Do you have the key?" I asked Paulette.

She waved a small key ring at me.

"Let's go then," I said.

She led me to a door beside the garage, one I hadn't even noticed. She unlocked it with a small key, then stepped inside and turned on the garage light.

The place was spotless. I had never seen a spotless garage before. Directly in front of us stood a workbench, tools hanging above it on a pegboard. A chair was tucked beneath it.

The car parked inside looked like it hadn't been driven in a long time. It was a Woody, which surprised me, and it was as clean and neat as the garage. The wooden side panels shone as if they had been polished.

At least it smelled like a garage, slightly musty tinged with gasoline.

Shipley closed the door behind us. I finally got a chance to take him in. He was as frail as his thin frame implied. His hair was naturally straight and his eyes were blue, but his skin was as dark as mine.

It was a striking combination, one that drew immediate attention to his face.

Paulette was a surprise. She looked like Marvella, which I remembered from the time I met her before the Nefertiti Ball. Paulette and Marvella shared their build, as well as the high cheekbones and dramatic bone structure. But I had thought Paulette the less attractive sister. I might have been wrong.

She turned slightly, beckoning us forward, and I realized with a start that she was about four months pregnant.

"I don't think he'd keep anything out here," she said.

She led us up three concrete steps to the back door. This too she unlocked, and started to push it open, but I caught her arm.

"Let me go first," I said.

She looked at me as if I were crazy, but moved aside.

I had no idea what I was expecting, but something warned me to be cautious.

"The light's to your left," she said.

I felt around and found the switch, one of those push-button kinds that dated from the first days of electricity. The light came on with a snap, shedding a pale light throughout the kitchen.

It was a disaster, cupboards open, food scattered, dishes broken.

Behind me, Paulette gasped, and I heard Shipley's worried voice ask what was wrong.

"Give me your flashlight," I said quietly, wishing I hadn't left the gun in the glovebox.

Shipley handed me the flashlight without a word. It was solid steel, heavy enough to do some damage if I used it as a club.

"What happened in here?" Paulette asked.

"Stay by the door," I said.

I slipped inside. It was impossible to move silently, my boots crunching on cereal and broken glass. Other footprints marred the flour someone had poured all over the floor. The room stank of syrup and coffee grounds and the shattered jar of grease.

"My God," Paulette said. She had followed me inside and Shipley was beside her. "Who did this?"

"Stay there," I said, this time with more emphasis.

The kitchen had two doors beside the one we came in, one on my left and the other directly in front of me. The door on my left was closer. I approached it carefully, trying to avoid the glass. When I reached it, I debated turning on the flashlight, then changed my mind.

If someone else was in the house, all the flashlight would do was make me a target.

I felt for a wall switch, found it, and pushed it on.

Another overhead light, just as pale as the one in the kitchen, this one revealing a ruined living room. Couch cushions upended, chairs on their sides, picture frames smashed. In the far corner, a desk had been swept clean, its surface contents spilled on the floor around it. The drawers were half open, and in one, I saw something glint.

I would come back to that.

The curtains were closed, which was a blessing. I didn't feel as conspicuous that way, and it didn't reveal the mess to the neighbors. I didn't want anyone to see me, see the destruction, and call the police.

A large rug covered hardwood floors. As I crossed it, the glass, cereal, and flour came off my boots. My footprints were the only ones outlined in white. Whoever had done this had destroyed the kitchen last.

I kept my back to the central wall, and worked my way right. A staircase bisected the room, leading into darkness above. I hurried past the stairs, and found myself in the dining room.

It was almost intact. The chairs had been moved, and one of the glass doors on the built-in china cabinet had been shattered, but whoever had done this had stopped before going to full-scale destruction.

A small bathroom stood just beside the dining room, obviously added to the house years after it was built. Nothing was disturbed in there, not even the medicine cabinet.

I came back into the kitchen. Shipley was standing in front of Paulette, as if he could protect her with that thin frame.

His gaze met mine.

"No one downstairs," I said. "Is there a basement?"

"Storm cellar in the back," Paulette said. "You can only get to it from the outside."

I'd leave it alone then, unless I saw a reason to go inside. "Have you heard anything?" I asked, and pointed upward.

Shipley shook his head. I nodded once, then eased myself back into the dining room. I could be quieter approaching the stairs from this side.

The light was at the bottom of the steps, just like I expected. I touched the wall plate, then decided against turning the upstairs lights on.

The stairs were a well, and I was at the bottom of it. Anyone with a few brains and a well-placed kick could put me out of commission immediately.

If the floor was made of wood, the stairs would be also. The house was old, which meant that it had soft spots, probably in the middle.

There was a banister on the left, but none on the right. I used the banister as a brace, set my left foot on the left side of the third step, and climbed, three steps at a time, never touching the middle of the wood.

The stairs didn't creak once.

When I reached the top, I found a closed door. All my caution had been for nothing.

I grabbed the knob—it was large, old, and metal—and turned it silently. Then I slammed the door inward as hard as I could, planning to knock anyone standing near it off balance.

No one was there.

I found the upstairs wall switch and flicked it on. The mess continued up here. Storage cupboards had been emptied onto the floor—clothing, linen, and yellowed envelopes mounded in the narrow hallway.

There were two rooms up here. I turned on the lights in each. The first was a study—papers scattered everywhere, the desk ruined, a safe knocked on its side, but still closed.

The second was Johnson's bedroom. The mattress was half off his bed, and a chair was tipped over. A television, which he had perched near the window, lay on the ground, its screen shattered.

I checked the closets, and let out a small sigh.

The Shipleys and I were alone.

I made my way back down the stairs and into the kitchen. The Shipleys hadn't moved.

"Whoever did this is long gone," I said.

Shipley's shoulders moved in a visible sigh. Paulette's eyes narrowed, her face becoming a replica of Marvella's just an hour ago. They had the same fierceness.

"Truman will—would have hated this. He's always so neat."

"What were you going to look for?" Shipley asked.

"I don't know," I said. "Clues, files, anything to help me. But now, I have no idea what to do."

"We have to clean it up," Paulette said.

"Not yet," I said. "How often were you here?"

She shrugged. "Often enough, I guess. Less after Tru and Val split up."

"This is going to be hard," I said, "but I'd like to know if anything important is missing."

Shipley nodded, his hostility to me clearly forgotten.

"I'm going to start with the papers," I said. "Which desk did he use most? The one upstairs?"

"For work," Paulette said. "He usually had that room locked. Is it open?"

"Yeah," I said. "Do you have the combination to the safe? They didn't get in that."

"I think maybe Val might," Paulette said, and then she flushed. "I hate this."

Shipley rubbed his hand on his wife's back. "Go easy, babe."

"I'm fine." As if to prove her words, Paulette walked away from him, heading out the door that led into the living room.

"My God," she said again.

"What's going on?" Shipley asked me quietly.

"Obviously something more than a gang hit," I said.

"If we call the police now, do you think they'll take your theories more seriously?"

I had a hunch it wasn't that simple. "Let's see what we find first."

"What a mess," Paulette said from the front room. "What an awful mess."

"Leave the desk for me," I said as I walked into the room. She was already standing beside it, her feet hidden by a mound of papers.

The glint in the half-open desk drawer caught my eye again, and I walked over to it. This time, I pulled the drawer out.

"What's that?" Paulette asked, reaching inside.

I held up my gloved hand, stopping her. Inside the drawer, I found medical syringes, candles, rubber tubes, and soot-blackened spoons. Behind those were specially folded sheets of paper, packets of citric acid, and a large package wrapped in brown paper.

I grabbed the package. It was soft, which I had expected, feeling like a bag of flour. With a letter opener, I made a small slit in the middle of the package, revealing a whitish-brown powder inside.

I scooped a bit of the powder into my gloved palm, then gingerly sniffed, careful not to get any up my nose. The powder had a bitter odor.

"Is that what I think it is?" Shipley asked, sounding shocked.

"Heroin," I said. "Probably enough to make us all rich."

TWENTY-FIVE

W hy would he have that?" Paulette asked, panic in her voice. "Why would he have that? Truman's not like that. He wouldn't have that stuff here."

I looked at the other items. The specially folded paper was used as packaging for smaller amounts. Anyone finding this stash would think that Johnson wasn't just using; he was also dealing.

"All the equipment's here, too." I poured that tiny bit of powder back into the wrapper, then wiped off my gloves on the brown paper, cleaning them as best I could.

Shipley waded through the mess toward us. "This isn't right."

"Truman's a good man, Mr. Grimshaw," Paulette said. "He hates drugs. He volunteers at the Teen Challenge Center as much as he can. He works with the kids who're getting clean. He wouldn't do this. He wouldn't."

"I know that," I said, "but someone wants us to think he does."

They looked at me, shock on both of their faces.

I waved my hand over the drawer. "It's a plant, and an obvious one, not, I think, that anyone would care. Whoever did this wanted the drugs found."

"Then why didn't they throw them on the floor?" Shipley asked.

"Because," Paulette said, "the next logical question is if someone found it, why didn't they take it?"

"Exactly," I said. "Better to leave the drawers intact here—upstairs they've been pulled out—so that it looks like they've been interrupted, and they missed the prize. Leaving the drawer conveniently open, though, so that police or anyone else coming in here would find the drugs."

"Why?" Paulette asked. "Why would anyone do this to Truman?"

"I don't know," I said, "but I have a guess."

They both looked at me again. I had apparently become trustworthy to both of them.

"What's your guess?" Shipley asked.

"They wanted to leave us an explanation for that gang hit, in case anyone wondered why someone would target Truman," I said.

"So they did this after you asked questions?" Paulette asked.

It was my turn to look at her. My stomach twisted. "I hope not. But I'm not sure we'll ever know."

"Now what'll we do?" Shipley asked. "We can't call the police. They'll jump all over this, and it'll convince them that Truman was a bad cop."

"We look for more," I said. "And then we get it out of here."

Shipley put his hands up as if we were in the old West and I was about to arrest him. "I'm not carrying that stuff out of this house. This is a good neighborhood, but my skin color has not changed in the last ten minutes, and if I get caught with it, I'll never see my kid grow up."

"I'm not asking you to take it out of here," I said. "Just look for it. If you find anything, call me. I don't want you touching it."

"Are you going to look, too?" Paulette asked.

"Yeah," I said. For more drugs and for other things, although I still wasn't clear on what. "Why don't you two start upstairs?"

"Don't you think we should look separately?" Paulette asked.

I looked at her stomach. "No," I said, "I don't. Some of this stuff is dangerous, and the less you and your baby are exposed, the better."

"Why don't you put the couch back together and just wait for us?" Shipley said.

"Because I'm not the waiting kind," Paulette snapped, sounding just like her sister.

She pushed past her husband.

"Upstairs?" she said to me. "The office?"

"Bedroom first," I said. "Sometimes they put things in closets and under mattresses. That's the best place to plant evidence."

She nodded, and headed across the ruined room. Shipley started after her, but I caught his arm.

"I know he was a relative," I said quietly, "but I need you to be honest with me. Is Paulette right? Or is she remembering the cousin she knew before he became a cop?"

Shipley's pale eyes widened. "I thought you and Truman were friends."

"We worked together. We never socialized, and honestly, he has a tendency—had a tendency—" I was having as much trouble referring to him in the past tense as everyone else was. "He liked to bend the rules sometimes. That's how we worked together in the first place. And I think he was willing to push things a bit farther than I ever would."

Although I wasn't sure if that was true or if it just depended on the situation.

Shipley thought for a moment. Then he glanced at the stairs, as if he didn't want his wife to overhear us.

"All right." He was nearly whispering. "I'll tell you this. Truman was a hard man. Had to be, I think, because of the job. We didn't have a lot in common, but the girls—Paulette and Marvella—they adored him. They were constant companions when they were kids."

The floor creaked above us. He started.

I nodded, trying to keep him talking.

"It got rough with Val," Shipley said. "He was never quite right after she left. Most guys would at least acknowledge the end of the marriage, but he told her that he made the vow before God, and he wasn't breaking it just because she wanted to find herself. Which was not at all why she left. They weren't suited. It was obvious to anyone who'd ever met them."

The floor creaked again.

"How hard do you want me to look?" Paulette called. "Should I be pulling up floorboards?"

"No!" Shipley yelled before I could say anything.

"If there's anything," I said loudly, "it'll be in plain sight, like this was. Half hidden, but easily found. No need to pry open secret doors."

"Good," she said, and the floor creaked as she walked back to the bedroom.

"She's going to be the death of me," Shipley said. "It's our first child, and she's acting like she's not even pregnant. I wouldn't be surprised if she signs up to skydive tomorrow."

It sounded like a line he said often, but there was real frustration in it. I understood the urge to protect. I felt it now more than ever.

"Truman and drugs," I said quietly.

"Paulette's right." Shipley lowered his voice. "Truman hated the stuff. He found one of the other cousins smoking weed once, and gave the kid a tongue lashing like I've never heard. I almost thought he was going to haul off and hit the kid, but he didn't."

I nodded.

"But," Shipley said, "I wouldn't put it past him to have something here if he was doing a sting or something. Although that doesn't really fit, because if he had something that dangerous in the house, he'd make sure no one could find it. It would be in his office or in his safe—"

"The safe," I said. "Whoever did this couldn't get it open. Do you know the combination?"

Shipley shook his head. "I don't think anyone does except Truman. Maybe Val."

Another dead end.

"All right, thanks." I nodded toward the stairs. "You'd probably better help your wife before she lifts something she shouldn't."

He paled, then hurried toward the stairs. I waited until he was out of my sight before I went into the kitchen.

First, I wanted to see if the white powder on the floor really was flour. The white powder was everywhere, but the bulk of it was near the stove. I crouched, and scooped up a fingerful into my left glove, being careful not to get any residue from the heroin in this small handful. I pushed it around with the fingertip of my right glove. No visible glass. Then I looked, and saw that the texture of the granules differed. One was small and fine, a crystal, and the other was a powder.

I sniffed, gently enough so that none of the powder got into my nostrils. Flour, sugar, and salt.

Somehow that relieved me. I pushed my way through the mess to a pile of grocery bags. I took one out of the middle, shook it off, and carried it back into the living room.

My black clothes were covered with white dust. I resisted the urge to wipe it off, not wanting to get any more residue on me, then opened the grocery bag and set it on the floor. I put the heroin package inside it, along with the paraphernalia, wrapped the bag up tightly, and set it near the back door leading into the garage.

I felt as nervous as Shipley about carrying heroin, but I didn't see any other choice. I didn't want to flush it here, in case I spilled some and didn't find it, and I wasn't about to hide it on the property. Johnson was being set up as a dirty cop, and he hadn't been.

I hadn't been able to prevent his death, but at least I could protect his family from this.

Then I went back into the living room, and went through the rest of the drawers. They had been emptied out. Obviously, whoever had done this fig-ured that no one would worry about the details.

As far as I was concerned, the details were always the most important thing.

I picked up the papers, finding mostly bills and bank records. The bank book had spilled open beneath several account ledgers. I looked at the ledgers first.

Johnson, like most honest cops, had only two accounts—his savings and his checking. His savings was meager. Less than a thousand dollars. But I could tell from the bills he had listed in there that he owned the house and had about five years left on a fifteen-year mortgage.

I wondered who would get the estate. Probably Valentina, since Johnson claimed not to believe in divorce.

I sighed and set the ledger down. Then I picked up the bank book and compared its account number to the numbers listed on the deposit and with-drawal slips nearby.

They all matched. He didn't appear to have another account, unless infor-mation for that was upstairs.

I took the withdrawal slip out of my wallet and compared that number to these.

It did not match.

I frowned, compared again, and the numbers didn't change. Then I went through the account balances. They didn't match the balance written on the bottom column of the withdrawal slip.

There was another account.

That was information I had not wanted.

I pushed aside the bank records, and looked at the remaining pieces of paper. Most of them were letters from family, birthday cards, and newspaper clippings about the Cubs and the Sox. I had had no idea that Johnson had been such a baseball fan.

"Mr. Grimshaw?" Paulette called from upstairs. "I think you need to see this."

I set everything down, stuck the withdrawal slip back in my wallet, and climbed the stairs. My heart was pounding. I wasn't sure what I was going to find.

She and Shipley were standing in the entrance to Johnson's bedroom. They had replaced the mattress on the bed, and set the chair back up. The television had been pushed to a corner, the broken glass from the screen piled against the molding.

"What?" I asked.

She handed me a large gold picture frame. The glass was shattered. It was a wedding picture, or what was left of it. The photograph had been ripped down the middle. All that remained of the bride was part of her veil, and her train, artfully wrapped around the groom's shoes.

It took me a moment to realize the groom was Johnson. He looked impossibly young. He was much thinner, although the thickness in his back, shoulders, and neck spoke of his football history. His eyes sparkled, and he had the biggest grin on his face that I had ever seen.

In fact, I had never seen Johnson smile like that.

"They're all like this," Paulette said.

"What are?" I asked, still thinking about Johnson, the man I hadn't known.

"The pictures." She swept a hand around the room. "Even after the divorce, he kept the pictures up in here."

I looked at the wall for the first time. Most of the frames hung crookedly. Many of them had shattered glass as if a fist went through them. On some, nothing else was wrong. Those were pictures of Johnson, fishing or—in one case—carrying a Christmas tree on his back like a jolly old St. Nicholas.

Empty picture hangers tilted sideways in a few places, and below others were broken frames, obviously thrown to the floor. The pictures in those had been ripped in half. Most of them had Johnson staring at the camera alone. Two of them, though, were ripped down the middle, leaving Paulette on one side and Marvella on the other. All that remained of the person who had been between them were two brown hands, pulling the other women into a hug.

"The pictures that are missing," I said, "are they of Valentina?"

"Every one of them," Shipley said.

I didn't want to ask the next question, but I saw no choice. "Are you sure Truman didn't do this himself, maybe after the divorce?"

"No," Paulette said. "I've been here a lot since then. He never touched them. He loved her, Mr. Grimshaw."

I took a deep breath. I had one more question to ask, and they weren't going to like it.

"This is important," I said, "and I need you to consider it. Marvella said he was crazy when it came to Valentina. You had both said something similar."

Shipley threaded an arm through Paulette's, almost as if he knew what I was going to ask.

I treaded gently. "You both know what happened to her on Sunday, right?"

Shipley nodded. "Marvella's been keeping us up-to-date."

"We know about the abortion, if that's what you're wondering," Paulette said.

"And the rape?" I asked.

"I guessed as much," Shipley said.

"Yes," Paulette said at the same time.

I swallowed hard. Here was the question I didn't want to ask. "Is it possible that what Valentina called a rape was something that happened between her and Truman, something he might not consider to be a rape?"

"Jesus, no!" Paulette pulled away from Shipley. "I thought you were his friend. How can you ask that?"

But Shipley caught her arm. "Paulie, settle down. It makes an odd kind of sense, you know? The relationship never was healthy."

She glared at him. "No," she said. "No. It wasn't Truman. He *worshipped* her. That was part of the problem. He treated her like she was going to break. He wasn't going to do something like that to her. He wouldn't."

"I was just wondering," I said, "because in that case, the abortion might have angered him—it being their child—and then her rejection of him might have pushed him over some edge."

"Which made him trash the house and run out to get murdered?" Paulette raised her voice.

"I think that's unrelated," I said, "although maybe not to the abortion."

"What?" Shipley said.

"I'm getting ahead of myself. Paulette, I'm sorry to ask these kinds of questions, but—"

"It wasn't Truman," she said, whirling on me. Her face had gone gray, and now I was getting worried about her. Shipley reached for her and she moved away. "I know it wasn't Truman. It was some creep who started following her after Nefertiti's Ball. An ugly creepy man who she made the mistake of dancing with once and he wouldn't leave her alone after that. He's the one, about a month later. And she couldn't get him to go away."

"Paulette, sit down, honey, you're not looking good," Shipley said.

"I'm not feeling good," she said. "My cousin was murdered today, and then we learn that someone's trying to make him out to be a bad cop, and now this so-called friend of his just accused him of rape."

"I had to ask," I said.

"Well, it doesn't make any sense. Why would he plant this stuff? Why would he trash his own house? And why would he go to Woodlawn if he was that kind of crazy?"

"I thought maybe he was tracking down the abortionist," I said. "I was trying to find one in that area just the other day. Maybe the gangs recognized him as a cop and—"

"They'd shoot him?" She put a hand on her own belly. The movement seemed to subconscious. "He didn't go to Woodlawn for that."

"How do you know?" I asked.

"Because the guy she went to lives in Hyde Park," Paulette said. "And he's white."

TWENTY-SIX

ow do you know this?" Shipley asked.

"Val told me." Paulette brought a hand to her face. "I need to sit down."

Both Shipley and I went to her side, easing her toward the bed. She lay on the bare mattress, her stomach looking larger in repose than it had when she stood.

"Why would she tell you and not Marvella?" Shipley asked. "I thought Marvella was her best friend."

"Because Marvella butts in where she's not wanted," Paulette said, her eyes closed. "She was afraid Marvella would go to Truman, and Truman would go after the guy who raped her."

"He should have," Shipley said.

Paulette shook her head. "Val didn't want him to. She didn't want him anywhere near that guy."

"What was the guy's name?" I asked. This was all tied together, but I wasn't sure how yet.

"The creep?" Paulette sighed. "I don't know. Something foreign."

"Would you remember it if you heard it again?" I asked.

"No," she said. "I only heard it the once, in December. He asked me to dance, too, and I said no. Then he tried to talk to me, and he sounded—I don't know—coarse, which didn't suit his name. That's all I remember. I wasn't paying a lot of attention. I was wishing that Mike had come along."

"I wish I had, too," Shipley said. "Now."

"Told you you should've learned to dance." She said that with affection, then reached out with one manicured hand and clutched his.

"You okay, baby?" he asked. "Do I need to take you somewhere?"

"Long day," she said. "I just got dizzy. I think I got so mad I forgot to breathe."

Her hand clutched his hard. I felt guilty for bringing her here. I hadn't known about her condition. I probably shouldn't have pushed her, either.

"I'm sorry," I said. "Those weren't fair questions about Truman."

"You're right," she said. "They weren't."

Then she opened her eyes and propped herself up on one elbow. With her other hand, she still held Shipley's.

"Truman would never have trashed this place. He loved it too much. And he wouldn't have destroyed Val's pictures, no matter what she did."

"Who did then?" I asked. "Have any ideas?"

"Maybe you're wrong," Shipley said to me. "Maybe this wasn't done after he died. Maybe it was done before."

"By someone who knew him," Paulette said. "Someone who knew this would make him so mad that he would have to respond."

I looked at the mess, straightened by Paulette and Shipley but not fixed. It spoke of rage to me, particularly the kitchen, but not uncontrolled rage. If the rage had been completely out of control, no one would have left the heroin behind.

Or ripped up the pictures that methodically.

I frowned. "You said there were individual pictures of Valentina in here?"

Shipley nodded. "A couple of studio portraits, really lovely."

"She wanted them back, but Truman wouldn't give them to her," Paulette said. "They're missing, too."

"I don't see studio-sized frames," I said.

Shipley prowled the edge of the destruction. "They're not here."

"Could someone have taken Valentina's pictures—not destroyed them, but taken them for some reason?"

Paulette's lips thinned. She had both hands on her stomach again. "Val wouldn't have taken them."

"I wasn't suggesting that," I said, wondering how I could regain their trust, particularly Paulette's. I had crossed a line, questioning her that way about Johnson. And it wasn't as if I hadn't been warned. I had. Shipley had made it clear downstairs that Paulette didn't care for someone speaking ill of her cousin.

She had her eyes closed again.

"Do we need to take you somewhere?" I asked.

"I'm fine," she snapped. "It's just been a hell of a day. I keep thinking if I hadn't let Truman convince me to talk to him, everything would have been all right."

"Talk to him about what?" I asked.

"He found Val's withdrawal slip." Her voice was tired.

My heart lurched. I reached into my back pocket, removed my wallet, and pulled out the slip. "This one?"

Shipley rejoined us. He sat on the edge of the bed, and took the slip out of my hand.

"Hey," he said. "What the hell is this?"

Paulette opened her eyes and watched him. Then she pushed herself upright, as if she wasn't comfortable having this conversation lying down. "I wasn't going to say anything, because she was going to pay us back on Friday. You wouldn't have even noticed."

"That's your withdrawal slip?" I asked.

Paulette nodded. She did look tired. There were shadows under her eyes that I hadn't noticed before. "Yeah," she said. "I loaned Val the money."

Shipley crumpled the slip in his right hand. "You paid for that butchery?"

"How was I to know?" Paulette asked. "Val was in trouble. She came to me, and I could help."

"You should have told her to go to Marvella. You know better than that." His cheeks were red, and he spoke with great precision. "Marvella would never have allowed this."

"It's not my fault," Paulette said. "Val had it all worked out. She didn't want to see Marvella. She didn't want Truman involved. She knew this guy—"

"The guy who did the abortion?" I asked.

"Yes." Paulette spit the word at Shipley, even though she was answering my question. "She went to school with him. She even dated him a few times."

"That white asshole?" Shipley asked. "The guy whose Daddy greased some palms so they'd look the other way to get him into fuckin' med school? That guy?"

Paulette set her jaw. "He's an intern now, and he knows what he's doing. At least, that was what Val said to me. She was sure it was going to be all right. She said he did it all the time."

"If he did that all the time," I said, "then he's killed a lot of women."

Paulette glared at me. "All I know," she said with great precision, "is that he went to med school and Val trusted him. Hell, half the guys on Marvella's list have never been to school in their lives."

"Did Truman know who this white doctor was?" I asked.

"He found the slip," Paulette said. "He came to me, and I told him what I told you. I can't even remember the boy's name. Greg something."

"Nikolau," Shipley said.

"Would Truman know that?" I asked.

"He made it a point to know everyone Val dated, before and after the marriage," Shipley said.

"You don't think this has something to do with that, do you?" Paulette asked.

"I don't know right now," I said. "Truman asked me to help him find out who hurt Val. I refused, even though I was already looking for Marvella. I—we, actually—were worried about how Truman would react when he found the guy."

"Smart," Shipley said.

"It seemed smart at the time," I said. "I have no idea now. If I had helped him, maybe he'd still be alive."

"Or maybe the gang stuff is completely unrelated." Shipley put a hand on top of Paulette's. "I keep telling Paulie that."

Her gaze met mine. She looked as convinced as I felt.

"Do you mind if I check out the office up here?" I asked, feeling like my privileges had fled with my rude questions.

"Go ahead," she said. "I'm just going to rest here for a few minutes."

"I won't be long." I directed this to Shipley. "Then you can take her home."

He gave me a rueful nod. Something in his expression told me he understood that nothing would be the same for this family again.

I went into the office and studied the mounds of paper. Someone had worked very hard at trashing this house, and searching for anything felt like looking for the proverbial needle in the haystack.

I approached the desk and started looking through the papers. Lists in Johnson's neat handwriting, many of them with names I didn't recognize, names crossed out. Many of the crossed-out names I did recognize. They had been on Marvella's good list. Apparently Johnson had been investigating, after all.

I didn't see any Greg Nikolau on the lists that I found, though, and no notes to help me. Nikolau hadn't been on Marvella's lists, either, or on Laura's. I would have remembered the name.

I pushed aside sheet after sheet—some of which had to do with our investigations last December, some with older cases. None of them seemed, to my superficial glance, to be gang-related.

Then I went to the safe. It was closed and locked. I tried to right it. It was too heavy. The door had a built-in combination lock which, even though I turned it, didn't magically spring open the way that safes did in the movies.

I moved aside a few more files, and saw nothing in them that looked related. I couldn't be certain, however, without more research. Besides, the gang angle felt wrong to me, although I couldn't quite say why. Perhaps because of my own guilt and Johnson's intensity when we had been talking in the hospital cafeteria.

Underneath the files, I found a phone book. I thumbed through it, located an address for Greg Nikolau. The address was in Hyde Park, just like Paulette had said.

Johnson had made his lists, but he hadn't found Nikolau that way. He had found the withdrawal slip and gone to Paulette. And nothing in this haystack was going to help me more than she would, at least tonight. I stood and walked back to the bedroom.

Paulette and Shipley were lying side by side. He had his arm around her waist, and his head on her shoulder. Her cheeks were covered with fresh tears.

I cleared my throat as I stepped inside the room. They looked at me, but didn't move apart.

"I think I've done all I can tonight," I said. "I want to thank you both for allowing me to come in here."

"Did you find anything?" Shipley asked.

"Nothing useful," I said, and then thought of the heroin. "Look, before you notify anyone about this mess, I'd make sure there's nothing more here."

"We plan to," Shipley said.

"And I'd clean all of this up yourself. Don't let anyone outside of the family in. Especially before you clean up that mess in the kitchen. God knows if someone deliberately spilled another bag of heroin under all that flour."

"What do we do with it?" Paulette asked.

"You," I said, "let other people deal with it. You shouldn't touch the stuff in your condition."

Her eyes narrowed, but Shipley nodded.

"The rest of you make certain you dump that flour somewhere far from here, and make sure it can't be traced to you or this house. Make sure you scrub the floors, and clean your clothing. Don't track anything into the living room."

"Gotcha," Shipley said.

"Paulette," I said, "I have one more question for you."

She wiped at her cheek with the back of her hand. "If it's about Truman's character—"

"It's not," I said. "I was just wondering how he got your withdrawal slip."

She nodded. She looked exhausted. "I've been thinking about that. There are only two ways he got that withdrawal slip. He either took it from Val's purse—"

"I'm the one who brought her to the hospital," I said, "and she didn't have a purse with her."

"Then he got it from her apartment." Paulette sounded tired. "Stupid idiot. He knew he wasn't supposed to go inside."

"Did he have a key?" I asked.

Paulette shook her head.

"I don't get it," Shipley said. "How did he go from searching for stuff about Val to gangs?"

"I don't know," I said. "But I mean to find out."

TWENTY-SEVEN

I didn't ask the Shipleys if they had Valentina Wilson's key. I knew what their answer would be—the same as mine would have been in that circumstance: Wait until she wakes up.

I might have been able to convince them to come with me while I searched, but I didn't like how tired Paulette looked. The last thing that family needed was another tragedy.

So, that meant my next stop was Greg Nikolau. I wasn't sure what I would find.

I had a hunch that he was my link. A man who was willing to perform abortions for five hundred dollars an operation might also have been willing to break other laws. I would find out when I saw him—if Johnson hadn't gotten to him first.

Nikolau might also have had the connections to get Johnson killed. The heroin still didn't quite fit in, but I was certain now that I would find the answers I wanted.

I left Johnson's house before the Shipleys did. Paulette didn't want to go yet, and Shipley was inclined to let her rest. I agreed with him. Her exhaustion and sadness showed. I hoped that she—and the baby—would make it through what promised to be a long and difficult week.

I went out the way I came in, deciding to avoid the front door and the prying neighborhood eyes. As I left, I picked up the grocery bag.

Just holding it made me nervous, and I wished I could ask Shipley to take care of this. But all I knew about the man was his relationship to Marvella, Paulette, and Johnson. I had no idea what Shipley did for a living and how really trustworthy he was.

Better that I took care of this, so that I would know that it got done.

After a moment's deliberation, I decided to put the bag under the driver's seat. First, I took off my gloves, turned them inside out, and stuck them in the bag. Then I got into the car first, closed the door, and slid the bag under my seat.

I disabled the interior light, taking out the tiny bulb and putting it in the glove box. My hand lingered over my gun, but I didn't take it out. If I did get caught, it would be better to have the gun concealed and hope that no one found it.

Every once in a while, I had to rely on sheer good luck, and I hated it. I knew that one day, my luck would run out.

I drove north to downtown, sticking to main streets. My car was rusty and filthy, and I was a black man, wearing black, with a gun in his glove box, and thousands of dollars in heroin under the driver's seat. I was every white policeman's cliché.

Hell, I was every white policeman's nightmare.

I drove as carefully as I could, even though I wanted to go as fast as possible. Skill had to augment luck; speeding would only guarantee that I got caught.

I was heading to the Chicago River. I was going to stop on one of the bridges right over the river, and dump this stuff into it. I didn't dare walk down to the river, for risk of having the package float, and I didn't want to stop on Michigan or State, with all the lights and the nearby city buildings.

So like a fool I went a little west, where the city and state office buildings were. But they were dark as I passed, and I didn't see a single police car.

My memories from Sunday night were accurate: This part of the Loop was a wasteland after ten P.M.

The bridges over the river here were short, only about a block long, but I figured that would do. I chose LaSalle, not because I had planned to, but because it was nearby.

Before I got to the bridge, I shut off my headlights and waited a few minutes, wondering if anyone had seen me. It didn't appear that they had.

The Sherman House was lit up, but there were no taxis parked outside. Some of the streetlights were out, and I blessed the city's disorganization.

Then I drove the car to the middle of the bridge, and stopped.

The storms had passed long ago, but the clouds still covered everything. It was one of the darkest nights of the year. Rain dribbled onto the windshield, almost as if it were pretending to be spray from the filthy river below.

First, I unlatched the car door so that I could push it open with my hip. Then I reached under the driver's seat without looking down. I opened the bag, took out my gloves, and turned them right-side-out again as I put them on.

My gloved fingers were clumsy, and I couldn't take the package out by itself, like I had planned. Instead, I grabbed the entire bag, and holding it tightly, got out of the car.

I did not shut off the ignition, nor did I let the car door close all the way. I walked to the edge of the bridge as I reached inside the bag, my fingers hitting the spoons, causing them to clank.

The rain ping-pinged on the concrete. My boots made a hushing sound as I moved, and I could hear my own breathing. I tried to keep it quiet, but I was having trouble.

Of all the risky things I had done in the last six months, this one felt the most dangerous.

The bag crinkled as I reached inside it and pulled out the package. I reached inside the slit I had made earlier and ripped the package open all the way. The last thing I wanted this package to do was float.

I held the package over the water. My hands were shaking. I turned the package upside down, heroin spilling from it, somehow missing the bridge— and, I hoped, me.

I leaned as far forward as I could—and flung the package as hard as possible.

The package soared through the air, the brown wrapping looking white against the darkness. The heroin spilled like rain from the package's gut, creating an arc that stayed in the air long after the package vanished into the blackness below me.

I never did hear a splash.

Then I upended the grocery bag, pouring the paraphernalia into the water below. The spoons and the candles splashed as they hit, but the paper, the citric acid, the rubber hoses, and the syringes floated. My stomach twisted, and I resisted the urge to look around me like the guilty man I was.

I wadded up the grocery bag and tossed it as well. All I had left were my gloves. They would get trace all over my car. I had another pair in the glove-box—real winter gloves, not work gloves. I would need gloves later this evening.

I pulled the gloves off over the river, trying to keep anything from spilling on me. Then I let them drop.

The Chicago River, one of the nation's dirtiest, could contaminate the evidence for me. Even if someone found the bag, they wouldn't know what it held or why it was there.

I was shaking, and still breathing hard, but so far, I seemed to be alone.

I got back into the car and let out a deep breath. I put the car into gear, drove north across the bridge, and turned east, stopping on Illinois to catch my breath.

An old drunk staggered down the sidewalk, clutching a bottle in his right hand. He didn't seem to see me.

No one else was on the road.

Still, I waited almost ten minutes before screwing the bulb back into my interior light and closing the car door properly. Then I turned on my headlights and drove to Hyde Park.

TWENTY-EIGHT

Even though most of the residents of Hyde Park were mostly upper- and middle-class, the neighborhood was the only voluntarily integrated one in the city. The University of Chicago, located here, filled many of the stately houses—now discreet apartment buildings—with students, most of whom drove cars as decrepit as mine.

As I entered this neighborhood in the middle of the night, I no longer felt like a target. I actually felt like I was coming home.

Greg Nikolau lived just north of the university in an area filled with student housing. Even though it was late, most of the apartments still had lights burning. On one front porch, a young man sat, his feet on the brick railing, his chair tilted back, as he read a textbook under the porch light.

I parked two buildings away from Nikolau's, which was the closest parking spot I could find. I got out and walked up the sidewalk, and didn't even feel conspicuous.

The streetlights here were dim, but the porch lights more than compensated. Nikolau's building—a Victorian house converted into apartments— had lights all around its circular porch. Bicycles were chained to the wrought-iron rails beside the brick steps leading up to the porch, and the front door was open, revealing more bicycles parked in the hallway.

Nikolau's apartment number, number four, was one flight up what had once been the house's grand staircase. It was worn now, with a faded carpet covering the graying wood.

I took the steps two at a time, the adrenaline that I had felt since I parked on the bridge still pouring through my system.

Nikolau's door was the first on my right. Several large boxes were stacked outside, their flaps overlaying each other as if someone had closed them hastily.

I knocked loudly, not sure what I would find here. I assumed if Nikolau ran an abortion service, he did it away from his home, and any backup he had would be there, not here. Besides, in bed asleep was where he was most likely to be at one A.M. on a Thursday morning.

Something shuffled behind the door, then it creaked open. A pistol pointed at me, its muzzle shaking.

"Go the fuck away." The words were indistinct, as if the speaker never learned to enunciate.

The gun's shaking bothered me, until I saw the hands clutching it. They were supporting each other and, even though a forefinger was on the trigger, the safety was still on.

I grabbed the pistol and twisted it out of the shooter's hand at the same moment I shoved the door open. The shooter screamed and staggered backward.

He was a young man, no more than twenty-five, thin and short, maybe 130 pounds soaking wet, certainly not someone who could handle me in a fair fight.

I stepped inside and let the door close behind me, hoping no one had heard that cry of panic.

All the lights in the apartment were on. The young man backed away from me, then tripped over his own tennis-shoed feet and toppled to the rug. He never took his gaze off me.

His face was swollen, his eyes so black and blue that they were nearly closed. His lips were three times their normal size, and his nose appeared to be broken.

"Greg Nikolau?" I asked.

"Can't you people leave me alone? Jesus. I'm doing everything you want." He had trouble speaking around those swollen lips.

"Really?" I asked, deciding to play along. "It doesn't look like it."

"Fuck!" He scrambled backward in a crablike crawl, still not taking his gaze off me. "It takes a while to pack, man. I'll be out of here by noon, I promise. He never said someone would come in the middle of the fucking night."

"Noon." I almost smiled. I suddenly understood what happened, and it felt like the only victory in a day filled with defeats. "Johnson gave you until noon? How kind of him."

"Kind?" Nikolau braced one hand on the wall as he got to his feet. His legs shook. The hand he used as a brace had a bandage wrapped around the wrist. It didn't look too steady. He swept the other hand down his body. "Does this look kind? He beat the shit out of me. I thought he was going to kill me."

"I'm surprised he didn't," I said truthfully, "considering what you did to Val."

We had misjudged Johnson after all. He hadn't killed Nikolau, but he'd made Nikolau understand the kind of pain he had put Valentina through.

"It was an accident," Nikolau said. "God, how many times do I have to say that? I liked Val. I even fucking asked her out a few times. I never meant to hurt her."

"You nearly killed her." I kept my voice level.

"Look," he said, extending his hands. The other hand was swollen and had bruises that showed purple against his pale skin. Maybe he needed both hands to hold the gun because neither hand was working well. "She was nearly three months gone. That's a lot of fucking tissue. And I don't use anesthetic. She knew that."

"That seems pretty stupid," I said.

"See, that's where you assholes don't know anything." He wiped his mouth with the back of his hand. He generated a lot of spittle as he tried to speak. "Anesthetic is dangerous if you don't know what you're doing. It takes special training."

"Like abortion," I said.

"Hell, women do that on their own. I was just helping out. Providing a service."

"Without anesthetic," I said.

"I didn't want to hurt her. Don't you get it? I'm not trained."

"But you're trained in abortion."

He gave me a baleful look—at least, that seemed like what he intended. "No one is, but that doesn't stop people. I've been interning at Cook County. You know how many self-induced I saw there?"

"No," I said, "and I don't care. It sounds like what you did was worse."

"It was not. Most of the self-induced die."

I clenched my fists. "Tell me again how what you did was different?"

"It wasn't me on this one! It wasn't. It was Val." His whiny voice grated on my ears. "She knew I didn't use anesthetic. If she couldn't take the pain, she shouldn't've come. I told her not to move. Be perfectly still, I said, and you'll be all right."

"You're saying that the damage that nearly killed Valentina Wilson was her fault?"

"She had some training. She knew what she was getting into."

"And how many women have you done this to who didn't have training? Who squirmed too?"

"You're twisting my words, man."

The anger I had been suppressing all day rose to the surface. I said, "Maybe I'll just kill you myself."

"Go ahead," he said. "Like I got anything to live for. Your friend took care of that. No medical license—not now, not ever. He got ahold of my advisors at the university and told them what I did. He called Cook County and told my boss. They're pressing charges, but I'm doing what your friend Johnson told me to do. I'm leaving town."

My fist slammed into his already-injured mouth. The teeth mushed beneath my fingers, and he banged into the wall. He held one hand over his lips, looking as surprised as I felt.

"What the hell was that for?"

I had no idea how I understood him. The words he spoke didn't sound like English. "So that you'll think twice before ever attempting an abortion again."

"Like I can do any surgery ever again. It's a finesse thing. Look at this hand. Look at it!" He held up his swollen, bruised right hand. "He stomped it. A bunch of the tiny bones are broken, but I can't do anything. I'm scared to go to the hospital, because they'll make me stay, and he said if he found me anywhere in Chicago after noon tomorrow—today, I guess—he'll kill me."

I wanted to cheer Johnson. His revenge was better than anything Marvella and I could have done.

"Then you'd better get the hell out of here," I said.

"But my stuff!" Nikolau said.

"Isn't worth your life," I said.

"Oh, Jesus." He slid down the wall and huddled in a fetal position.

"That's all I wanted to tell you," I said. "The sooner you get out of town, the happier the rest of us will be."

"This isn't fair," he said, huddled against the wall.

"Considering that you're guilty of attempted murder, it's very fair," I said, and walked to the door. I wanted to beat this kid senseless. Hell, I wanted to kill him with my bare hands.

But it wouldn't accomplish anything. This kid—and that's all he was, some idiot punk kid with no sense of the people he was trying to help—had no community ties, no gang connection. If I killed him, no one else would be discouraged from doing abortions.

Nothing would change, except that he would stop injuring innocent women. But Johnson had already taken care of that. Johnson, whom I hadn't trusted enough to take into my confidence.

Johnson, who was dead.

"Hey!" Nikolau cried. "What about my gun?"

I hefted it and looked at it. It was a nice piece, expensive, even if it had been poorly cared for.

"My gun now," I said, and let myself out of the apartment.

TWENTY-NINE

I got into my car and sat for a moment, letting the anger course through me. It wasn't all I felt. I also felt respect for Johnson, respect I wasn't sure I wanted to feel.

He had proven me wrong. I had listened to Marvella's worry about her cousin, thought about the times I had seen him angry, and forgotten that I hadn't really known him.

Maybe if I had given him a chance, he would be alive now. I would have had the benefit of Johnson's complicated brain, and he wouldn't be a potential statistic in a war no one would win.

I sighed, and checked Nikolau's gun. It wasn't even loaded. I tucked it under the seat. Then I took one last look at the neighborhood.

The textbook reader got up, picked up his chair, and went inside his building. Another man, young by the look of him, unlocked one of the bikes on a nearby porch and rode it down the stairs. He bounced off the curb and into the street without even looking for traffic. He disappeared into the darkness.

I wondered if Nikolau had operated here or somewhere else. He didn't look sophisticated enough to have a separate office. How deceptive this was. Safe and intellectual, easily middle class, concerned with class times and homework assignments instead of women, lying on a bed in an upstairs apartment, clenching their fists against a pain so intense that they involuntarily tried to get away from it.

Valentina had trusted that asshole, and I didn't understand why.

As I sat there, trying to calm down, Nikolau lurched out the front door. He carried a suitcase in his least injured hand. He tried to open the trunk of his car, gave up, and kicked the back. Then he leaned on it, defeated.

After a moment, he set the suitcase down and opened the trunk with his good hand. Then he picked the suitcase up and set it inside. He got into the driver's side, looked up at the building, and shook his head.

He seemed to struggle for a minute with the ignition before the car started. He reached across the column with his left hand and shifted, then the car jerked forward, narrowly missing the others parked around it.

I smiled.

"Nice work, Johnson," I said as if he were sitting beside me. "Nice work."

I started up my own car, made a U-turn, and headed out of the neighborhood. Nikolau was the proof I needed; I had been right. Johnson hadn't gone back to work. Whatever he had been doing on the Gaza Strip during the afternoon had been related to Val.

Johnson had gotten the withdrawal slip from Val's apartment, and then confronted Paulette. She hadn't known exactly who raped Val, although she probably could recognize the man. Had she told Johnson that? I wasn't sure.

My next stop, then, would be Val's apartment.

I felt like I was retracing Johnson's last steps, walking behind him, missing the clues. I wondered if we had worked together whether he would have made this much progress or if my methods would have held him back.

I shook the thoughts away and, with them, a feeling of loss so intense that my fingers dug into the steering wheel's hard plastic. I couldn't think about Johnson. Instead, I had to concentrate on finding his killer.

And the next place I had to find was Valentina's apartment.

I had been having luck with the phonebook, so I decided to continue with that particular investigative tool. I parked in front of my own apartment, locked the car, and went inside.

The building was silent. A single light burned in the hallway. Marvella's lights were off, and some circulars leaned against her door. I picked them up and carried them inside my own apartment, which was considerably cooler than it had been earlier in the day.

I had left the windows open, and the heavy rain had soaked the windowsills. I closed the windows slightly, still letting the breeze come in. I felt restless here, as if I didn't belong. It was a strange feeling, but one I recognized from my stint in Korea.

Things always felt different after the shooting started.

I ate an apple as I thumbed through the phonebook. Sure enough, Valentina Wilson was listed—as Val Wilson, which was smarter than initials on her part. Val could be either a male or female name; initials tended to shout that the inhabitant was female.

She lived a few blocks away from Johnson, apparently unable to leave that neighborhood. Thoughtfully, Ma Bell had even provided an apartment number in the form of a ½. Valentina Wilson lived in a two-flat on the second floor.

I finished the apple, tossed the core, and went into my bedroom. From my closet, I took a black jacket and my shoulder holster. I also took the last of my cash from the top drawer.

I had no idea if I would need any of that, but I didn't want to come home again until I was certain.

Then I left, heading back to one of Bronzeville's nicer neighborhoods to break into an apartment.

It was after two A.M. I couldn't go to the hospital in the middle of the night and get Marvella's help. I didn't want to disturb the Shipleys again, not with the way Paulette had looked when I left. Valentina had been a cop's wife, and Paulette had made a point of telling me that Johnson did not hide an extra key outside his door. I doubted Valentina did, either.

If I wanted to get inside that apartment, I had to do it myself.

I got my extra set of gloves out of the glovebox and put them on. They were thicker than the pair I had discarded, and would make my movements difficult. But they were all I had left.

Valentina's neighborhood looked as different from Nikolau's as possible. It also differed from Johnson's. On this block, only the stumps of the old trees remained, and no one had planted any younger trees. The two-flats had been built in the 1920s and, from the look of them, hadn't been altered at all.

Only the streetlights illuminated this block. All of the porch lights were out, and no lights shone in apartment windows. Everyone was asleep. People here worked; they didn't go to school, and couldn't skip class to sleep in.

I drove around the block, scoping it out, then parked on a side street. I snuck through the alley behind the apartment buildings, staying in the shadows, moving as quietly as I possibly could.

When I reached the back of Valentina's building, I studied it, seeing what I had hoped to find—a wooden fire escape built onto the outside of the building nearly three decades ago.

Those old fire escapes were sturdy. They had platforms near large windows or doors so that the tenant could easily escape in case of an emergency.

They also made entering exceptionally easy.

For a moment, I toyed with trying the front door. There had to be a main entrance with a main staircase. But I didn't want to be seen, and the light out front was good enough that someone might catch me going in. I had a hunch that not a lot of people went in and out of apartment buildings this late at night—especially large men, dressed all in black.

The only lights in the alley were on both ends—streetlights, placed so that passing cars could see cars merging from the alley. Valentina's two-flat was in the center of the block. Unless someone was looking out a back window, no one would see me here.

The backyard was a mass of puddles from the afternoon's deluge. The ground squished as I walked on it, and I cursed quietly, hoping that the sound wasn't as loud as I thought it was. The wind had died down and there hadn't been any rain for hours now.

An eerie silence had fallen across the city, as if it were waiting for something.

The fire escape was as soaked as the ground. The wood looked swollen, as if the water had gone inside its very pores. That made my climb easier. Wet wood didn't creak and groan like dry wood did.

I was careful, making certain to step lightly so that my boots didn't make a sound. I was especially quiet as I passed the first floor's window.

It took me only a moment to get past the first floor and up to the second. The fire escape butted up against a large, old-fashioned, double-hung window. A flip lock had been installed on the lower half, and the lock appeared to have been turned.

I cursed under my breath and studied the window. It operated on a rope-pulley system, and there were no screens or storms. I could touch the rope if I wanted to.

The window had been installed in the 1940s and, even though someone had tried to improve the window's security with that lock, they had failed. All I had to do to get inside Valentina's apartment was pull down the window's top half.

I climbed farther up the stairs, grabbed the top of the window frame, and pushed down. This part of the window wasn't attached to the lock, which had been installed to prevent someone from opening the bottom half of the window by pushing up. The top half went down easily, and didn't even squeal from lack of use as I thought it might.

I levered myself over the now-open window and into the apartment. It was warm inside and smelled faintly of lilies. I felt for the ledge with my foot, not wanting to jump down, afraid that the sound of my weight hitting the floor would awaken the tenants below.

My foot found the frame. It wasn't very wide. I brought the other foot all the way down and hit something before I reached the floor. It was the toilet. I used it as a step on my way to the floor.

In all my preparation, I had forgotten a flashlight. The apartment was dark, and I couldn't see anything. I would either have to find Valentina's flashlight or risk turning on a light.

I left the window down in case I had to make a quick escape. There didn't appear to be anything in the bathroom that would help me see better, so I slipped out of the room, trying to walk lightly, and found myself in a long narrow hallway. I pulled the bathroom door closed, and turned on the hallway light.

Quickly, I scanned my surroundings. The hallway had no windows, only doors. If anyone saw this light from outside, they might not register where it was coming from.

Still, I would have to move quickly. The longer I left the light on, the easier I would be to catch.

The room to my left off the bathroom appeared to be an extra room. Books lined the wall and spilled off a desk. An overstuffed chair sat in the corner against what must have been the chimney. A reading light stood above it, and more books tumbled along the side.

The fact that Valentina was a reader finally sunk in. Johnson had told me she was, but I had dismissed that. People who didn't read much often thought the presence of a book or two meant someone else read all the time. I figured since Johnson didn't read for enjoyment, he had misstated Valentina's preferences.

I had been wrong.

I passed that room, even though it would be the one I would need to search the most. First, though, I wanted to figure out the apartment's layout.

I continued down the hallway. The next room, on the right, was Valentina's bedroom. The hallway light illuminated the bed, which had been turned down as if a maid had come in to take care of it. Something small and square cast a shadow on the pillow.

Another door on my left proved to be a large closet. On the top shelf, after much fumbling, I found a flashlight. I flicked the switch. A small beam of light appeared before me.

I used the last moment of hallway light to see the rest of the apartment—the high-ceilinged living room with a formal dining area, complete with chandelier, and the square, comfortable kitchen.

Then I shut off the hall light, and used the flashlight only.

Except for the book room, the apartment was excessively neat. The sofa's cushions were dented, with a pillow downturned facing the television, but the rest of the living room didn't look used. Fresh flowers sat on every table, most of them lilies. Their scent was overpowering. I had no idea how anyone could live with that many flowers.

Even more decorated the kitchen, and a gigantic vase of hothouse roses covered the kitchen table. A water ring around the vase suggested that someone had refreshed the water recently. I trained the light on it, and saw a card tucked among the leaves.

With one hand, I reached in and pulled out the card.

To brighten your homecoming, my love.

—A.

A? No one had mentioned a current boyfriend, a lover, or anyone close to Valentina. But then, I had been talking mostly with Marvella, and generally around Johnson. Maybe she had chosen not to mention a boyfriend around the ex-husband.

I retraced my steps through the apartment, finding nothing else of interest as I went. More flowers in the bedroom, and a box of chocolates on the pillow, also from the mysterious A.

Then I went into the book room, pulled the curtains and the shade, and risked turning on the reading light.

Most of the books around the chairs were novels—thrillers, mysteries, classics. Several of the books on shelves were texts—biology, medicine, and legal. The books on the desk were an eclectic mixture of the same, with some history and several books in other languages thrown into the mix.

The desk drawers revealed neatly kept ledgers, just like Johnson's, outlining bills and payment in a double-entry bookkeeping system. I scanned the accounts and saw why Valentina had borrowed the money from Paulette. Valentina had no money in savings at all, but she was paid once a month, in a sum large enough to cover rent, food, and repay Paulette over time.

I didn't understand why a woman with a job that paid so well didn't have more cash put away. I scanned the ledgers and didn't find the answer to my question.

Then I opened another file, and did.

Her savings had gone to two places: a private detective agency and a lawyer. The detective agency had sent her short written reports attached to expense sheets that looked padded. The lawyer had written a letter to someone named Armand Vitel, demanding that he stay away from Valentina Wilson or legal steps would be taken.

I took the file to the reading chair and sat down. The detective reports were mostly accounts of Vitel's earnings, and other information that could be obtained through telephone calls. The detective, who did not sign his reports, seemed hesitant to follow Vitel or even approach him, citing concerns about "safety."

A short, general report closed with this:

> Although Mr. Vitel's actions are invasive, they are not illegal. His unwanted advances simply make him a persistent suitor, something the law can do nothing about. Unless Mr. Vitel breaks the law in his contact with you, you cannot bring any authorities in to dissuade him from his behavior.
>
> Given Mr. Vitel's profession, he probably knows this. We suggest that you continue to politely rebuff his attentions until he finds another target for his affections.

The report, dated in February, was the last in the detective's file. The lawyer's letter followed, with a March date. There was no apparent response to that, either from Vitel or from Valentina. The lawyer's letter was vaguely worded, probably because the lawyer knew he did not have much legal standing to back up his threat of suit.

I got up and put the file back. Then I dug in the drawer. There were a few more files in there, mostly personal papers, insurance documents, and a copy of the divorce decree. Nothing unusual.

Behind the files, however, I found a box. Inside were letters, all written in the same childish hand, all signed *A*. Some had been torn up, one had been burned, and a few remained intact, as if Valentina couldn't decide what to do with them.

I read the intact letters—or as much as I could stomach of them. They began as love letters and quickly turned into something pornographic. The first one was dated December 9, 1968:

> *Ever since our magical dance under the lights of Nefertiti, I have been unable to get you out of my mind. Who knew that such an unromantic place as Sauer's Brauhaus could be the site of a world-class meeting between two lost souls?*

The first letter was almost poetic. The pornography didn't begin until it became clear to Vitel that Valentina did not share his passion.

The letters were disgusting and left me feeling filthy. I set them back in their box, tucked them in the back of the drawer, then leaned on the desk.

Vitel was the person Johnson had gone after, I was convinced of it, perhaps even the person Johnson had met in the Gaza Strip. Something had gone wrong, though, and I wasn't certain what that something could have been.

I turned off the reading lamp and headed back to my window. Then I stopped.

The flowers on the kitchen table spoke of homecoming. The Easter lilies looked fresh. Valentina had been gone most of Saturday, and at Marvella's all of Sunday. It was now Wednesday. Some of the flowers should have wilted.

Who had placed the flowers in the apartment? Why were the flowers here instead of at the hospital?

My heart started to pound. I walked back into the living room and read all of the cards.

The cards had the same writing as the letters had, and the same signature: *A.* Most of the sentiments were expected: get well, miss you, happy Easter.

But the flowers on the dining room table, a large spray that seemed to be mostly leaves and baby's breath, had this tucked in its massive cut-glass vase:

> *I pray for you from afar. I cannot sit at your bedside because it is guarded by the man you have discarded. When you come home, I shall care for you like you should be cared for. When you come home, I shall love you even more.*
>
> *—A.*

He had been in the apartment, trespassing, just like I was. He had prowled these rooms, touched her things.

She was in as much danger as she had ever been. More, perhaps, because Johnson was gone.

I pocketed the card and headed out of the apartment. I had to see Marvella, and I hoped she had the answers I needed.

THIRTY

The storm clouds over Lake Michigan were turning a violent pink as I drove to the hospital. While I had been in Valentina's apartment, the air had turned cold. Another storm front was moving in, just ahead of the dawn.

The radio disk jockeys were discussing the storms of the day before, promising that today's rain wouldn't be similar. Because the storm was so early in the year, the damage had been minimal—the storm sewers had been able to handle it, for the most part, and only a few tree limbs had come down, knocking out power to Rogers Park.

The early-morning newscaster reported Johnson's death by calling it another gang shooting involving a police officer. Johnson's name was left out of the report, pending notification of relatives. The newscaster spent little time on his death. Instead, the newscast focused on Black Panther leader Fred Hampton getting out on bond after his indictment for stealing seventy dollars' worth of ice-cream bars last summer, and an unrelated bombing yesterday afternoon at Goldblatt's Department Store.

The chatter was a welcome distraction. I wanted a little bit of time to gather my thoughts before I confronted Marvella.

As I pulled in the hospital's nearly empty parking lot, I realized that visiting hours hadn't even started. I grabbed my black coat in an effort to make

myself look respectable. I felt filthy and ragged, but not tired. Still, I probably had the air of a man who had been up all night.

The hospital's front entrance was not locked. I was going to cite a family
emergency to get me to Marvella, but my made-up story was wasted—no
one sat at the front desk.

I scooted past it, though, and once inside the main part of the hospital,
tried to look as if I belonged. A resident no older than Nikolau stood beside
me as I waited for the elevator; he looked like he had had less sleep than I had.

We got on the elevator together, and he got off on the second floor. I rode
the elevator all the way to five.

The hallway was quiet. A nurse sat at the nurse's station, reading a chart
as if it were a good novel. I eased past her and walked quietly down the
hall.

I half-expected Marvella to be outside of Valentina's room, sitting in
front of it like a security guard. But she wasn't. My heart started to beat
harder, and I worried that I had found this information too late, worried that
Vitel had come here in the middle of the night and done something while I
was away.

Carefully, I pushed the door open. Marvella, who had been sleeping in a
chair, sat up even before she was fully awake. When she saw me, she blinked,
and then whispered, "I told you to stay out of the room."

"I have to talk to you," I said, glancing at Valentina's bed. She had tubes
hanging out of her arm, and a large bag of fluid above her. She looked thinner than I remembered, her head turned sideways in sleep.

The room smelled of rubbing alcohol and illness.

"You're not supposed to be here," Marvella whispered. She made a *shoo*
motion with her hands.

I crooked my finger. "It's important."

She tossed aside the rubber hospital blanket she had been using to keep
warm, stood, and stretched. Her movements were catlike, her hair frizzed.

When she reached me, she put a hand on my arm and shoved me out of
the room.

"How is she?" I asked.

Marvella's features relaxed. "Better. She opened her eyes shortly after you
left."

"What does the doctor say?"

"It's still touch and go," Marvella said. "But more go."

I felt myself relax slightly.

She pulled the door closed and stepped away from it, into the hallway.
"What do you need me for?"

272

There was no easy way to approach this. I hoped I would be able to talk with Marvella, but if she didn't know anything, I might have to go to Val.

"Who's Armand Vitel?" I asked.

"How the hell should I know?"

"He's been sending Valentina love letters ever since Nefertiti's Ball. I think he's the guy who raped her."

Marvella rubbed the sleep from her eyes, and as she did, I realized she had never asked me to find Val's rapist. Only the abortionist.

If Marvella had thought the rapist was still a threat, she would have asked for help with that, too.

She probably didn't know as much as I hoped.

"Okay," Marvella said. "So the guy has a name. There's not much we can do about it. Like Truman said, it's too late to press charges, not that I would recommend it anyway. No one ever listens to the woman. They always think she asked for it."

"That's not why I want to know," I said. "I'm pretty sure Truman was going after Vitel when he got murdered."

Marvella frowned. "What?"

I told her about Johnson's house being torn up, about the missing pictures, and everything Paulette had told me.

"Paulette helped Val?" Marvella sounded stunned.

"Paulette said that Valentina swore her to secrecy. And that she wasn't worried because Valentina had met the guy in college. He was in medical school then."

"Greg?" Marvella's voice rose. "She went to Greg?"

I nodded. "Truman found out, and took care of Nikolau."

"Shit," Marvella said, and leaned against the wall, clearly bracing herself for more bad news. "Is the kid dead?"

"No," I said. "We both misjudged Truman. He did better than we would have."

"What'd he do?" Marvella asked.

"He roughed him up a bit, got his license revoked, and forced him to leave town."

"How do you know this?"

"Because," I said, "I administered the final kick to make sure Nikolau won't bother anyone again."

Marvella shook her head slightly. "What has this to do with Vitel?"

"I couldn't find anything in the house that led me to believe that Truman was back doing police work. He spent part of yesterday bullying Nikolau. The rest of the time, he had to be going after Vitel."

"But you don't know that for sure."

"No, I don't," I said, "but I have pretty good intuition."

"Intuition isn't enough."

"It's a start," I said.

An orderly walked by. He looked at us, but didn't say anything.

I waited until he was out of sight before speaking again. "You're probably going to be mad at me, but I went to Val's apartment."

"You what?"

My only hope was to slide past that part as quickly as possible. "And it's full of flowers, all of them from Vitel. One of them had this note."

I handed it to her. Marvella read it and turned ashen.

"He's going to come here?" she asked.

"He might," I said. "I need to know who he is. I need to know if I'm right about him. If we're going to protect her, Marvella, we have to have the facts now."

"Dammit," she said.

Her hand, clutching the note, shook. Her eyes moved back and forth as she debated with herself. I waited, hoping she would think this through and come up with the right answer.

"You really think he killed Truman?" Marvella asked.

"He might have ordered the hit," I said. "Think about it. If Val knows something about this guy, she might have remained silent, not to keep Truman out of her life, but to protect him."

"Because this guy is involved with gangs?" Marvella read the note again. "And he ordered a hit on Truman?"

I nodded.

"If that's true, then we don't have any options," Marvella said. "If Truman can't protect Val, then who can?"

Present tense. I wondered if she had even known she had used it.

Johnson couldn't protect anyone anymore.

"We don't know what's true and what's not," I said. "Only Val does."

Marvella kept staring at the note.

"Look," I said. "For all we know, Truman might have gone down to the Gaza Strip to follow up on this case, and gotten killed because of some other case he was working on. At this point, anything is possible. The one thing I am certain of is that this Vitel is dangerous to Val, and he might come here now that Truman's gone. You have to know that."

"You're not going to tell Val that she's in danger," Marvella said.

"All I'm going to do is ask her if he was the one who attacked her."

Marvella nodded. "Make it quick, and don't tell her about Truman, either."

"Thank you."

She waved a finger in my face. "Remember."

"I will."

"Okay," she said. "I'm going to see what I can do about keeping her protected. Maybe hospital security will keep an extra eye on the room."

Then she hurried down the hall. I watched her go.

After Marvella turned the corner, I pushed the door open. The scents of rubbing alcohol and illness hit me again. The room had a twilight grayness—morning light was trying to filter through the orange curtains over the outside window, and hallway light blended through the brown curtains over the inside window.

The room was warm—I had no idea how Marvella had slept under a blanket—and oddly humid.

I sat in the wooden chair someone had pushed next to the bed. I hadn't realized this was a private room until just now. It was probably a recovery room used for extremely ill patients. Marvella didn't have to tell me to go lightly. It was clear that Valentina was still very sick.

The tubes sticking out of Valentina's arm had bruised her skin. The remains of nail polish colored her fingertips, which rested on top of her own rubber blanket.

I reached across the metal railings and gently took the hand nearest mine. Her skin was cool, which I hadn't expected. I thought she would feel feverish.

"Valentina?" I said softly.

She didn't move.

"Valentina, can you wake up?"

She moaned and slid her hand away from mine. With her other hand, the one not tied to a legion of tubes, she wiped off her face.

Then she turned her head slowly and looked at me, blinking herself awake.

I didn't know how many painkillers she had taken or how clear her perceptions were. I didn't want to frighten her.

"I don't know if you remember me, Val," I said gently. "I'm Bill Grimshaw, Marvella's neighbor. My friend Laura and I found you Sunday night."

Valentina frowned. "I thought Smokey found me."

"They call me that sometimes," I said.

"Then who's Dalton?"

I started. Laura had used my full name that night. I had forgotten.

"Marvella gave me permission to talk to you, but only for a few minutes," I said, ignoring that last question. "I have something really painful to ask you, and I wouldn't do it if it weren't important."

Her expression grew wary. She blinked again, as if she were trying to clear cobwebs from her brain.

"The man who attacked you a couple of months ago," I said, "was his name Armand Vitel?"

She closed her eyes and licked her dry lips. I grabbed the glass beside the bed.

"I have water," I said.

She opened her eyes, didn't meet my gaze, and grabbed the glass with her good hand. Then she tried to inch herself upright. I put a hand behind her neck and held her up so that she could take a drink.

Even though she was medicated, even though she had just awakened, she seemed more alert than I expected, as if she were stalling.

Then she handed me the glass. "Where's Marvella?"

"She had to talk to hospital security. I found some stuff that leads me to believe Vitel might come here."

Valentina bit her lower lip.

"Marvella and I won't let him. We're doing everything we can to prevent it. But I need to know if he was the one who—" I found I couldn't be as blunt as I wanted to. "—who got you into this situation."

"Raped me," Valentina whispered. "He raped me, Mr. Grimshaw."

"I'm sorry," I said.

She shrugged, as if it didn't matter, even though we both knew that it did.

"Why didn't you tell Truman?" I asked.

She plucked at the blanket. "What could he do? I met Armand at a dance. We were seen together. He sent me flowers and letters. It would be his word against mine. And, believe me, his word would win."

It usually did in these cases. Few rapes ever came to trial, and if there were no witnesses, it always came down to which party was the most credible. The victim had her entire life's history paraded before the court. Most of the accused's life history—particularly his arrest record—often was excluded under the rules of evidence.

Valentina's history probably wouldn't seem that sympathetic. She was black, lived alone, and she was divorced, which many still saw as a sign of promiscuity.

But the way she answered my question bothered me. Not her words—

which were nearly identical to Marvella's—but her attitude. She wasn't telling me everything.

"Truman might have been able to take care of the problem privately, had you thought of that?" I asked.

"I was afraid of that," she said. "He has to stay away from Armand. Armand hates him."

"Truman can take care of himself." I had to struggle with both the present tense and the sentiment. In this case, Johnson hadn't been able to take care of himself.

She stopped plucking at the blanket. She shoved her pillow back with her elbows, propping herself up more efficiently than I had done. Even though she was small and thin, she didn't seem frail.

"Tell me something," she said. "I know Marvella wants to keep me all cocooned and safe, but I have to know. Truman's dead, isn't he?"

It was my turn to be surprised. It must have shown on my face, because her mouth turned downward.

"I'm sorry," I said, and my voice broke. I cleared my throat, swallowed, and spoke in a firmer tone. "Marvella made me promise not to tell you."

"How?" Valentina whispered, and she wasn't talking about Marvella.

"He was shot," I said, deciding to leave out as many details as possible.

"When?"

It was harder for me to answer that. I felt like it had been weeks ago, even though it had been less than twenty-four hours. "Yesterday afternoon."

"I thought so." Her eyes were dry. She nodded, just a little, then sighed. "When I was—asleep, you know?—I thought I heard something like that. And when I asked about him, Marvella acted weird."

"I'm sorry," I said.

She shook her head. "He found out, didn't he? About Armand."

"I think so," I said.

"And he was going to fix it." She sounded bitter. "Goddammit, Truman."

We were both silent for a moment. Her reaction to Johnson's death surprised me. I hadn't expected her to be protecting him. I thought she was the angry wife who wanted nothing to do with him.

She seemed calmer than I would have expected, given the news. Perhaps the drugs blunted her emotions—or perhaps she was waiting until she had a private moment to let her guard down.

She was saying, "I managed to avoid Truman for the last few months so he didn't know, because if he had found out, he would have done something. He did do something, didn't he?"

"He beat the hell out of Greg Nikolau," I said.

She smiled. It was a fond smile. "That was my mistake. I thought I could take care of this alone. And I knew Greg. The procedure isn't complicated, and he'd done a few. I figured he'd be all right. I should have listened to Marvella."

"How come everyone defers to Marvella on this?" I asked.

Valentina gave me a sideways glance. "She never told you?"

"No," I said. "Did she have a bad experience?"

I meant the question euphemistically. I wasn't quite able to ask if she had had an abortion, too.

"You could say that." Valentina's eyes narrowed. "She was eighteen and poor, and nearly died from appendicitis. She came out of the surgery missing one appendix and one uterus."

I went cold. "They can't do that."

"They did," she said. "They do, a lot. She signed something when she was that sick, and they figured why let a poor girl breed? You should check sometime. It happens all over—and not just to black girls. White ones, too, if they've had too many babies and they don't have enough money."

I couldn't quite wrap my mind around this. Too much had happened or I was too tired. "I don't get it," I said. "How does that tie to . . . what happened to you?"

"Because Marvella, bless her, gets angry." Valentina said this in a toneless voice. "And when she gets angry, she takes action. She's been after legislators for years, talked to lawyers, and she keeps track of doctors and hospitals, which ones do these procedures, and which ones don't, for whatever reason."

Valentina rubbed her hand on the blanket. So she wasn't as calm as she appeared.

"Turns out botched abortions are the most common justification." A tear ran down her cheek but her voice didn't change. "So Marvella started making lists of who did a good job, so a woman wouldn't be in this—in my—you know."

She waved her hand at me. "I was stupid. I was stupid all around. I was stupid to dance with him, and stupid to not confide in Marvella."

But not, I noticed, stupid in failing to tell Johnson.

"You were doing the best you could."

"I kept thinking of Truman. I wasn't thinking about me. It's like I wasn't even involved in any of this. Cut off, you know?"

I did know. I had felt that a time or two myself.

"I still don't understand," I said. "What were you trying to protect Truman from? What was Armand into?"

"Into?" Valentina blinked, frowned, as if she had to concentrate. "He's into everything. Don't you know who he is?"

I shook my head. "I never heard of him before today."

"That explains it," she said, more to herself than to me. "That's why you thought you could protect me."

"What do you mean?" I asked.

"Armand Vitel," she said. "He can get in anywhere."

"Why?" I asked.

"Because," she said slowly as if she were speaking to a child, "Armand Vitel is a cop."

THIRTY-ONE

Whatever I had expected Valentina to say, it hadn't been that. I stood up, suddenly restless. The implications were larger than I wanted to consider. A cop, a gang hit—had I made the wrong assumption? Had Truman Johnson been killed because he was with someone else?

Who was first out the door? I had asked the bartender.

Couldn't see it. Would've thought the other guy, because your friend waved to me, but don't know that for sure.

Didn't know it for sure. But if it had been Johnson when everyone else had been expecting Armand Vitel, then the boys had hit the wrong man. Vitel would have saved his own life by coming back into the bar, getting his things, and going out the back door.

The police wouldn't have known, and the gangs wouldn't have found out until it was too late.

Valentina was wiping the tears off her face. "This is just an awful mess," she said, "and no one can make it right."

"I know," I said. "But you didn't start it. Vitel did."

She ran her thumb under her lower eyelid. "You're kind."

"It's true," I said. "None of this would have happened if he had left you alone."

"He's not the type to leave people alone. God." She wiped her other eye. "I've got to stop this, or Marvella will know you told me."

"It's all right," I said.

She shook her head. "Marvella needs to do something right now. I'd rather have her take care of me than go after Armand."

"Don't worry about Armand," I said.

"You can't go after him." Valentina reached for me. Her fingers were shaking. She wasn't as strong as she was pretending to be. "Look what happened to Truman. You don't know how smart he is."

She meant Vitel.

"I don't care how smart he is," I said. "He loses control. Anyone who loses control isn't all-powerful."

"But he covers it, and he's ruthless." Her hand caught my arm. "You can't. Promise me you'll stay away from him."

"You see how good I am at keeping promises." I put my hand over hers. "I promised Marvella I wouldn't tell you about Truman."

"Don't," Valentina said. "Don't play these kinds of games. You don't know who Vitel is."

"And he doesn't know who I am, which gives me a hell of an advantage." I eased Valentina's hand off my arm. "Truman was a good cop. I'm not a cop at all. I don't have to follow the same rules."

She shook her head. "Don't do this for me."

"All right," I said quietly. "I won't. I'll do it for Truman."

And then I walked out of the room.

Marvella came back just as I stepped out of the door. She looked tired and flustered. "How's Val?"

"Upset," I said.

"Understandably," Marvella said. "She got upset just telling me a little bit about it on Sunday. Did she give you enough information?"

I nodded. "Vitel's a cop."

"Oh, God," Marvella said. "Then hospital won't be able to do anything."

She was quick.

"That's right. You're going to need your own guards," I said, "and not just people like Shipley. You'll need someone big, like me."

"You're not staying?" Marvella asked.

"No," I said. "I'm going to work on it from a different angle."

And before she could ask me any more, I headed off down the hall.

I needed information, and I wasn't going to get it here. I had to find out who Vitel was, what his cases were, and how they connected to Johnson. I also had to find out what kind of trouble I would be in if I took care of the problem myself.

The elevator was fuller than it had been on the way up. Two nurses, their white uniforms ironed, their little caps starched, stood to one side. A man wearing a rumpled suit and reeking of cigar smoke leaned against the elevator wall.

I stepped inside and rode down, staring at myself the whole way, a black smudge in the stainless steel doors.

For the first time in months, I felt out of my depth. Valentina's statement had the weight of history and Chicago politics, things I still wasn't as up on as I should have been. The fact that Armand Vitel was a cop—and, I was assuming, a black cop, since no one had mentioned his color, and he attended the Nefertiti Ball, which had been a benefit for the South Side Community Art Center—shouldn't have stopped Johnson from going after him.

In fact, it should have made Johnson's job easier. He could have used the letters as proof of unwanted attention, and gone to the union or to the Afro-American Patrolman's League. The fact that Valentina felt he couldn't, and that even knowing Vitel's identity had been dangerous, meant there was something here I didn't understand.

So when the elevator stopped on the first floor, I went to the pay phone near the cafeteria, and called Jack Sinkovich.

I didn't have his home phone memorized, but he was listed—the phonebook was still my friend. The phone rang four times before someone picked up and fumbled against the receiver.

A faraway voice cursed, then the phone line crinkled as the receiver moved.

"What now?" Sinkovich's sleepy voice asked.

"I need a piece of information from you," I said.

"Je-Zus, Grimshaw, it's six-forty-five A.M. My alarm is set for seven. Couldn't you at least have waited till then? Don't you fuckin' know how awful it is to wake up fifteen goddamn minutes before the goddamn alarm? It's a sign of how your entire day is gonna go. Shitty."

I waited until he paused for a breath before I said, "Who's Armand Vitel?"

"He's a cop, you know that." Sinkovich sounded even more annoyed.

"I don't know anything about him," I said.

"Yeah, you do. I introduced you to him yesterday."

"I didn't meet any Armand Vitel," I said.

"You talked to him for a long time," Sinkovich said. "He's Chaz Yancy's favorite gopher on the Red Squad. That's how he got his nickname."

I felt cold. Very cold. "Jump?"

"What's going on?" The annoyance in Sinkovich's voice had vanished.

"Is it Jump?" I repeated, articulating each word slowly.

"Yeah, of course." Sinkovich had moved closer to the phone. He sounded louder. "They call him that because Yancy says, 'Jump,' and Vitel asks—"

"How high." We spoke the last two words of the old joke in unison.

"Can Jump Vitel operate without Yancy's permission?" I asked, leaning against the wall so no one could hear me.

"Sure," Sinkovich said. "They aren't joined at the hip, at least not anymore. They used to be. We've called him Jump long before there even was a Red Squad."

"What do you think of him?" My voice was even lower.

"Jump? Or Yancy?"

"Jump," I said.

"I wouldn't let him shake my hand without counting my fingers afterwards, if you know what I mean," Sinkovich said.

"Is it just theft or is there other stuff?" I asked.

"What's this all about?" Sinkovich sounded wide awake and suspicious now.

"You don't want to know, Jack. Just answer me."

"Does this have something to do with Johnson?"

"Answer me, Jack."

He was silent. I could hear his breathing, harsh and ragged, as if he had been running. "There's rumors," he said after a moment.

"What kind of rumors?"

"There's rumors about the whole Red Squad," Sinkovich said. "They like their job too much, they're trigger happy, they like the power. There's those kind of rumors about every special unit, you know that."

"I do," I said. "I'm asking about Jump."

Sinkovich sighed. "You didn't hear nothing from me."

"Why do you think I called you at home?"

Again he was silent. I could imagine him thinking it through.

Pots clanged in the cafeteria, and the smell of institutional eggs filtered toward me, mixed with coffee and baking bread. My stomach growled. I couldn't remember the last time I had eaten.

"A bunch of excessive-force complaints," Sinkovich said so softly I almost didn't hear him. "That's one of the reasons he was put on the Red Squad, because nobody cares what he does to ghetto kids."

"All in the past, before the Red Squad?" I asked.

"No, there've been more," Sinkovich said. "But no one pursued them, you know? He was one of a handful of cops not assigned to the Democratic National Convention."

The fact that Sinkovich brought up the convention was serious. He was very sensitive about his own behavior during it.

"Because . . . ?"

"I don't think, for all the mayor's tough talk, that he wanted any dead white kids." Sinkovich's voice sounded empty. "Especially rich white kids."

My stomach felt hollow. The concrete wall was cold through my black shirt sleeve.

"What else?" I asked.

"You hear about that black kid, the one who got arrested two weeks ago and died in jail? The Stone?"

"Yeah," I said.

"He was Jump's. Word around the House is that Jump brought him in like that, denied him medical treatment, and sat there, watching."

I leaned my forehead against the wall. "Why hasn't anyone done something about him?"

"They did." Sinkovich's voice was bitter. "They assigned him to the Red Squad. Now you gonna tell me what's going on?"

It was my turn to be silent. Two interns, looking exhausted, walked into the cafeteria. A nurse, her uniform splotchy with dried blood, followed them.

"How about I ask you a question instead?" I was huddled as close to the phone as I could be. Now I wished I had made the call from my apartment.

"Shoot."

"Could a guy like that have the right kind of gang connections to set up a hit?"

"Oh, God." There was panic in Sinkovich's voice. "You're not suggesting—?"

"I'm not suggesting anything," I said. "It's a hypothetical. I mean, the gangs would all hate him, right?"

"Except for a handful of informers, yeah. But those kids were too young to be informers. Why the hell would he kill Johnson?"

"I never said that." I kept my voice down.

"Jesus, Mary, and Joseph. You can't go up against a guy like this," Sinkovich said. "You can't even bring your pet photographer up against him. It won't stick."

Sinkovich was referring to Saul Epstein, who had helped us with the case last December. Saul was a nationally known photojournalist, whose pictures from our case, published outside of Chicago, caused a scandal nationwide.

"Saul is in New York City, getting an award for December's story," I said.

"Well, there you go. And no other journalist'll touch it. They don't dare. Hell, everyone's afraid of the Red Squad."

"I'm not asking them to touch it," I said, as levelly as I could. Another intern walked past, and the emergency-room doctor from Sunday night. He looked like someone who had been up all night as well. "I'm asking you if such a thing were possible."

"The hit?"

"Something like that, yeah," I said.

"Of course Jump can set one up," Sinkovich said. "He'd know who to go to. Those kids aren't loyal yet, and if one of the informers did the ordering, they'd never know who was behind the setup. Even if it wasn't them, even if it was Jump himself, the kids might do it. They're not human anymore. They'll do damn near anything for a fuckin' candy bar."

"Thank you, Jack," I said, and started to hang up.

"No! No!" His voice got even louder. "You can't hang up yet!"

I stopped. "I only have a minute, Jack."

"Look," he said, panicked. "Look, you mess with those guys, you can't live in this city. You got that? They'll go after you, your kid, your family. They'll shred you and everyone who ever said hello to you. Even if they don't kill you, they'll fuckin' destroy you. And you're a guy with secrets, Grimshaw, don't tell me you ain't. God knows what they'll do to you."

"Thanks, Jack," I said.

"No! Wait! I'm serious, Grimshaw. They'll burn you. That rich girlfriend of yours can't stop them. They'll use their own pet journalists to take her down, and she's got a lot to lose." He paused, as if he were trying to get ahold of himself. "And so do you, Grimshaw. That kid of yours is a piker, but he's somethin' worth fightin' for. You can't take a bullet on this one. This one you gotta walk away from."

"I get it, Jack," I said.

"But you're not going to listen, are you?" he asked, his voice getting smaller as I moved the receiver away from my ear.

I set receiver in the cradle and stayed beside the phone. It was worse than I had ever imagined. No wonder Valentina had been trying to protect Johnson.

Truman Johnson walked into a wall so big he couldn't have busted through it no matter how hard he tried. The problem was the timing. He probably felt flush after his victory with Nikolau. Valentina needed protection, and Johnson, not realizing how truly sick Jump Vitel was, set up the meeting beforehand. Johnson probably went to that bar to warn Vitel away from Val.

Johnson probably told him that he would be protecting her from now on.

He had no idea how much Vitel hated him. The trashing of the house came after Johnson's death, not before. Johnson had no way of knowing that, by setting up the meeting, he had given Vitel the opportunity he had been waiting for.

My stomach was churning, and my head ached. I hadn't had any sleep and I didn't know when I would get any. What I needed was a few moments to myself.

I needed a chance to think.

I left the phone and walked into the cafeteria alongside a white woman with a beehive hairdo, wearing a green dress that ended just above her knees. One of her false eyelashes had come unstuck, and her pancake makeup had pooled in her laugh lines, like makeup often did at the end of the day.

Night shift had to be ending.

I stood in the short line, tray in hand, but I wasn't thinking about food. I was thinking about arriving at that crime scene, Johnson on what was left of his belly, and Jump Vitel lying through his teeth about trying to save Johnson's life.

It must have seemed so simple to Vitel. He did go up the stairs first, like the bartender thought, signaled the kids, all the while talking to Johnson. Then, the moment the bike pulled close, and Johnson's attention was on it and his tiny assassin, Vitel launched himself down the stairs, probably low enough to prevent himself from getting hit by bbs, blood, or guts.

"Mister?" the middle-aged white woman behind the counter asked me in a tone that suggested she had said something before. "Did you want something?"

Jump Vitel's head, I thought, but I didn't say that. I looked at the steam tables instead.

The scrambled eggs were runny, and the toast had been burned. The oatmeal seemed almost like an extension of the crime scene.

My stomach twisted again.

"The French toast," I said, pointing. It, at least, looked edible. "Lots of butter. Please."

She served four small pieces on a plate, put a pad of butter beside them, and set the whole thing on my tray. I grabbed some orange juice and milk, as well as a cup of coffee.

After I paid for everything, I had to go back for my silverware and napkins. I spread the butter on my toast while standing at the condiments table. The syrup bottles were sticky and nearly empty, but I used one anyway.

By the time I got to a table, I no longer wanted to eat. But I forced myself to, ignoring my queasy stomach.

I wished I could also ignore the images in my mind.

After Johnson had been shot, Vitel had hurried down the stairs, remembered his coat and his gun, and ran out the back door. Yancy might already have been running down the alley or he had been waiting for Vitel.

Yancy could have known about the hit, or he might not have. He might have simply thought that Vitel was inside, having a private meeting, something the two of them felt had to be kept secret, or not. He could have been innocent of this crime. Or not.

I had no way of knowing.

All I knew was this: They had come out of that alley, and one of them—maybe even Yancy—had seen the bike turn the corner. Whether the two men saw the shooter get into a car was something I probably wouldn't know.

Not that it mattered. The Gang Intelligence Unit knew how these hits worked, what the routine was, and what the getaways were. They didn't have to make anything up, because their version was probably accurate.

I didn't even taste my food. It went down like paste and sat like a lump in my stomach. The orange juice gave me some energy, though. I used the milk to cool down my coffee, and made myself sip.

Sinkovich was right. I couldn't take on the entire Gang Intelligence Unit myself. Even if I managed to report this, no one would believe me. I hadn't seen it, and the evidence I had would make a judge laugh me out of court.

It wasn't even enough to go to Saul Epstein with, even if he had been in town. We would have to do weeks of investigation, word would leak out, and we would both be in danger—as well as Epstein's wonderful grandmother, Ruth Weisman, and all of the Grimshaws.

Not to mention Jimmy. I couldn't jeopardize myself like that, not with Jimmy around. I believed Sinkovich. If I went after Vitel, he would come after me. And mine, and the life I had built here.

But I couldn't let this go, any more than Johnson had. Anyone who had seen those notes knew that Vitel wouldn't stop until he either possessed Valentina or killed her.

And I wanted to hurt him for what he had done to Johnson.

I wanted to kill him for what he had done to Johnson.

I set my coffee down and put my head in my hands. I didn't know how to fight Vitel. Everyone was afraid of him. No one would help me.

I was truly on my own.

Valentina had explored two different routes while she tried to protect Johnson. The detectives she had hired were afraid to take on Vitel, just like

Sinkovich was. And the lawyer didn't have the ability—not that I believed for a single moment that threatening Vitel with a lawsuit, even if the lawyer had grounds, would have frightened him.

Valentina could move out of the city. Vitel didn't seem to have a grudge against Marvella or the rest of Johnson's family. Vitel would simply turn his attention to some other woman, and do to her what he had done to Valentina.

And if that happened, he would get away with his crimes—all of them: the fear tactics, Valentina's rape, and finally, Johnson's murder.

I couldn't let Johnson's murder go unavenged.

I supposed I could just walk up to Vitel and shoot the son of a bitch. He didn't know me. He would probably remember seeing me with Sinkovich, but that would allow me to get close, not hinder my strategy.

But what would happen after I shot him? Either I'd have to be cunning enough to get him alone—and not even Johnson managed that (although he probably thought he had)—or I would have to kill Vitel in front of God and everyone.

Either way, I would become another one of Vitel's victims, a man who lost everything for a single moment of revenge.

There had to be another way. I had to find someone as angry at Vitel as I was, someone who could take action against him. Someone who had more clout than I did.

That wouldn't be anyone in government. Nor would it be the police, who already knew this psychopath was on the loose, and didn't want to do anything constructive to restrain him.

The only people Vitel hurt were people who couldn't fight back—or if they could, could only use illegal methods, which simply escalated the war the Gang Intelligence Unit seemed to believe they were involved in.

Then I leaned back in my chair. Sinkovich had used the word "loyalty," and he had been right. Loyalty was everything to the gangs. That was why, when they caught informers, they killed them so viciously and left their bodies to be found. Why they stood up for each other, even when turning other gang members in would make a situation better.

Gangs believed they were family because the gang replaced a nonexistent family—and loyalty was the only real currency that the gang had.

Vitel had violated that loyalty. He had taken something that belonged to the gang—the hit squad—and had used it for his own purpose.

And in gang parlance, that was worse than the murder itself.

THIRTY-TWO

The official headquarters of the Blackstone Rangers was on Sixty-seventh and Blackstone. There were others, including the First Presbyterian Church of Woodlawn, and the Southmoor Hotel. But the large warehouselike building on Sixty-seventh and Blackstone was where petitioners went when they needed to bargain with the Stones.

I had been there once before.

I drove there now as the city woke up. The traffic around me went north instead of south. Mine seemed to be the only car on my side of the road.

When I left the hospital, I had stopped at my apartment briefly enough to get ready for this meeting. I had taken both guns, my shoulder holster, and my jacket inside. Then I had cleaned up so that I looked somewhat presentable—it had been a long night—and changed into less obvious clothing. Black worked for the middle of the night. On a tall, wide black man in the middle of the day, black clothing forced people to make the wrong kind of assumptions.

It made me noticed instead of invisible.

So from my closet, I removed a pair of pants, hand-me-downs from Franklin that he had given me the summer before. They were loose, and a bit short, revealing a good inch of my socks, which was precisely how I remembered them to be. I tucked a white shirt into them.

Then I got the guns ready.

I was going alone into the Black P. Stone Nation, as it called itself, a gang four thousand members strong. I had gone in once before with Malcolm Reyner as backup, and we had come out alive.

This time, I would have no backup at all.

I took Nikolau's gun and put it in my shoulder holster, then slipped the holster on. I hadn't had time to buy ammunition for that gun, and I doubted I would need it. If I did indeed find some members of the Stones' leadership group, the Main 21, someone would frisk me. They would find Nikolau's gun and confiscate it until the meeting was over.

Then I strapped my own gun, loaded with a full clip, on the inside of my left calf. It would take two quick moves to reach it—and two quick moves might be two too many—but it would be the only backup I had.

I hoped they would take me at face value—a forty-year-old man wearing bad clothing—and decide that I was too dumb to carry any other weapon other than the one in my shoulder holster.

I made sure the pants covered the gun no matter how I moved my leg. When I was satisfied, I put the suit coat on and left the apartment.

My mouth had a metallic dryness as I drove. My own gun weighed heavy against my leg, feeling like a scab that needed picking.

Overhead, the clouds remained, as dark and ominous as they had been the day before. A light breeze blew, swirling last fall's leaves and the dirt that got stirred up from yesterday's storms.

As I got closer to Sixty-seventh and Blackstone, the morning crowds thinned, and I found myself once again in one of the worst neighborhoods in Chicago.

No one made a pretense at cleanup here. Empty lots glistened where buildings had burned or been torn down. Graffiti decorated the remaining walls—most of it blue against the red walls, all of it with a variation of Blackstone Rangers or Black P. Stone or simply Stones.

The last time I had been here, it had been a December twilight, and I had thought I had entered hell. But hell looked worse in the daytime. All the details were visible—the dirty streets, the broken windows, the ruined businesses.

A few destroyed cars—most of them burned out or robbed for parts—hugged the curbs. Others, newer, were parked nearby. I kept an eye out for the Gang Intelligence Unit's white van—or anything large enough to be used by the Unit. The last time I had been here, the van had been spying on the building.

I didn't want the van anywhere close this time.

Of course, at this time of day, the van was usually near schools. I hoped it followed its usual plan.

The pawn shop that served as a front for the headquarters was closed. I was too early to get in that way. Still, I parked in front of it, and sat for a moment, my hands on the steering wheel.

This was my chance to change my mind. If I backed out now, Vitel would continue doing what he had been doing, but the city wouldn't have another police casualty in its so-called gang war.

Of course that war was being manipulated by the Unit, grabbing members of rival gangs and dropping them in each other's turf so that the murder and attempted murder rate went up. And of course, placing others in the line of fire—innocent people, like Truman Johnson, who would be counted as a police casualty in that self-same war.

No matter how long I sat there, as the chill morning air seeped into my car, I wasn't going to change my mind. I had only one way of stopping this bastard, and I was going to take it.

I got out of the car. I didn't see anyone on the street—no red tams, no faces peeking out of the broken windows, no one stepping out of the tavern next door. But I knew I was being watched. A place like this always had its guards, and they were always on alert.

I didn't even try the door to the pawnshop. The tavern's main door was closed as well.

Instead, I went around the side of the building to the door that led to a stage in the meeting room, a door through which Malcolm and I had escaped the building four months earlier.

The door was metal, and it was closed, too. The winter hadn't been kind to it. Bullet holes had shattered its diamond-shaped window, and others had penetrated the center of the metal.

Rust from the harsh winter streaked the door's white paint, and the lock beneath the doorknob itself looked like someone had tried to tamper with it.

I knocked, hating the way my back was exposed to the alley. Again, I saw no movement out of the corner of my eye, but the hair behind my neck rose. Someone was watching, and that someone was close.

Shuffling behind the door caught my attention. Movement near the base of the diamond window suggested that someone tried to peer out of it.

Then there was silence.

I knocked again.

More silence.

I had no idea what I would do if I couldn't locate the Stones. Did I go to the Southmoor Hotel or the First Presbyterian Church? Or did I wait here until the pawnshop opened and try again? How long before my activities in this part of town drew attention?

How long before the Gang Intelligence Unit knew I was here?

Then the lock clicked, and the door banged open. The Stone who had talked to me first in the pawnshop, a man in his twenties whom I knew only as Charles—and whom I would never call that to his face—peered out.

"This better be important, Gramps," he said. "Because you be waking up some brothers."

"You said I should come back if I had information." I pitched my voice low, almost submissive.

"I didn't say." But he held the door open anyway, and I stepped inside.

It was dark, and I had to blink for a moment before my eyes adjusted. We entered behind a stage that had once been part of a tavern. The wings still existed, and were probably used for dramatic entrances during some of the larger Stones meetings.

Charles pulled back a dusty old velvet curtain, showing me the three flat wooden steps that led to the floor below. Then he clicked on overhead lights.

"Wait here," he said, and disappeared into the blackness behind the stage.

The room he had left me in was huge. Metal folding chairs lined one wall. On another, someone—or several someones—had painted a dramatic mural. Words mixed into a flowered backdrop, and in the foreground, dozens of faces, including famous ones—Aretha Franklin, Malcolm X, Martin Luther King, and the Stones' official leader, Jeff Fort.

I had been in this room before. It had three exits—the one I had just used, another to the right, and one hidden in the mural itself. The place still carried the musty beer smell of the tavern it had once been, and I thought I caught the sickly sweetish odor of marijuana floating in the air.

The wait seemed to take forever. I wondered if Charles had to wake the leaders up to bring them down here. I paced the room, studying the mural, trying to see if more than one artist had worked on it. I still wasn't able to tell.

Finally, two Stones I hadn't seen before, both built like linebackers and wearing ratty black leather jackets, came in from the main door. Their red tams were pulled over large afros, and one of them wore sunglasses, which he removed when he saw me.

"Arms out, Pops," he said.

I stuck my arms out as if I were about to do jumping jacks. I extended my legs also.

"I have a shoulder holster," I said before they started searching. "I always carry my gun."

They could understand that. The Stone who spoke pulled the left side of my jacket open and saw the holster. The other Stone reached in and removed Nikolau's gun.

Then the first Stone patted me down, his big hands hard against my skin. He stopped just shy of the second gun, and I tried not to sigh with relief. He would have wondered why I hadn't told him about it.

"Will I get my gun back?" I asked, letting the nerves that had just rattled me into my voice.

"Depends," he said, and carried the gun out of the room. The other Stone stayed by the door, arms crossed, watching me as if I were a part of an extremely interesting experiment.

We stood like that for another long time, although how long I wasn't certain. I didn't wear a watch, and I didn't want to be looking at it if I had.

After a while, the Stone who had taken my gun returned. He whispered to the remaining Stone, and then stood beside him, hands clasped behind his back.

Five Stones walked across the stage. I recognized two of them, although I didn't know their names. One had a long goatee, and the other coke-bottle thick wire-rim glasses. The remaining three were strangers to me, but considering the way the others treated them, they were important.

"Gramps," Glasses said. "You said we wasn't gonna see you again."

"You said my family's protection was contingent on good information."

Glasses smiled, revealing astonishingly white teeth. "I did, didn't I?"

"Awfully early in the morning for information," said one of the Stones I didn't recognize. He had a deep voice, and he kept his hands tucked in the pockets of his leather jacket.

"I didn't want the Red Squad to see me," I said.

"Why? They spying on us again?" Goatee asked.

"I don't know," I said, "but it would be better if I stayed out of their way right now."

"You in trouble with them?" Deep Voice asked.

Charles came in the side door and leaned against it, blocking it. He watched me closely, as if he expected me to make a quick move.

"We don't get along," I said.

"Your information checked out last time," Glasses said, and I felt relieved. I had told the Stones that the Gang Intelligence Unit was planning a raid on one of their headquarters—a lie on my part, but a logical one. I figured the

Unit would eventually do that. Apparently, I had been right. "How can you get information from them if you don't get along?"

"I have friends in low places," I said, using one of Malcolm Reyner's favorite phrases.

"What have you got this time?" Goatee asked.

"Something that disturbs the hell out of me," I said, not lying. "Does our deal still stand?"

"Protection in exchange for information? You got it, Gramps," Glasses said. "Ain't we been livin' up to our end of the deal?"

He was asking me, wanting me to tell him if someone had crossed the line.

"Yes," I said. "You have, and I'm grateful."

I was, too. The gang harassment in December had been ugly, and I hadn't been certain then that I had enough tricks to keep Jimmy away from them.

"So what you got, Gramps?" Goatee asked.

"The hit on the cop yesterday," I said. "The one in the Gaza Strip. You know it?"

The two Stones who hadn't spoken nodded. Glasses said, "We don't care about Disciples' business."

"It wasn't a Disciples' hit," I said. "I was led to believe it was Stones."

Goatee rolled his eyes, and shook his head. Deep Voice crossed his arms. "We'd know if we took on a cop. We didn't even know that one."

"But it was your method," I said. "Two kids on a bike, a getaway car, and a van, right?"

Two of the Stones on the stage looked surprised. For the first time in our two dealings together, Glasses looked nervous.

Goatee didn't seem to notice. "So they copied our method, so what?"

Deep Voice wiped his nose on the sleeve of his jacket. He looked nervous, too.

"The Disciples weren't the ones who copied your method," I said. "It was hijacked."

"What the hell does that mean?" Goatee asked.

Glasses stood up straighter. He exchanged a glance with Deep Voice. Charles pressed closer to the wall, on the floor level near me.

"It means someone convinced two of your shooters to pull this off," I said.

"Which two?" Goatee asked. He was speaking to me, but he was looking at the Stones around him.

"Heard a rumor that it was Squeak and his brother," Deep Voice said. He was studying me.

"Have you checked out the rumor?" I asked.

"Ignored it," one of the other men said. "Thought it was a Disciples' lie."

Glasses glared at Deep Voice. He shrugged.

"I was planning to look into it today," Deep Voice said. "It's my turf."

"Those boys didn't do it on their own," I said. "It was a hit, and you'll probably find out they were paid. They might even have gotten the information from one of your men."

"Might?" Glasses sounded angry.

"I'm not sure about that part," I said. "But if it was one of your guys who ordered the hit, he's a police informant."

"What?" All five Stones said that in unison.

"That's a hell of a charge," Glasses said. "How do you know this?"

"Because, as you said, you all had no reason to hit this cop. I know who had the reason. He met with the cop in Greenwood's, and he led the cop outside for the hit."

"You think a cop killed a cop?" Deep Voice asked.

"Yes," I said. "I know that a cop did this."

"Who?" Glasses asked.

"Jump Vitel." My words echoed in the large room.

"That's not possible," Deep Voice said. "No Stone would listen to a member of the Red Squad."

"No Stone would, but an informant would."

"You said you weren't sure about the informant," Glasses said.

"And I'm not," I said. "But those kids are what—ten? How easily did you guys buy them? Maybe Vitel bought them for twice as much."

"Son of a bitch," Deep Voice said.

Goatee held up his hand. "That's a hell of a charge, Gramps. What's your proof?"

"Vitel's girlfriend." I mentally apologized to Valentina for that small lie—although, probably, from Vitel's perspective, I was telling the truth.

"So let's talk to her," said one of the other Stones.

"Are you kidding?" Glasses snapped without looking at him. "Bringing a cop's girlfriend down here?"

"We can't act on this crap without confirmation," the Stone said.

"No, we can't," Deep Voice said. "We also can't let some cop mess with our business."

"Vitel's been in our face too much as it is," Goatee said.

"Not to mention what he done to Charles's brother, here," Glasses said.

They all looked at Charles, who was studying the floor.

"Your brother was the one who died last month?" I asked, guessing.

Charles nodded.

"I'm sorry," I said.

He shrugged.

"We let that go," Deep Voice said, "because we thought the cops would take care of their own."

"We woulda," one of the other Stones said.

"But they're dogs. They didn't do nothing. Jump's back on the street like he done something good." Deep Voice was gaining a preacher's cadence.

"Maybe to them he did," Glasses said.

"Panthers been saying the cops want to level the ghetto. I hear lots of talk of war," Goatee said.

"Panthers are crazy, man," Glasses said. "Panthers just want to take over the Main 21. Make us 'po-litical.'"

"That don't mean they're wrong," Goatee said. "They been right about this crap before."

"The city's talking about declaring an official war against the gangs," I said, adding the information Sinkovich told me. "They've already increased their firepower, and they may do it again. They've also added more than a hundred men to the Red Squad."

"Shee-it," Glasses said. "I thought I seen more of them fuckers around."

"They got a hundred plus, they won't miss one," Deep Voice said.

"Hey," Goatee said, holding up a hand. "We don't go offing cops. Not for no reason, not without proof, and not on the word of some old fart who thinks he's got so-called information."

I didn't like the old-fart characterization, even though my clothing supported that description. Still, I had to get this group moving.

"So check the story out," I said. "Then take action."

"Sounds like great advice, Gramps," Deep Voice said. "I think we'll take you up on that."

He jumped off the stage and walked toward me. I held my position, my heart pounding. His eyes were dark, but they were clear.

"And you be coming with us," he said, grabbing my arm. He snapped his fingers and half a dozen guns were pointed at me.

I forced myself to breathe evenly, but I couldn't suppress an involuntary swallow.

"If your information don't check out, they gonna find one dumpy fuckin' corpse on the Gaza Strip." Deep Voice grinned. "Shoulda dressed up, old man. This might be the last fuckin' thing you ever wear."

THIRTY-THREE

The Stones were going to just keep a single gun trained on me as they led me out of the building, but Charles reminded them that I had once beaten up several of their members, one badly enough that he still didn't walk well. So they tied my hands behind my back, and shoved me into the alley where yet another Stone had pulled a large gray sedan up to the door.

The rain that had threatened all morning had started, small drips that didn't seem to know they were part of the same storm. Two Stones held me as we walked forward—the two who had guarded me while we waited for the members of the Main 21 to arrive.

Charles flanked me, and Glasses, Goatee, and Deep Voice followed. The other two were supposed to stay behind, in case I had set up some kind of scam that got them to empty their headquarters.

The Stones shoved me into the backseat of the sedan and forced me to straddled the center, my long legs on either side of the mound in the middle of the car. I hoped my pants didn't rise up too far on the left, revealing the gun. The short pants leg had stopped the initial search, like I had hoped, by revealing that bit of sock so that no one thought I was carrying a second weapon, but if that weapon got revealed now, I would be in even bigger trouble.

The car bounced and shook as the other Stones crawled inside. It was a tight squeeze in the back—the two that were guarding me, and Deep Voice and Charles, both sitting by the windows, both with shotguns across their laps.

A gun was still pressed against my side as well.

I didn't want to be along. I had hoped to set everything in motion and then go home, letting Vitel's past sins catch up with him.

Instead, I was riding along to interview two ten-year-olds, the actual murderers of Truman Johnson. And if they confessed to working for Vitel, I wasn't certain what the Stones would do to them.

I had a hunch the boys would become victims of the same kind of street justice that I wanted the Stones to inflict on Vitel. And I wasn't sure how I felt about it. They were children, but they were also hired assassins who had learned to kill in cold blood.

We drove farther north than I expected, up to the Robert Taylor Homes, a two-mile-long housing project that loomed over the South Side of the city. The complex was sandwiched between the Rock Island Embankment and State Street, sixteen-story concrete buildings with narrow windows marking each floor.

People warehouses, with no yards, no playgrounds, nothing but concrete and roads beside them, as dismal a place as I had ever seen.

We pulled into the parking lot just off Fifty-fourth and Pershing. Burned-out cars, broken glass, and garbage covered the asphalt. A little girl sat on the steps leading into the building, her dress dirty, her hair tangled. She held a headless doll as filthy as she was, but she wasn't playing with it. She was just staring straight ahead, as if the nothing before her mesmerized her.

She was about the same age as Norene.

The car cruised the parking lot, until it finally stopped by the main doors to this building, marked with a number over the top.

"Squeak lives here?" Glasses asked, surprising me. The car had been quiet up until that point.

"Yeah," Deep Voice said, looking out the window, his hand clutched on his shotgun.

"Shit," Glasses said. "I don't want to go into Stateville. You go, Brass. And you go with him, Chico."

Goatee slid his shotgun to Glasses and got out. "You comin', Brass?"

Brass, apparently, was Deep Voice. He held onto his shotgun as he got out of the car. I was still looking at Goatee, wondering if he got the nickname Chico because he had Puerto Rican blood.

They closed the car doors and went into the building, looking both ways as they stepped across the threshold.

"You ever been to Stateville, Gramps?" Glasses asked me.

"I take it you don't mean the Illinois State Penitentiary," I said.

The Stones around me laughed, all except the one who had the gun pressed into my side.

"He means the Congo Hilton, my man," the Stone said.

"No," I said. "I've never been inside this housing project."

"Ain't he nice and formal?" the driver said. " 'I've never been inside this housing project.' You'd almost think he was gonna call you sir, Nate."

"Ain't nobody calls me sir without saluting first," Glasses said. He, apparently, was Nate.

The others laughed again, but there were nervous edges to the laughter. Everyone kept a watch out, as if expecting trouble.

I didn't move. Through the windshield, I could see the side of the building. On the tenth floor, several windows were missing and the concrete had been charred by fire.

Graffiti covered much of the lower walls, and there was only one piece I could read from this distance. In big red letters, someone had spray painted BLACKSTONE IS STONE BLACK.

After a few minutes, the rain started in earnest, a shower that sprinkled fine drops on the windshield. The driver turned on the wipers, and the Stones near the side windows rolled them down. The second of my bodyguards—the one who wasn't holding a gun on me—turned so that he could see out the back window.

I didn't ask any questions. I knew better. I just waited with the rest of them, watching gangs of kids who should have been in school run past. There appeared to be no adults here, except for an elderly man who was making his way out of the front door.

It took nearly half an hour before Goatee and Deep Voice—Chico and Brass—reappeared. They loped across the parking lot and got into the car.

Chico hit his hand on the roof, making a pounding echo inside. "Let's go."

The driver didn't have to be told twice. He spun out of the lot, his tires peeling.

"You take care of it?" Nate asked.

I felt cold.

"Nothing to take care of," Brass said.

"You didn't find them?" Nate asked.

Rain came in the windows, hitting everyone, including me. The Stones nearest the windows rolled them up.

"They turned up last night in Disciples turf," Chico said, taking his gun back from Nate. "Squeak and his little brother, both dead."

"Mom's so broke up about it, she asked us for some smack." Brass sounded disgusted.

I continued to stare out the windshield, watching the road. Cars passed us, many of them heading toward the Loop. We were driving south again.

I tried to stay motionless. The last thing I wanted to do was call attention to myself.

"Dead how?" Nate asked,

"Now this is the interesting part," Chico said. "Shotgun."

"Disciples don't warning-kill like that," Nate said.

"No shit," Brass said. "This is a cop trick."

Nate wrapped one arm around the seat and turned toward me. "You know about this, Gramps?"

"No," I said, not willing to add more.

"Shit," Nate said. "Ain't no way to check your story now, old man."

"Don't need to check it," Brass said. "Cops took Squeak and his brother to Disciple country, shot 'em, and left 'em there. We can blast Jump just to even everything out."

"We ain't going after him without proof, and I don't know how we're getting proof now." Nate was still looking at me. "Do you, old man?"

"What do you want?" I asked. "Confirmation that he was there?"

"Shit, we know the Red Squad was there. We seen 'em," Chico said.

"You drove by?" I asked.

"Shooting on the Gaza Strip," Nate said. "Had to make sure it wasn't one of ours."

No, I thought, it was one of mine. And the anger flared again. Vitel had thought this all through. He knew someone would check on who ordered the hit, and he got rid of his witnesses.

All except one.

"The bartender," I said.

"What? You goin' senile, Gramps?"

"There's still one witness," I said. "The bartender at Greenwood's."

"Old Julius?"

"I don't know what his name is." I felt an urgency, wondering if Vitel had taken the bartender out as well. "But he saw Vitel talking to the other cop."

"Ain't nothing unusual about cops talking," Nate said.

"Unless one leads the other into an ambush," I said.

Nate studied me for a moment, his eyes distorted by the thickness of his glasses. They made his face vulnerable, almost soft.

"You want Vitel bad, don't you, Gramps?"

"Don't you?" I asked. "He used two Stones to kill an enemy of his, then killed the Stones so there weren't any witnesses. Finally, he leaves the bodies in places that'll make you guys and the Disciples escalate tensions."

" 'Escalate tensions,' " the driver said, mocking me. "Shit, man, talk like a human being."

"Nice picture you're painting, Gramps, but we don't know it wasn't you what did it." Nate tilted his head as he studied me. "How come you ain't taking out Vitel yourself?"

It was a sign of my exhaustion that I almost told him. I blinked, forcing myself to remain alert. "I didn't say anything about taking anyone out. I promised you information. I delivered. You're the ones who are talking about taking people out."

Nate grunted and turned around.

"Where're we going?" the driver asked.

No one answered for a minute. Then Brass said in his deep voice, "Greenwood's Tavern."

Nate looked over his shoulder at him.

"Hey, you made a deal with the old man. Let's find out if his information is right. If he's feeding us a line of bull, then we get to mess with his kid." Brass gave me a sideways look, filled with cunning.

I forced myself to breathe evenly, to remain calm. "All I'm doing is keeping up my end," I said, glad my voice didn't betray my anger. "If you need proof of that, fine. But my goal here is the same as it's always been. I take care of my family. Giving you information when I have it is part of that. There's no way I would jeopardize anyone I know to bring you false information."

"Let's just see." Nate waved a hand at the driver. "Brass's right. Greenwood's Tavern. Let's see what Old Julius has to say."

THIRTY-FOUR

Even though it was only ten-thirty in the morning, the tavern's doors were open. The driver passed the alley door first—it was propped open with a box—and then he turned onto Woodlawn.

There were no other cars on the road. It looked deserted. No one watched from the windows, and the ruined buildings made the entire place look empty.

The driver pulled up in front of the tavern. The Stones opened the car's doors, and everyone got out. The Stone with the gun trained on me pulled me out curbside, and I nearly lost my balance without my hands to steady me.

The air was cooler down here, and the rain felt like a fine mist. All I saw, though, was the sidewalk. Despite the rain and yesterday's flash-flooding, a large stain still marked the concrete where Truman Johnson's body had fallen.

My shoulders straightened. The Stone next to me looked at me with alarm, but I didn't move. I kept studying that stain. It was why I was here, the reason I had chosen this path.

Johnson had tried to protect the woman he loved, and had failed.

I would make certain the job got done right.

"Whassamatta, Pops?" My Stone bodyguard asked. "You never seen filth before?"

I didn't answer him. I couldn't answer him, and tell him that what he had called filth was the spot where a good man had lost his life.

"Inside, Daddy-O," said Charles, pushing me forward. I stumbled up the curb.

"I'm not going to fight any of you here in this neighborhood," I said. "I'm not suicidal. And I know you could shoot me if I tried to leave before I was excused. So would you mind untying my hands? I promise not to do anything funny."

"We like funny," Brass said as he passed me, heading down the stairs into the tavern.

"But we don't need it right now." Nate snapped his fingers, and the other bodyguard untied my hands.

I brought them around the front of my body and rubbed my wrists. The rope hadn't been tight, but it had chafed. I was gonna have rope burns for the next week.

The two Stone guards and Charles led me down the stairs. This door was propped open as well. The tavern's scent of stale beer and old cigarette smoke reached me before I stepped inside.

An overhead light was on, and the candles on the tables weren't lit. The bartender I had seen the day before was standing near the edge of the bar, wiping his hands on a rag.

"I can't serve you liquor until noon," he said to Nate.

He probably, legally, couldn't serve Nate liquor at all. I seemed to be the only person in the room, besides the bartender, who was of age.

"Like you're afraid of the Liquor Commission." Nate clapped a hand on the bartender's arm. "Old Julius, meet Gramps. Gramps, this here be Julius Hammond, proud owner of this lovely establishment."

"We've met," I said.

"Gramps here says you seen Jump Vitel leading a cop out of this place right into a hit. Is that right, Old Julius?"

The bartender glared at me. "I didn't recognize nobody," he said between clenched teeth.

"Really?" Nate's hand tightened on his arm. "Not even Jump Vitel, who's in here all the time?"

"I don't even recognize you," the bartender said.

"Good boy," Nate said. "You ain't supposed to recognize me."

Then he shoved his glasses up his nose and frowned.

"Of course," Nate added, "I doubt you're supposed to recognize Mr. Jump Vitel, either."

"I can serve you some food," the bartender said. "That's about all I can do."

My frustration built. I wanted to cross the room and shake the bartender. He had seen Johnson lying dead out front. How could he pretend he didn't know what happened?

"You could," Nate said, his voice very smooth. "And your little bar here could suffer a suspicious fire, too, while you was cookin'. What would your money-bags brother say about that, Old Julius?"

"Wouldn't say nothing if Old Julius got trapped in the kitchen, didn't make it out 'cept as a corpse." Chico smiled as he spoke, as if he were talking about the weather.

The bartender kept wiping his hands on that towel.

"Don't threaten him, boys," Brass said. "You threaten him, he'll make up any damn thing."

"Just want him to tell the truth, don't we, Gramps?" Nate said.

I moved slightly so that the bartender could see the gun trained on me. "It would help," I said.

"If I tell you what I saw, you aren't going to do anything to me, right?" the bartender asked Nate.

"Except let you go on, pretending to get along with the Red Squad, the Disciples, and us." Nate pulled him close. "Now, I asked you a question. Did you see Jump Vitel lead that cop out into that hit yesterday?"

The bartender closed his eyes. He looked like he was praying. "Yes."

Nate raised his eyebrows and tilted his head at me, as if he was surprised. "Then what did our friend Jump do?"

The bartender grimaced, opened his eyes, and looked directly at me. "Came back in here, got his gun and his coat, and went out the alley door."

"What was out the alley door?" Nate asked.

"The Red Squad's van. He told the cops who showed up later that he tried to stop the hit."

"But you know better," Nate said.

The bartender nodded.

"Was the rest of the Red Squad involved?"

"I don't think so," the bartender said. His cheeks were flushed. "My brother was back there. Paying them."

Protection money. How did this tavern survive, paying protection to the gangs and the police?

"Sooo," Nate said to the other Stones. "We got Officer Jump Vitel breaking our code, killing cops and blaming it on us, and killing kids and blaming it on the Disciples. Ain't it interesting how much shit one law-abiding man can get away with in his lifetime?"

Then, with one quick move Nate grabbed the bartender by the neck and slammed his face on the bar. I started, not expecting the violence. My Stone bodyguard shoved his gun deeper into my ribcage.

"He been dealing out of here again, our buddy Jump?" Nate asked, his face pressed close to the bartender's.

"Yeah." The word was muffled against the bar.

"He been sharing the profits with you?"

"Yeah."

Nate let the bartender go. The bartender wiped his mouth with a shaking hand. The entire left side of his face was crimson from the force of the blow against the bar.

It took me a moment to understand Nate's last two questions. If the bartender hadn't been getting the drug money, he would have had a reason to set up Jump Vitel.

For the first time, I was relieved that Vitel had paid his debts.

Nate grinned at me. "Looks like you were right, Gramps. You done real good. That little family of yours must be awful proud of you."

"You have your proof," I said. "May I go?"

"Shit no." Nate walked over to me and wrapped an arm around my neck. He had to reach up to do it. The gesture was meant to be a friendly hug. "Why would you want to leave, old man? The party's just getting started."

"It's not really my party," I said.

"Bullshit." Nate pulled on my neck so that he could lean his head close to mine. His glasses brushed my cheek. "Don't give me none of that jive, bro. It's all your party."

"And," Brass said with a grin, "you get to stay until the very end."

THIRTY-FIVE

Nate let me go, then clapped his hand on my back, as falsely friendly with me as he had been with the bartender.

"Let's give Gramps a good seat for the show," Nate said.

Brass grabbed one of the wooden chairs and set it against the brick wall, facing the entrance. "This good, Nate?"

"Perfect." Nate grinned at me. "Watch and learn, old man. Watch and learn."

The bodyguard guided me to the chair, and I sat down. The chair creaked beneath my weight. I could see through the door, up the steps and into the empty street. If I had been sitting here the day before. I would have seen Jump Vitel lead Truman Johnson up those steps—probably talking all the way—and pause as they got into the street.

I would have seen the bike, the kids, the shotgun, the shot—and then Jump himself running back in here, grabbing his own gun, waving to the bartender, and disappearing out the door beside me, off to be a failed hero, someone who tried to stop a shooting, and missed by only a few seconds.

Nate peered at me. "Comfortable?"

"I could use a beer," I said, not exactly lying.

He laughed. "You heard Old Julius. It's against the law to drink this early in the morning in the City of Chicago. But this is the Gaza Strip. Get my man a beer, Julius."

The bartender didn't even look at me as he went around the bar. He grabbed a stein off the pile of glasses and filled it.

"And I need the phone," Nate said.

The bartender grabbed the phone and set it on the bar. Then he brought me my beer. Foam poured down the sides and pooled underneath the glass. The smell was awful, cloying and grainy, but I took a sip anyway, to continue my bravado.

Nate picked up the receiver, looked at it, and handed it to the bartender as he came back to the bar.

"You need to make a call," Nate said to the bartender. "You need to call your friend Jump Vitel and inform him that my man Chico here just scored some stuff and wants to sell it. You thought you'd be a citizen and let Jump know about it, so he can pocket some cash along with you. Can you do that for me, Old Julius?"

The bartender took the receiver. "Jump's gonna know something's wrong."

"No, he ain't," Brass said. "You've made this call a hundred times before. Stop with the bullshit or I really will see how easy it is to torch this place."

The bartender shot me a frightened glance. I picked up my beer and saluted him with it, then took another sip. It tasted as bad as it smelled.

The bartender dialed—from memory—and said, "Patch me through to Jump."

Everyone watched him. The bartender leaned against the bar, looking tired and older than he had fifteen minutes before.

"Jump? Julius. I got Chico down here with some stuff. You wanna risk coming down here after yesterday?"

A warning sentence. Nate flicked his fingers against the bartender's ear. Brass reached into the ashtray next to him, pulled out a book of matches, and opened it. He lit one and stared at the flame.

The bartender's eyes widened.

"Okay," the bartender said, although I wasn't sure it was to the Stones or Jump Vitel. "You better come fast. He's not gonna stay here long."

"Right on, man!" Chico yelled. "I don't get my money in twenty, I'm doing business elsewhere."

Brass lit another match and waved it under the bartender's nose. The bartender moved his head away, trying to keep from getting burned.

I was holding my breath.

"Okay," the bartender said again, sounding calmer than most people would have if a match was near their nose hair. "See you in fifteen."

Then he hung up.

"You didn't tell him to come alone," Chico said.

Brass pushed the match closer.

"I never do. He would have thought that was weird," the bartender said.

"Fifteen. Don't give us much time." Nate leaned over, blew out the match, and looked up at the bartender as if he was flirting with him. "For this crap, he come in the front or the back?"

The bartender's eyes were still wide. He was watching Brass, not Nate. "Front, mostly."

"Mostly," Nate said. "Do that mean like half-and-half or eighty-twenty or what? How much does he come in the front?"

"Nine out of ten times," the bartender said.

"Good." Nate moved away from him. "Brass, I need three shooters, rooftop, triangled on the front door. Bop"—he was looking at the second bodyguard—"you get the alley door and the shotgun. Make sure you got the right target before you shoot, man."

Bop looked at him as if the direction insulted him, then grabbed the shotgun from Brass. Brass went with him out the back door.

Nate reached around the bar and yanked the phone out of the wall. Then he said to the bartender as if nothing had happened, "I could use a brew myself."

The bartender glanced at the front door, licked his lower lips, and didn't move.

Nate slammed his hand on the bar, and the bartender jumped.

"Do I gotta do it?" Nate asked.

The bartender looked at me. His face was pinched, his cheek beginning to bruise. "I thought you were better than this."

"Than what?" I asked, my hand tightening around my glass. I could, I supposed, reach for my gun, stop everything now, get the bartender out, get me out, and leave.

And then I'd lose protection for Jimmy, and Vitel would still be walking the street.

There would also be no guarantee that the bartender would survive another week.

"Why aren't you doing anything?" the bartender asked me.

"I am doing something." I raised the beer, and took one more sip.

Nate grinned at me. "I'm beginning to like you, Gramps."

Then he pulled at the bartender's sleeve. "But you, you get to work, or I swear I'm shoving you out to join your friend Jump."

The bartender scurried behind the bar and poured another beer. He handed it to Nate, who carried it toward me. As Nate approached, he grabbed a chair and slid it next to mine.

He sat down, tilted the chair back, and sipped his beer. "Gotta tell ya," he said after a minute, "didn't expect you to kick back and enjoy the show, Gramps. Figured you for a runner right out."

I didn't know how to respond to that, so I didn't.

"But you got balls. Charles's been saying that, I seen it in December, I see it now. You got balls." He took another sip of his beer, some of the foam staying on his lower lip. He licked it away. "You ever seen anyone shot, Gramps?"

"A few times," I said.

"No wonder you're cool." He set his glass down. "You go out that back door there, take the second door, not the one that goes to the alley, and you'll find the car. You can go there, you can walk to yours, whatever you wanna do. You don't gotta stay, Gramps. I was just testin' you, you know?"

"I know," I said.

"If Vitel don't listen to our friend there, it could get ugly. You don't wanna get caught in a shootout with us and the Red Squad."

He was serious. He was going to let me leave.

But he had been right earlier. I had put all of this in motion. This was the only kind of justice Johnson would get. I had to see it to the end.

"I'll risk it," I said.

Brakes squealed outside, and a bumper appeared in view. Then a car door slammed.

"Heads up," Charles whispered.

I saw black-booted feet appear around the bumper from the driver's side. It took a moment for the entire person to come into view, but I didn't have to see all of him to recognize him.

It was Jump Vitel.

And he was alone.

THIRTY-SIX

I could have called out to Vitel. I could have run through the back door, getting out before the shooting started.

I could have gotten my gun in two moves, grabbed Nate, and pulled him into the street. Once Vitel saw Nate, this entire thing would have ended.

And the sharpshooters wouldn't have had a chance. They wouldn't dare shoot, not with Nate in the way.

I didn't do any of those things.

Instead, I set my beer on the checked tablecloth, wiped my moist hands on my too-short pants, and let out a small breath.

Jump Vitel had his hands in his pockets as he walked toward the bar. He was whistling. With his toe, he brushed the stain on the middle of the sidewalk and then he grinned.

He took one more step, and the back of his head flew off. The crack of a rifle followed not a half-second later. He fell forward, slamming into the iron railing beside the steps, his body making a thudding sound as he hit.

Then there was something like silence. The crack of the rifle still echoed, but no one else had fired. Nate's shooters had gotten Vitel on the first try.

Beside me, Nate let out a breath. I was still holding mine.

Jump Vitel's hand hung over the stairway, his arm swinging back and forth.

Nate took one more sip of his beer, then set it down. He stood, threw a dollar on the table, and said, "C'mon, Gramps. We have to be going."

But I wasn't ready to leave. Instead, I walked forward. My bodyguard didn't shoot me. Chico stood aside to let me pass. Charles joined me halfway there.

I stopped when I was close enough to see Vitel's face—or what was left of it. Half of his skull was missing, his left eye was gone. Blood coated the remaining skin.

He didn't look human anymore.

Not that he had ever been human anyway.

"Gramps!" Nate called from the back of the bar. "Last chance."

I turned. All of the Stones but Charles and Nate were gone. Charles was beside me, staring as well. He had gotten revenge, just like I had, revenge for his brother.

I took his arm and pulled him with me. The bartender was watching.

"You mention me," I said to him as I walked by, "and I'll tell Chaz Yancy who made that phone call."

"C'mon," Nate said again. He held the door open, and we hurried through it.

There weren't any sirens yet. The neighborhood was deadly quiet. I wondered how long Jump Vitel would lay there before anyone noticed he was dead.

I didn't care. I followed Nate and Charles out the second door, into a series of burned-out hallways that led to the street behind the tavern.

The car was waiting, just like Nate said it would be. We climbed in, getting into the same positions we had been in when we arrived. Only now there wasn't a gun in my ribs, and Brass wasn't with us.

The car pulled out slowly, as if nothing had happened. Nate turned around, said to me, "Where're we taking you, Gramps?"

"My car's at your place." My voice sounded normal, but my breath smelled like beer. It made me feel like someone else.

"Okay, man. Whatever you want." He held out a hand. "You're a Stone now, bro, and we protect yours like they're our own."

I clasped his hand, like I was supposed to, but I felt no victory. Only exhaustion, and a feeling that, in some ways, I had just made things worse.

THIRTY-SEVEN

First, I went to the hospital.

Valentina's room hadn't changed since the morning. The curtains were still drawn, and it still felt like night. The air smelled of sickness and greasy chicken soup, the remains of which sat on a tray on the nightstand.

Marvella had a light on over her chair. She had been reading *The Confessions of Nat Turner*, apparently aloud. When I came in, she had set the book, face-open, on the floor.

I stayed by the door. I didn't want to be here long. I was tired and numb, and I wanted nothing more than to go home.

But Marvella and Valentina had to hear the news, and they had to hear it from me.

Valentina watched me from the bed, her tiny features blank as I told her that Armand Vitel was dead.

Marvella leaned forward, her long body nearly touching mine.

"How do you know?" she asked.

"It's on the radio," I lied, knowing that the news would pick the story up eventually. GANG SHOOTS COP: SECOND DAY IN A ROW. SECOND COP DEAD IN GANGLAND WAR. What the city would see as an escalation, I saw as justice, and Valentina saw only as relief.

When I gave her the news, she turned her head away from me, but not before I saw tears in her eyes.

She never said a word. Marvella went to her side, taking her hand.

"What happened?" Marvella asked me.

I shrugged. "There weren't a lot of details."

Her lovely eyes narrowed. "Sometimes you're just like him, you know."

"Who?" I asked, thinking of Vitel.

"Truman," she said. "Not sharing information, protecting the women."

I almost denied it—it seemed like such a ridiculous charge. But I had protected Valentina. I made sure that Vitel would never attack her again. And I saw no reason that anyone who hadn't been present at Greenwood's should know what really happened.

"I'm sure there'll be a write-up in the papers tomorrow," I said. "They'll have everything."

Marvella shook her head, a thin smile on her lips. As I headed out the door, Valentina turned toward me.

"Smokey," she said, and it sounded odd, hearing my real name come from her lips.

I stopped, still holding the doorknob.

Valentina's gaze met mine, and I was struck again by the intelligence in her eyes—intelligence, and knowledge. I hadn't fooled her any more than I had fooled Marvella.

They both knew I had something to do with Vitel's death, and they both knew I wouldn't tell them what it was.

"Thank you," Valentina said.

I nodded. "I only wish I could have done more."

More. Sooner. Before we lost Johnson. Before all of this had spiraled into something ugly, and inevitable.

There wasn't anything else to say. I left them, drove home. It felt like I hadn't been to the apartment in days, even though it had only been hours.

As I unlocked the deadbolts and let myself inside, I heard the phone ringing. I closed the door and hurried across the room, banging my leg against a kitchen chair, nearly tumbling over the edge of the couch as I reached for the phone.

"What?" I said. I didn't feel like having a real conversation.

"Mr. Grimshaw?" The woman on the other end of the line sounded hesitant, as if my rude greeting had convinced her she had the wrong person.

"Yes." I tried to soften my tone.

"It's Anna Shay at Helping Hands. You told one of our volunteers you had some questions for Helen Bell."

Helen Bell. I didn't know any Helen Bell. And then I remembered. The starving woman with the two children. Helen and Carrie and Doug. I had wanted to ask Helen about the baby we had found outside the building.

The corpse that I would take custody of in a few weeks.

"Yes," I said.

"She's willing to talk to you, if you want to come down here."

I had planned to ask Helen what she knew about that child. I had planned to be discreet, in case the baby had been hers. But I had seen a lot in the last twenty-four hours, and I wasn't sure discretion was possible anymore.

"How is she?" I sat on the arm of the couch. My legs ached. I was even more tired than I had realized.

"What do you mean?" Anna Shay said.

"Is she doing all right?"

"She's really bright, sir. She's one of the most gifted seamstresses I've seen. She learned it from her mother, who apparently disowned her when the first baby—oh, you can guess the story."

I could. "How are the children?"

"Douglas doesn't care for school, but he's joined Grace Kirkland's group and he likes her. Carrie needs some special help. She's been underfed her entire life."

I thought not of the little girl clinging to her too-thin mother, but of the child sitting on the steps at the Robert Taylor Homes, her eyes staring at nothing, too tired, too sick, too defeated already to play with the ruined doll in her arms.

"What's their prognosis?" I asked.

"Prognosis?" Anna Shay asked, clearly not understanding me.

"Do you think they're going to make it through the program? Be able to take care of themselves, have a real future?"

"Oh, yes, sir. They're determined to make it. They don't want to go back." I could hear the smile in her voice. "They're going to do just fine."

I clung to the phone. More street justice. If I ignored the baby, Helen Bell and her children would have a chance at a good life.

Who was it that said to me that you took care of the living? I couldn't remember anymore.

"Sir? Did you want to come down here and meet with her? I was supposed to ask when you want the appointment." Anna Shay sounded a little breathless.

I sighed. Sometimes partial victories were all that we would get. And some questions would go forever unanswered—forever unasked.

"I don't need an appointment right now, Mrs. Shay," I said. "You've answered my questions. Give Helen my best, will you?"

"Yes, sir," Anna Shay said.

"And thanks for calling." I hung up, then stood beside the phone for a long time.

What had Helen Bell thought? Had she known I was going to ask about the baby? Did she even know about the baby? Or did she have no suspicions at all? I didn't know. I would never know if she was going to face my questions with courage or just with simple curiosity at someone else's interest.

I would have to call Laura and tell her about all of this—or at least about some of it. But that could wait.

Before I talked to anyone else, I had to see Jimmy.

THIRTY-EIGHT

I could have picked Jimmy up at the church where Grace Kirkland taught. Then I would have been able to see Doug Bell for myself, talked to Grace, found out how things were going there.

But I didn't want to. I was tired of getting involved in other people's lives, other people's problems.

Instead, I drove to the Grimshaws' house at five-thirty. The "Happy Easter" sign was still in the window, looking festive and welcoming.

I sat in the car for a long moment, feeling like I didn't belong—as if I were a patch of darkness on the Grimshaws' bright day.

But I had to get Jimmy. It was time to bring him home, and hold him close, time to apologize for leaving him with friends yet again.

As I got out of the car, I ran my hands over my sleeves. I had showered and changed, but I still felt as if I had Vitel's blood spattered across my front, even though I hadn't been close enough to get touched by any spray.

I made myself walk up the sidewalk. The air smelled of rain, but the clouds weren't heavy like they had been for the past two days. The sky was simply gray. The rain would be a mild cleansing instead of a violent fury.

Someone had cleaned the green Easter grass off the porch, but the shoes were still there—or maybe these were new pairs, left outside so that no mud would get tracked across Althea's floors.

As I knocked on the door, I heard laughter inside. The delicious scent of split-pea soup filtered out the doorway, and my stomach growled. I had forgotten to eat once again.

Through the door, I heard someone yell, "I'll get it," followed by another voice, apparently arguing. Then footsteps slapped toward me, and the front door banged open.

Norene faced me. Her braids were coming loose, and she had a milk mustache over her tiny mouth. She was wearing some kind of brown uniform, and she looked very serious.

"Uncle Bill!" she cried and pulled back the screen door. Then she wrapped herself around my legs—her favorite greeting.

I put my hand on her braids and let her hug my knees. The faint odor of chocolate reached me, and it seemed to come from her.

She held on tightly, and I was beginning to realize there was more to this hug than a greeting. But I couldn't move, not with her iron grip on my legs.

"Can I come in, hon?" I asked.

"Only if you buy some cookies," she said.

I wasn't sure I had heard her correctly. "Cookies?"

Mikie had come down the hall, a crumpled paper in her hands. She was wearing a brown uniform, too, only hers was neater. It had badges on a scarf, and she wore knee socks that were falling down.

"Girl Scout Cookies, Uncle Bill," Mikie said.

Lacey sauntered into the room. She wore the green uniform I associated with the Girl Scouts.

I had never seen the girls in uniform before, although Althea told me they were all proud members of the Scouts. When I lived with the family last summer, no one dressed up like this. Maybe it was only a school thing.

Lacey held a piece of paper in her hands. She looked younger than usual, probably because she wasn't wearing makeup or clothing that I didn't approve of.

"We're all selling the cookies," Lacey said. "But Mom says it's not fair for all of us to expect you to buy some."

Girl Scout Cookies. Little girls learning—what? How to survive in the woods? I had no idea what Girl Scouts did, although somehow, I found the entire concept refreshingly innocent.

"You'll get mine, right, Uncle Bill?" Norene let go of my knees. I wondered if I would get the circulation back anytime soon. "I gots the best."

"I have the best," I said, correcting her as I stepped all the way into the dining room. The Easter baskets were gone, but the tablecloth bore some candy stains that hadn't been there before.

The pea soup smell was stronger in here. My stomach rumbled again. All this talk of cookies and the smell of soup warmed me.

"And," I added, looking at all three of them, "I think I'll eat enough Thin Mints to justify more than one order."

Lacey smiled, and Norene jumped up and down. Mikie held out her order form. "Now?" she asked, with the finesse of a used-car salesman.

"Leave him alone," Franklin said. He appeared in the kitchen doorway. He was wearing a suit. The jacket was wrinkled, and he looked tired.

His eyes didn't twinkle like I would have expected them to. Usually his daughters' antics amused him.

He studied me as if no one else was in the room. "What happened this time?"

The girls glanced at each other, then slid into the living room. They started discussing the cookie order forms.

I took that as a cue. Franklin was still angry at me.

Jimmy walked past Franklin into the dining room. Jimmy wore clothes I didn't recognize—a shirt that seemed too big, and pants that were a little too short. Had I forgotten to bring him a change of clothes?

I probably had.

He stood between me and Franklin, glancing back and forth between us.

I extended a hand to him. Jimmy crossed the room and took it. His hand was warm and sticky. "You okay?"

"I'm fine," I said.

"You don't look fine," Jimmy said.

"I haven't had much sleep."

Franklin leaned into the living room.

"Girls," he said. "Go help your mother."

"Da-ad."

I could recognize Lacey's disgusted tones even though I couldn't see her.

"Daddy, we're just—"

"I said go, Mikie." Franklin crossed his arms. Even I wouldn't mess with him when he was in that mood.

Norene skipped out of the living room, across the dining room floor toward the kitchen door. She waved at me as she passed, flashing me a bright grin.

Mikie still clutched her order form and stomped past her father, head down. Lacey opened her mouth to argue with him, but Franklin pointed at the kitchen.

"Go," he said again.

Jimmy's grip grew tighter on my hand.

Franklin waited until Lacey's voice rose in the kitchen, reciting her protest to her mother. There was laughter in Althea's voice as she responded.

But I couldn't concentrate on them. Instead, Franklin came up behind Jimmy and put his hand on Jimmy's shoulder.

"I think we should have a conversation, Smokey," Franklin said.

I shook my head. "Not tonight."

"What happened, Smoke?" Jimmy asked.

Franklin's gaze met mine. He hadn't said anything to Jimmy, just like I had asked him to. But now Franklin was staring at me with disapproval.

He would never have run off like I did. He would have reported what little he knew and hoped the authorities took care of it. At best, he would have gone to some of Bronzeville's leaders, and asked them for help.

But he wouldn't have left Jimmy with friends while he went to find a killer.

Jimmy was looking up at me. He was a good kid. He had a difficult life, but he was making the best of it. And he was stuck with me, a man who didn't always do the right thing.

I owed him an explanation. Secrets wouldn't help either of us.

This wasn't about Franklin. This was about me and Jimmy.

I crouched, so that I was at Jimmy's eye level. I didn't have to go as low as I did a year ago. He had grown significantly since Martin died.

Jimmy's brow was furrowed. His eyes were wide as he studied me.

I took his other hand, so I was holding both of them now. I said, "Truman Johnson got killed."

Jimmy's head went backward just a little, the only sign of his shock. His expression didn't change, however, and I worried that he was learning the wrong things from me.

"The policeman?" Jimmy asked.

I nodded.

Jimmy frowned. He had met Johnson, but they hadn't really known each other. Oddly enough, Jimmy knew Sinkovich better.

Jimmy blinked a few times, his frown growing deeper. I recognized the look. He was thinking about the times he had met Johnson.

After a moment, Jimmy said, "I liked him. He was a good man."

I tensed. Franklin crossed his arms. Here it was, yet another example for Jimmy of men who did the right thing and died. But I had started this conversation. I had to finish it.

"Yes," I said to Jimmy. "Truman Johnson was a good man."

Jimmy nodded. He seemed to think for a moment, and then he asked, "Did you get the guy that killed him?"

Franklin shook his head slightly, as if he couldn't believe this conversation was going on in his dining room.

"Yes," I said. "I did."

And as I spoke. I braced myself for his reaction. Jimmy had been so unpredictable lately, so difficult. I had no idea what he would think of being left alone so that I could "get the guy" who had killed a good man.

To my surprise, Jimmy smiled slowly. He nodded, and squeezed my hands, as if he were comforting me.

"Okay, Smoke," he said softly. "I can live with that."

And, I realized, I could, too.